PRAISE FOR
The Dead Romantics

"I LOVED this book. A beautiful, poignant story, full of beautiful, poignant characters. Florence is exactly the type of lovable, endearing, relatable lead I want to fall for, and her journey through learning how to love again had me squealing, sighing, [and] laughing. *The Dead Romantics* is like a beautifully crafted puzzle: at the end all the pieces fall perfectly into place, and the picture that they form is at once touching, funny, breathtaking, hopeful, and dreamy."

—Ali Hazelwood, *New York Times* bestselling author of *The Love Hypothesis*

"*The Dead Romantics* was an absolute and unexpected delight. Voicy and quirky and *fun*; the pages will probably sparkle (but with black glitter)."

—Christina Lauren, *New York Times* bestselling author of *The Unhoneymooners*

"This book made me fall in love, broke my heart then reassembled it at least twice, and left me swooning. A hauntingly romantic, hilariously heartwarming story. Ashley Poston is the real deal."

—Gwenda Bond, *New York Times* bestselling author of *Not Your Average Hot Guy*

"*The Dead Romantics* takes so many things I love—quirky heroines, found families, cozy small towns, fanfics, GHOSTS (!!!)—and gives them all a fresh, fun, thoroughly modern spin. This is truly a rom-com to die for!"

—Rachel Hawkins, *New York Times* bestselling author of *Reckless Girls*

The Dead Romantics

• • • • •

ASHLEY POSTON

JOVE
New York

A JOVE BOOK
Published by Berkley
An imprint of Penguin Random House LLC
penguinrandomhouse.com

Library of Congress Cataloging-in-Publication Data

Names: Poston, Ashley, author.
Title: The dead romantics / Ashley Poston.
Description: First edition. | New York: Jove, 2022.
Identifiers: LCCN 2021035584 (print) | LCCN 2021035585 (ebook) |
ISBN 9780593336489 (trade paperback) | ISBN 9780593336496 (ebook)
Classification: LCC PS3616.O8388 D43 2022 (print) |
LCC PS3616.O8388 (ebook) | DDC 813/.6—dc23
LC record available at https://lccn.loc.gov/2021035584
LC ebook record available at https://lccn.loc.gov/2021035585

First Edition: June 2022

Printed in the United States of America
1st Printing

Book design by Daniel Brount

To every author
who asked us to believe in
Happily Ever Afters

The Dead Romantics

A Buried Story

IN THE BACK-LEFT corner of the Days Gone Funeral Home, underneath a loose floorboard, there was a metal box with a bunch of old journals inside. To anyone who found them, the scribbles looked like some teenager venting her sexual frustrations with Lestat or that one guy from *The X-Files*.

And, if you didn't mind ghosts and vampires and blood oaths and leather pants and true love, the stories were quite good.

You could wonder why someone would shove journals full of smutty fan fiction underneath the floorboard of a century-old funeral home, but never question the mind of a teenager. You wouldn't get very far.

I hid them there because—well—I just did, okay? Because when I left for college, I wanted to bury that part of me—that dark, weird Addams Family side—and what was a more fitting place than a funeral home?

And I almost succeeded, too.

1

....

The Ghostwriter

EVERY GOOD STORY has a few secrets.

At least, that's what I've been told. Sometimes they're secrets about love, secrets about family, secrets about murder—some so inconsequential they barely feel like secrets at all, but monumental to the person keeping them. Every person has a secret. Every secret has a story.

And in my head, every story has a happy ending.

If I were the heroine in a story, I would tell you that I had three secrets.

One, I hadn't washed my hair in four days.

Two, my family owned a funeral home.

And three, I was the ghostwriter of mega-bestselling, critically acclaimed romance novelist Ann Nichols.

And I was *sorely* late for a meeting.

"Hold the door!" I shouted, bypassing the security personnel at the front desk, and sprinting toward the elevators.

"Miss!" the befuddled security guard shouted after me. "You have to check in! You can't just—"

"Florence Day! Falcon House Publishers! Call up to Erin and she'll approve me!" I tossed over my shoulder, and slid into one of the elevators, cactus in tow.

As the doors closed, a graying man in a sharp business suit eyed the plant in question.

"A gift to butter up my new editor," I told him, because I wasn't someone who just carried around small succulents wherever she went. "God knows it's not for me. I kill everything I touch, including three cactuses—cacti?—already."

The man coughed into his hand and angled himself away from me. The woman on the other side said, as if to console me, "That's lovely, dear."

Which meant that this was a terrible gift. I mean, I figured it was, but I had been stranded for too long on the platform waiting for the B train, having a small panic attack with my brother on the phone, when a little old lady with rollers in her hair tottered by selling cacti for like a dollar a pop and I bought things when I was nervous. Mainly books but—I guess now I bought houseplants, too.

The guy in the business suit got off on the twentieth floor, and the woman who held the elevator left on the twenty-seventh. I took a peek into their worlds before the doors closed again, immaculate white carpet or buffed wooden floors and glass cases where old books sat idly. There were quite a few publishers in the building, both online and in print, and there was even a newspaper on one of the floors. I could've been in the elevator with the editor for *Nora Roberts* for all I knew.

Whenever I came to visit the offices, I was always hyperaware of how people took one look at me—in my squeaky flats and darned hose and too-big plaid overcoat—and came to the conclusion that I was *not* tall enough to ride this ride.

Which . . . fair. I stood at around five foot two, and everything I wore was bought for comfort and not style. Rose, my roommate, always joked that I was an eighty-year-old in a twenty-eight-year-old body.

Sometimes I felt it.

Nothing said Netflix and chill quite like an orthopedic pillow and a wineglass of Ensure.

When the elevator doors opened onto the thirty-seventh floor, I was alone, grasping my cactus like a life vest at sea. The offices of Falcon House Publishers were pristine and white, with two fluorescent bookshelves on either side of the entryway, touting all of the bestsellers and literary masterpieces they'd published over their seventy-five-year history.

At least half of the left wall was covered in books by Ann Nichols—*The Sea-Dweller's Daughter*, *The Forest of Dreams*, *The Forever House*, ones my mom sighed over when I was a teenager writing my smutty Lestat fanfic. Next to them were Ann's newer books, *The Probability of Love*, *A Rake's Guide to Getting the Girl* (I was most proud of that title), and *The Kiss at the Midnight Matinee.* The glass reflected my face in the book covers, a pale white and sleep-deprived young woman with dirty blond hair pulled up in a messy bun and dark circles under tired brown eyes, in a colorful scarf and an oversized beige sweater that made me look like I was the guest speaker at the Yarn of the Month Club and not one of the most distinguished publishing houses in the world.

Technically, *I* wasn't the guest here. Ann Nichols was, and I was what everyone guessed was her lowly assistant.

And I had a meeting to get to.

I stood in the lobby awkwardly, the cactus pressed to my chest, as the dark-haired receptionist, Erin, held up a finger and finished her call. Something about salad for lunch. When she finally hung up, she looked up from her screen and recognized me. "Florence!" she greeted with a bright smile. "Nice to see you up and about! How's Rose? That party last night was *brutal*."

I tried not to wince, thinking about Rose and I stumbling in at 3:00 A.M. "It sure was something."

"Is she still alive?"

"Rose has survived worse."

Erin laughed. Then she glanced around the lobby, as if looking for someone else. "Is Mrs. Nichols not going to make it today?"

"Oh no, she's still up in Maine, doing her . . . Maine thing."

Erin shook her head. "Gotta wonder what it's like, you know? Being the Ann Nicholses and Stephen Kings of the world."

"Must be nice," I agreed. Ann Nichols hadn't left her small little island in Maine in . . . five years? As long as I'd been ghostwriting for her, anyway.

I tugged down the multicolored scarf wrapped around my mouth and neck. While it wasn't winter anymore, New York always had one last kick of cold before spring, and that had to be today, and I was beginning to nervously sweat under my coat.

"Someday," Erin added, "you're going to tell me how you became the assistant for *the* Ann Nichols."

I laughed. "I've told you before—a Craigslist ad."

"I don't believe that."

I shrugged. "C'est la vie."

Erin was a few years younger than me, her Columbia University publishing certificate proudly displayed on her desk. Rose had met her a while back on a dating app, and they'd hooked up a few times, though now from what I heard they were strictly friends.

The phone began to ring on her desk. Erin said quickly, "Anyway, you can go ahead—still remember the way, yeah?"

"Absolutely."

"Perf. Good luck!" she added, and answered the call in her best customer service voice. "Good morning! You've reached Falcon House Publishers, this is Erin speaking . . ."

And I was left to my own devices.

I knew where to go, because I'd visited the old editor enough times to be able to walk the halls blindfolded. Tabitha Margraves had retired recently, at the absolute *worst* time, and with every step closer to the office, I held tighter on to the poor cactus.

Tabitha knew I ghostwrote for Ann. She and Ann's agent were the only ones who did—well, besides Rose, but Rose didn't count. Had Tabitha passed that nugget of secrecy to my new editor? God, I hoped so. Otherwise this was going to be an awkward first meeting.

The hallway was lined with frosted glass walls that were supposed to be used for privacy, but they provided extraordinarily little of that. I heard editors and marketing and PR shadows talking in hushed tones about acquisitions, marketing plans, contractual obligations, tours . . . reallocating money from one book's budget to another.

The things in publishing that no one ever really talked about.

Publishing was all very romantic until you found yourself *in* publishing. Then it was just another kind of corporate hell.

I passed a few assistant editors sitting in their square cubicles, manuscripts piled almost to the top of their half walls, looking frazzled as they ate carrots and hummus for lunch. The salads Erin ordered must not have included them, not that editorial assistants made enough to afford eating out every day. The offices were set up in a hierarchy of sorts, and the farther you went, the higher the salary. At the end of the hall, I almost didn't recognize the office. Gone were the floral wreath hanging on the door for good luck and the stickers plastered to the frosted glass privacy wall that read TRY NOT, DO! and ROMANCE ISN'T DEAD!

For a second, I thought I'd made a wrong turn, until I recognized the intern in her small cubicle, stuffing ARCs—Advance Reader Copies, basically rough drafts of a book in paperback form—into envelopes with a harried sort of frenzy that bordered on tears.

My new editor didn't waste any time peeling off those decals and tossing the good luck wreath in the trash. I didn't know if that was a good sign—or bad.

Toward the end of her tenure at Falcon House, Tabitha Margraves and I butted heads more often than not. "Romance *believes* in happy endings. Tell *Ann* that," she would say, tongue in cheek, because, for all intents and purposes, I was Ann.

"Well *Ann* doesn't anymore," I would quip back, and by the time she turned in her resignation and retired down to Florida, I'm sure we were both plotting each other's demise. She still believed in love—somehow, impossibly.

And I could see right through the lie.

Love was putting up with someone for fifty years so you'd have someone to bury you when you died. I would know; my family was in the business of death.

Tabitha called me crass when I told her that.

I said I was realistic.

There was a difference.

I sat down in one of the two chairs outside of the office, the cactus in my lap, to wait and scroll through my Instagram feed. My younger sister had posted a photo of her and my hometown mayor—a golden retriever—and I felt a pang of homesickness. For the weather, the funeral parlor, my mom's amazing fried chicken.

I wondered what she was cooking tonight for dinner.

Lost in my thoughts, I didn't hear the office door open until a distinctly male voice said, "Sorry for the wait, please come in."

I bolted to my feet in surprise. Did I have the wrong office? I checked the cubicles—the brown-haired workaholic intern cramming ARCs into envelopes to the left, the HR director sobbing into his salad on the right—no, this was definitely the right office.

The man cleared his throat, impatiently waiting.

I hugged the cactus so tight to my chest, I could feel the pot beginning to creak with the pressure, and stepped into his office.

And froze.

The man in question sat in the leather chair that for thirty-five years (longer than he'd been alive, I figured) Tabitha Margraves had inhabited. The desk, once cluttered with porcelain knickknacks and pictures of her dog, was clean and tidy, everything stacked in its proper place. The desk reflected the man behind it almost perfectly: too polished, in a crisp white button-down shirt that strained at his broad shoulders, the sleeves rolled up to his elbows to reveal rather intimidatingly sexy forearms. His black hair was swept back out of his long face and somehow accentuated his equally long nose, black square glasses perched on it, and there were very faint freckles speckled across his face: one by his right nostril, two on his cheek, one just above his thick right eyebrow. A constellation of them. For a second, I wanted to take a Sharpie and connect them to see what myth they held. The next second, I quickly came to the realization that—

Oh.

He was hot. And I'd seen him before. At publishing functions with Rose or my ex-boyfriend. I couldn't place the name, but I'd definitely run into him more than once. I held my breath, wondering if he recognized me—*did* he?

For a second, I thought so, because his eyes widened—just a fraction, just enough for me to suspect he knew *something*—before it vanished.

He cleared his throat.

"You must be Ann Nichols's assistant," he greeted without missing a beat. He stood and came around the desk to offer his hand. He was . . . *enormous.* So tall I felt like I'd suddenly been transported into a retelling of "Jack and the Beanstalk" where he was a very hunky beanstalk that I really, *really* wanted to climb—

No. No, Florence. Bad girl, I scolded myself. *You do not want to climb him like a tree, because he's your new editor and therefore very, incredibly,* stupendously *unclimbable.*

"Florence Day," I said as I accepted his hand. His almost completely enveloped mine in a strong handshake.

"Benji Andor, but you can call me Ben," he introduced.

"Florence," I repeated, shocked that I could mutter anything above a squeak.

The edges of his mouth quirked up. "So you said."

I quickly pulled my hand away, mortified. "Oh *god.* Right—sorry." I sat down a little too hard in the uncomfortable IKEA chair, cactus planted firmly on my knees. My cheeks were on *fire,* and if I could feel them, I knew that he could see I was blushing.

He sat down again and adjusted a pen on his desk. "It's a pleasure to meet you. Sorry for the wait, the subways were hell this morning. Erin keeps telling me not to take the B train and yet I am a fool who does every single time."

"Or a masochist," I added before I could stop myself.

He barked a laugh. "Maybe both."

I bit the inside of my cheek to hide a smile. He had a great laugh—the kind that was deep and throaty, like a rumble.

Oh *no,* this was not going as planned at all.

He liked me, and he wasn't going to like me in about five minutes. I didn't even like myself for what I was here to do—why did I think a *cactus* as a gift would make this easier?

He scooted his chair in and straightened a pen to be horizontal with his keyboard. Everything was neat like that in this office, and I got the very distinct feeling that he was the kind of person who, if he found a book misplaced at a bookstore, would return it to the shelf where it belonged.

Everything had its place.

He was a bullet journal guy, and I was a sticky note kind of girl.

That might've been a good thing, actually. He seemed very no-nonsense, and no-nonsense people were rarely romantic, and so I wouldn't get a pitying look when I, eventually, tell him that I no longer believed in romance novels and he would nod solemnly, knowing *exactly* what I meant. And I would rather have *that* than Tabitha Margraves looking at me with those sad, dark eyes and asking, "Why don't you believe in love anymore, Florence?"

Because when you put your hand in the fire too many times, you learn that you only get burned.

My new editor shifted in his seat. "I'm sorry to hear that Mrs. Nichols couldn't make it today. I would've loved to meet her," he began, wrenching me from my thoughts.

I shifted in my seat. "Oh, Tabitha didn't tell you? She never leaves Maine. I think she lives on an island or something. It sounds nice—I wouldn't ever want to leave, either. I hear Maine's pretty."

"It is! I grew up there," he replied. "Saw many a moose. They're huge."

Are you sure you aren't half moose yourself? my traitorous brain said, and I winced because that was *very* wrong and *very* bad. "I guess they prepared you for the rats in New York."

He laughed again, this time surprising himself, and he had a glorious white smile, too. It reached is eyes, turning brown to a melting ocher. "Nothing could prepare me for those. Have you seen the ones down in Union Square? I swear one had a *jockey* on him."

"Oh, you didn't know? There's some great rat races down at the Eighteenth Street Station."

"Do you go often?"

"Absolutely, there's even a squeak-easy."

"Wow, you're a real mice-stro of puns."

I snorted a laugh and looked away—anywhere other than at him. Because I liked his charm, and I definitely didn't want to, and I hated disappointing people, and—

He cleared his throat and said, "Well, Miss Day, I think we need to talk about Ann's upcoming novel . . ."

I gripped the cactus in my lap tighter. My eyes jumped from barren wall to barren wall. There was nothing in the office to look *at*. It used to be full of things—fake flowers and photos and book covers on the walls—but now the only thing on the walls was a framed master's degree in fiction—

"Does it have to be a romance?" I blurted.

Surprised, he cocked his head. "This . . . is a romance imprint."

"I—I know, but like—you know how Nicholas Sparks writes depressing books and John Green writes melodramatic sick-lit, do you think I—I mean *Mrs. Nichols*—could do something in that vein instead?"

He was quiet for a moment. "You mean a tragedy."

"Oh, no. It'd still be a love story! Obviously. But a love story where things don't end up—'*happily ever after*'—perfect."

"We're in the business of happily ever afters," he said slowly, picking his words.

"And it's a lie, isn't it?"

He pursed his lips.

"Romance is dead, and this—all of this—feels like a con." I found myself saying it before my brain approved, and as soon as I realized I'd voiced it aloud, I winced. "I didn't mean—that isn't Ann's stance, that's just what I think—"

"Are you her assistant or her editor?"

The words were like a slap in the face. I quickly snapped my gaze back to him, and went very still. His eyes had lost their warm ocher, the laugh lines having sunk back into a smooth, emotionless mask.

I gripped the cactus tighter. It had suddenly become my buddy in war. So he didn't know that I was Ann's ghostwriter. Tabitha didn't tell him, or she forgot to—slipped her mind, whoops! And I needed to tell him.

He was my editor, after all.

But a bitter, embarrassed part of me didn't want to. I didn't want him to see how much of my life I didn't have together because, as Ann's ghostwriter, shouldn't I? Have it together?

Shouldn't I be better than *this*?

When I was growing up, my mother read Ann Nichols's books, and because of that, I did, too. When I was twelve, I would sneak into the romance section in the library and quietly read *The Forest of Dreams* between the stacks. I knew her catalog back and forth like a well-played discography of my favorite band.

And then I became her pen.

While Ann's name was on the cover, I wrote *The Probability of Love* and *A Rake's Guide to Getting the Girl* and *The Kiss at the Midnight Matinee*. For the last five years, Ann Nichols had sent me a check to write the book in question, and then I did, and the words in those books—my words—had been praised from the *New York Times Book Review* to *Vogue*. Those books sat on shelves beside Nora Roberts and Nicholas Sparks and Julia Quinn, and *they were mine*.

I wrote for one of romance's greats—a job anyone would *die* to have—and I . . . I was failing.

Perhaps I'd *already* failed. I'd just asked for my last trump card—to write a book that was anything, everything, but a happily ever after—and he said no.

"Mr. Andor," I began, my voice cracking, "the truth is—"

"Ann needs to deliver the manuscript by the deadline," he interrupted in a cold, no-nonsense voice. The warmth it held a few minutes before was gone. I felt myself getting smaller by the moment, shrinking into the hard IKEA chair.

"That's tomorrow," I said softly.

"Yes, tomorrow."

"And if—if she can't?"

He pressed his lips into a thin line. He had a sort of wide mouth that dipped in the middle, expressing things that the rest of his face was too guarded to. "How much time does she need?"

A year. Ten years.

An eternity.

"Um—a—a month?" I asked hopefully.

His dark brows shot up. "Absolutely not."

"These things take time!"

"I understand that," he replied, and I flinched. He took off his black-rimmed glasses to look at me. "May I be frank with you?"

No, absolutely not. "Yes . . . ?" I ventured.

"Because Ann's already asked for three deadline extensions, even if we get it tomorrow, we'd have to push it quickly through copyedits and pass pages—and that's only *if* we get it tomorrow—to keep to our schedule. This is Ann's big fall book. A romance, mind you, with a happily ever after. That's her brand. That's what we signed for. We already have promotions lined up. We might even have a full-page spread in the *New York Times*. We're doing a lot for this book, so when I prodded Ann's agent to speak with her, she connected me with you, her assistant."

I knew that part. Molly Stein, Ann's agent, wasn't very happy to get a call about the book in question. She thought everything had been going smoothly. I hadn't the heart to tell her otherwise. Molly had been pretty hands-off with my ghostwriting gig, mostly because the books were part of a four-book deal, this being the last one, and she trusted that I wouldn't mess up.

Yet here I was.

I didn't want to even *think* about how Molly would break the news to Ann. I didn't want to think about how disappointed Ann would be. I'd met the woman once and I was deathly afraid of failing her. I didn't want to do that.

I looked up to her. And the feeling of failing someone you looked up to . . . it sucked as a kid, and it sucked as an adult.

Benji went on. "Whatever is keeping Mrs. Nichols from finishing her manuscript has become a problem not only for me, but for marketing *and* production, and if we want to stay on schedule, we need that manuscript."

"I—I know, but . . ."

"And if she can't deliver," he added, "then we'll have to get the legal department involved, I'm afraid."

The legal department. That meant a breach of contract. That meant I would have messed up so big that there would be no coming back from it. I would've failed not just Ann, but her publisher and her readers—everyone.

I'd already failed like that once.

The office began to get smaller, or I was having a panic attack, and I really hoped it was the former. My breath came in short bursts. It was hard to breathe.

"Miss Florence? Are you okay? You seem a little pale," he observed, but his voice sounded a football field away. "Do you need some water?"

I shoved my panic into a small box in the back of my head, where everything else went. All of the bad things. The things I didn't want to deal with. The things I *couldn't* deal with. The box was useful. I shut everything in. Locked it tight. I pressed on a smile. "Oh, no. I'm fine. It's a lot to take in. And—and you're right. Of course you're right."

He seemed doubtful. "Tomorrow, then?"

"Yeah," I croaked.

"Good. Please tell Mrs. Nichols that I send my regards, and I'm very happy to be working with her. And I'm sorry—is that a *cactus*? I just noticed."

I looked down at the succulent, all but forgotten in my lap as my panic banged on the box in my head, lock rattling, to get free. I—I thought I hated this man, and if I stayed in this office any longer, I was going to either throw this cactus at him or cry.

Maybe both.

I jerked to my feet and put the succulent on the edge of the desk. "It's a gift."

Then I gathered my satchel and turned on my heels and left Falcon House Publishers without another word. I held myself together until I stumbled out of the revolving door of the building and into the brisk April day, and let myself crumble.

I took a deep breath—and screamed an obscenity into the perfectly blue afternoon sky, startling a flock of pigeons from the side of the building.

I needed a drink.

No, I needed a *book*. A murder-thriller. Hannibal. Lizzie Borden—anything would do.

Maybe I needed both.

No, *definitely* both.

2

.....

The Breakup

IT WASN'T THAT I *couldn't* finish the book.

I just didn't know how.

It'd been a year since The Breakup—everyone has at least one in their lives. You know the one, right? The kind of breakup from a love you thought would last your entire lifetime, only to find your heart ripped out with a spork by your former lover and placed on a silver platter with FUCK YOU written in ketchup. It'd been a year since I'd hauled my luggage out into the rain on that shitty April evening and never looked back. That's not the part I regretted. I will *never* regret ending things with him.

I just regretted being the kind of girl who fell for someone like him in the first place.

The time had crawled by after that. At first, I had tried to get up every day and sit down on the couch with my laptop and write, but I couldn't. I mean, I *could*—but every word felt like pulling teeth, and every one of those words I deleted a day later.

It was like one day I knew how to write; I knew the scenes, I knew the meet-cutes and the swoony moments, exactly how the hero tasted when my heroine kissed him . . . and then the next day, it was all gone. Iced over in a blizzard, and I didn't know how to thaw out the words.

I couldn't remember when I stopped opening up the Word document, when I stopped trying to look for a romance between the lines. But I did, and now I was here between a rock called despair and a hard place named Benji Andor.

Absently, I brushed my fingers along the spines of the books at McNally Jackson, a bookstore nestled in the thick of Nolita. I followed the rows of titles and last names around to the next aisle—romance—and quickly moved on to sci-fi and fantasy. If I didn't look at them, they didn't exist.

I never imagined being a ghostwriter. Hell, when I first got my agent and sold my first book, I thought I'd be invited to literary panels and I thought I'd go to book events, and I thought I had finally found the door to the stairs that would take me up and up and up into my forever career. But the door closed as quickly as it opened, and sent an email saying, "We regret to inform you . . . ," as though my book flopping was *my* fault. As though me, a girl with a nonexistent social media following, less money, and almost no connections, was responsible for the fate of a book published by a multimillion-dollar company with every resource and connection available to it.

Maybe it *was* my fault.

Maybe I hadn't done enough.

And anyway, I was here now, writing for a romance author I'd only ever met once, and I was about to screw that up, too, if I couldn't finish the damn book. I knew the characters—Amelia, a smart-talking barista with dreams of being a music journalist, and

Jackson, a stability-shirking guitarist disgraced from the limelight—trapped together on vacation on a small Scottish isle when their Airbnb host accidentally double-books the property. The isle is magical, and the romance is as electrifying as the storms that roll in from the Atlantic. But then she finds out that he lied to her about his past, and she lied to *him*, because while the booking was indeed happenstance, she decided to use it to try to win over an editor at *Rolling Stone.*

And I guessed the plot hit too close to home. How could two people reconcile and trust each other when they fell in love with the lies the other person told them?

Where did you go from there?

Last time I tried to write that scene—the reconciliation one, the one where they face each other in a cold Scottish storm and pour their hearts out to try and repair their damage—lightning struck Jackson dead.

Which would've been great if I ghostwrote revenge fantasies. Which I didn't.

I began to nose through the used J. D. Robb section when my phone started to vibrate in my satchel. I dug it out, praying it wasn't Ann Nichols's agent, Molly.

It wasn't.

"Great timing," I said, answering the phone. "I have a situation."

My brother laughed. "I take it your meeting didn't go well?"

"Absolutely not."

"I told you that you should've led with an orchid and not a succulent."

"I don't think it was the plant, Carver."

My brother snorted. "Fine, fine—so what's the situation? Was he hot?"

I pulled out a book that did *not* belong in political thriller—*Red, White & Royal Blue* by Casey McQuiston—and decided to walk it back to the romance section where it did, in fact, belong. "Okay, we have *two* situations."

"Oh Lord, he's *that* hot?"

"You know that book I let you borrow? The one by Sally Thorne? *The Hating Game*?"

"Tall, stoic yet quirky, has a bedroom wall painted to match her eyes?"

"That's it! Though *his* eyes are brown. Like *chocolate* brown."

"Godiva?"

"No, more like melty Hershey's Kisses on like the worst day of your period."

"Damn."

"*Yeah*, and when I introduced myself, I said my name—*twice*."

"You didn't."

I groaned. "I did! And *then* he didn't give me another extension on my novel. I have to finish it. And it has to have a happy ending."

He guffawed. "He said that?"

"Yeah."

"I don't know if that turns me on more or less . . ."

"*Carver!*"

"What?! I like a man who knows what he wants!"

I wanted to strangle him through the phone. Carver was the middle of the Day siblings and the only one who knew I ghostwrote—and I made him *swear* to secrecy or I'd print all of his embarrassing middle-grade fanfic starring Hugh Jackman in the town paper. Friendly sibling blackmail and all that. He just didn't know *whom* I ghostwrote for. Not that he didn't constantly guess.

I made my way into the romance section, half-naked men glowering down at me from their shelves, and slipped the book into the M section.

Carver asked, "So, I hate to be *that* person, but what're you going to do about that manuscript?"

"I don't know," I replied truthfully. The titles on the shelves all seemed to run together.

"Maybe it's time to branch out again?" he suggested. "Obviously, this writing gig isn't working for you anymore, and you're too brilliant to be hiding behind Nora Roberts."

"I don't ghostwrite for Nora."

"You wouldn't tell me if you did," he pointed out.

"But it's not Nora."

"Mm-*hmm*."

"It's really not."

"Nicholas Sparks? Jude Deveraux? Christina Lauren? Ann Nichols?—"

"Is Dad around?" I interrupted, my gaze falling to the Ns. *Nichols.* I ran my fingers along the spine of *The Forest of Dreams.*

I could hear Carver frowning in his voice. "How did you know I was at the funeral home?"

"You only ever call me when you're bored at the funeral home. Not enough work at the tech firm today?"

"Wanted to leave early. Dad's wrapping up a meeting with a client," he added, which meant he was talking with the bereaved about funeral arrangements, caskets, and pricing.

"Have you talked to him yet?"

"About the chest pains? No."

I made a disapproving noise. "Mom says he keeps refusing to go see Dr. Martin."

"You know Dad. He'll make the time eventually."

"Do you think Alice could pressure him?"

Alice was *really* good at getting Dad to do things he didn't want to do. She was the youngest of us, and she had Dad tied around her pinkie so tightly, just the mere *thought* of upsetting her would drive him to pull down the moon if he had to. She was also the one who decided to stay in the family business. She was the only one who wanted to.

"Already asked," Carver replied. "They've got something like three funerals this weekend. I'm sure he's going to go next week when he's a little less busy. And he's fine. If anything happens, Mom's right there."

"Why does he have to be so *stubborn*?"

"Funny coming from you."

"Ha *ha*." I picked out two sci-fis and a charming-looking paperback. *Howl's Moving Castle* by Diana Wynne Jones. Buying books always made me feel better, even if I never read them. "Can you try at least? To convince Dad to go sooner rather than later?"

"Sure, if you can convince him to take a day off work—"

In the background, I heard Dad yell, "Convince who? Of what?"

And Carver replied, covering the receiver to shout back (not that it helped my eardrums), "Nothing, old man! Go drink your Ensure! Hey—I was joking—oh, what's that, Mom? I should come help you with something? Sure! Here's your second favorite—"

"I am *not* second favorite," I interjected.

"Okay, bye!"

I heard a scuffle on the other end of the phone as Carver very quickly handed it over to Dad. I could imagine the exchange—Carver tossing his cell phone to Dad as Dad tried to swat him in the arm and missed to catch the phone, and Carver slinking away into one of the other rooms after Mom, laughing the entire way.

Dad raised the phone to his ear, and his bold, boisterous voice boomed through. "Buttercup! How's the Big Apple?"

My heart swelled at the sound of his voice, chorused with Carver laughing away in the background. I missed my family, more than I really cared to admit most days. "It's good."

"Eating enough? Staying hydrated?"

"I should be asking *you* that." I exited the aisle and sat down on the bookstore step stool, satchel and books in my lap. "*Old man*."

I could almost *hear* him roll his eyes. "I'm *fine*. These old bones haven't quit on me yet. How's my eldest doing? Found a nice catch in the city yet?"

I snorted. "You know my life is more than who I date, Dad. Love isn't everything."

"How did my beautiful eldest daughter become so bitter? It's so tragic," he lamented with a heavy sigh. "She was made from the loins of love!"

"Gross, Dad."

"Why, when I met your mother, I was so smitten with her—"

"Dad."

"—we didn't leave the hotel room for three days. *Three days!*"

"Dad."

"Her lips like fresh rose petals—"

"I get it, I get it! I just . . . I don't think I'm ready for a new relationship. I don't think I'll ever be."

"Maybe the universe will surprise you."

For some reason, the angular face of my new editor came to mind. Yeah, right. I ran my thumb over the pages of one of the books in my lap, feeling them buzz softly. "How's the family business?"

"Good as it'll get," Dad replied. "Remember Dr. Cho? Your orthodontist?"

"Alice said he passed."

"Was a good funeral, though. *Beautiful* weather for April. The wind danced through the trees, I'm telling you. A great send-off," he said, and then he added a little softer, "He thanked me afterwards."

I swallowed the knot in my throat because anyone else hearing that would've thought he was crazy. Maybe he was a little crazy, but if he was, then I was, too. "Did he now?"

"It was nice. Got some ideas for my own funeral myself."

"It'll be a while," I joked.

"I should hope! Maybe then you'll come home."

"I'd be the talk of the town."

He laughed, but there was a little bitterness there. One that we both shared. It was why I left, after all. Why I didn't stay in Mairmont. Why I went as far as I could, where no one knew my story.

As it turns out, when you solved a murder at thirteen by talking with ghosts, the newspapers printed exactly that.

LOCAL GIRL SOLVES MURDER WITH GHOSTS

You can imagine how that sort of thing could haunt you. I wasn't exactly the popular kid in high school, and after that I didn't stand a ghost of a chance of being asked to prom. Carver and Alice couldn't see them, and neither could Dad's younger sister Liza, or Mom. It was only the two of us.

We were the only ones who could understand.

Another reason why I was better off alone.

"Please go see Dr. Martin next week—" I began, when he interrupted me.

"Oh, there's another call coming in. I'll talk to you soon, okay, buttercup? Don't forget to call your mother!"

I sighed, more out of resignation than regret. "Love you, Dad."

"Love you more!"

He hung up, and I finally noticed the bookseller glaring at me for sitting on the stool. I popped up and quickly apologized for taking up real estate, and scurried off toward the cash register.

One of the only good things to come out of this writing gig was the fact that I could write books off on taxes. Even if I never read them. Even if I used them to build book thrones and then sit down and cry on them while pouring myself glass after glass of merlot.

It was still worth it.

And the small hit of serotonin *did* make me feel a little less murderous. Tucking the books into my backpack, I left for the closest station that would take me back to Jersey. It was about a twenty-minute walk up to the Ninth Street station, but the afternoon was sunny and my coat was heavy enough to protect me from the last biting chill of the season. I liked the long walks in New York. It used to help me work through a plot inconvenience or figure out a scene that never quite worked, but all my walks in the last year couldn't jostle my brain into creating again, no matter how far I went. Not even today, on the eve of everything coming unraveled.

At Ninth Street, I descended into the bowels of the subway. It was much hotter in the station than outside, and I unbuttoned my coat and tugged down my scarf to keep myself cool as I took the steps down two at a time to the platform.

The train pulled up to the platform and the doors dinged. I elbowed my way into the packed car, shoved myself up against the far door, and hunkered down for the long ride. The train began to move again, rocking gently back and forth, and I stared out of the door window as light after light passed.

I didn't pay attention to the shimmering transparent woman standing a few people away, somehow inhabiting a free space. She kept looking at me, intently, until the train pulled up to the next station, and I sat down in a newly empty seat and pulled out one of the books I'd bought.

My dad would've hated what I just did. He would've told me to give her a chance. To sit down, to listen to her story.

All they wanted, usually, was for someone to listen.

But I ignored the ghost, as I had done for almost a decade in the city. It was easier when you were surrounded by people. You could just pretend like they were another faceless person in the crowd. So I pretended, and as the PATH train crossed under the Hudson River to Jersey, the ghost flickered—and was gone.

3

.....

Dead Romance

I DRAINED MY glass of wine and poured myself another one.

I used to be good at romance.

Every one of Ann Nichols's new novels had been praised by fans and critics alike. "A dazzling display of passion and heart," the *New York Times Book Review* called *Midnight Matinee*, and *Kirkus Reviews* said *A Rake's Guide* was "a surprisingly enjoyable romp"—which, hey, I'll take as positive. "A sensational novel from a well-loved storyteller," *Booklist* wrote, and never mind all of the blurbs from *Vogue* and *Entertainment Weekly* and a million other media outlets. I had them all posted on my dream board in my room, cut out from magazines and email chains over this last year, hoping that seeing them all together could inspire me to write one last book.

Just one more.

I was *good* at romance. Great at it, even. But I couldn't for the life of me write this one. Every time I tried, it felt wrong.

Like I was missing something.

It should've been easy—a grand romantic gesture, a beautiful proposal, a happily ever after. The kind my parents had, and I'd spent my entire life looking for one just as grand. I wrote them into novels while I looked for my real-life equivalent in men at bars wearing sloppy ties or wrinkled T-shirts, and strangers who stole glances at me on the train, bad idea after bad idea.

I just wanted what my parents had. I wanted to walk into a ballroom dancing club and meet the love of my life. Mom and Dad weren't even *assigned* to each other as dance partners until their respective partners both came down with the flu, and the rest, they say, was history. They'd been married for thirty-five years, and it was the kind of romance that I'd only ever found again in fiction. They fought and disagreed, of course, but they always came back together like a binary star, dancing with each other through life. It was the small moments that tied them together—the way Dad touched the small of her back whenever he passed her, the way Mom kissed his bald spot on the top of his head, the way they held hands like kids whenever we went out to dinner, the way they defended each other when they knew the other was right, and talked patiently when they were wrong.

Even after all of their kids moved out, I heard they still cranked up the stereo in the parlor and danced across the ancient cherrywood floors to Bruce Springsteen and Van Morrison.

I wanted that. I *searched* for that.

And then I realized, standing in the rain that April evening, almost a year ago exactly—I'd never have that.

I took another gulp of wine, glaring at my screen. I had to do this. I didn't have a choice. Whether it was good or not—I had to turn in *something*.

"Maybe . . ."

> The evening was soggy, and the cold rain struck through her like a deathly chill. Amelia stood in the rain, wet and shivering. She should've taken her umbrella, but she wasn't thinking. "Why are you here?"
>
> Jackson, for his part, was equally as wet and cold. "I don't know."
>
> "Then leave."

"That's not very romantic," I muttered, deleting the scene, and drained the rest of my glass. Again.

> Nighttime on the Isle was supposed to be magical, but tonight's rain was especially cold and heavy. Amelia's clothes clung to her like a second skin. She wrapped her jacket around herself tighter, to shield against the biting cold.
>
> Jackson said, his breath coming in a puff of frost, "I didn't think the ice queen could get cold."
>
> She punched him.

"Yeah, great job." I sighed, and deleted that one, too. Amelia and Jackson were supposed to be reconciling, coming back from the dark night of the soul, and stepping into the light *together*. This was the *grand romance* at the end, the big finale that every Ann Nichols book had, and every reader expected.

And I couldn't write this fucking scene.

I was a failure, and Ann's career was dead in the water.

There was little more depressing than that, save for the state of my refrigerator and cabinets. All that we had left was dino-shaped mac and cheese. Perfect depression food, at least. As I pulled the box from the cabinet, my roommate burst in through the door, slinging her purse down on the couch.

"Fuck the man!" she cried.

"Fuck the man," I intoned religiously.

"All of them!" Rose stormed into the kitchen, opened the refrigerator, and began to stress eat carrots out of the container. Rose Wu had been my roommate in college, but she'd graduated a year early and moved up to NYC to pursue a career in advertising. A year ago, she had a spare room. So, I moved in, and that was that. She was my best friend and the best thing about this whole damn city rolled into one.

She was the kind of person who demanded to be looked at—the kind who could walk into a room and command it with a single look. She knew what she wanted, and she always went for it. That was her mantra. "You see it, you reach for it."

That might've been why she was so successful at the advertising firm where she worked. Only two years in, and she was already the social media marketing manager.

"*Michael*," she began, shoving another carrot into her mouth, "came in today and was telling *me* I did wrong with our client—you know, the actress Jessica Stone? We're working on advertising for her clothing line—and how it's *all* my fault. Bitch, she's not even my client! I'm not even in publicity! She's *Stacee's* client! God, I hate white men being unable to tell one Asian from another."

"I can murder him if you want," I replied with absolute sincerity, opening the box of macaroni, extracting the cheese packet, and dumping the noodles into a pot full of water. I didn't even wait for it to start boiling. It would eventually.

Rose shoved another carrot into her mouth. "Only if we don't get caught."

I shrugged. "Grind up the body. Host a barbecue. Feed the remains to your office. There, done."

"That sounds like the plot to a movie."

"*Fried Green Tomatoes*," I admitted.

Rose cocked her head. "Did it work?"

"Oh, hell yeah, and I've got a *great* barbecue recipe we can try."

She sighed and shook her head, twisting the carrot bag closed and shoving it back into the refrigerator. "No, no. I don't want to risk food poisoning innocent people. I've got a better idea."

"Wood chipper?"

"Drinks."

The water began to boil. I stirred the pot with a spatula, since everything else was dirty. "Do you mean arsenic or . . . ?"

"No, I mean *we're* going out. For drinks."

I gave her a baffled look. Me, standing in our kitchen, making deadline mac and cheese in my comfy flannel pajama bottoms and an oversized Tigger sweater, no bra, and yesterday's hair. "*Out . . . ?*"

"Out." Rose went to the doorway of the kitchen and stood there like Gandalf to the Balrog. None shall pass. "*We* are going *out*. Clearly I had a bad day, and by the looks of the new books on the counter, you did, too."

I groaned. "No, Rose, please, let me stay in and eat my mac and cheese and die. Alone."

"You are *not* going to die alone," my roommate replied adamantly. "If anything, you'll at least have a cat."

"I hate cats."

"You love them."

"They're assholes."

"Much like every ex-boyfriend you've ever had, and you loved all of *them*."

I couldn't argue with that. But I did *not* have cats, and I did *not* want to go out drinking, either. I ripped open the powdered cheese packet. "My bank account is about as lacking as my love life. I couldn't even afford a Natty Light, Rose."

She gave a loud sigh and took the packet from my hand, scooting the boiling pot of noodle water onto an off burner. "We're going *out*. We're going to have *fun*. I need fun, and I know you do, too. I'm sensing, from the mac and cheese, that the meeting with your editor didn't go well today, did it?"

Of course it didn't. Why else would I be making depressing mac and cheese? I gave a shrug. "It went fine."

"Florence."

I exhaled through my mouth. "Ann has a new editor. I think you might know him or something—he seems familiar. His name is Benji something or other. Ainer? Ander?"

Rose gawked. "Benji *Andor*?"

I pointed at her with the wooden spoon. "That's it."

"You're kidding."

"I kid you not."

"Lucky!" Rose barked a laugh. "He's *hot*."

"Yeah I know—how do *you* know?"

"He was in a whole Thirty-Five Under Thirty-Five thing in *Time Out* a year ago. He used to be an executive editor over at Elderwood Books before they folded. Where were you?"

I gave her an exhausted look. She knew exactly where I was a year ago. Making depressing mac and cheese for a *different* reason.

She waved her hand dismissively. "Anyway, it's nice to see he's still in publishing, but at Falcon House's romance imprint? Wow."

I shrugged. "He probably likes romances? Do I know any books he worked on over at Elderwood?"

Rose put the packet of powdered cheese back into the box. "*The Murdered Birds*? *The Woman from Cabin Creek*?"

I stared at my roommate. "So . . . gothic murders?"

"Gruesome, *morbid* gothic murders. Like I'm talking Benji Andor is a modern-day Rochester, but without the wife in the attic. I hear he even had a *fiancée* once, but *he* left *her* at the altar."

I gave Rose a look. "Do you even know what happens in *Jane Eyre*?"

"I've sorta half seen the movies. Anyway, that's not the point. So, you have publishing's hottest bachelor editing Ann's books now. I can't *wait* until he gets to your sex scenes. Seriously, they're some of the best I've ever read, and I read a *lot* of smutty books. And fanfic," she added as an afterthought.

"He won't," I deadpanned. "I have until tomorrow evening to turn in the book."

"Wow, you really couldn't get another extension, huh?"

I groaned and put my face in my hands. "*No*, and if I don't turn it in, he's getting legal involved. And then the cat's out of the bag! Hi, I'm the ghostwriter! But I can't even do *ghostwriting* properly, and then they'll start wondering where Ann is, and then some really grizzled detective will come around questioning me and then everyone'll start wondering if I *murdered* Ann Nichols—"

"Hon, I love you, but you're jumping the shark here."

"You never know!"

"*Is* she dead?"

"I don't know! No!" Then, a bit calmer: "Probably not?"

"Why don't you just tell *your editor* about being her ghostwriter?"

I sighed. "I couldn't. You should've seen the way he *looked* at me when I asked to write a sad romance instead. It was like I killed his favorite puppy."

"You say that like he'd have more than one puppy."

"Of course. He seems like a multi-dog kinda person. But not the *point*. The point is, I didn't. Couldn't."

"So instead, you're going to ruin your career and disappoint your *one* literary hero."

My shoulders drooped. "Yeah. Now can I *please* eat my mac and cheese and wallow in my despair?"

Rose's face turned to stone. "*No*," she said as sharply as her cat eyeliner, and grabbed me by the wrist and dragged me out of the kitchen and down the hallway to our bedrooms. "C'mon. We are going out. We are forgetting our worries. We are going to conquer this stupid, loud, exhausting city tonight! Or die *trying*!"

At the moment, I'd rather have died.

Rose's closet was full of fashion. It was a runway in our apartment. Beautiful sparkly dresses and soft blouses and pencil skirts with a slit *just* low enough to be work appropriate. Rose took out a short black dress, the one she had been trying to make me wear for at least a month now, and finally her evil plan was coming to fruition.

I shook my head. "No."

"*C'monnnn*," Rose pleaded, presenting the dress to me. "It'll really make your ass pop."

"I think you mean my ass will pop *out* of it."

"*Floreeeeeeence*," she whined.

"*Roooose*," I whined back.

She frowned. Narrowed her eyes. And said—

"Catawampus."

My eyes widened at the word. "Don't you *dare*," I whisper-warned.

"Cat-a-wam-*pus*," she enunciated, and there it was. Our emergency word. The word with no arguments. It wasn't a request anymore—it was an order. We allowed each other one a year. "You aren't an old spinster in a tower, and you've been acting like it for too long, and honestly? I should've done this sooner. If you aren't making progress on your stupid story—"

"It's not stupid!"

"—then there's no use sitting here eating depression mac and cheese and getting drunk alone on Two-Buck Chuck. *Cat-a-wam-pus.*"

I glared at her. She smirked, crossing her arms over her chest, triumphant.

I threw up my arms. "*Fine!* Fine. I will only do this if you promise to do the dishes for the next month."

"Week."

"Deal."

We shook on it.

Somehow, I had the feeling that she got the better end of the deal, and my suspicions were confirmed when she said, "Now get naked and put this on. We're going to get you in trouble tonight and find you some inspiration to kiss."

"I don't need trouble to—"

"Naked! Now!" she cried, and pushed me out of her room and into my own and shut me inside. I stared down at the dress in my hands. It wasn't *that* bad. Sure, it was way too short for my liking and it had at least a hundred too many sequins, and it probably cost more than an entire month of *rent*, but it wasn't the gaudiest thing in Rose's wardrobe. (That went to the rainbow number she broke out every June for the Pride Parade. There were strangers we never saw the rest of the year who recognized her in that dress every single Pride.) The dress wasn't really my taste, but maybe that's exactly what I needed.

To forget that I had failed at the one thing I was ever good at. To pretend like tomorrow wasn't the last day of the best career of my life. To be someone else for a while.

Just for a night.

Someone who didn't fail.

4

Fated Mates

ROSE WAS LIKE an encyclopedia of the night. She knew exactly what restaurant had the best deconstructed burger, and which warehouses housed the most recent silent rave. (And how to get there.) She knew which cellar jazz bars made the best sidecars and the best diner for 3:00 A.M. hangover cures and the cheapest cocktails at the local artisanal bar where the next Franzen lamented about not having the time to pen his Great American Novel. She came from a small town in Indiana, with only a duffel bag and money stuffed into her shoes, and somehow, she'd made New York City her home in a way I never could.

I think it was the stars. I missed the stars too much. Especially the way they looked from the brick steps of my parents' front porch.

There really wasn't a sight like it.

There also wasn't a sight like whatever murder back alley Rose led me to that night. There were three streetlights, and every single one of them flickered like they were all auditioning for the world's most cliché horror movie. I followed Rose down the narrow alley, one hand stuck in my purse, around my pepper spray.

"You're going to murder me," I said. "That's it, isn't it? You want my Gucci crossbody bag."

She snorted. "I don't know how many times I have to tell you that it's fake."

"You can barely tell."

"Yeah, if you close your eyes." Then she stopped at what I realized, a moment later, was a door, and knocked.

"Who are your murder accomplices?" I asked. "Is it Sherrie from HR? Or my new hunky editor—"

The almost-hidden door gave a creak and swung open to reveal a tweed-dressed grad student with small round glasses and gelled-back hair. Rose motioned with her head for us to go inside, and I followed her.

I didn't know what I expected, but it definitely wasn't a narrow low-lit bar with wooden round tables. It was crowded, but everyone was whispering, as if they didn't want to break the mood, so it was surprisingly quiet. Rose found us a table near the back, a single flickering candle in the center. At the front of the bar, where we came in, there was a stage with a microphone and a single amp. The crowd was a strange amalgamation of tweedy-professor types and boho artists who painted themselves naked and pressed their tits to a canvas to make art. Some of those art pieces were on the walls, actually.

"What *is* this place?" I asked, baffled.

"Colloquialism," she replied.

"Bless you."

She rolled her eyes. "A bar, Florence. It's a bar."

I looked for a menu on the table, or maybe it had fallen to the ground—but there wasn't one. "I'm definitely not cool enough for this."

"You are *more* than cool enough," she replied, and when the bartender slipped out from behind the slab of cherry oak that served as a bar to greet us, Rose ordered something that sounded very fancy.

"Oh, I'm good with Everclear—"

Rose put a hand on my arm, giving me a warning look, because the last time we'd gotten drunk on Everclear was in college and it had been dumped into a tub of Jungle Juice. Neither of us remembered how we'd gotten from Bushwick to the Lower East Side that night, but some mysteries were better left unsolved.

I shifted uncomfortably at the table, feeling so incredibly out of my element in a too-tight black dress, ordering a too-expensive cocktail, in a quiet hole-in-the-wall bar full of people who probably all were so much cooler than me. I was half-afraid someone would come up and ask for my artistic credentials, and when I took out my Costco card and a cardboard-printed membership to a smutty book club—

Well.

Much like with Ben Andor, I feared I was not tall enough to ride this ride.

Rose slipped a credit card out from her glittery silver clutch and handed it to the bartender. "Put everything on this, please."

The bartender took her card with a nod and left. *Everything?* How long were we going to stay? I guessed it didn't matter anymore, did it? We could stay all night, or only a few minutes, and I would still wake up tomorrow not knowing how to write that scene. The bartender returned with two very fancy drinks named the Dickinson, and Rose held hers up to cheers with me. I stared at her like she was no longer my roommate, but an alien entity who had assumed my dear Rose's smokin'-hot body. She gave a one-shouldered shrug. "What? It's a Mastercard."

"I thought you were trying to get *out* of debt."

"Florence Minerva Day, you deserve someone to take you out and treat you nice once in a while."

"Are you going to take me back to your place and have your way with me after?" I teased.

"Only if I get to be the little spoon and you let me make you pancakes in the morning before I leave and never call you again."

"Perfect."

"Cheers," she said, raising her cocktail. "To a good night."

"And a good tomorrow," I finished.

We clinked our cocktails together. The drink tasted like strawberries and awfully expensive gin. Definitely not the ten-dollar handle I used to buy at the bodega in college. This stuff was dangerous. I took a larger gulp as a woman in a brown shawl stood from one of the tables near the front and made her way toward the microphone.

"Is this an open mic or something?" I asked.

Rose took another sip of the Dickinson. "Sorta."

"Sorta . . . ?"

Before Rose could reply, the woman in the brown shawl leaned in toward the microphone and said, "Thank you all for staying with us through our break. Now, for our next reading, I'd like to welcome Sophia Jenkins," she said in a soft voice that reminded me of a patient kindergarten teacher.

People snapped as she relinquished the mic and a brown-skinned woman with short gray hair came up to the microphone and took out a journal.

"It's a *poetry reading*?" I whispered to Rose.

"A reading of anything, really," my best friend replied with a half shrug. "I figured you needed some inspiration. Writing's lonely, I hear. It's nice to listen to other people's words."

The woman's short story was about a fish in the ocean who dreamed of being a siren, or maybe she was a siren who thought she was a fish. It was beautiful, and simple, and the entire bar had quieted to listen.

When she was done, everyone snapped politely.

I didn't realize I needed that until this moment. Just quiet art, spoken to quiet people to appreciate. No secrets. No exchange. No expectations. "You're a really good friend, Rose Wu."

She grinned. "You're right, and any good friend would tell you to go up next."

"What?"

"I said what I said."

I hesitated, but it didn't sound like a terrible idea, when all day writing had felt like pulling teeth. The artisanal Dickinson helped. I *could* go up there. I could read something that I jotted down on my phone a while back. I could put a little bit of creativity into the world that seemed to want to suck it from your very marrow.

I could go up there and be someone—anyone—other than Florence Day tonight.

Because Florence Day would be curled up on the couch with a bowl of mac and cheese, her laptop balanced precariously on a pillow on her lap, trying desperately to write a story she didn't believe in. Because storybook love only existed for a lucky few—like my parents. They were the exception to the rule, not the rule itself. It was rare, and it was fleeting. Love was a high for a moment that left you hollow when it left, and you spent the rest of your life chasing that feeling. A false memory, too good to be true, and I'd been fooling myself for far too long, believing in Grand Romantic Gestures and Happily Ever Afters.

Those weren't written for me. I wasn't the exception.

I was the rule.

And I guess I finally understood the kinds of lies I told people with my witty prose and promise of a happy ending. I promised them that they were the exception. And every time I looked at that blinking cursor in my Word document, trying to unite Amelia and Jackson, all I could see was my reflection on the screen.

The reflection of a liar.

But for one night—one moment—I didn't want to be that girl I saw in the reflection of my computer screen. I wanted to go back. To pretend that there was true love waiting for me somewhere out in the world. That souls separated by space and time could come crashing together with the force of a single kiss. That the impossible was not quite out of reach. Not for me.

That there was love, true and fierce and loyal, in a world where like called to like . . . and I was no longer the rule.

Where I was the exception.

As if the universe answered, I stood when the emcee called for another volunteer, another person to bare their heart. And so did someone else. Someone near the front of the bar, where the tables were so tightly packed the tweed suits blended together.

I froze.

"Oh, my!" the emcee cooed. "What a treat. Which one of you'd like to go first?"

The man in question turned to see who else had volunteered. Our eyes met. I knew then that it *was* him.

I could recognize him anywhere.

Even after a hundred years, after I'd scrubbed my brain of everything he was, I would know him.

Platinum-blond hair and a loose-cut V-neck and tight jeans and a birthmark just below his left ear in the shape of a crescent moon that I had kissed so many times my lips hurt just thinking about all of the nights I rubbed them raw, trying to forget about it. About *him*.

It was the universe telling me that I couldn't forget. That if love was true, then love was a lie. That I had been happy once, happy then, but not happy forever. Because that wasn't my story. That even my stories weren't mine.

Perhaps they never were.

5

.....

Dead Serious

THE FIRST TIME I met Lee Marlow, I was at a party with Rose and Natalie, our other roommate, who had since moved to South Korea. The party consisted of a lot of publishing people, though it wasn't a mixer. There were authors, editors, quite a few assistants, and agents. It was for some milestone, but I couldn't for the life of me remember what. They all blended together after a while, party after party, book launch after book launch, swanky bars after rooftop restaurants after extravagant apartments in Midtown.

I had grabbed Rose by the upper arm and brought her close. "Oh my god, four o'clock. Red Vans. I *told* you I could've worn my Converses."

"But those Louboutins make your ass look amazing," she replied.

"I can't feel my feet, Rose," I complained, envying the guy in the red Vans. Then he turned around and my breath caught in my throat. "Oh."

"He'd look better in a nice pair of Gucci leather loafers."

"That sounds so pretentious."

"Says the girl wearing her best friend's Louboutins."

"You *made* me!"

She inclined her head. "And I don't regret it for a second."

I did, however, regret it a few hours later when my feet had gone from numb to stabbing pain. The party was in someone's swanky Midtown apartment, and while most people were in the living room or on the balcony, I had hobbled my way into the library and sank down on the leather high-back chair that probably cost more than my NYU tuition, and taken off those priceless Louboutins, and I never felt more relief in my life. I leaned back in the plush leather chair and closed my eyes, and basked in the quiet.

Rose thrived on parties, on the energy, the loudness, the people. I liked them sometimes—on special occasions, like at concerts or Comic-Cons, but there was nothing quite like the silence of a well-loved library.

"Guess I'm not the only one looking for a little quiet," came a good-humored voice from the other side of the library.

My eyes flew open and I sat up straight—only to find the man in the red Vans sitting on one of those ridiculous bookshelf ladders, the autobiography of some dead poet in his hands. It was like a scene from one of those cheesy nineties rom-coms—light streaking in between the dark velvet curtains, painting his face in angles of pale moonlight.

I felt myself blushing even before I registered how picturesque he looked. It was his eyes, I think. When he looked at me, the world around us blurred. All I saw was him, and all he saw was me. And he *saw* me. It felt like one of those moments I wrote about in romances, one of those destiny-calling feelings, where like called to like. And I knew—I *knew*—I was the exception to the rule.

He noticed my shoes abandoned by the chair. "Bold of you to take your shoes off in a stranger's house."

"These aren't shoes, they're torture devices," I argued, feeling myself go rigid in defense. "And I don't see it bothering you."

He studied my shoes. "They do seem to be rather pointy."

"Great for stabbing men alone in a library."

"The pretty girl with the blond hair and the Louboutins in the private library?" He grinned. "No one'll see that coming."

I narrowed my eyes. "Are we flirting or is this a game of Clue?"

He did that thing—the thing people did sometimes when they ran their tongue over their teeth, just under their lips, to hide a smile. "Which do you want it to—"

"Marlow!" A tall woman with strawberry hair strode into the library, two drinks in her hands, immediately breaking the spell with her soft honey voice. I quickly looked away, down at my bare feet, as he greeted her. "There you are. I thought I left you by the head editor from Elderwood."

"*You* try holding a conversation with that guy," the man in the red Vans replied, and accepted one of the drinks the woman handed to him.

"I've had to talk to worse." She then took him by his coat sleeve and tugged. "C'mon, there's still a lot more people to meet."

I wondered who she was. His girlfriend, perhaps? Fiancée? She was beautiful, with blunt-cut bangs and a loud yellow jacket, paired with high-waisted tartan-print trousers. I later came to find out that she was his assistant editor before he left Faux, where he had steadily climbed the ladder for years.

If the man in the red Vans had gone with her, things would have been so, so different. But he glanced back at me, a smile tucked into the corner of his mouth, and said, "I'll be there in a minute."

"Ugh, *fine*," she said as someone caught her eye in the crowd in the living room. "Oh! Ohmygod, that's him. That's the author. Mr. Brown!" she called, hurrying back into the fray of people.

And then we were alone again.

He watched her go, setting his drink on the mahogany bookshelf—that should've been my first warning sign, a blatant disregard for someone else's books—and came over to me. I felt my chest constrict; I wasn't sure if I'd rather be left alone with my painful feet or if I wanted him to stay.

"So," he asked, "do you have anywhere to be tonight?"

"Here."

He snorted a laugh. "Anywhere else?"

I inclined my head. "Are you asking?"

"Are you saying yes?" He arched a very pointed eyebrow. It was the kind of arch a feature writer would call *belletristic* when they sat down to pen his profile in *GQ*.

I should've told him to leave. I should've said I needed to stay and keep an eye on Rose. But I didn't know, and he looked at me with this genuine sort of curiosity—who could this girl be, in Louboutins and a discount black dress? And he was a mystery, too, in his red Vans and his loose brown suit and his wild blond hair.

He outstretched his hand to me, as if wanting me to take it. "I'm Marlow—Lee Marlow. C'mon, let's go somewhere shoes aren't required."

I smiled at him, and I knew then—I just *knew*—that this was something special. I felt like a star that had come unhinged from the night sky and started to fall, and I couldn't stop myself. I didn't want to.

This was the moment. The one we'd tell at dinner parties. Of how we met, and fell in love, and knew we'd grow old together, and even when we died it wouldn't be the end. Because if there was one thing more powerful than death itself, it was true, undeniable love.

I could feel it in my bones.

I just wanted to talk to him, to breathe in his words, to understand what made his brilliant mind tick.

I was, as the French say, *une putain d'idiote.*

"Florence Day." I took his hand.

And that was how I, the girl perpetually used as the backup date, who would rather hide in a burrito of blankets and watch trashy reality TV on a Friday night, began to date one of the hottest men I had ever met in my entire life.

But as I got to know him, as the dates turned into months, turned into anniversaries and sweet kisses, I thought it was the kind of love story worthy of my family's legacy. A romance novel in the real world. It had the perfect meet-cute, the most charming love interest, and the most beautiful setting—a brownstone in Park Slope with a rooftop garden where I would sneak out and write chapters upon chapters of whimsical words.

Sometimes he would find me up in the garden and ask in that smooth tenor of his, "What're you doing up here, bunny?"

And I'd close my laptop or my journal or whatever I was using to write that evening, and smile at him, and say, "Oh, just thinking up stories."

"What kinds of stories?" He'd sit down on the bench beside me, between a busy azalea and a pot of curling devil's ivy. "I hope they're naughty," he said as he burrowed his face into my hair and kissed the side of my neck at the tenderest spot.

It always made me shiver.

"Very," I'd laugh.

"I could take a peek. Make them better."

"Bold of you to assume they aren't already perfect."

He laughed into my hair and murmured, "Nothing's perfect, bunny," and kissed me so softly, I would've called him a liar if my lips weren't preoccupied, because this was damn near perfect. The way the evening light crept over the rooftop, orange and golden and dreamy, and how his fingers were gentle as he cupped the sides of my face.

This was perfect. *He* was perfect.

Even so, I kept my ghostwriting secret.

There was never a right time to tell him, I felt, because every time a book he edited hit the list, I had been on there for a few weeks more. It felt like lying, even though I had signed NDAs and bundled myself in cautionary tape.

And so, because of that, I told him everything else. I laid my heart bare to him because I wanted to make up for the one secret in my life I didn't know how to vocalize. I told him all of my other secrets, and my nightmares, and finally—after a year of kisses and dates and promises we always intended to keep—as we sat on the couch watching *Portals to Hell*, I confessed, "They don't really like people yelling at them to appear."

"Hmm?" He looked up from a book he was reading, his glasses perched low on his nose. Years later, I realized he didn't actually *need* them—a small lie, being built on. "What was that, bunny?"

"The ghosts. They really don't like it when people yell." I was half a bottle of pinot grigio into the night, so I was a little braver than usual. I'd never talked about ghosts with anyone other than my father and Rose, and I thought—stupidly—that if I exchanged one for the other, my secret ghostwriting with a story of actual *ghosts*, it would make up for it.

He gave me a strange look over his black-framed glasses. "*Ghosts?* Like the haunting kind?"

I nodded, swirling my wine around in my glass. "Dad and I've danced with them in the funeral parlor."

"Florence," he chided.

"Most of them just want to talk, you know, to have someone listen. It's not as creepy as it looks in the movies. I wasn't always able to see them, but it started when I was eight? Nine? Somewhere in there."

He took off his glasses and turned to me on the couch. "You . . . you're saying you saw ghosts? Like actual spirits. The"—he wiggled his fingers in the air—"*wooooo* kind?"

"I see ghosts. Present tense."

"Like—right now?"

"No. Not now. Sometimes. I don't talk to them anymore. I haven't since I left home—"

He was chewing on the inside of his cheek, as if to keep himself from laughing, and I felt my heart sink then. Some things you just couldn't tell even the people you loved the most. Some things no one would ever understand. *Could* never understand. And Lee was giving me the look I'd seen every day in high school, that pitying look, verging on curious, wondering if I was crazy.

I grinned then, and kissed him on the mouth. "Ha, what do you think of my story?" I asked, shoving down the part of me that began to fracture. The part I could never—would never—share with anyone again. "It's a book I'm working on."

More lies. But close to the truth. Truer than I'd ever been with anyone outside of Mairmont. But somehow, it still made me feel ashamed. And alone. I drained the rest of my glass and started to get off the couch, but he took me by the wrist and pulled me back down onto the cushions again.

"Wait, bunny. It's really interesting." And then, very softly, he asked, "Tell me more?"

I paused. "Really?"

"Absolutely. If this story means something to you, I want to listen."

Always the perfect words at the perfect time. He was good at that. He knew how to make you feel important and cherished.

"But," he added, "third person, please. The first-person kind of threw me off," he admitted with a laugh.

So, I took a deep breath and I started. "She knew she would see a ghost when the crows came."

And that was how I told him about the part of my life I couldn't.

I told him about the ghosts of my childhood, and how rare they really were—some years without any at all. I'd seen a few in the city, but I never stopped to ask if they wanted anything. I didn't really have it in me anymore, not after what I went through in Mairmont. I wanted to get away from that life—that part of me. And the best way to do it was to ignore them.

I never should have told him anything. I shouldn't have even pretended that they were a story.

My younger sister, Alice, always said I was too gullible. Too generous. Too like the tree in that picture book, who kept giving and giving until there was nothing left. She said one day it would come back to bite me in the ass.

Lee Marlow did like to bite, but never my ass, and anyway I loved him, and he loved me, and we had a brownstone in Park Slope and he kissed me with such intensity that any echo of doubt fell silent between our lips. I might have been that weird girl who saw ghosts, but to him I was perfect.

Once he said, while we were out to dinner together and I had just told him about the time I had been woken up by the ghost of the recently deceased mayor, "You should try to publish this story. You might just make millions off it."

"I tried publishing once. It didn't work out. And I definitely did *not* make millions."

He had barked a laugh. "Well, that's because you wrote a romance."

"What's wrong with that?"

"Oh, bunny, you know you can do better."

I faltered. "Better . . . ?"

"No one's remembered for a *romance*, bunny. If you want to be a good writer, you gotta make something that lasts."

I didn't know what to say. Honestly, I should've said something—anything—to rebuke him, but then if I did, he would ask how I knew, and I'd have to tell him that I ghostwrote for Ann Nichols. By then, we were two years into our relationship, and he knew I was always writing *something*, but I'd been sneaky enough to keep him oblivious. So I pressed on a smile and said, "I don't know. I kind of like keeping this story to myself."

"Someone else'll beat you to that story if you don't write it."

Maybe if I'd pressed him, he'd have given up the ghost, too.

For the record, he never told me about the book he was writing. He didn't tell me until it sold at auction for a million dollars—exactly what he said mine would sell for. It sold to his own publishing house. Where he was a senior editor. And when I read the deal report, I realized it didn't tell me anything.

> Gilligan Straus, at Faux Publishing, has acquired in a twelve-house auction world rights to Faux senior editor Lee Marlow's untitled debut, and a second novel. William Brooks of AngelFire Lit brokered the deal.

And Lee wouldn't tell me, either.

"It's a book, bunny," he laughed. "Be happy for me!"

"Of course I am," I replied, because I was silly—so silly. I should've been happy for him. Ecstatic. It was a life-changing deal! He could quit his job, write full-time, do all of the things he'd told me he wanted to but couldn't because work weighed him down.

And now he was successful.

I should've been happy—no, I *was* happy.

Genuinely.

Then one night, a few months after the deal, he left his computer open while he went to go pick up his laundry. I'd never snooped before—I never wanted to. I trusted him.

I was a fool.

Because he'd taken what he'd said to me to heart. That if I didn't write the story that I wove for him, then someone else would.

I just didn't think . . . I didn't think it'd be *him*.

Three years and a day after I met Lee Marlow, I realized that I had gotten our story all wrong. I was the main character, but not in my own story.

I was the main character in *his*.

I was sewn into the pages, into every word, laced into every sentence. The book he sold was a book about my family's funeral home. About the stories I'd told him. The ghosts. The funerals. The graves. The bullies who picked on me and called me Wednesday. Who poured ink on my hair. The memories of my parents dancing in the parlor late at night, when they thought their kids had gone to bed. Of me and my sister fighting over the urn of our grandmother, and the ashes scattering all over the floor. Of the stray cat named Salem who must've been hit by a car at least once a year and *never* died—until cancer took him fourteen years later.

It was all there. All of my secrets. All of my stories.

All of *me*.

He used me as inspiration, and then he just used me.

He used the book deal to quit his job, become a full-time writer, and when I confronted him about the story, he said to me—and I'll remember it until the day I die—"Bunny, you can still write your romance."

"That's what you think I'm mad about?"

"*You* weren't going to write this book."

"You don't know that!"

"Bunny, c'mon, aren't you being a little unfair?" He had tried to soothe me as I elbowed past him on the way down the steps of our brownstone. *His* brownstone.

And maybe, yeah.

Maybe I was, but—

"What happens at the end? To your Florence in your book? Does some guy come in to save her, only to steal the one story that's hers?"

His demeanor changed then. He was still charming, still looked at me like I was the center of the universe in which everything else orbited, but suddenly I was something that was no longer precious. "I can't steal a story you'd never write, Florence."

And that was it. I had been an utter fool. Whatever I felt was nothing, it was imagined.

Then he shut the door on me.

Literally.

He didn't even try to explain or beg for me to come back. He simply left me on the sidewalk on a cold April evening with my one jumbo suitcase and two pots of devil's ivy I'd stolen from the rooftop garden.

And all of his stories began to make sense if I thought of them the same way he thought about my stories.

Fictional.

I thought I knew Lee. He had studied at Yale, and left because he wanted to teach French to orphans in Benin. He only came back because his mother died of cancer, and he wanted to help his father grieve. He had a sister in a group home in Texas after she suffered a brain aneurysm on her wedding day, and he always donated to the ASPCA because he used to volunteer there in high school, and I ate all of it up like candy. I never questioned it.

Why would I? I trusted him.

I began to figure it out, though, after the night he left me in the rain. I put together his lies, piece by piece, until they finally began to add up. I mean, he didn't even know the *capital* of Benin. (It's Porto-Novo, by the way.)

Here was the truth: Lee Marlow flunked out of Yale. His parents lived in Florida, and his sister was married to a librarian in Seattle. He never chased a master's at Oxford. He never interned at the *Wall Street Journal.*

And I was heartbroken.

Standing there on the sidewalk in the April rain, I did the only thing I could think of—I called Rose, and she had a roommate who was moving out. It did cross my mind to go home, of course it did, because with one big hug from my parents I would be okay again, but if I went back home, it meant that everyone who said I wouldn't make it in New York, who expected me to return so they could whisper behind their hands about the girl who talked to ghosts, would be right. And that was a story I couldn't face. Not yet.

So, I showed up on Rose's doorstep that rainy Wednesday evening, and that was that.

I haven't been able to write a romance since.

6

The Death Toll

I HADN'T SEEN him since that rainy April evening. I'd tried not to think about his blue eyes, or his artfully disheveled blond hair, or how his calloused fingers felt when they touched me—

Suddenly, the bar seemed much too small. The walls were closing in. I couldn't stay here. What was I *doing*? I was Florence Day, and Florence Day didn't live her life like this. She didn't share her stories—whether they were real or not—she didn't wear tiny black dresses, and she didn't drink artisanal drinks named after dead poets.

The universe reminded me of that.

Rose saw Lee Marlow a split second after I did, and I heard her whisper, "*Shit*. We can go if you want—Florence?"

"I—I need some fresh air."

"I can go with you—"

"No." I said it a bit too sharply, but I didn't care. The people at neighboring tables were staring at us now, sipping on their dead poets like I was part of the dinner show. "I'm fine. He can—he can go first. I need to go to the bathroom." It was a bad lie, and we both knew it, but she let me go anyway.

I tore my gaze away from Lee Marlow and made my way toward the back of the bar, where the bathrooms would be. The emcee welcomed Lee up to the microphone, and he introduced himself, and said he would be reading from—from—

"*When the Dead Sing*. It's a little book you might've heard buzz about. It's coming out in a few months, so please be gentle with me," he said modestly.

A few months? That soon? This past year, time seemed to slip through my fingers like sand. How could it be a *year* already and still my heart hurt this much? I could barely breathe. I didn't watch where I was going. I just knew I needed to leave, and I needed to leave *now*—

But the line to the women's bathroom was ten people long. That was at least thirty minutes. And I felt the tears at the corners of my eyes burning. I couldn't wait.

And I refused to break down where Lee could see me.

I *wouldn't*.

Beyond the women's bathroom was a glowing emergency exit sign, and I took it as a girl in a sparkly purple dress asked if I was okay. "No," I mumbled truthfully, slipping past the line to the emergency exit, and burst out into the cold April air.

I had to breathe. I had to calm down. So I did. I filled my lungs up with so much frigid air, I felt they might burst, then I let it out again. And again. I tilted my head back and blinked the tears out of my eyes, hugging myself tightly so I wouldn't rattle apart. Not here. Not anywhere.

Never again.

I hated that I cried when I was angry, or upset, or annoyed. I hated that I cried at the slightest flux of emotional nuance. I hated how helpless I felt. I hated how I wanted to both march up to him and give him a fistful of my thoughts and run as far away from him as I could.

I hated how I couldn't do both.

"I *told* you," sighed a soft male voice, "I don't need to hear you read from your damn book agai—oh. Hello."

I spun toward the man—and froze. A tall shadow sulked against the brick wall. He quickly pocketed his phone and stood straight, making himself even taller, and with my eyes already blurry with tears, he looked like a shadowy nightmare.

Oh no. Narrow, darkly-lit alley. No one around. My life spinning out of control.

This was where I got murdered.

"If you're gonna kill me, do it already," I hiccuped a sob.

He paused. "Come again?"

"No one's around. Do it quick."

He sounded baffled. "Why would I want to do that?" He stepped out of the shadows, and I could see his face finally. And that made it all the worse. It *was* a murder-y stranger, but not of the life kind. He was the kind to murder a career. *My* career.

Benji Andor.

And worse yet, he could see *my* face now, too. His thick eyebrows knit together. "Miss Day?"

"*Shit*," I cursed, quickly looking away. Oh no, could he see me *crying*, too? That was mortifying. I wiped my eyes. "What are you doing here, Mr. Andor?"

"Ben," he corrected, "and same as you, I suppose."

"Crying in a back alley?"

"Not that, no . . ." He judged his words carefully, frowning.

Why—why did he have to be *here* of all places? I had half a mind to turn around and go back inside but . . . Lee would still be reading from that stupid book. I didn't want to hear it. I didn't want to remember it existed. I just wanted to disappear.

I pressed the palms of my hands against my eyes and took a deep breath. *It's okay, Florence. Calm down. It doesn't matter. It doesn't matter—*

Then his voice, soft and a little hesitant, asked, "Is there anything I can do?"

No.

Yes.

I didn't know.

I wanted to get away from Lee Marlow and his words. I wanted to get away from his memory. Everything about him—because he reminded me that I only had myself to blame. And I didn't want to remember that. I didn't want to remember any of it. My heart still felt like it was freshly broken, shattering all over again, the jagged pieces falling deep into the pit of my stomach like fresh pains.

And I didn't want to feel that anymore. It had been a year. Why wasn't I *over* him? Why did I still want him to look at me like I was the only story he wanted to learn (irony, that one), and tuck my hair behind my ear, and kiss me like I was the heroine in a romance, and tell me I was loved? That he loved me.

I missed that the most. I missed it so much, the closeness, the certainty that I mattered.

And I wanted to matter again.

To someone, to anyone.

For a moment.

"*Yes*," I decided, and reached up—because he was so damn tall and I was very much not—and took his face in my hands and pulled him down to crush my lips against his. They were warm and soft and dry, and my fingers brushed against the stubble on his cheeks. My stomach burned, but it filled the ache.

He made a surprised noise, jolting me to my senses. I quickly jerked away. "Oh my god—I'm so sorry. I—I didn't . . . I wasn't . . . I usually don't do this."

"Make out in back alleys?"

"Kiss tall strangers."

He gave a snort that sounded like laughter. "Did it help?"

My lips still felt wet and tingly, and he tasted like a rum-and-Coca-Cola sort of dead poet (Lord Byron?), and I didn't mind. I gave a nod. "But it doesn't mean anything," I added quickly. "It doesn't—this doesn't mean—I'm not going to fall in love with you."

"Because romance is dead?" he asked, tongue in cheek.

"Six feet under."

"So you say . . ."

And his mouth found mine again. He pressed me up against the side of the wall, and kissed me like I hadn't been kissed in—well, at *least* a year. The night was cold, but he felt like a furnace. I curled my fingers around the collar of his dark coat and pulled him closer. As close as I could. His hands were warm as his fingers came up to cradle the sides of my face, and we danced in the dark alley while standing still.

We didn't talk. We didn't think—or I, at least, didn't think. Not about Lee Marlow, or the book due, or anything else, even though Ben didn't even know it was *me* doing the writing. I wasn't his author. Not the one who was going to turn the book in late; Ann was. He thought I was her assistant. The middleman. No one.

I wanted to be no one for a moment.

He broke away, breathless. "Miss Day?"

"It's Florence," I gasped. My lips throbbed.

"No, um—that's not—your phone," he said rigidly. "It's ringing."

Oh. Was it? I just noticed. It was my Mom's ringtone. That struck me as odd through the haze of kissing Benji Andor. Why was she calling this late? It *was* late, wasn't it? I untangled my fingers from his coat and dug for my phone in my crossbody purse. He still hovered over me, bent near, shielding me against the world, and it was . . .

Nice.

It was nice in a way few things had been tonight.

When I found my phone, I realized I had over twenty missed calls from my mom—

And Carver.

And Alice.

Please call Mom, Carver's text read.

Wait—what? Why?

I was more confused than anything else. It was 11:37 P.M. Was something wrong with Mom? The funeral parlor?

"Is something wrong?" Ben asked.

"I—excuse me," I muttered, dipping out from underneath him and moving away a few feet. It was nothing, I told myself. Just—it was nothing. I quickly pressed her speed-dial number. The phone barely rang once before Mom answered.

"Sweetheart," she began.

Something was off.

It was off before she said anything.

"It's your father."

And then—

"You need to come home."

The dread in my stomach bloomed into a sickly, cold flower. "Is he okay? What hospital is he at? I can—I can be there on the first flight in tomorrow and—"

"No, sweetheart." And in those words, I knew. It was the way Mom's voice dipped. The way it halted suddenly at the end. It was like finding yourself at the edge of a cliff—a sharp drop, and then nothing. My lips were numb, and I still had the memory of Ben's fingers in my hair, and Dad was—

"H-He had a heart attack. We tried . . . the ambulance . . . it was during his poker game and he was winning and . . . Alice and I followed the ambulance but—" Her words were sporadic, trying to piece together an evening of horror while I had gotten tipsy on Dickinson martinis. "They couldn't—he was gone. He was gone by the time we got there—by—he was . . . he's gone, darling."

Gone.

The word was so quiet, I barely heard it. Or maybe my heart, thundering in my ears, was too loud. But whatever it was, the word didn't register, not really, not for a long, long moment. And then, like the cold wind, it burrowed deep into my bones, and I could feel my heart beginning to crack. Right down the center, breaking off all the pieces of me that were my father, all of the memories—the late nights in the funeral home, when I couldn't sleep because of a thunderstorm, when the wind howled between the cracks in the house and made them moan, so I'd quietly go down to the kitchen and get myself some milk, and sometimes I'd see Dad there at the kitchen table. He would be sitting there, watching the trees outside of the window bend in the storm.

"Oh, buttercup, can't sleep?" he'd ask, and when I shook my head, he patted his lap and I climbed up to sit on it.

Lightning lit the skies, making the thin summer trees look like bony skeleton hands reaching up toward the clouds. I curled myself up against my dad, who was sturdy and round and safe. I always felt safe with his arms around me, where nothing bad could ever get me. He was the kind of man who gave the best bear hugs. He put his whole heart into them.

"What're you doing up?" I had asked, and he'd laughed.

"Listening to the dead sing. Do you hear them?"

I shook my head, because all I heard was the wind howling, and the bushes outside scraping against the side of the house. And it was terrible.

He hugged me tighter. "Your grandma—my mother—told me once that the wind is just the breath of everyone who came before us. All the people who've passed on, all the ones who've taken a breath—" And he took a breath himself, loud and dramatic, and exhaled. "They're still in the wind. And they'll always be in the wind, singing. Until the wind is gone. Do you hear them?"

And he tucked his head down by my ear, and rocked me gently back and forth, humming a strange and soft tune, and when I strained to listen, I could start to hear it, too—the dead singing.

As I shuffled out of the alley to sit on the curb, numb, a breeze swept an empty potato chip bag across the ground. I watched it go, but I didn't hear any sort of music. I heard my name. "Florence?"

I glanced back, though my eyes were blurry, and all I could see was a massive hulking shape. He came closer, and knelt to me, putting a hand on my shoulder before I realized who it was.

Ben Andor.

Right. He was here. I'd been kissing him. I wanted to forget and now—

"Hey, is everything okay—"

I shrugged his hand away and stumbled to my feet. I forced out, "I'm fine."

"But—"

"I said I'm *fine*," I snapped. All I wanted to do was break into pieces and be carried off by that silent, dead wind. Because there wasn't a world without my father's stupid parlor playlists and his cheesy jokes and his bear hugs.

That world didn't exist. It couldn't.

And I didn't know how to exist in a world without him in it.

A moment later, Rose was there, shoving Ben Andor away from me. "What the hell did you do?!"

He was baffled. "Nothing!"

"The fuck you did!" She dug into her purse for the pepper spray. He quickly held up his hands and hurried back into the bar. She turned then to me and hugged me tightly, asking me what he'd done, what had happened.

"He died," I said.

"Ben?"

"Dad." I felt a sob bubble up in my throat, like a bird wanting to be set free, and then I gave a wail and buried my face into my best friend's shoulder, on the curb of an empty street, while the world spun on, and on, and on, without my dad in it.

And the wind did not sing.

7

Days Gone

DAYS GONE FUNERAL Home sat at the perfect junction between Corley and Cobblemire Roads. It sat there so patiently, like an ancient ward on the corner, looming over the rest of the small town of Mairmont, South Carolina, like a benevolent grim reaper. It stood at exactly the right height in exactly the center of the plot of land, and it looked the way it always had: old and stoic and sure.

The funeral home had been a staple in Mairmont for the last century, passed from Day to Day to Day with love and care. Everyone in Mairmont knew the Days. They knew Xavier and Isabella Day, my parents, and knew that they loved their job, and us children—Florence, Carver, and Alice Day—who didn't love the funeral home as *much* as our parents, but we loved it enough. We Days dealt in death like accountants dealt in money and lawyers dealt in fees. And because of this, we Days weren't like the other people of Mairmont. Everyone said that when a Day was born, they were already wearing funeral clothes. We treated death with the kind of celebration most people only ever reserved for life.

No one understood my family. Not really.

Not even me, to be honest.

But when it was time, everyone in Mairmont agreed that they'd rather be buried by a Day than anyone else on earth.

I never thought I would come back to Mairmont. Not like this, with a small carry-on suitcase and a backpack with my laptop and an extra toothbrush in tow. My hometown sat in the liminal space between Greenville and Asheville, so close to the state line you could walk up to the Ridge, spit off it, and hit North Carolina. It was the epitome of nowhere, and I used to love it.

But that was a very, very long time ago.

Somehow, I had managed to snag an Uber who'd drive me from Charlotte to Mairmont, and when the Prius pulled down Main Street, it looked just like it did in my memories. South Carolina was warmer than New York; the Bradford pears that lined the roads already unfurling their green leaves, speckled with white flowers. The sun had set, but it still bled reds and oranges into the horizon like a watercolor painting, and my dad was dead.

It was weird how the thought just appeared like that.

My flight was almost empty, and they gave us pretzels, and my dad was dead.

The Uber driver's car smelled like lavender incense to cover up the weed, and my dad was dead.

I had already been standing in front of the steps to the Days Gone Funeral Home for ten minutes, watching the figures inside the glowing windows walk in and out of the parlors less and less, because the reading of the will had already started, and Dad was dead.

The funeral home was a renovated Victorian mansion, repainted white every summer so it looked fresh and ghostly for whatever happy haunts decided to arrive. The shingles were a deep obsidian that, when the sun hit the roof just right, sparkled like black sand. The patterns in the foundation's brickwork were faded reds and oranges, and the wrought iron railings curved sweet deathly designs across the upper windows and dormers. On Valentine's it was festooned in paper-cutout hearts and pink and red balloons, on the Fourth of July we set off purple fireworks, and at Christmas it was outlined in lights of red and green, like the grumpy old grandfather who didn't want to admit he was enjoying the holidays but very much was.

It looked just as it had the day I last left for college a decade ago. I still remembered the way Mom kissed my forehead and left a bloodred stain in the shape of her lips, and the way Dad hugged me so tightly, like he didn't want to say goodbye.

I couldn't wait for him to hug me again—and then I remembered, like a stone dropping into my stomach—that he wouldn't. Ever again.

It knocked the breath out of me.

I should've come back sooner. I should've taken weekend trips like Carver suggested. I should've gone fishing with Alice in the summer, I should've helped Dad re-stain the front porch, and I should've gone with Mom to those ballroom dancing classes.

I should've, should've, *should've* . . .

But I never did.

The funeral home looked the same as when I last saw it, the stained glass windows and the dormers and the turrets, but there was something inherently wrong as I stood there on the porch, mustering up the courage to step inside.

Dad was gone, and there were crows sitting in the branches of the dead tree beside the house, crowing, prodding me to go inside. I didn't think much about the crows.

Maybe I should have.

It's just—the world felt all wrong. Dad should've been answering the door. He should've been outstretching his arms and bringing me into a rib-crushing hug and telling me what a *treat* it was to have me back home.

But instead when I rang the doorbell, a large and long *gong* that reverberated through the house's old bones, my little sister answered the door. She'd cut her black hair short since the last time I'd seen her, and her gauges were a little larger than last time, though she didn't have on her dark gothic eyeliner. But that might've been because she'd cried it all off.

"Oh, it's you," Alice greeted, opening the door wider for me to come in with my suitcase, and retreated into the foyer.

"Hello to you, too." I stepped inside. I took off my coat—I didn't need it in Mairmont at all, it turned out—and hung it on the coatrack. There were about ten other coats hanging there—so I could only guess who was waiting in the parlor. People I didn't want to see.

Which was, like, *everyone.*

Alice waited in the foyer for me to hang up my coat and made a *hurry up* motion with her hand. She was dressed in black, from the oversized sweater she pulled over her hands to her black jeans to her black Doc Martens, and for a moment I could trick myself into thinking this was just another day, another family meeting, because Alice always wore black. She had the most Dad in her. Alice wearing black was like a blue sky—it was just right.

I hated the color. For a multitude of reasons. Turns out when you were known for being like that kid in *The Sixth Sense*, everyone expected you to dress in all black and quote Edgar Allan Poe.

Dad loved Edgar Allan Poe.

Don't. Don't think. I took a deep breath, smoothing out the front of my wrinkled light blue blouse, and followed my younger sister toward the largest parlor in the funeral home.

The inside was finished with stately oak floors and dated red floral wallpaper. There was a staircase past the foyer that led to the second—and third—floor of the funeral home, but those parts were reserved mostly for my family. We lived here until I was twelve, as weird as it sounded. The stairs up to the other levels of the house looked tempting in that supernatural-murder sort of way. My bedroom was the second one on the left, the third on the left my brother's, the two doors on the opposite side my parents' room, a bathroom with a claw-foot tub, and a small study, and then on the third floor Alice had the loft all to herself. The rooms were all vacant now, filled with decorations and spare furniture, dust-covered and forgotten. I knew every creaky floorboard, every rusted hinge. Electric lamps hung on the walls, giving off a subtle yellow glow. On the first floor—the funeral home part of the house—there were three parlor rooms, the biggest to the left, where I reckoned everyone was waiting for me, and a smaller one to the right, beside the stairs to the second floor, and then one just beyond that. Past the third parlor room was a kitchen with a gas stove and old tiled flooring, and across from the kitchen was the door to the basement. Dad used to joke about having skeletons in our closets because we basically did. The basement was where Dad, undertaker and funeral director, prepared the bodies, and I'd been down there a few times, but not enough to really think much about it. I wasn't the cadaver type, not like Alice, who always loved to watch Dad work.

I wondered, absently, if Alice was going to prepare Dad, too.

"I'm surprised you came back," Alice said, her voice guarded, and motioned toward the largest parlor room—the red one. "We're almost done."

"Sorry, my flight was delayed."

"Sure." Then she turned away from me and returned to stand beside Mom, and I let out a long breath. Alice and I weren't always this unfriendly. She used to follow me around everywhere when we were kids, but we weren't kids anymore.

And Dad was dead.

Mrs. Williams, a Black woman with short natural hair, was already reading the will when I came into the parlor and stopped in the doorway, her neon-yellow glasses low on the bridge of her nose. Karen Williams had been Mairmont's sole lawyer for as long as I could remember. I went to high school with her daughter, who ended up marrying a friend of mine, Seaburn Garrett, the caretaker of Mairmont's cemetery. Beside Seaburn, sitting in a wingback chair, was Carver and his boyfriend, Nicki. Mom's parents were in a retirement home in Florida, so I doubted they would be making the trip, and Dad's parents had passed when I was really little. So this was it.

My family.

My heart floundered. It swelled and deflated and felt strange. And I felt so wrong to be here, gathered in this parlor room that smelled like roses and the softest, barest hint of formaldehyde, without Dad.

Mom looked up from her lap when I came into the parlor, and quickly jumped to her feet. "Darling!" she called, opening her arms, and rushed over to me. She drew me into a hug, so tight it was rib cracking, and I buried my face into her warm orange sweater. She smelled like apples and rose perfume, the smell of my childhood—skinned knees and pancakes in the breakfast nook and Sundays at the library, sitting in the stacks reading romance novels. She hugged me so tightly, it felt like every memory was a bone in my body that she needed to hold on to, to make sure they were still here. Still real.

"I'm so glad you're here," she said softly, and finally let me go.

She tucked my hair behind my ears, and her eyes were a little wet. "You're still skin and bones, though! What do they feed you in New York—lettuce and depression?"

"About," I replied, unable to hide a laugh. She squeezed my hands tightly, and I squeezed them back. "I'm sorry I'm late."

"Nonsense! We were just getting to the good part, weren't we?" Mom finally let go of my hands, and turned to Karen to ask her to start from where she left off again. Leave it to Mom to find a *good part* in reading Dad's will.

Seaburn bumped his shoulder against mine and gave me a nod. "Nice to see you home."

"Thanks."

Karen gave me a sad smile and said to us, "It *seems* like Xavier left some instructions for his funeral." She took out a list from the manila envelope on her lap, and showed it to us.

Carver gave a groan from his seat in the high-back velvet chair. "*Chores?*"

Alice massaged the bridge of her nose. "Even from beyond the grave, he's making us work for free."

"*Alice*," Mom chided. "He's not even in the grave yet."

"Bless his soul," Karen lamented, and pulled her glasses down a little to read from the list. I was surprised she could read his handwriting at all—it was revoltingly bad. "One. For my funeral, I would like one thousand wildflowers. Bouquets are to be organized by color."

A murmur of confusion crossed the room.

A thousand? Why would—*oh*. Wildflowers, like the ones he picked every Saturday for Mom. I glanced over at her, and she hid a smile as she looked down into her lap. Alice and Carver were blanching at the request—they hadn't realized its significance.

Why a *thousand*, though, I didn't know.

"Two. I want Elvis to perform at my funeral."

Seaburn murmured to his wife, "Isn't he dead . . . ?"

"Very," she replied.

Dad would've tsked at that and said, "Only mostly dead," in that cryptic way of his. Because music was a heartbeat, too, in its own way, and death wasn't a send-off without some good tunes.

I was beginning to get the worst sort of feeling.

"Three. I want Unlimited Party to supply decorations. I put in the order on January 23, 2001. You can find a receipt in the envelope with this will." And then Karen Williams took the yellowed receipt out of the envelope.

I remembered Dad once saying, "When I go out, there'll be streamers and balloons, buttercup. There won't be any tears."

My throat tightened. I curled my hands into fists.

Karen put the receipt back, and kept reading, "Four. I want a murder of twelve to fly during the ceremony."

"A murder?" Alice asked.

"Of crows. Twelve crows," I translated. The same murder that kept stealing our Halloween decorations, and gave Dad shiny things when he fed them spare corn on the cob, and sat on the old dead oak tree outside of the funeral home whenever a ghost appeared—how were we supposed to catch those birds?

They *hated* me.

Karen went on. "Five, my final request. Buttercup"—I felt my heart skip at my nickname, and even though Karen was reading, I could hear Dad in the words, the soft love there, the lopsided grin—"I have left a letter to be read aloud at the funeral. Not a moment before—"

The doorbell rang.

Seaburn asked the group, "We're not expecting anyone else, are we?"

I checked my watch. It was 9:00 P.M. A little late for visitors.

"Could be flowers," Carver pointed out.

"Or someone canvassing for mayor," Karen added.

"Our mayor's a dog. Who would want to run against a *dog*?"

Mom said, "Florence, you're closest."

"Sure," I replied, and made my way to the front door to answer it.

A *letter*? What kind of letter did Dad want me to read for his funeral? I didn't like the sound of that. For all I knew, it could've been mortifying stories from my childhood he'd been keeping as blackmail—like the time I got a marble stuck up my nostril and then shoved a marble in the other one because I was afraid my nose wouldn't look even. Or the time Carver was playing in a coffin and it closed on him. Or the time Alice thought she was a witch and gathered all the stray cats in the neighborhood as her familiars and they ate the neighbor's canary. He was that kind of person. And he *definitely* was the kind of person to include a PowerPoint presentation in the letter, too.

And that just made me miss him more. He couldn't be gone, could he? He—he could still be here. As a ghost. Lingering. He had unfinished business, didn't he? He hadn't said goodbye. He couldn't be *gone.* I hadn't talked with him enough, laughed with him enough, soaked in the stories he had and the cryptic wisdom he espoused and—and—

When I opened the door, I didn't see anyone at first. Just the porch and the moths that fluttered around the porch lights, and the rocky cobblestones that led to the sidewalk, and the soft streetlights and the wind that rushed through the oak trees.

Then a crow cawed in the oak tree out front, and my eyes focused, and barely—*barely*—I began to make out an outline. Of a shadow. A body—

A man.

A ghost.

My heart leapt into my throat—*Dad*?

No—it wasn't. The man was . . . too tall, too broad. Slowly, like adjusting the focus on a pair of binoculars, the shape took form, until I could see most of him, and my eyes traveled up to the face of the towering stranger, framed by dark hair and a chiseled jaw. It only took a moment to recognize who he was—

Well, who he had *once been*.

I paused. "Benji . . . Andor?"

And he was most definitely dead.

8

.....

Death of a Bachelor

BEN'S GAZE FELL on mine as soon as I said his name. His eyes were dark and wide and—confused. The slightest crease between his eyebrows deepened as he recognized me. "M-Miss Day?"

I slammed the door closed.

Oh, no. Oh *no, no, no.*

This wasn't happening. I didn't see anything. It was a trick of the light. It was my overworked brain. It was—

"Florence?" Mom called from the parlor. "Who is it?"

"Um—no one," I replied, my hand curling tighter around the doorknob. The faintest outline of the figure still stood in the doorway, shadowed in the stained glass. He wasn't gone. I closed my eyes, and let out a breath. Nothing was there, Florence.

No one was there.

Not your dad, and not the crazy-hot editor who was most *certainly* not dead.

I opened the door again.

And there Benji Andor stood as he had before.

Ghosts didn't look like they did in the movies—at least from my experience. They weren't mangled, flesh rotting off their bones. They weren't pale as if some unfortunate actor had a bad run-in with baby powder, and they didn't glow like Casper. They shimmered, actually, when they moved. Just enough to make them look a little wrong. Sometimes they looked as solid as anyone living, but other times they were faded and flickering—like a lightbulb on its last wire.

Benji Andor looked like that, standing on the welcome mat to the Days Gone Funeral Home. He looked like how his memories remembered him, the night in Colloquialism, his dark hair neatly gelled back, his suit jacket fitted to his shoulders, his black slacks pressed. His tie was a little askew, though, just enough to make me want to straighten it. My gaze lingered on his lips. I remembered them, the way they tasted.

But now he was—this man was—

The spring wind that rattled through the dead oak tree didn't mess up his hair, and the light from our foyer didn't sit right on his face, and his shadow was gone. He shimmered, slightly, like a holograph in glitter. I reached out toward him, slowly, to touch his chest—

And my hand went through him. It was cold. A burst of frost.

He stared down at my hand in his sternum, and I whispered just as he cursed—

"Fuck."

9

Dead on Arrival

"FLORENCE?" MOM CALLED from the parlor. "Is everything okay over there?"

I blinked, and Benji Andor was gone. I quickly drew my hand back and rubbed at my fingers. They tingled from where I'd touched—and gone through—him. He wasn't really here. He wasn't really dead.

I was losing my goddamn mind.

"Florence?" Mom put a hand on my shoulder, and I jumped in surprise. She gave me a worried look. "Are you okay? Who was that at the door?"

I shook my head, crossing my arms over my chest to warm my cold hand. "No one—I'm fine. It was, um—someone ding-dong ditched."

She squeezed my shoulder.

"I'm fine," I reiterated, and tried to shake off the encounter. Benji Andor wasn't *dead*. I'd just groveled in his office yesterday. *Kissed* him last night behind the bar. He couldn't be dead.

He wasn't.

But if my mother was good at anything, it was seeing right through my lies. "You saw one, didn't you? A ghost."

"What? No—I mean. No," I decided, because it was easier than trying to explain whatever had happened. Mom had enough to deal with already—she didn't need her eldest daughter coming off the rails already. I had to be there for her. Not the other way around. I grabbed her hands and squeezed them tightly. "I'm fine," I said again, and this time I put my heart into it. "I'm okay. Glad to be home."

"I know it's a lot," she replied, and we moved out of the foyer and back toward the parlor again. "But things have changed. People have changed."

But how much had stayed the same?

I couldn't tell her that, at the airport, I had debated on whether or not to turn around and go back to my apartment. Skip the funeral. Burrow myself in a murder podcast. Try to forget that Dad was dead. That he was never coming back. That I would never get to, not ever, not while he was alive, tell him about my career, and my ghostwriting, and share with him all of the starred reviews and—

Stop. Stop thinking.

"Besides," I said, trying to bury my thoughts, "I couldn't let the family fall apart without their favorite disaster child."

"You aren't a disaster," Mom chided.

"No, she definitely is," Carver argued, and Mom hit him in the shoulder. Karen called her over and she left us for the parlor. Carver asked, putting his hands in his worn jean pockets, "Who was at the door?"

"A ghost."

He blinked. As if he wasn't sure whether I was lying or telling a particularly bad joke, but then I smiled and he barked a laugh. "Ha! If it was Dad, I hope you thoroughly chewed him out."

"Gave him what for."

"Really?"

"No. No one was at the door," I lied, and he melted a little.

My brother was a lot of things—a smartass, a computer tech guru, and a gullible mess. He was like the glue that kept the Day siblings together. I couldn't remember the last time Alice talked to me of her own volition.

"You never know. I mean, when we were kids—"

"How are you and Nicki?" I interrupted.

"Good," he replied, annoyed that I'd changed the subject, but he took the hint as he led me back into the parlor. "So, did you figure out what to do with the editor for Christina Lauren?"

"Christina and Lauren write their own books," I replied automatically. "But no, I didn't."

"So what happened?"

"Dad died. I came home."

"You never turned it in?"

"Can't turn in half a book."

"Do you think you could—I don't know—copy and paste the same chapter fifty times, turn that in, and by the time your editor realizes you turned in the wrong thing, you'd have the book done?"

I stared at my brother in surprise. "That's . . ."

"A great idea, right?"

"A *terrible* idea," I replied. Then I frowned, and thought about it for a moment. "It might work."

"Ha! See? You're welcome. I'm a genius."

Maybe Carver's ploy could give me enough time. Not much—but *enough*. The ghost I saw at the door—it wasn't a ghost. It was a hallucination. Benji Andor couldn't be *dead*. I'd kissed him last night! And he looked healthy, and he wasn't *that* old, and as far as I could tell, it would take a lot to murder someone akin to a tree trunk.

He was fine.

It was a trick of my brain—the imaginary ghost of my new editor whom I'd accidentally made out with in a back alley in Brooklyn coming to haunt me because I was already stressed out and chugging along on three hours of sleep and four cups of airplane coffee.

That was all.

"Uh-oh, what now?" Carver murmured under his breath as we came back into the parlor. Everyone had left their seats and was huddled around Karen and the will. Mom was pacing back and forth on the other end of the parlor, her heels clipping on the hardwood floors like a metronome, never missing a beat. That was bad. She rarely paced. Most of the time she just floated between rooms like an ethereal Morticia Addams.

"What's the commotion about?" Carver asked, looking around.

Nicki looked up from the will, and handed it to Seaburn. "Well, we've sort of got a problem."

"What kind?"

Alice sighed, massaging the bridge of her nose. "Dad didn't give anyone instructions on any of this," she said in her deadpan voice. "He just—I guess—thought we could read his freaking mind."

"We've got a receipt for the party stuff, but that's it. I'm not sure about the wildflowers or the murder of crows or . . . Elvis? I dunno what to do about that one." Seaburn shrugged and handed the will off to me.

Dad's script was long and loopy, and all I wanted to do was move my fingers across the words, memorizing the way he dotted his Is and crossed his Ts. It was written on the yellowed cardstock that I'd gotten him a few years ago for Christmas.

"He always liked live music—maybe he meant an Elvis impersonator," I thought aloud to myself. "And the flowers . . ."

Carver snapped his fingers. "He always picked them out on the old walking trail."

The Ridge. I didn't want to think about the Ridge.

"Murder of crows, then?" Alice asked, crossing her arms over her chest. Everyone shrugged.

Mom joked, "Perhaps we could use the crows he always fed in the evenings. They're never very far."

"Someone else'll have to catch them," I said. "They don't like me."

"They don't *know* you. You haven't been home in ten years," Alice pointed out.

"Crows can live up to twenty years."

"Sure, it's about *you*, then," Alice said with a roll of her eyes.

"That's not what I meant," I snapped as I passed the will back to Karen. She tucked it neatly into a manila folder, where the receipt and a few other pieces of paper resided.

"We'll figure Xavier's funeral arrangements out tomorrow," Mom assured us, clapping her hands together to dismiss everyone for the evening, before Alice and I could get into a fight. "That's enough for one day, I think."

After everyone had left, Carver, Alice (steadfastly ignoring me), and I went around the house and turned off the lights in every room. It was second nature to us at this point, even if I hadn't been around for ten years. Carver took the back rooms, I took the left, Alice took the right. We checked the windows to make sure they were closed; we locked the doors.

I would be lying if I said I wasn't looking for Dad as I did.

Though I was about as subtle as an elephant, apparently.

"If you want to see him, he's just down the hall, you know,"

Alice said, breaking our silent fight. She hugged herself tightly, pulling her sweater sleeves over her hands again. "Third freezer on the left. The one with the shaky handle."

I closed the door to the second parlor room behind me, and my cheeks burned with embarrassment. I was glad that most of the lights were off, so hopefully she couldn't see them. "I wasn't looking."

"You were. For his ghost."

"Maybe I was," I admitted.

She pursed her lips and looked away. "Well, I don't think he's here."

"I don't think so, either," I admitted.

"Who's not here?" Carver asked, stomping loudly out of Parlor C. He stomped everywhere loudly. It was just what he did. Nicki followed out into the hall behind him, quiet as ever. It always struck me how different Carver and Nicki were—like a square peg and a round hole—but I guess they were like pieces in a puzzle. They found grooves where the other person fit, and that's how they worked.

"No one. Everything's locked up on my end," Alice said, and left for the foyer, where Mom was putting on her boots and coat.

My brother gave me a sidelong look, and put his hands in his pockets.

"Don't worry about it," I sighed, and finished my rounds. I did pass the door to the basement—the mortuary—where we stored the bodies in cold fridges until it was time to prep them for burial. Those set for cremation went to a crematorium the next town over. The basement door was like any other, though the handle was different—a pull latch with a hard dead bolt.

For old times' sake, I checked the dead bolt again. Locked. Probably Alice's doing.

I hadn't been down into the prep room in ages. I hated the smell of it—a mix of disinfectant and formaldehyde, and a distinct undercurrent of something you weren't really born recognizing. It was a smell you found in the hospital, too, and extended care homes.

There's a certain smell to death.

You didn't really recognize it at first, but the longer you existed in those spaces, the more acquainted with it you became. I didn't realize death had a smell until we moved out of this house. I always thought it was what the world smelled like—a little sad and bitter and heavy. On spring mornings, Dad would open up all of the windows, and turn up the radio, blasting Bruce Springsteen, and try to breathe life into the house again, wake up the old wooden floors and the creaky attic beams.

It was about that time again, when the mornings were crisp but the sun was already warming up the buds on the trees. The air in the house felt heavy with incense and disinfectant and that sad, soft smell of death, waiting to be let out into the wind.

My hand closed tightly around the handle to the basement. Maybe Dad was down there, sitting on one of the cold steel tables, smoking a cigar and wondering when one of his kids would realize he'd been playing us the whole time. He'd laugh and say, "I couldn't die, buttercup, until I'm good and ready."

But he was dead, and he wasn't ready.

And his ghost was not here.

"We're leaving," Carver called from the front of the house. "Florence? You still back there?"

I let go of the handle. I'd come back later when it was light out. When I was in a steadier state of mind.

"Coming," I called and hurried down the hallway to the foyer, where everyone else had already put on their coats and shoes. Carver handed me my heavy winter coat, so misplaced here in

Mairmont where everyone had already brought out their cute spring cardigans and jean jackets.

He kissed me on the temple and said, "It's good to see you home."

"*Grossssss*," I complained. "Sibling *affection*."

As we left the funeral home, Mom locked up behind us. We meandered down the stone pathway to the sidewalk. The crows were gone from the oak tree. Had I actually seen them? Or were they just a part of my messed-up head, like my editor?

Mom said as she caught up to me, wrapping her arm around my shoulder, "Oh, it'll be so nice to have you home! Right, Alice?"

I gave a start. "She's home, too?"

My sister said pointedly, "Some of us fail quieter."

"That's not what I meant—"

"Oh, yikes!" Carver interrupted me, his arm interlocked with his boyfriend's. "It's past Nicki's and my bedtime. We'll see you in the morning? Over at the Awful Waffle?" Code for Waffle House. "Ten?"

"Sounds beautiful," Mom replied. Carver kissed her on the cheek as he said his good night, Nicki telling me how nice it was to see me, and they left down the sidewalk in the opposite direction.

Mairmont wasn't terribly busy in the evenings. Most of the restaurants down Main Street closed up around eight, and the ones that stayed open were packed with sports fans watching a late-night basketball game or families gone for a late-night ice cream run. Nicki and Carver had bought a house together just on the other side of the town square, on a cute road with rainbow-colored houses and white mailboxes, and in five years I could see them fostering a few kids and introducing some pandemonium to their quiet little street.

Honestly, I couldn't wait for it.

When they had disappeared down the sidewalk, Mom pulled Alice and me close to her, a daughter on each arm, and led us home. The walk was quiet, the night air chilly but not cold like it would've been in New York. The flowering Bradford pears did stink, though. A *lot.* In that unpleasant way teen boys' bedrooms did. But the trees did look beautiful with their small white buds glowing in the streetlights that lined Main Street. The soft golden glow reflected off the windows, and the wind was quiet, and the sky was wide.

My parents moved into the unassuming two-story house around the corner from the funeral home when I was twelve. Neither Carver nor Alice really remembered ever living in the funeral home—they didn't remember that the third stair creaked, or that at night when the wind rattled the old rafters they moaned, or that sometimes you could hear footsteps in the attic. (Though, later, I managed to get rid of them.) I was the only child who remembered living—truly *living*—in the funeral home. Dad chasing me across the hardwood floors, and Mom humming as she restored the stained glass window above the door. Alice wandering around the front yard in her underwear, a funeral bouquet fixed onto her head like a flower crown. Carver drawing great stick figure epics on the parlor walls, improving the fifty-year-old wallpaper filled with flowers and orchids. Me, with my bedroom door locked, whispering to the ghosts who came to find me.

Alice and Carver didn't remember why we moved, but it was because of me. Because one night, when I had been pulled out of bed by a mischievous young spirit, I had found myself wandering toward the basement.

"Are you sure this is your unfinished business?" I had asked the ghost. "To see—to see you?"

He had smiled at me. "Absolutely—I wanna see. I have to see," he said as he led me down into the mortuary. I had gone down there a few times with Dad, but never alone. It was where the dead were stored in narrow freezer boxes until their funeral came. I didn't know the facts yet. I just knew Dad prepared them for the rest of their journey—like Charon over the river Styx.

There were only two guests in the mortuary that night—Dad called them "guests." They were bodies. Obviously. I had guessed the right freezer box on the first try, and pulled the drawer out. On the narrow table lay a boy who looked a lot like the one who stood beside me. Young—twelve, maybe. Dad had already fixed him up, painted his blue lips tan, and covered the bruises on his neck.

"Does that help?" I asked the ghost—and he looked . . . "Are you okay?"

"I wanted to wear my *Transformers* T-shirt," he replied, and looked away. "I'm really dead, aren't I?"

"I'm sorry."

He took a large breath (or as much as a large breath looked), and then he nodded—just once. "Thanks—thank you."

And like the dozens of ghosts before him, the sparkling bits that made him began to break away like dandelion tufts, and dispersed into the room—and he moved on. A firework there, then gone. And I was left alone in the frigid mortuary.

I climbed the steps to the door again, but it had locked itself when it closed the first time—I had forgotten to unlock it. I pushed on it—once, twice.

Banged on it—called for help.

Nothing worked.

Dad found me the next morning. Apparently, they had looked everywhere once they realized I was missing, until they finally came down into the mortuary and found me curled up on the steel table in the middle of the room, a blanket over me, asleep.

Mom and Dad decided that maybe—just *maybe*—raising a

family in a funeral home might not be as eclectic and wholesome as they were expecting.

Luckily, there was an old two-story house down the street, built in 1941, so it gave Mom things to renovate and fix around the house as we grew up. That was her college major—architectural renovations. She was really good at it, too. I used to wonder if she ever regretted marrying Dad, and moving to a small nowhere town with nowhere people, but she never gave the slightest hint she did. She took unloved things, like the stained glass window above the door in the funeral home, and the stone and brass fireplace in the new house, and turned them into wonders.

The new house was less showy than the funeral home. It sat on a side road off Main Street, beside the Gulliver family and the Mansons, built with old crumbling bricks as red as clay, and pristine white shutters. But at night, when Carver and Alice's respective room lights were on, the house looked like it had eyes and a grinning red mouth for a door.

The house was exactly as I remembered it as we came up the cobblestone pathway. Bare threads of ivy clung to the brick walls, and a lone spider hung from the sconce beside the door. Alice's red convertible was in the driveway, though it looked a lot worse for wear these days, beside Mom's unassuming SUV. Dad had a motorcycle, though I didn't see it in the driveway. I wondered where it was.

"Ah! That thing," Mom said as she fished into her heavy purse for the keys. "He took it to the shop this week before . . . well, you know. Before." She smiled, but it didn't quite reach her eyes. "I'll ask Seaburn to get it tomorrow."

"I'll get it," Alice said.

"Oh, Alice, you know how I feel about you riding that thing."

"Mom."

"Fine, fine." Mom unlocked the front door, and it creaked wide open. She walked into the foyer and flipped on the lights. Alice marched inside, not even bothering to take off her boots as she stormed through the house to the kitchen, and flung open the liquor cabinet. She asked Mom if she wanted anything. "Oh, a nice whiskey would be lovely . . . Florence?"

"That sounds amazing," I agreed, taking off my coat.

The house was warm and it smelled like it always had—of pinewood and fresh linens. The walls were a bright gray, and the furniture was hand-me-down and restored, worn and loved. A staircase off the main hallway led up to most of the bedrooms, while the master was on the first floor, across from the living room. There were photos of all of us on the stairway wall—from elementary school through college graduation, smiling moments frozen in time. Years where we went through bad hair, and blue hair, and braces, and acne.

I looked at one of the earliest photos of us—so early, Alice was an infant. It had been taken outside of the funeral home, Mom in a sleek red dress and Dad in a terrible tweed suit, Carver in one to match. I had pitched a fit that day because I wanted to wear my rainbow unicorn house shoes instead of the white dress shoes that hurt my feet, and I'd won. There I was in a fluffy red dress and . . . unicorn slippers.

On the hallway table there were a few framed newspaper clippings. Dad getting the keys to the town. Mom being presented with a local restoration award. Carver winning a robotics competition. And—

LOCAL GIRL SOLVES MURDER WITH GHOSTS

Along with a photo of thirteen-year-old me smiling for the papers. It made me sick to my stomach.

"Here you go," Alice said, offering a glass of whiskey on the rocks.

I jumped at her voice, and spun to her. She rattled the ice in the glass, waiting for me to take it. Suddenly, I was very much not in the mood. "I—I think I'm going to go to the bed-and-breakfast."

Mom poked her head out of the kitchen. "What? But it's so late . . ."

"I'm sure they have a room." I grabbed my coat where I hung it on the coatrack, and shrugged it back on. "I'm sorry." I stepped back out into the brisk night with my suitcase. "I have a book due and—I'll keep all of you up."

"Writing can't be *that* noisy," Mom said, frowning. "And I even blew up the mattress in your old bedroom for you!"

"Bad back."

"Since when?"

"Mom," Alice said, downing my glass of whiskey, "let it go. There's a hole in the blow-up mattress anyway."

Mom gave her a surprised look. "There is?"

Alice shrugged. "Was gonna let her figure it out herself."

"Thanks," I replied, not sure if she was lying to cover for me or if there actually was a hole in the inflatable mattress upstairs. I wouldn't put it past her.

I just couldn't stay here. In this house. After the episode at the funeral home, I didn't want to test being home. Mom already had enough to worry about with the funeral. I didn't want her to have to worry about me, too.

"I'll see you tomorrow morning?" I promised. "At the Waffle House?"

Mom relented without persisting. She was good at that—at seeing when people were shutting down, and letting them. "Of course, darling. See you in the morning."

I smiled a small thank-you, trying not to meet Alice's hard gaze, and wheeled my suitcase down the cobblestone steps again, back toward Main Street. Mairmont was quiet at night, but walking the sidewalk alone, while all the storefronts were closed, reminded me how out of place I felt here in the town that never really accepted me. In New York, I could walk down any street and find another creature of the night walking, too. But here, everyone had their cozy houses and their cozy families, all sequestered for the night, and I was alone.

I told myself I didn't mind it.

I packed my bags and left the day after high school graduation. I never visited. I never looked back. Not when Carver proposed the idea of TP'ing my bully's yard for my birthday a few years ago, not when my parents had their thirty-year anniversary.

Not when Alice begged me to come home.

We had been best friends once, but that was a lifetime ago. I didn't regret leaving—I *couldn't* regret leaving. It was for my own sanity. But looking back on it, I could've handled it a little better. That I did regret. I could've not shut Alice out of my life. I could've visited once in a blue moon. I could've . . .

Would've, should've, could've.

Hindsight was such a bitch. Because everything I ran from had caught up with me. Even the crows that now sat on the roof of the bed-and-breakfast, looking down at me with their beady black eyes.

I tightened my grip on my suitcase. They were just birds. They didn't mean anything. And even if they did, I had nowhere else to go.

10

Dead and Breakfast

THE MAIRMONT BED-AND-BREAKFAST was a small B and B on the corner of Main and Walnut. It was tucked into a garden that was green even in winter, its blue vinyl siding barely visible beneath all of the ivies that grew on it. I pushed open the wrought iron gate and made my way up the stone pathway to the front door. A soft golden light spilled in through the front windows, which meant Dana was still minding the desk. They were the night kind of person that sat up reading Stephen King and obscure nonfiction on Queen Victoria or Lord Byron's lovers. They were sitting on a stool behind a heavy wooden desk when I finally elbowed the screen door open and wiggled my suitcase inside. They looked up, large round glasses perched on the bridge of their nose, secured with a golden chain that draped down on either side of their pale, long face. Dana had short curly brown hair and a wide smile with a gap between their two front teeth, and when they saw me, their smile widened even more.

"Florence! I can't believe it," they said, putting a sticky note into their book and closing it. They wore a sweatshirt with HARVARD on the front and rib-hugging jeans, and somehow always looked more stylish than I ever could. Even in high school, they were immaculate. "I thought you were up in New York!"

"I was. Had to come home, though. For—um—"

They winced. "Right, oh shit. I'm sorry. I knew that. Sorry. It's just—surprising. To see you."

I fixed on a smile. "Well, I'm here."

"Right! You are. And I'm betting you want a room."

"If you wouldn't mind?"

"Absolutely! I know how it is. Parents getting rid of your room and all. The second I moved out, my mom turned my bedroom into her knitting room. *Knitting!* She even took down my *Dawson's Creek* posters. I'll never forgive her for that, you know." They pulled up an app on their iPad, and tapped at a few screens. "How long will you be staying with us?"

"Probably until the end of the week?"

If I make it that long, I thought as I took out the last credit card I owned and painfully handed it to them. I'd just climbed out of my credit card debt too, but I couldn't stay at home. Not right now. Not when Dad wasn't . . .

I just couldn't.

Dana checked me in, asking whether I'd want one bed or two—one, preferably on the second floor of the three in this house, and not beside the stairs if they could help it. "And the least spooky one," I added, sort of joking.

Sort of not.

They laughed. "Don't want to solve any more murders?"

"Don't remind me," I begged, taking the key they handed me.

"I dunno. I thought you were kind of cool in high school." They leaned in, then, secret-like. "Could you really speak to the dead?"

"No," I lied. "I just solved a murder. It was luck."

"Still kinda rad."

"And weird."

"Weren't we all? Anyway, you can have my favorite room—we call it the Violet Suite."

I looked at the key, and the key chain that hung from it—a wooden violet. "Let me guess, there's purple in the room?"

"Not as much as I'd like," they replied indignantly. "Breakfast is in the morning from seven thirty until ten. I'll be here all night, and John will be here in the morning—remember him? He was a few years younger than us. Scruffy guy, but he's got a heart of gold once you get to know him."

"Oh, right—you two got married."

They wiggled their ring finger. It was a black band made out of meteorite. Of course they'd be cool like that. "Alas, off the market."

"Well, congrats."

They smiled. "Thanks! If you need anything, we're the two you talk to."

"Whatever happened to Mrs. Riviera?"

Dana gave a sad smile. "Oh, she passed a few years ago. Gave the whole damn inn to me."

"Damn indeed," I replied, startled. "Well—belated congrats again. The place looks great."

"Didn't think I'd stick around here for the rest of my life but . . ." They shrugged modestly, and sat back on their barstool again, absently opening their book to their bookmarked page. I caught a peek of the book—*The Kiss at the Midnight Matinee.* "Sometimes life takes you unexpected places. Let me know if you need anything, okay, hon?"

"Absolutely. Thank you." I put the keys into my coat pocket, and rolled my suitcase over to the stairs. They weren't as steep as the steps to my walk-up apartment, thank god, so I made it up to the second floor with my thighs of steel and rolled my suitcase down to the end of the hall. Each door had a cute little flower on it, carved into a plank of wood with an artistic hand, and they were all plants that could kill you. Oleander. Bloodroot. Foxglove. Iris. Marigold. Hemlock. The flower on the door at the end—the Violet Suite—was wolfsbane. I opened the door and, having not forgotten the crows perched on the roof, hesitantly peeked my head inside.

"Hello . . . ?" I whispered.

The room was dark, with only the golden glow from the streetlight on the sidewalk shining in through the window. There was no movement. No ghostly apparitions.

Coast was clear.

I flicked on the light beside the door and rolled my suitcase inside. The room was bigger than the one I paid for with blood and tears every month in Hoboken, New Jersey. There was a full bed big enough to fit me and all my baggage, a dresser, a floor-length mirror, and even a closet. There was a coffeepot on top of the dresser, and a boutique assortment of teas and instant coffees, as well as a flat-screen TV mounted on the wall. The bathroom was beautiful, too, with a claw-foot tub and a large vanity. I was definitely going to take advantage of that. Traveling made me sore, and the stress from today had cramped my neck badly, and my orthopedic pillow was five hundred miles away. Dana was right, though; there *wasn't* enough purple in a room they called the Violet Suite.

As I began to unpack my carry-on luggage, putting my underwear in the top drawer and hanging my black funeral dress in the closet, I honestly forgot about the crows on the roof. My hands were busy, and my head was—for the first time all day—mercifully blank.

And then I heard a noise.

I quickly grabbed my razor for defense—what could a razor do?—and rounded the bathroom doorway slowly.

"Hello?" I called hesitantly.

I'd be lying if I said I wasn't looking for a six-foot-three romance editor in oxford leather loafers, argyle socks, a crumpled white shirt, and neatly pressed trousers. But there was no one in my hotel room.

"I'm losing it," I muttered, and finished putting up my toiletries.

My dad was dead, and I didn't need ghosts to complicate that. I didn't need *anyone* to complicate that. My family was already complicated enough—never mind my history with Mairmont. If I started talking with ghosts again, I was sure to land in the Mairmont gossip circles within the week: "Did you hear, Florence is back and talking to herself again?"

Poor Florence and her imaginary friends.

Florence and her ghosts—

I swallowed the knot in my throat, and without saying another word, I turned off the lights and fell onto my bed and pulled the covers over my head.

All I could think of was how quiet the inn was, and how my thoughts were so loud against it, and how in New York I never had to hear silence. I never had to think about Mairmont, or the people here, or why I left.

For ten years, I hopped from one apartment to the next, chasing after a love story that wasn't mine, trying to force myself to be the exception instead of the rule, and over and over again all I found was heartbreak and loneliness, and never once did I see a murder of crows in a dead oak tree, or a ghost on my front steps, because I was like everyone else, normal and lost, and my dad was still alive.

And just for a second—*one second longer*—I wanted to be that Florence, and live in that pocket of time again.

But it was gone, and so was my dad.

11

……

Past Tense

I SLEPT FOR almost three hours.

Almost.

I knew how ghosts worked. They always popped up in the most unexpected places, and I wasn't sure when Benji Andor would show up again. *If* he showed up again. A very small, very unreliable part of me well and truly hoped I'd imagined him. But tell that to my anxiety, which was dead set on not letting me get a full REM cycle of sleep. Every groan and crack of the old house startled me awake, until my phone finally went off at 9:30 A.M.

And I felt like a truck had run me over, backed up, and hit me again.

At least I had packed my heavy-duty concealer—the good stuff. I slathered it under my eyes and hoped I looked at least a little alive as I traipsed down the steps to the foyer, where a larger redheaded man sat on the stool Dana occupied last night. He had on an anime T-shirt and about half a dozen piercings in his face, and it took me a moment to recognize him.

"John?"

He looked up from his magazine at the sound of his name, and put on a smile. "Flo-town! Dana said you were staying here!" He stood and quickly hurried around the desk to give me a bear hug. Approximately three of my ribs cracked and I died. He set me down with a laugh. "It's been—how long, ten years?"

"About," I conceded. "I barely recognized you!"

He blushed and rubbed the back of his neck. He had on a hat with a pizza design on it, and a loud floral button-down. Miles from the guy I dated in high school—polo shirts and short buzzed hair and a football scholarship to Notre Dame. "Ah, yeah, a lot's happened."

"You're telling me. Congrats on you and Dana!"

"Yeah, can't *believe* my luck. How's New York been treating you?"

"Good. Well—not bad," I amended.

He laughed. "That's good to hear. And how's your wr—" The old rotary phone at the desk began to ring, and he apologetically excused himself to go take the call. "Mairmont Bed-and-Breakfast, John speaking . . ." Then he put his hand over the receiver and whispered to me, "It's good to see you, though I'm sorry about your dad. He was a real good guy."

The words hit me like a hurricane, because for a moment I'd forgotten. "Thank you," I forced out, fixing a smile onto my face.

He went back to the person on the phone, and I left as quickly as I could. I think he shouted after me about breakfast, but I was already late to the Waffle House to meet my family, and no offense to the breakfast at the inn—nothing topped hash browns scattered, smothered, and covered.

The WaHo was at the end of Main Street, near the elementary school and the bookstore, and the parking lot was jammed with travelers stopping through Mairmont on their way through South Carolina to North Carolina and Tennessee. It was close enough to Pigeon Forge to visit Dollywood whenever you wanted or pop over to Asheville to tour the Biltmore. Mairmont was situated just on the outskirts of the Appalachian Mountains, hilly enough to have great walking trails but flat enough for the mountain roads to not kill a Prius. My family sat in the farthest booth at the diner, already eating their cheesy hash browns and sausage-and-egg omelets. I quickly hurried over and slid into the booth beside Mom.

She said, “We already ordered you a waffle and hash browns,” as she slid over a cup of coffee.

I took a long drink. “Mmh, battery acid.”

“Late as usual,” Carver added dryly, mocking a look at his expensive Rolex.

Alice agreed. “Some things never change.”

“No one said there was a *hard* meeting time,” I scoffed. “Ooh, yum,” I added as the waitress came over with my waffle and a side of hash browns. They smelled absolutely delicious, and my stomach grumbled, reminding me how many meals I skipped yesterday. (Three, all three.)

“Blessed nutritious breakfast sugar,” I said, starved, as the waitress left for another table.

Carver gave me a strange look from across the table. “That hungry?”

“They don’t have Waffle Houses up in New York,” I replied, digging my fork into the soft waffle, cutting off a piece so large I had to angle it to get it into my mouth. It was syrupy and sweet and soggy, just like I remembered.

Mom asked, “So how’s the bed-and-breakfast? I heard it was renovated after Nancy Riviera passed. Is it pretty?”

“Gorgeous,” I said between mouthfuls. “Dana did a great job.”

"Your father and I talked about spending the night there on our anniversary and . . ." Mom frowned into her almost-empty cup of tea. "Well, I guess that won't be happening."

Alice gave me a pointed look, as if it was my fault.

"Anyway," Mom went on, "staying in hotels *always* gives me such sore muscles. You know, your room *is* exactly as we left it. Well, with the exception of a sewing machine in the corner. And some paints. And some reclaimed furniture pieces I found on the side of the road—"

Alice interrupted, "She turned it into her art room."

"It's my crafting office," she corrected nobly.

"That's fine. I like the bed-and-breakfast." I took another large bite of waffle. "So, what's the family meeting this morning?"

Mom clapped her hands together. "Right! The schedule."

I blinked. "Come again?"

Alice said, "There's two funerals we have to get through first. Mr. Edmund McLemore and Jacey Davis."

Carver shook his head. "I know no one else'll point this out—but don't you think it's a bit insane that we have to do other people's funerals when Dad's dead? Can't they get someone else?"

Alice gave him a tired look. "Who, exactly? There's not another funeral home in town."

"Then the *next* town? Asheville? Pop on the interstate and you're there in no time. C'mon, Mom," he said to our mom when he realized that he wasn't gonna get Alice to budge, "you can't honestly be expected to work right now."

But Mom was having none of it. She waved her hand dismissively. "They want to be buried by a Day, and it's an honor and a privilege to do so! I won't send them somewhere else when we can give them the best ending."

It was next to impossible to argue with Mom when she had her mind set. Much like Alice, she was immovable. Carver was the sensible one, but he also knew when it was a lost cause. He shook his head and mumbled something under his breath (that sounded suspiciously like "this is why we never went on vacation"), and I was left sopping up the syrup and asking, "Can I do anything to help?"

"Oh, sweetheart, I don't think so," Mom replied. "Besides, Alice has most of the funerals this week under control. I just have to be there to—to be there. Xavier would haunt me if I didn't. Though I don't think I can do all the heavy lifting."

"I can do that," Carver suggested. "I have some time accrued."

I frowned down into my waffle. Business as usual, even though one of us was gone, and it was strange in the way that *The Twilight Zone* was strange. As though, on the plane ride home, I'd fallen into a parallel dimension. Everything was off-kilter enough to be wonky. How everyone's life was still running, still going, still pushing forward when Dad—

I fisted my hands. "But what about Dad's funeral arrangements?"

"Aren't they just so eccentric?" Mom sighed wistfully.

"Someone needs to do them, Mom."

"Meaning us," Carver guessed, and stirred his glass of water. "I'm afraid I can't help all that much. I have a tech report due at the end of the week, and if I'm helping with the other funerals . . ."

"I won't have time between the two services and the embalming processes," Alice added, somewhat annoyed. "His requests are just—just so—so *inane*."

"They're what Dad asked for."

"I know, but we don't have the time, Florence."

That struck a nerve. "Well, *I* have time, so I'll do all of them."

My younger sister rolled her eyes. "You don't have to do *all* of them. I just meant—"

"You don't have time, I get it."

She threw up her hands. "Sure! Whatever! Do it yourself. Florence Day, always being the lone hero!"

"That's not what I meant and you know it—"

"Girls," Mom interrupted in her steady, soft voice. Alice and I both sank back into the booth. "Fighting about this won't solve anything."

No, but I wasn't the one picking the fights. I began to say as much, when Carver checked his smart watch and said, "Karen's supposed to come by with Dad's finances in a few. Want to go ahead and head over there, Mom?"

"If we must," Mom sighed. "Xavier could've at least given us a *hint* on how to go about the Elvis one . . ."

Yes, but I'd figure it out.

I wanted to ask about the lawyer, and the finances—I hadn't heard anything about a meeting, but it seemed like my siblings had. Maybe they didn't want me to be a part of it, or I'd missed the memo, or . . . I didn't know. A myriad of things.

But whatever—I tried to brush off the feeling that I was missing out on something that I should've been a part of as I grabbed the ticket for the bill.

"Go on, I'll pay," I said. "I think it's my turn, anyway."

My family scooted out of the booth and started talking about the funeral and how widely to send out the invitations. To the relatives in the Lowcountry, and the poker club, and most of Mairmont (including the mayor, Fetch, a bubbly golden retriever who had won reelection three times).

Mom sighed as she followed Alice and Carver out of the WaHo. "I wonder if it would be frowned upon to dance with his portrait at the wake? You know the picture—him in the dovetail tuxedo? So dashing."

"*No*," Carver and Alice replied, and the door chime dinged as they left.

I bit the inside of my cheek to keep from smiling. I was still angry with Alice—she was hurting, we all were—but I missed them. I missed mornings like this, and bad soggy waffles, and I missed Dad.

I didn't think missing him would feel so lonely, though.

I leaned on the counter, beside a guy muttering to himself—small towns, they always had at least one weird guy—and handed the cashier a twenty. She smiled and said, "You must be Florence!"

The man beside me went rigid.

"Your dad comes here every Saturday," the cashier went on. "Always orders the same thing—the All-Star with extra hash browns. Scattered, smothered, and covered. Where is the old man today?"

"He passed away the other night," I said, and the man glanced over. We locked eyes. Dark hair, brown eyes, an angular face. He didn't have anything in front of him—no food or coffee—and no one seemed to pay him any attention. And that was a feat when you sat up at the counter at a Waffle House. You had to be either highly disliked or—

Or not really there.

And worse yet, I recognized his dark hair and navy trousers and the articulate way he had rolled up his sleeves tightly to his elbows. He looked like he could've been a painting of a forlorn businessman . . .

. . . of the slightly dead variety.

I paled.

"M-Miss Day?" Benji Andor asked.

The cashier's smile faltered. "Oh, no. I'm so sorry to hear about your father—"

Suddenly, the jukebox gave a loud screech, and the lights flickered with a start. It picked a random album and inserted it into the player. The neon lit up, and a song crackled from the forty-year-old speakers.

I winced. And whispered, "Stop it."

His wide eyes darted to the jukebox, then back to me. "I—that's not me."

"It *is*."

"That thing keeps acting up," the cashier apologized as she counted out my change. "Got a mind of its own sometimes, I think."

The piano beat. The tambourine. And suddenly I'm back in the red parlor after a wake, dancing on Dad's feet as he sings "buttercup, don't break my heart" in an awful key, golden afternoon light streaming through the window. It fills me with bitterness, because it's gone. The moment's gone—all those moments are gone.

My throat constricts.

"Four dollars and thirty-seven cents is your change. Have a great day, miss," the cashier said as she handed me a few bills and coins. I quickly pocketed them into my coat and left the diner. Ben followed, squeezing through the open door as it swung shut.

"Last night—at that door—it was you, wasn't it? You answered the door," he said, following me.

I trained my eyes at the sidewalk in front of me. "This isn't happening."

"*What's* not happening?"

Don't look at him. Don't look at him.

An older gentleman walking his dog decided to cross to the other side of the street, and I didn't know if it was because of *me* or because the dog had to take a poo in an azalea bush on the other side, but it didn't stop me from guessing. I fished my phone out of my pocket and mimed answering a call.

In two steps, he had caught back up with me. "Please don't ignore me—everyone is. *Everyone.* I sat in that diner for—for *hours*—trying to get someone to see me. No one could! No one! What's happening to me? Last I remembered I was at your front door, and then I was in the diner and—things don't make sense—and you're not listening—"

"I *am*," I interrupted. "I just can't be seen, you know, talking to myself."

His shoulders slumped. "So it's true . . . no one can see me. Except you? But—why?" About fifty emotions crossed his face, from disbelief to confusion, before he finally settled on accusatory. "What makes *you* special?"

"Wow. You're charming, you know that?"

"I am when I'm not scared out of my mind, Miss Day."

I winced. Even though I was walking at a pretty fast pace, he was keeping up on his long legs without even breaking a sweat. There was no way I'd outpace him. Sometimes, I hated being short.

Often, actually.

On top of my father's funeral, Benji Andor's ghost was something I didn't need.

But . . . I couldn't *ignore* him, either.

Especially hearing his voice crack like that, begging for me to see him because—

My dad would tell me to help him. My dad would say it was our job, our duty, our *responsibility*. A responsibility I hadn't risen to in about ten years. Not since I left Mairmont. And of course I felt like I had to now, because if Dad was here, *he* would have.

I stopped at the street corner, and decided, well, to make my dear dead dad proud, and spun on my heels to face Benji. He came to an abrupt stop a few inches away, and I realized just how silly I probably looked to him from his angle. I didn't care. "You're a ghost," I started. "A spirit. Working through a post-living experience."

"Working through a post-living—*what*?" Baffled, he ran his fingers through his hair. "I'm not *dead*. This is a bad dream. A nightmare. I'll wake up and—"

"Everything will be exactly the same," I interrupted. "Because you won't wake up."

"No—*no*."

His voice wound tight again, like Alice's used to when she began to have a panic attack. I'd never encountered a ghost this adamant about being alive before. When I was a child, every ghost that came looking for me knew they were dead. It wasn't a hard leap to make, but Benji Andor seemed to be the kind of straitlaced guy who dealt in facts and figures instead of midnight ghost stories and myths.

And I couldn't believe I was doing this.

"Mr. Andor," I said, because Benji or Ben sounded too informal, and I wanted to keep as much distance as I could. "I'm sorry."

"I'm *not dead*—"

I punched my fist straight through his chest.

"That tingles," he murmured, frowning down at my fist that should've been massaging his heart in his chest if he were alive.

"See?" I pointed out. "Dead."

"I can't be. I don't—I don't *feel* dead."

I removed my fist. Touching a ghost tingled for me, too. It felt cold, and a bit crackly—like my fingers had fallen asleep. "Not even inside? Not even a little?"

He ignored my very funny joke. "I can't be dead because I don't remember dying, thank you very much. And ghosts don't exist. It's scientifically proven."

"Is it now."

"*Yes*."

"Then, buddy, I'm not sure what to tell you."

We came to the roundabout in the middle of town. There was a green park in the middle with a white gazebo, and a man who looked like my old orchestra teacher on the steps practicing a rousing rendition of Journey's "Don't Stop Believin'" on his cello. He was really tearing up the strings.

"If I'm dead," Ben proposed smartly, "then how can you see me?"

What a question.

One that Lee Marlow never asked as I told him all of my ghost stories. He simply suspended his disbelief as I weaved my memories into his fiction. Did he ever find a reason for why I could see ghosts? Did his editor ask how? Did Lee finally have to make something by himself?

I didn't know—and I didn't want to know.

But leave it to an editor to ask the questions that burn into plot holes.

"I don't know," I admitted, "but what I do know, Ben, is that you're dead. Very dead. Dead-as-a-doornail sort of dead. *Ghost* dead—"

He held up his hand to stop me, his other massaging the bridge of his nose. "Okay, okay, I get it. I just . . . I want to know why. And why *you*."

"That makes two of us, then." I crossed the street, back toward the bed-and-breakfast, and he followed slightly behind me with his long, leisurely legs. "The only thing I can think of is that manuscript—but if you're dead, I don't have to turn it in anymore."

"Not that you had it finished to begin with," he muttered.

I opened the wrought iron gate to the inn—and froze. "Wait . . ." I turned back to him. "You *knew*?"

"That you were Annie's ghostwriter? Yes," he replied, a bit perplexed. "I'm her editor—of course I knew. I just didn't expect . . . well, it was a surprise when you walked in."

I blinked. "*Oh*. Well then."

"No, wait, that's not what I meant—"

I whirled around and marched up the front walk to the veranda. "No, no, I definitely get what you meant. Me, the failure that I am."

"Why didn't you just tell me you ghostwrote for her?"

"Would it have changed anything?" I challenged, and he pursed his lips in reply. Looked away. Because I was right—it *wouldn't* have changed anything. "See? It didn't matter anyway. Whether I told you or not, you knew I was a failure."

"That's *not* what I think of you," he stressed somberly.

I wanted to believe him. Wished I could. But I knew myself better than someone who had talked with me for thirty minutes and kissed me behind a hipster bar, and I knew exactly what I was—*who* I was.

A coward who ran away from the only home she ever knew. A gullible idiot who fell for guys who promised her the world. And a failure who couldn't finish the one thing she was good at.

Suddenly, a strange look crossed his face. Confusion. Then curiosity. He cocked his head. "Do you hear th—?"

The next second he was gone, and I was left standing on the veranda alone.

12

Emotional Support

THE PHONE RANG four and a half times before Rose picked up.

"Oh thank *god* you called. I was beginning to worry the town swallowed you up," she said. In the background, I could hear bathroom noises, and realized that she must've been . . . at *work*?

I checked my watch. "What're you still doing at the office? Isn't this your lunch?"

"*And* Saturday," she said with a tragic sigh. "But ohmy*god*, I have some news—but first, I want to ask how you're doing. How's the family? Is everything . . . well, not *fine* because of course not, but is everything fine?"

"As fine as it can be." I flopped onto the bed in the Violet Suite. It creaked loudly. I would've hated to be in one of the neighboring rooms if any honeymooners ever got this suite. The hinges needed some WD-40 and duct tape. "Alice is rearing for a fight, but I figured she would be. We haven't really seen eye to eye in a few years."

"Yeah, my money's on Alice—no offense."

"You haven't even met her! And I'm your best friend!"

"Yes, and I love you, but you're about as threatening as a chipmunk."

"Rude," I said, but I didn't say she was wrong. Because she wasn't. Of all the fights Alice and I had had over the course of our contentious relationship, Alice had won the majority of them. "Though she probably could murder me and never get caught. She did go to Duke for forensic chemistry."

"Wow, so badass. And your brother's a swanky tech bro—what happened to you?"

"Unequivocal failure," I replied bluntly. "And apparently the only one who's willing to prepare Dad's funeral as he planned out in his will."

"That is *so* metal."

"It's exhausting." I recounted to Rose what I needed to do, and she listened sagely as I ranted about the wildflowers, and Elvis, and murders of crows, and the party supplies. I told her about the Waffle House conversation this morning, and how I was saddled with doing all of it by myself. "I mean, they have stuff to do, too, but—so do I!"

"Maybe it's too hard for them."

"It's hard for me, too."

Rose gave a hard sigh. "Yeah, I know, but you're the big sister, right? You've always been really good at pushing through whatever feelings you have and getting things done. I mean, remember when that guy—Quinn—stood you up on a date and you had to finish edits for *Midnight Matinee* in like twelve hours?"

"Quinn sucked."

On a long laundry list of guys that I fell for that sucked.

"You pushed through and *aced* those edits. And the time our toilet literally exploded and you fixed it with the power of YouTube and sheer determination *while on deadline*. And the time I got that horrendous stomach bug and you ended up making ends meet by writing all those terrible self-help articles and paying all the bills for *three months*. You just do things. You finish them. You pull through."

"Tell that to Ann's book I didn't finish."

"One thing in a *very* shitty year."

"Wish I could tell Ann's agent that. I'm just waiting for Molly to call me again once Ann finds out to tell me all the things I already know—how I'm a failure, how Ann should never have put her trust me, how the *one job* I had was the one I failed at and I know I failed and—"

"And *as I said*, you've had a very shitty year. You're *good*, Florence! You're reliable. Most of the time. Maybe your family doesn't realize you want help with your dad's funeral."

At the mention of help, I bristled. "Who said help? I don't need *help*. And anyway, what are you doing in the offices on a Saturday?" I wanted to change the subject, to get away from the things that I might've once been good at but wasn't anymore. Which, as it turned out, happened to be everything. "And are you—are you in a stall?"

"Absolutely. You know how my boss hates me talking on the phone in the office," she added in a hushed tone. "And everything is *super* nuts today over here. Jessica Stone's freaking out over her clothing line launch, so my boss called us all here to work, on our Saturday, because apparently she's auditioning for a role in the remake of *The Devil Wears Prada*."

"Yikes."

"But that's not the *ohmygod* part. You would not believe what happened yesterday."

I rolled over on the bed, and the springs creaked. I stared up at the speckled ceiling. "You . . . got a promotion?"

"Benji Andor got hit by a *car*."

Ben.

I bolted up in bed. "He did?"

"Yes! You know Erin? At Falcon House? Yeah, she saw it happen. Like, you know right in front of the building? The intersection? She happened to look up at the *exact* right time—and *wham*! She's so distraught. Like, *so* distraught. Poor thing. I'm getting drinks with her tonight to see how she's *really* doing—maybe I can finally convince her to leave publishing. She could do *so* much better literally anywhere else."

I was still way back on Ben Andor getting hit by a car. Blood everywhere. For some reason, that one scene from *Meet Joe Black* played in my head, over and over again, but instead of Brad Pitt, it was Benji Andor in a dark blue suit and striped tie being flung across the road again and again and again—like a football game's fourth-quarter touchdown instant replay.

So he really *was* dead. I mean—of course he was. But it also meant I wasn't going crazy. That he was actually here, haunting me. He hadn't showed up until last night. And that meant he was sticking around because his unfinished business had something to do with me.

"*Shit*," I whispered, because there was only one thing it could be. The *Jumanji* drums began to play in my head, coming from my backpack where I left my laptop. A dirge of absolute dread.

"I *know*," Rose agreed. "The world lost another fine ass."

"Oh my god."

"I know—oh, *shit*," she muttered, and I heard her cover her phone with her hand so what she yelled was a little muffled. "Um—yes, it's me! I'll be out in a minute, Tanya."

There was a voice on the other side, and then the clip of heels out of the bathroom.

Rose picked up the phone a moment later with a morose tone. "The boss just came to check on me. I gotta go—but if you need me, let me know, okay? I'll catch the next flight down and be there with you."

"You don't have to."

"I know I don't have to, but I'm offering. I'll be your emotional support best friend. I can get some wine and you can go show me around your weird little town."

That sounded so tempting, but plane tickets were expensive, and she was needed at her job. I'd be fine. I always was. "Nah, but thank you, though."

"You don't have to do everything alone, Florence."

"I've got so much baggage, I'm never alone," I replied jokingly, and she laughed.

"You're ridiculous. Love you."

"Love you more."

I waited for her to hang up, and flopped back down on the squeaky bed. Having some help would be nice, but I didn't need it. Xavier Day was my father. His funeral was *my* responsibility. So instead I pulled up Google on my phone and punched in where to find the nearest flower shop. I could do things on my own—I didn't need to bother anyone else. Alice was up to her gills in funeral preparations and Carver had his own job and Mom—Mom couldn't do everything.

I wasn't sure if my siblings could see it, but she was barely holding herself together.

No, this was my job. I was the eldest. I could do this. Alone.

I had for this long, anyway.

13

Ghoul Intentions

THE CROWS WERE on the roof when I left the bed-and-breakfast that afternoon, and that meant Ben was lurking around somewhere. Though at the moment, either he didn't want to be perceived, or he was hiding in a bush somewhere crying. I would be, if I found out I was dead and the only person who could see me was a failure of a ghostwriter who gave him a plant instead of, you know, the manuscript that was due.

I should tell him what Rose told me—about his accident. He had disappeared so suddenly this morning, I didn't get the chance to ask if he remembered how he died or not. Though, the fact that he thought he was still alive, somehow, definitely tilted that answer toward *not*.

Google Maps on my phone said that the Main Street Flower Emporium was still open after all these years, so I left for the center of town. My senior year prom date bought a corsage from them that ended up being haunted.

I didn't want to think about how that happened.

Just like I didn't want to think about the deep, twisting vein of sadness in my stomach, and how as time passed in Mairmont and Dad wasn't here, it kept growing. Would it go away someday? Would the dagger in my side slowly shrink to a paper cut? Would the grief ever disappear, or was it stagnant? Would it always be there, just under the surface, lurking in the way only grief could?

I'd always written how grief was hollow. How it was a vast cavern of nothing.

But I was wrong.

Grief was the exact opposite. It was full and heavy and drowning because it wasn't the absence of everything you lost—it was the culmination of it all, your love, your happiness, your bittersweets, wound tight like a knotted ball of yarn.

The bell above the door chimed as I came into the flower shop. It smelled like roses and lilies and my grandmother's potpourri that she always kept in the bathroom. There was an older gentleman behind the counter, fixing up a flower arrangement. An old-timey radio played Elvis in the background.

"Mr. Taylor," I greeted, wondering if he remembered me from seventh-grade English class.

He looked at me over his thick glasses, and his eyebrows jerked up. "Miss Florence Day! If it isn't you, I swear."

I fixed a smile over my mouth. "It's me. How are you?"

"As good as I can be, as good as I can be," he replied, nodding. "Been doing up flower arrangements as quick as I can, but it don't seem quick enough these days. So much going on. Are you here to place an order?"

"I—oh. No. Well . . ." Movement caught the corner of my eye, and I turned to watch Ben not so subtly try to hide behind a bouquet of roses on a table. Because that wasn't conspicuous at all. I studiously turned back to the florist, intent on ignoring him. "I was wondering if you knew where I could find a thousand wildflowers?"

"A *thousand*?" Mr. Taylor scratched the side of his head.

"I know. It's a lot."

"I don't really stock *that* many wildflowers, and if I did that'd be . . ." Before I could stop him, he took out a beat-up old calculator and punched in some numbers. "About fifteen hundred dollars."

I blanched. That was more than my part of the apartment rent for the month, and I most *certainly* didn't have that kind of money. "Well—um. That's good to know, I guess."

"Is this for your father's funeral? I could pull something together—"

"Oh, no. No, no, no, I couldn't possibly."

"Of course you can! Xavier was a good man. I'm sorry. I know it's tough. How's Bella hanging in there?"

"Mom's okay," I replied, but it struck me that I didn't really *know* if she was fine or not. I tried calling her after my chat with Rose, but she didn't pick up. She and Carver might've still been in the meeting with the lawyer. I didn't know how long those things took. "And anyway, I'm just running some errands for her. Trying to make things easier. Dad left a laundry list of things to do for his funeral."

Mr. Taylor barked a laugh. "Course he did! Mind if I ask what else you need doing?"

So I told him—the flowers, and the murder of crows, and the party decorations, and Elvis—

"You know, there's an impersonator who always sings up at Bar None. Your dad loved him. He'd stop by every Thursday night before heading to his poker game and make the poor guy sing 'Return to Sender.'"

"Bar None," I echoed, remembering that Dad *did* love to go have a drink or two before poker nights.

"Yep. Always got them hips goin' and everything." He mimicked the impersonator as best he could without throwing out a hip. "Maybe that's who your dad meant?"

"Maybe," I said. It was worth a try, at least. I'd go first thing tomorrow. "Thanks—that's a big help."

"Always. Lemme know if you change your mind about those wildflowers," he added as I waved goodbye, and then he gave a start, as if he remembered something. "Oh, Florence—I'd hate to ask . . ."

"Yeah?"

"As I said," Mr. Taylor fretted, "we're up to our gills in orders and running a bit behind—those flowers your dad ordered may arrive a bit late."

My heart jumped into my throat. "He ordered flowers?"

"Earlier this week," Mr. Taylor replied. "A bouquet of daylilies, to Foxglove Lane."

So, not wildflowers. Of course Dad wouldn't make it that easy. But Foxglove Lane . . . I knew where it was. But why would he send flowers there? I didn't know why I said what I did next. Maybe it was to glimpse into the everyday life I'd missed. Maybe it was to walk, for a moment more, in Dad's shoes. I said, "I'll deliver the flowers."

"Oh, I couldn't ask you to—"

"It'd be a pleasure. Besides, I've nothing else to do today, and it'd be good to explore the town a bit since I've been gone." I smiled to really sell the point, and he must've been really strapped for help, because he handed me the address written in Dad's loopy script and a single arrangement of daylilies, and thanked me profusely.

It really wasn't that big a deal, and I really *didn't* have anything else to do today. I didn't want to go to Bar None, because it was

Saturday in the late afternoon, and I was sure it was already getting a bit crowded. And while I loved Mairmont, I didn't want to see many of the people in there. I didn't know who from my graduating class left the town or stayed—and most of them, unlike Dana and John, hadn't been very nice.

I'd been lucky to have not run into them thus far, but considering that I'd only been here about twenty-four hours . . . I knew my luck was shit, and it'd run out sooner rather than later.

As I left the florist, I tried to ignore my untimely shadow, and Ben was *really* hard to ignore. Especially because he was pretending to *not* follow me, and that just made it creepier.

"I see you, you know," I said when I reached the end of the block. I looked over my shoulder, and he quickly whirled on his heels and pretended to go the other way. "Seriously?"

He winced and turned back to face me. "Sorry. I was . . . I just saw you and I . . ."

"You've been following me since the bed-and-breakfast."

He wilted. "I have no excuse."

"Admitting there is a problem is the first step to recovery, good job."

"I'm not sure what else to do." He put his hands in his pockets, his shoulders hunched. He looked a bit more unraveled than he had this morning, his hair floppy and his eyes tired. "Or where else to go."

There was nowhere else. It was me and then . . . whatever came after. *If* anything came after. My family was the spiritual but not religious sort. We all had our different ideas of what happened—whether we returned to the world, or became part of the wind, or just . . . if we just stopped.

And anyway, whatever I could've said wouldn't have helped him.

He was, on all accounts, dead. Rose had verified it. And at least

I knew I wasn't going crazy—he really was here. For the moment, however long it took.

And I was his last stop.

I hugged the arrangement tighter. "Well, you can come with me," I offered.

"Can I?" He perked, like a golden retriever who'd finally been asked to go for walkies.

"Yeah. We can get to the bottom of this thrilling mystery together," I said, referring to the arrangement. "Why would my dad send flowers to a stranger's house?"

"Maybe he knew them from somewhere?" Ben guessed.

"He *did* have poker games. Maybe it's one of his buddies from that?" But I doubted he'd send them daylilies. He'd send them orchids or corpse flowers or—*something* a bit more his brand. Daylilies weren't his style at all.

My frown deepened as I thought, prompting Ben to propose, "We'll see when we get there, I suppose."

"I hate surprises," I agreed with a sigh.

Foxglove Lane was one of those quiet streets adjacent to the main drag where you could just see yourself buying a house behind a white picket fence and growing old in it. The houses were all different colors of Charleston-type designs, with porches that faced the west and narrow builds. When I was eight or nine, I went to a birthday party for someone who lived on Foxglove Lane. Adair Bowman, maybe? It was a slumber party and they broke out the Ouija board and I sat back and had absolutely nothing to do with it.

One, because Ouija boards were mass-market trash made by a toy company to sell the occult to the middle class.

Two, because even though Ouija boards were mass-market trash made by a toy company to sell the occult to the middle class, I still refused to poke the bear.

Adair called me a scaredy-cat. I definitely was. But I also slept perfectly well that night while the rest of the kids had nightmares about old General Bartholomew from the cemetery coming to haunt their dreams.

The house in question was halfway down the lane, far past Adair's old family home—though I think they moved the year after I'd solved the infamous murder. It was smaller than the others, but very well loved. The front lawn was quaint, with trimmed azaleas around the house and a colorful flower bed, newly planted for spring.

I climbed the brick steps to the front door and rang the doorbell.

It took a moment, but an old lady finally answered. She was hunched over, wrapped in a fluffy pink housecoat and darned slippers, and had the most beautiful wide brown eyes. "Oh," she said, opening the glass door. "Hello."

"Mrs.—" I checked the name and address on the card, written in Dad's sloppy handwriting. "Elizabeth?"

"Yes," she replied, nodding, "that's me, dear."

I offered up the daylilies. "These are for you."

Her eyes lit up at the arrangement, and she took it gently with gnarled and bruised hands. There was dirt under her long fingernails. She gardened. Alone?

"*Florence*," I heard Ben whisper, because he saw the gentleman first.

There was a shimmer in the hall behind her, an older man in an orange sweater and brown trousers, the hair that was left on the sides of his head combed back. He mouthed, "Thank you," his eyes glistening with tears.

Oh. I understood now.

Mrs. Elizabeth smelled one of the lilies and smiled. "Charlie always gave me lilies on our anniversary. I think that's today? Oh, my. Time's always a bit wonky when you get older," she added with a laugh. "Thank you, dear. You know, I get these every year but I still don't know who from!"

"A friend," I replied.

"Well, this friend of mine has very good taste," she decided, and gave me one of her lemon biscuit cookies before I left.

Sometimes, a spirit's final business wasn't talking to someone, or exposing their murderer, or seeing their own dead body—sometimes it was simply a waiting game.

Ben was playing a different sort of waiting game on the sidewalk. He looked paler than he had a few minutes before. "That man—he looked like I do. Shimmery and . . ." With a hard inhale, he sank into a crouch, his hands on the back of his neck. "I really am dead, aren't I?"

I finished my bite of cookie, and sank down next to him. "Do you really not remember how you died?"

He shook his head. "No. I mean—I—I remember leaving work, and then . . ." He inhaled sharply. Halted. Clenched his jaw. "It was . . . just outside of the building, wasn't it? My accident?"

Silently, I nodded, but I wasn't sure he saw me. If he saw anything, really. His eyes had this distant look to them, a thousand-mile stare to a place and time he'd never be again.

"I—I was typing an email on my phone when . . . the van popped the curb and . . ." He blinked, his eyes wet with tears, as he looked up at me. His voice cracked as he said, "How did I forget that?"

"I don't know," I replied gently, wishing that I did know something—*anything*—to help him. I knelt down beside him, curling my arms around my knees. "I'm sorry."

He bent his head, as if he could hide the fact that he was crying, but his too-big shoulders shaking gave him away. I wanted to reach out for his shoulder, to comfort him in one of those *there, there* pats, but I couldn't even touch him. I wasn't good at other people's emotions because I didn't know how to help, usually. When someone was in pain, I wanted to fix it. And I couldn't.

Which made me frustrated.

And when I was frustrated, I cried. If I was not already mortified enough. This had to stop—now. I tried the only way I knew how. "A-At least you're still kinda hot," I sobbed.

He jerked his attention to me. His eyes were red rimmed. "W-*What*?"

The tears just kept coming. I pushed them away as quickly as I could. "D-Drop-dead g-gorgeous, really."

"I . . . I don't—are you—?"

"I b-bet you s-strike a k-k-killer silhouette."

"You're crying and trying to hit on me?"

"I'm trying to make you laugh so you stop crying, because then I'll stop crying," I lamented, but it sounded more like *I'mtryingtomakeyoulaughsoyoustopcryingbecausethenillstopcrying*, and it was a miracle he even understood me at all.

But he did—and he laughed. It was soft, and weak, more of a *pah* than a laugh, but it was there. He rubbed his palms over his eyes. "You're the weirdest woman I've ever met."

"I know," I sniffed. "But d-did it work?"

"No," he said, but he was lying. In the afternoon light, his cheeks were turning a very delicate shade of red despite the tears in his eyes, and it only made the mark above the left side of his lip look that much darker.

"Oh, don't you die of mortification on me," I teased.

"I'm apparently already dead," he replied softly. "So that's impossible."

"I don't know, your cheeks are a dead giveaway."

He pursed his lips together, and then said, surprising me, "I'm afraid you're gravely mistaken."

I barked a laugh, a real laugh that I didn't know I had in me anymore, and it surprised me. It surprised him, too, because he looked away to hide a smile, rubbing the tears out of the corners of his eyes. While the mission wasn't accomplished, I think I did get him to feel a little better, and at least he wasn't crying, and that meant I wasn't crying, either.

I said, shaking my head, "That was a terrible pun."

"Yours weren't much better. And you're supposed to be a writer for a living."

"*Ex*-writer," I reminded. "My editor didn't give me another extension."

"Ex-editor," he reminded. And then he said very softly, gently, "Thank you, Florence."

I couldn't touch him—this wasn't my first ghost, and probably wasn't my last—but it was instinct. To comfort him. Even though I wanted someone to comfort *me*, too. I just wanted someone to stop me, and sit me down, and tell me that things would hurt for a while, but they wouldn't hurt forever.

I wanted to tell him that this wasn't forever.

My fingers slipped through his shoulder, numb and cold—

And then he was gone.

Again.

14

Moonwalks

FINDING A THOUSAND wildflowers would be the death of me.

I didn't want to take Mr. Taylor up on his offer because I didn't want anyone to go out of their way for me. If I was going to do something, I didn't want to inconvenience anyone else. It might've been because I was stubborn, or because I just didn't like help, but I resolved to do all these things on Dad's list alone. So, I called a florist within twenty-five miles from me and asked about the price and delivery fees of a thousand fucking wildflowers. Turns out, they cost more than my first apartment in Brooklyn, and *that* was the place that I shared with a cockroach big enough to contend with Godzilla.

"They're *weeds*!" I cried, slamming my phone down on the bar. "Why do *weeds* cost so much?!"

After Ben disappeared, I went back to the inn, where I returned to my search for a thousand wildflowers. I had moved from my room to the tiny bar downstairs that didn't have a bartender, but a bell I could ring to summon Dana and ask them for another rum and Coke. Which I did. Often. I had my laptop with me, opened to Yelp and Google Maps and twenty other tabs that I'd rather not mention.

Could I pick the flowers in the wild? Where even *was* a wildflower field? Maybe the Ridge? But it was April. And there had already been more than one cold snap. They'd be dead and crispy by the time I found them. And it was the *Ridge.*

I didn't want to go there. Not ever.

Dana poked their head through the doorway behind the bar that led to the check-in counter. "Everything okay in here?"

"Weeds!" I cried, throwing my hands up. "They want a thousand dollars for *weeds*!"

"I think I got a dealer who can cut you a deal—"

"Wildflowers," I corrected.

"*Ooh.* Yeah, I'm afraid I can't help you there." The front door opened, and Dana glanced back and smiled. "But you know what *can* help?"

"A bullet to the head?"

"The mayor! Dun, dun, DUN!" they sang as the clatter of paws came up behind me on the hardwood floor.

I turned around on my stool.

And there sitting so perfectly behind me was a golden retriever named Fetch. A little grayer than I remembered around his snout, he was still just as *fetching* as he had been the day I met him, before I left for college.

That was ten years ago—holy shit, I suddenly felt old.

"Doggo!" I cried, sliding off my stool onto the ground. He gave a soft yip, tail wagging, and smothered me in kisses. A laugh bubbled up from my throat. There was no way to *not* feel a little happy when you're being licked by a dog with breath that could knock an elephant out cold.

"You remember me, boy? You miss me?" I asked, scrubbing him behind the ear, and in a happy reply, his tail went *thump thump thump*. "Of course you remember me, right, boy? Have you been keeping the town safe?" *Thump thump thump!* "Pass any good laws?" *Thumpthumpthumpthump—*

"There is now officially a water bowl in front of every shop on Main Street that is changed daily," said a voice behind the dog.

I glanced up.

Seaburn, his owner, stood with his hands in his pockets. "Thought we'd find you here."

I looked up as the mayor tried to go to second base with his tongue. "Mom sent you?"

"Nah. She's busy with a funeral this evening. I asked to help but . . ."

"I also asked," I supplied. After the florist, I'd stopped by the funeral home to help out with the visitation today, but Mom was having none of it.

In fact, she seemed a little bit angry. "It's not like I can't run my own business!" she cried. "I'll be fine! I've been doing this for *thirty years*!"

It was all I could do to leave with my head intact.

Seaburn sat down on the stool next to me. "Your mom does things in her own way, on her own time. We should leave her to it."

That didn't mean I wasn't *worried*. And focusing on my mother felt a lot more constructive than focusing on my own sadness. Hers I felt like I could at least try to fix. Mine? It was a hole in my chest filled with all of the things that made my grief so heavy, it was hard to breathe sometimes.

I gave the mayor one last good scrub behind his ears before I resumed my seat and took another long gulp of my rum and Coke.

Seaburn and I had graduated within a few years of each other.

He was a junior when I started at Mairmont High. His family owned and maintained St. John's of Mairmont Cemetery on the other side of town, so it felt only natural that, when Dad needed someone to help manage the funeral business, he asked Seaburn if he wanted to work together. For the last seven years or so, Dad and Seaburn had managed the funerals and the gravesite services for the majority of the town. And apparently Dad had started to train Alice in the same thing.

"You're more than welcome to keep me company," I said. "I'm not up to much. Just . . ." I waved at my Word document.

Seaburn asked Dana for a beer, and asked me, "Still writing?"

"Stubbornly."

He barked a laugh. "Good! I liked your first book—*Ardently Yours.* So funny. Loved the romance bits, too."

"Oh no"—I burrowed my face in my hands—"please tell me you didn't read it."

"Don't worry, I closed my eyes during the sex scenes."

I groaned into my hands, mortified.

"We even did a book club for it when it came out," he went on. "Everyone loved it. It was—I dunno how to describe it." He tilted his head, taking another sip of his beer. "*Happy*'s a close word."

That was flattering, especially from Seaburn, who read so much and so widely my reading habits probably paled in comparison. "A romance leaves you happy—or at least content—at the end. Or it's supposed to. I think."

Because I didn't know anymore.

"It was good. You're a fantastic writer," he added. "I think everyone in Mairmont bought a copy." If only the sales in my small hometown could have changed the course of that book, my entire life could have been so, so much different.

I rubbed my thumb against the condensation on my glass.

The mayor came and put his head on my lap. I scrubbed him good behind the ears again, and his tail assaulted the floor. *THUMPTHUMPTHUMPTHUMPTHUMP—*

"Thanks," I said, because I felt as though I didn't deserve that sort of praise—not in my current predicament. "I'm trying."

"All anyone can do," Seaburn replied, and then took a deep breath. "And speaking of trying something . . . I heard from Carver that you're taking on the old man's will alone."

"No one else has time."

"That's not true."

I gave a one-shouldered shrug. "I can do it. Everyone else has things to do, and anything I can do to help out . . . I don't know if you know this, but I've been kind of MIA for the last ten years," I added sarcastically.

"The town ran you out. There's a difference."

"But I could've come back, right? It wasn't like I was ostracized or anything. I was just . . ."

Bullied. Called *ghoulie* behind my back. My social media was bombarded, day after day, with memes and names and joking questions of "Can you solve the Black Dahlia next?" And "Do you commune with the devil?"

Or, more commonly, *liar.*

All because I helped a ghost solve his own murder when I was thirteen—too young to know better but too old to chalk it up to imaginary friends.

"No one who knows you faulted you for leaving," Seaburn replied sternly. He reached over to my hand and took it tightly. My knuckles grated together, how hard he squeezed. "Especially not your dad."

A knot formed in my throat. "I know."

But it was still nice to hear.

"I just want to help my family," I said helplessly. "This is the only thing I know I can do. Or at least try to. Carver and Alice . . ." They had been talking about finances with Mom before I came to breakfast this morning, and had changed the subject *way* too quickly to be inconspicuous about it. They had meetings today with Dad's life insurance reps, and the budget for the funeral—and I wanted to do something, anything, to help. "They've already done a lot. A lot more than me. This is the least I can do, right?"

Seaburn sighed. "You don't have to do everything alone, love."

But oh, it was easier that way.

"Thank you," I said instead, with a soothing smile I'd learned over the years of saying, *I'm fine.*

"All right, just as long as you know," Seaburn said, and raised his glass. "To the old man. The weirder, the better."

"The weirder, the better," I replied, and we clinked glasses and drank quietly. When he'd finished his beer, he checked the time and figured he'd ought to start moseying home, so I thanked him for the conversation and went to give one last pat to the mayor—but he was gone.

"Now where did he wander off to . . ." Seaburn began to get up to look for him, when I said I would find the mayor. I needed to stretch my legs anyway.

"I'll go find the mayor. Stay for another beer—on me," I added, signaling to Dana, and went to go search for the mayor. He couldn't have gone far. Dana pointed outside, and I followed their direction. "Fetch," I called, clicking my tongue to the roof of my mouth, "here, boy."

I searched around the side of the veranda. It was a warm evening, and it brought quite a few lightning bugs out of hiding. They blinked between the blooming rosebushes and the hydrangeas in the garden.

Outside, I found Fetch—and a friend.

Ben was sitting in one of the rocking chairs, and Fetch had gone up and put his head on the armrest. Ben tried to pet him, but his fingers passed through the dog's ears, and he quickly jerked his hand away.

Fetch wagged his tail, anyway.

Dogs were pretty good judges of character. And I hated to admit that it was nice to see Ben, and see him not . . . losing it. Like he did earlier. Because real emotions were complicated. If someone started crying, I started crying with them, and it turned into a whole ordeal—like with Ben. Oh, that was *mortifying.*

I put my hands into my jean pockets, steeled my nerves, and wandered closer to him. "So, you like dogs, Mr. Andor?"

He seemed surprised that I'd noticed him because no one else had. "Oh—ah, Ben, please."

"Ben." I said his name and it sounded—friendly. Nice. Pointed at the front, and a hum at the end. I motioned to the mayor. "This is Fetch."

"He's a good boy. I heard that he's the mayor?"

"Yep, won reelection twice already."

"What a *good* dog," he told Fetch, whose tail began to whip the porch in a happy *THUMPTHUMPTHUMPTHUMPTHUMP*—

Oh yeah, Ben was definitely a dog kind of guy. Nailed it.

Fetch whined and I clicked my tongue to the roof of my mouth. He came trotting over and I scrubbed him behind the ears. He licked at my hand.

The night was soft and warm, like most spring nights in the South. There was still the undeniable snap of the last of winter's chill, but the lightning bugs were already out and performing loops in the garden outside. The moon was so bright, it looked almost like a silvery daytime, and a group of kids played kickball in the street.

There wasn't much to Mairmont. It was quiet, and the traffic was token, and the cicadas buzzed so loud you could barely think.

I don't know why I said what I said next—maybe it was the buzzing of the insects, or the kids kicking a ball down the street, or the two glasses of rum and Coke, but I said, "Dad used to say these kinds of nights were best for a good moonwalk."

Ben gave me a peculiar look. "A *moonwalk*?"

"It's a stroll—most of the time, through a graveyard. Dad says you can only take a moonwalk when there's a good moon. No clouds, no rain. Don't look at me like that—*yes*. Graveyard. My family runs a funeral home. My dad's the director." I stopped myself, and corrected, "*Was* the director." I shifted uncomfortably on the rail and shook my head. "It doesn't matter—"

"Do you want to go?" he asked suddenly.

"Go . . . where?"

"On this, erm, *moonwalk*. I have some questions about"—he motioned to himself—"and about you. I don't quite understand, and I'd like to. And maybe you need to talk, too. Besides, a change of scenery might be nice."

"Through a graveyard."

"I *am* dead. It seems apt."

I bit my lip to keep the smile from my face. He had a point. But him asking was . . . *unexpected*. And I didn't know what it was—probably the rum and Cokes—but it might've also been the way the silvery moonlight fell across his face, and the way his hair was a little floppy and his eyes were dark and deep and not at all cold or cruel, like I'd imagined in my head. As though he was actually looking at me, really looking, and wanted to know me and this weird life I lived. No lies, no walls of fiction—only this strange little secret no one knew.

And, anyway, I *did* need a change of scenery.

15

....

The Sorrows of Florence Day

ST. JOHN'S OF Mairmont Cemetery was a tiny little patch of green grass surrounded by an old stone wall. There were tombstones that stuck out of the gentle hills like white teeth. Some had flowers bursting from them; others hadn't been touched in decades. The cemetery was shadowed by oak trees that were large enough and thick enough that I was sure they'd been here long before any of the bodies below the lawn. And sitting in each one of them, perched so comfortably, were crows. A whole murder of them. Sitting in the budding branches and looking down at us with their beady little eyes, nestled in to watch us.

The wrought iron gates were closed and locked, but that had never stopped me before from creeping in. There was a crumbling wall about twenty feet down from the gate that I could get a foothold in and haul myself over.

"Oh, it's closed," Ben noted, reading the sign. "I didn't realize cemeteries closed—where are you going?" He followed me over to the place in the wall where it was a bit crumbled.

I pointed at the wall. "I'm scaling that sucker."

"Can't we . . . I don't know . . . ask permission or walk through a park instead or—"

"Park's closed at night, too, and besides"—I took off my flats and tossed them over the wall—"I know the guy who owns it. We'll be fine." I decided not to add the part where I'd been permanently banned from the cemetery after dark after the previous owner called me in for trespassing one too many times. Seaburn wouldn't care. Though it wasn't Seaburn I was worried about.

"I'm suddenly second-guessing this," he muttered.

"You're dead—what could you possibly be afraid of?" I asked.

He gave me a level look. "That's not the point."

I rolled my eyes and put my feet into the old climbing holds that I'd chiseled out when I was teenager, and began to work my way up six feet to the top, where I looped my leg over and straddled it. "You coming or am I going for a walk alone?"

He shifted his weight from one foot to the other as he debated. Ran the numbers. Debated his options. His shoulders were stiff, his eyebrows furrowed, as if it were more than *just* breaking into a cemetery that stopped him.

I swung my leg back over. "We don't have to, you know," I said, softer. "We can go to a park if you aren't comfortable. Or—the Ridge?"

I couldn't *believe* I just suggested that.

He shook his head. "No, it's fine. It's just . . . there aren't others? In the graveyard? Others like me, I mean."

"Ah, other people working through a post-living experience."

He pointed at me. "That."

I glanced back at the graveyard. The moon was so full and so bright, I could see from the gates to the far wall, and all of the off-white mausoleums and gravestones in between. "No, I don't see anyone—wait. Are you *scared* of ghosts?"

He stiffened. "No."

He said that *way* too quickly.

"You are! Oh my god, *you're* a ghost."

"Supernatural things upset me."

"I promise no *wittle ghostie* is going to hurt you, Benji Andor," I teased, "and if any of them do, they'll have me to contend with."

"You can punch ghosts?"

"No, but I'm a really bad singer. Unleash me with a microphone on any of your enemies and they're *toast*."

He snorted a laugh. "Good to know." Then he took a deep breath and said, "No, I don't go back on my word. This isn't turning out how I expected but—things rarely do, don't they?"

It sounded like he was referring to his own predicament. He couldn't have been much older than I was, and he was dead. He had plans—everyone has plans, even if they don't realize it. Even the ones who go because they think they don't have plans. There's always something that comes up.

I wondered what he regretted, what parts of his life he wished he'd done differently.

I wondered if my dad had any regrets when he went, too.

"Then c'mon." I nodded my head toward the graveyard, and looped my leg back over the wall. "Live a little."

"Yes, well, would that I could."

"Probably wrong choice of words. See you on the other side!" I pulled the rest of myself over and dropped down onto the grass. I was only 55 percent sure that he'd follow me—was he really such a stickler for the rules? He was *dead*. "Just walk through the wall, my dude," I called over to him. "You're a *ghost*—"

A moment later, he stepped through the wall and shivered. "That feels so weird," he complained, dusting invisible lint from his crisp button-down shirt. "I don't like it. It tingles. In weird places."

I headed up toward the path that looped the whole cemetery, and called back to him, "You're a terrible ghost."

"It wasn't as though I applied for this role. What if we get caught?"

"If *I* get caught," I corrected, "then I'll run. You're a ghost. No one else can see you."

He caught up in a few quick strides, and fell into pace beside me. Lee never did that. He always expected me to match his. "Right," he said, "about that. I have questions."

I took a deep breath. "Okay. I'll try to answer them."

"Can you summon ghosts?"

"No."

"Do you exorcise them?"

"No. Like I said earlier, most of them just want to talk. They have good stories. And they want someone to listen." I shrugged. "I like listening—don't give me that look," I added, sensing his gaze on me, as if he was trying to puzzle me out. As if I had surprised him.

He quickly looked away. "Is this . . . post-living part of your life a family business?"

I laughed at that. "No. My family owns the funeral home in town, but only me and my dad can see spirits. Ghosts. Whatever you want to call them—*you*. I don't know why. Maybe it has something to do with the funeral parlor? Who knows."

"Is that why you left? Not to be too forward," he added quickly, realizing that, in fact, it *was* a little too forward. "I just . . . picked up on it. People are surprised you're home."

"I guess they would be." For a few steps, I mulled over the question. What to tell him, and what to leave out. Though, what was the point of lying to a dead guy? "When I was thirteen, I helped a ghost solve his own murder. Before that, the whole mediator thing was kind of a family secret, but when your town paper writes 'Girl

Solves Hometown Murder with Ghosts,' it kind of blows that out of the water."

"So you became a local celebrity?"

I barked a laugh. "If only! No one believed me, Ben. Bestcase, they thought I was doing it for attention, worst case they thought I had something to *do* with the murder. Imagine being thirteen and on the witness stand and having to say, 'A ghost told me.' It was . . ." I tried not to remember much about that year if I could help it. The articles about me, the weird news stunt, the people calling me a liar. "Anyway, most people thought it was just a wild story. I guess it makes sense—I'd wanted to be a writer ever since I was little. I like words. I like shaping them. I like how the stories you create can be kind and good, and I like how they can never fail you, if that's how you make them." I kicked a rock, and it skittered off into the grass. "Or, you know, *in theory*."

I bit my thumbnail as we walked on in silence. The only sound was my footsteps soft on the grass.

After a while he said, "I liked that about your first book."

Surprised, I turned to him. "*Rake*?"

"No, your first book. What was it—*Ardently Yours*, I think was the title?"

My eyes widened. "You didn't."

"Why is that so surprising?"

"*No* one read that book, Ben. It never left its first printing."

"I assure you I did."

I wasn't sure how much of that I believed. First Seaburn said he read it, then Ben—two people who didn't know each other. Once my dad had said, "Don't worry, buttercup, your book will find the people it needs to," but I didn't believe him.

I was beginning to second-guess myself.

We mingled among the tombstones. I knew where Dad's plot

would be. It was already sectioned off at the top of the hill, under the large oak tree where the crows perched. I sat down on one of the stone benches throughout the cemetery, and Ben took a seat beside me.

I outstretched my hands toward the graveyard. "So? Worth it, right? One of the best views in Mairmont."

He pressed his mouth into a thin line, and his lips twisted a little. "I mean, it still isn't worth the trespassing charge but . . . it's nice."

I bit in a grin, and pulled my feet up under me to sit cross-legged. The sky unfurled in front of us, infinite and dark. The stars were much brighter here—so bright I almost forgot that you didn't need light out here in nowhere. The stars gave you all the light you needed. "Dad used to sneak in here with me when I was a kid. We'd stroll the graveyard. He called it his *exercise*. Sometimes when the ISS would pass overhead, we'd come out here and watch it. We've seen loads of comets and space junk falling in the sky. You really can't beat a view like this."

"No," he agreed. "You kind of forget in the city how many stars there are. I grew up in Maine where there were a lot of stars, too."

"Ann's in Maine," I pointed out. "Maybe you were neighbors and didn't even know it."

"There's a lot of writers in Maine. How do you know I wasn't neighbors with Stephen King?"

"Good point."

"Has anyone famous visited you as a ghost?" he asked.

"*Famous*?" I tilted my head in thought. "No . . . not that I know of. Most of the people I dealt with were from Mairmont, and I really didn't talk to ghosts in New York, so I wouldn't know. You're a weird outlier, come to think of it. You died in New York but you're haunting me five hundred miles away."

"I'm wondering the same thing," he mused, rubbing his chin. "I never imagined my afterlife would be walking cemeteries at midnight in the middle of nowhere."

"My ex hated this type of thing."

"What—sneaking into cemeteries and performing séances to summon the dead?"

"Wouldn't that have been fun? And no. He wasn't ever really into this scene. I mean, you aren't, either, *clearly*," I added, motioning to his rolled-up shirtsleeves and neatly pressed trousers, "but he wouldn't have even entertained the idea. Even if he knew I liked it, he wouldn't have asked."

He cocked his head. "True, he isn't really the graveyard type. I always thought it was strange how he wrote a contemporary gothic horror."

I stiffened. "Right—you know him. Lee Marlow."

"We are—were—work associates," he clarified, frowning as he had to correct himself to past tense. "We both got into publishing around the same time, so I saw him at functions—I recognized you when you walked into the office the other day," he added. "We never really crossed paths, though."

No, but I was never going to tell him that I recognized him, too, when I first saw him the other day. "Was that also why you were at that writing bar the other night?"

"Colloquialism? Yeah. I was there at the bar getting drinks with him because *apparently* he wanted to vent about the font they're using in his book."

I made a face. "God forbid it's *legible*."

He chuckled. It was a warm, throaty sound that reminded me of red velvet cake. In a book, I would've called it a *delicious* sound. "Did you read it?" he asked. "Marlow's book."

"Oh," I replied distantly, "I'm very familiar with it. You?"

"No—I have an advance copy but it never piqued my interest."

"Might've saved yourself there. The heroine in the book is so dry and salty and apathetic—about *everything*."

Ben winced. "He probably thought that meant a strong female character."

I threw up my hands. "I know, right? A woman can be emotional and vibrant and love things. That doesn't make her weak or inferior—*argh!* I'm not going to rant about it, it'll just make me upset," I added, forcing my hands down by my sides again. A blush crept over my cheeks. "Not that I care what he wrote. At all."

It's not like he wrote me into his book. I *wasn't* that dry and salty. At least I didn't think I was.

And I *definitely* wasn't apathetic.

"And," I added, unable to stop myself, "he made her a bad kisser. Like, *pathetically* bad. And I don't know about you, but I think salty bitches kiss *great*."

He nodded, agreeing. "In my experience, women with sharp tongues usually have soft lips."

"You kiss sharp-tongued girls often?"

His gaze lingered on my lips. "Not often enough."

My ears began to burn with a blush, and I glanced away from him. He was a *ghost*, Florence. Very much dead. And off-limits. "You know, if I was any other kind of person, I'd ask you to haunt Lee Marlow's hipster ass."

"A ghost for hire."

"You'd be chillingly good at it."

"I have a bone to pick with him, anyhow."

"Oh?" I laughed. "Were you in love with him, too?"

"No, but you were. And I can tell that it hurts."

That surprised me. "Am I that obvious?"

"No—yes," he admitted. "A little. You don't seem like the person who wrote *Ardently Yours* anymore. Not in a bad way, but in the way you feel when you're reading something and realize what you've been looking for—are you listening?" he added as I stood and began to pace in front of the bench. "I don't think you're listening—"

"Shush, wait." I held a finger up to him to get him to quiet. My brain was thinking, and it was connecting dots like a constellation. "The manuscript."

"What about it?"

"What connects us! It's not *Ann*, it's the manuscript. You're here because *I'm* not done with it. That's your unfinished business!"

He tilted his head. "Well, you're almost finished with it, right?"

"Um . . ."

"Florence," he said sternly, and a shiver went up my spine. "You've had over a *year*."

"Yeah, and a lot of things have happened in a year!"

"But—"

Suddenly, a flashlight blinded me. I shielded my eyes with the back of my hand and winced away from the blaringly bright light. There was the crunch of gravel, and the jingle of keys. *Shit.* I hadn't even noticed him unlocking the cemetery gate or coming inside. I'd been too wrapped up in flirting with this ship called *Disaster.*

I dove behind the bench. Ben hid with me.

"Hello?" the police officer called. "Hey, you kids, you're not supposed to be in here."

"*Shit,*" I whispered. "I think that's Officer Saget."

"Bob?"

"What? No—was that a joke, Benji Andor?"

"Too dated?" he asked, ashamed.

"A bit—*shit.*" I ducked down lower as the flashlight beam searched overhead again. How could I possibly explain to Ben the years of hate accumulated between Officer Saget and me? "So, fun story: I might be banned from this graveyard."

"Florence!"

"I was a kid!"

The police officer called out to us, but I pressed my finger to my lips and told Ben to be *quiet*. He wasn't going to trick me this time. I was an *adult*. With a functioning and fully formed brain this time!

Well, mostly functioning. On good days.

The officer walked closer, over the dark grassy hill, toward us. While I didn't have any outstanding warrants, I did absolutely have a parking ticket I hadn't paid in ten years. I didn't want to think about what that cost now. Never mind the other misdemeanors I had on my record. Starting a fire at school. Stealing Coach Rhinehart's golf cart. Trespassing in the Mairmont County Museum . . .

Enough to make me a public nuisance.

Suddenly, with a startled caw, the murder of crows sitting in the oak tree took flight at the same time. They scared Officer Saget, who cursed and ducked as they swooped in and broke out into the night sky. Then I saw Ben try to grab for my wrist, but his hand passed through it. He looked momentarily annoyed.

"Hurry!" he hissed.

He didn't have to tell *me* twice. I turned on my heels and leapt into a sprint toward the back of the cemetery, cutting around tombstones and fake flowers propped up against plaques, and headed for the back corner. It got darker the farther we ran, and a little sliver of wall had fallen down behind the old oak there—

I slipped through the crumbled wall and broke out onto Crescent Avenue, and hopped through a few backyards until I returned to the cross street with the inn. I didn't stop to catch my breath until I was inside the wrought iron gates and halfway down the path to the front door.

"I've never been so close to getting caught!" I clutched my sides as I dissolved into peals of laughter. "Did you startle the crows?"

"I would never," he replied indignantly, folding his arms over his chest.

I could've kissed him. "Thank you."

The tips of his ears burned red and he looked away. "You're welcome."

Trying to hide a grin, I wandered up the cobblestone path to the front door when I paused on the porch steps where we began, and glanced back at Ben. "I'm sorry," I said, "that I lied to you about getting caught in the cemetery."

"Well—at least now I know," he replied, and shook his head. "I'm going to—I don't know. Go see if I can haunt the diner or something. Smell some coffee. Question," he added as an afterthought.

"Answer," I replied.

"Is it normal to hear things? Chattering—voices—barely? Like they're just out of earshot?"

I frowned. "Not that I know of, but I never asked."

"Huh. Okay, well, good night. Try not to get into too much trouble," he added, and left down the sidewalk toward the Waffle House. I stood on the porch of the bed-and-breakfast for a while, watching as his transparent form slowly melted into the darkness and was gone.

I already had one dead person to mourn. Common sense told me that I shouldn't get involved with Ben, that my heart couldn't take another goodbye so soon, but I think I'd already decided to help him. I wasn't sure when I decided—yesterday? When he first showed up at the front door?

I was foolish, and I was only going to hurt myself, because if I knew anything about death, the goodbyes were harder with ghosts than corpses.

16

....

Songs for the Dead

SATURDAY ROLLED INTO Sunday, and I tried to convince Mom to let me help out with the funeral today—the second-to-last one Dad scheduled before he died—but she adamantly refused the entire breakfast. I hadn't been to a funeral in years. The dirges, the gospels, the crying widows and the grieving kids and the parents who had to bury their children and—

The ghosts.

I pulled on an NYU sweatshirt and texted Mom, **Are you sure?**

One more word and I will ground you, Mom texted back with a heart emoji.

Well, fine then.

Speaking of ghosts, I hadn't seen my resident haunt yet today, not even as I went downstairs to grab a bagel and some cream cheese from the breakfast selection in the dining room. (Second breakfast was always my favorite meal of the day.) I smeared a large helping of cream cheese onto my bagel, humming along with the morning radio murmur in the corner of the room. I poured myself coffee in a to-go cup and made my way back into the foyer.

"Florence! There you are."

I gave a yelp. Sitting at the front desk, his head propped up on his hand, was John. And beside him, leaning smugly against the desk, was Officer Saget.

"You look like you've seen a ghost," the police officer commented. In the daylight hours, he looked much older than I remembered. His hair was almost completely silver now, he kept his beard trimmed tight against his jaw, and he looked to be made of nothing but blocks put together. He was as square as they came.

"Ha, that's hilarious," I replied tightly. "Nice to see you, Officer."

"You, too. Did you have a busy night last night, Miss Day?"

"Absolutely not. Went to bed early. Had a great night's sleep—" Though I couldn't resist a yawn. "And now I'm up and about to go check out the town."

"Early, you say?"

"Absolutely."

He didn't get a read on my face last night. He didn't know it was me.

John watched the exchange back and forth like a badminton tournament, putting a bookmark into his current manga to watch.

"You know it's illegal to lie to an officer," Saget went on.

"Why would I lie?"

"So you didn't take any midnight strolls?"

"Oh, absolutely not," I lied.

He pursed his lips. His nostrils flared. But then, after a moment, he seemed to think better of his strategy. "You get off this once—this *once*, Florence. If it were anywhere else, I'd be getting you for trespassing. Try to act your age, okay?" he warned, and bid John goodbye, before he left out of the front door, climbed into his police car illegally parked on the curb, and drove away.

I let out a breath I didn't realize I'd been holding. "*Shit*, that was close."

John gave me a look. "Oh, girl, you just love chaos, don't you." This morning he had his red beard braided down his front like a Viking, and his pizza baseball cap again.

"It's in my blood," I replied, and took a long sip of coffee. "What *I* want to know is who ratted me out to the cops. Seaburn doesn't care if I go into the cemetery after dark, but I've trespassed so many times everywhere else I feel like Saget's just gunning to get me on something."

"I don't think he ever forgave you for bringing in that wild possum to the police station."

"I didn't know what else to do! I didn't think he had *rabies*."

Chuckling, he shook his head. On an embroidered doggie bed beside the front desk was our mayor. He looked up, his tail *pat-pat-patting* on the ground. I scrubbed him behind the ears. "So, I got a question."

"I might have an answer."

"Do you know when Bar None opens?"

He checked his smart watch. "I'm sure it'll be open for lunch in a few minutes. They've got pretty good cheese dogs. And their Tater Tots are—" He mimicked an A-OK signal. "Why don't you take the mayor with you? He's due for an inspection of those tots, anyway."

I guessed that Seaburn was helping out with the funeral, so the least I could do was bring his dog along. "Sure. Mayor, wanna go with me?" The dog popped to his feet. "Then let's go! Thank you, John!"

I wasn't looking forward to today's tasks. While Carver and Alice were helping Mom, I had to figure out how to do Dad's impossible tasks. I already miserably failed at trying to get the flowers yesterday. I couldn't wait to fail at finding Elvis today.

At least I had a good companion with me.

But the flower shop owner *did* give me a lead, and while he wasn't exactly Elvis, I knew my dad well enough to know that he didn't always mean what he said, and thank god Bar None actually did keep strict operational hours, because I got there right at ten in the morning.

I let myself in, the mayor at my heels. There was a DOGS SHOULD VOTE sign inside the bar, and I took that as permission enough to let the best dog in with me. A man stood behind the bar prepping for the day.

"Is that Florence Day I see?" he asked, and adjusted his glasses. "I don't believe my eyes! The famous Florence Day."

Dagger, meet heart. "You got me," I replied with a practiced smile.

"Perez. I'm sorry to hear about the old man," he said, offering out a hand.

I shook it. "Thanks. Um, I have a weird question for you. Mr. Taylor down at the flower shop said that there was an Elvis that plays here some nights?"

"Elvis . . . ? Ah! Of course!" He thumbed over his shoulder to a poster on the events board behind him. "You mean *Elvistoo*."

I glanced behind him to the poster he was referring to, and found myself staring at an aged-out version of Elvis in glittery sequins, about to eat a microphone. "Oh, that's—exciting?"

"Hey, Bruno!" he called in the back.

The chef poked his head out. "Yeah, boss?"

"This is Xavier's kid."

Bruno's dark eyes lit up like firecrackers on the Fourth of July. He quickly exited the kitchen, wiping his hands on his pristine white apron. "Well, I'll be! Florence Day!" His voice was velvety smooth. I had a feeling he was— "Your dad came to watch me sing every Thursday. Before the poker games," he added when confusion crossed my brow.

"That makes sense."

We shook, and he sat down on the stool beside me. Perez, the bartender, asked if I wanted a drink, and I told him a lemonade would be nice. Bruno said, "Your old man never missed a night—and when he didn't come on Thursday, we knew something was wrong," he said. "I'm sorry. I know it's not much and it's not a great word to express the shit that's happened, but it's all I got."

"It's really appreciated."

The bartender slid over a lemonade, and I curled my fingers around the cool, moist glass. The ice shifted, condensation pearling on the outside like rain droplets. He said, "Your dad always raved about you."

Bruno nodded. "Always said you were up in the big city, chasing your dreams. That you could write words that could wake the dead."

"He said that?"

"Absolutely."

I felt heat nibble at my cheeks. Of *course* Dad would say something like that. He didn't even know that I ghostwrote—that those books were sold in airport bookstores and at grocery store checkout counters—

And . . . now I couldn't tell him at all.

Ever.

He paused. "Xavier swore me not to tell anyone, but I gotta know if it's true that—"

"Bruno . . . ," the bartender warned.

I frowned. "Know if what's true?"

Bruno instead said, "He was so proud of you, Miss Day. So fuckin' proud he cried. He knew you were chasing your dream, like Carver and Alice, and he was so damn proud of all you kids."

But he never knew the full story. I never told him that I pulled inspiration from his and Mom's romance, that I memorized all of the stories they told me of their grandparents, all the love stories they had passed down from generation to generation. I had been so caught up with being the exception to the rule—the one family member who would never have a glorious love story—that I'd forgotten why I wrote about love.

Because a gray-haired woman in an oversized sweater asked me to, yes, but also because I *wanted* to. Because I believed in it, once upon a time.

"Did I upset you?" Bruno asked, and I realized I hadn't touched my lemonade.

I took a deep sip and shook my head. "No," I replied, and winced because my voice was anything but convincing. "I actually came to ask you a question about Dad. Would you be available Thursday around three?"

"I—I mean, I'd have to check with Perez—"

"Yes," Perez replied. "He is."

"I guess I am?"

"Then would you do the honors of singing at my father's funeral? I'll pay you, of course—is there a special rate you have for . . . strange venues?"

Bruno blinked at me. Once. Twice. Then he leaned forward and asked, "Lemme get this straight: You want me to sing at your father's funeral."

"Yes. In that." And I pointed to the poster.

His bushy black eyebrows shot up. "Huh."

"I know it's strange but—"

"Hell yeah."

That took me back. "And your going rate?"

The man grinned, and finally I noticed that his left canine was gold plated. "Miss Day, Elvistoo honors the dead for free."

17

Dead Hour

I CURLED MY fingers around the wrought iron gate to the cemetery. It was already locked—I forgot that it closed most evenings at 6 P.M.—and I didn't really want to walk the graveyard tonight, but I didn't know where else to go. There was a storm rolling in. Lightning lit the bulbous clouds in the distance, and there was a distinct smell in the air.

Damp and fresh, like clean laundry hung out to dry.

Thunder rumbled across the hills of the cemetery.

"A bit early for one of those moonwalks, isn't it?" asked a familiar voice to my left. I glanced over, and there was Ben, his hands in his pockets, looking a little worse for wear. His tie was a little askew, the top button of his shirt undone, exposing enough of his collar and a necklace hanging there—with a ring on it.

A golden wedding ring.

His? Or someone else's? I didn't know why, but I was startled by it. I really knew nothing about him, did I? I didn't know why it bothered me. I never cared before what kind of jewelry ghosts wore. *Silly*, I chastised myself, letting go of the gate, and turned to him. "Yeah. Storm's coming in, anyway."

He inclined his head toward the clouds. "You can tell?"

"You can smell it in the air. Want to walk me back to the inn?"

"It'd be an honor, Florence."

Again, he said my name, and again each vowel curled a chill up my spine in a not-too-unpleasant sort of way. It was actually very pleasant. I liked the way he said my name. I liked that he even *said* it. Lee only ever called me *bunny* this and *bunny* that.

But oh, what power there was when Ben said *my name*.

A gust of wind scattered a few green leaves. I pushed my hair behind my ear, to keep it out of my face, while it blew right through him. It didn't ruffle his hair, or his clothes. He was stagnant, forever like this. A portrait now, something never to be changed. Like my dad—forever sixty-four. His experiences ended. His life frozen.

Ben put his hands in his pockets and began, "You know, I've been thinking about our conversation in the graveyard."

"About how to help you move on?"

"Yes, and I was thinking that perhaps the reason I'm here has nothing to do with the manuscript," he proposed. He turned to me and said, very adamantly, "Maybe I'm here to help *you*."

I stared at him. Blinked. And then burst out laughing.

He looked indignant. "It's not that funny."

"It definitely is!" I howled, clutching my sides. Because if *that* wasn't the plot of a rom-com, I didn't know what was. "Oh my god—sorry. I just—that can't be right. What would I need help with?"

"Love. Help you believe in it again."

My laughter quickly died in my throat. It suddenly wasn't funny anymore. It was personal. I pursed my lips. "You're not the Ghost of Christmas Past, Ben."

"But what if—"

"That's not how this works," I dismissed. "I've never heard of a ghost coming back to help someone alive. It's always me helping you. Them. Whatever."

"And if you're wrong?"

"I don't need help with love. I'm perfectly content with my eyes wide open. It's not me stuck being unalive, it's you. So, *I* need to help *you*. Make sense?"

"Yeah," he said, not looking at me, clearly thinking that I was wrong. "I guess."

"Good. And I will get to the manuscript, I promise. I just—I need time."

"Well, you have plenty of that now," he replied wryly, and I winced a bit. He wasn't wrong.

We passed the ice cream shop, where a kid and her father sat at the table by the window sharing an ice cream sundae. When I was little, and Carver and Alice were littler, Dad used to take me to the parlor and split with me a chocolate bowl with sprinkles on top.

I wished I could ask Dad about how to help Ben. He would've known. The only lead I had was the manuscript but . . . I didn't know how to fix that. And if that *was* why Ben was sticking around, then I was afraid we were both shit out of luck.

And I was annoyed that Ben would even . . . that he would even *propose* that I . . . that he was here to—

Argh!

I tried love. It didn't work. The end. There were bigger things in my life that I had to tackle than something so frivolous.

"Did you find what you were looking for at that bar?" he asked after a moment.

"Somehow, yes. Managed to book Elvis for the funeral."

He gave a start. "Presley? Is he . . . a *ghost*?" he asked in an almost whisper.

Oh, why was that charming? Why was that so *charming*?

I bit the inside of my cheek to keep from grinning, because I was still annoyed with him. "No"—I took out a poster from my back pocket and unfolded it to show him exactly which Elvis I was referring to—"but he's the next best thing."

He held a hand over his mouth to hide a laugh. "An *impersonator*? For a *funeral*?"

"You didn't know Dad," I replied, pocketing the poster again.

"He sounds like a riot."

I smiled at the thought of Dad going to watch Bruno perform before his Thursday night poker games—and then my smile faded as I remembered that he never would again. I folded my arms over my chest and said curtly, "He *was*."

"Right—yes. Sorry."

We walked the next three blocks in silence, passing the bookstore with a poster of *When the Dead Sing* by Lee Marlow, and I lingered only for a moment. Only long enough for Ben to glance back to see why I'd stopped, and then I made myself put one foot in front of the other, and ignore the poster, the release date. Only a few more months before the whole world read my story ruined by his words.

"Oh, look! Annie's books."

"What?"

I stared through the window at the stacks of romance novels, with Ann Nichols's new books at the top. The ones I wrote—*Midnight Matinee, A Rake's Guide*—all of them. Dad walked by this bookstore every day on his daily lunch breaks to Fudge's. He must've seen this display, these books. I wondered if he ever ducked into the store and bought one. I wondered if Mom loved the dry humor in Nichols's new ones. Mom and I never really talked about books after mine failed. I didn't want to talk about books at all after that.

I turned to keep walking, when Ben backtracked and nodded his head toward the door. "Let's go in."

"Why?"

"Because I like bookstores," he replied, and stepped backward through the closed door.

I had half a mind to not follow him, but a part of me wondered what section he gravitated toward. Literary? Horror? I couldn't even imagine him in the romance aisle, towering and broody in his pristine button-down shirts and ironed trousers.

The bell above the door rang as I stepped into the cozy bookstore. The woman behind the counter, Mrs. Holly, had been there for twenty-odd years. She looked up from her book with a smile. "Well, I'll be damned! Florence Day."

Even my local booksellers back in Jersey didn't know my name, but it seemed like a decade away couldn't erase me from small-town memory. Everywhere I went it was "Holy smokes, Florence Day!" like I was Mairmont's local celebrity. Well, I guess I was.

"Hi, Mrs. Holly," I greeted.

"What're you in for?"

Have you seen a ghost float through, by any chance? Six foot sexy, with just the slightest hint of nerd? I wanted to ask, but instead went with, "Just looking."

"Could I help?"

"I don't think so," I began, before my eyes caught the pop-up on the counter for *When the Dead Sing* by Lee Marlow. PRE-ORDER TODAY! the cardboard stand-up announced, with the picture of the cover—a run-down Victorian mansion with a Wednesday Addams–looking girl standing in front of it, unsmiling. From one of the windows peered a ghoul of some sort, demonic eyes and sharp teeth.

Riveting.

"The author must've never visited a small town before in his *life*," Mrs. Holly said when she noticed what had grabbed my attention. She shook her head. "One of my booksellers *loved* it, though. I don't get why."

"Noted," I replied.

Of course he couldn't write small towns. He'd never lived in one—he thought every small town was either Stars Hollow or Silent Hill. There was no in-between.

"You write better than he ever could," she went on.

I stiffened.

"You know I still sell your book! Not as often these days, but I do. It's a pity it went out of print already. Barely made it to paperback."

"I didn't like the paperback anyway," I replied with a bit of bitter humor, because the paperback had been so ugly I couldn't imagine anyone picking it up on their own. You knew a publisher had given up on a book when they let their design intern make a book cover.

I told Mrs. Holly I wanted to browse, and made my way back through the aisles of memoirs and self-help, past sci-fi and fantasy, to the back corner of the store where the paperback romances were. And there was Ben, looking through the used romances with cracked spines and dog-eared pages.

"Weren't you a horror editor?" I asked as I slid up to him. "Why'd you come to romance?"

"My imprint shuttered." He attempted to take a book off the

shelf, but his hand fell right through it. He frowned, having forgot, and sighed.

"That can't be the *only* reason."

"I read a book once that changed me. And I realized I wanted to help writers write more books like that, and find more books like that, and give them the chance they wouldn't have otherwise."

"Must've been a great book. Bestseller? Have I heard of it?"

His mouth twisted into a grin, as if I'd said something funny. "If I've learned anything as an editor over my last ten years, it's that you never really hear of the good ones."

I roamed my gaze across the shelves—the Christina Laurens and the Nora Robertses and the Rebekah Wetherspoons and the Julia Quinns and the Casey McQuistons—until my eyes settled on the most familiar spine. I took it out for him. There were only two on the shelf. I wondered how much longer Mrs. Holly would be able to stock it before she couldn't find it anymore. *Ardently Yours.*

I smoothed my hand across the cover, across the embellished font and the laminated gloss. I remembered how much I loved this book. How every word sounded like a heartbeat, how every turn of phrase was a love song.

"You said you read mine—was it one of those you never hear about?" I asked quietly. "One of the good ones?"

He didn't answer at first. I glanced up to see if he'd even heard me, and to my surprise he wasn't even looking at the book. He was looking at—at *me*, with this soft, quiet sadness that made my stomach twist.

"Yes," he replied, as sure and certain as a sunrise. "It was."

My eyes burned, and I quickly looked away, and wiped the tears with the back of my hand. They were words I didn't think I needed to hear. Lee Marlow had never said as much—he said it was fluffy, it was lighthearted. It was candy, though even candy could be good—sweet and flavorful and exactly what you needed exactly when you needed it. But he never said as much.

Rose never understood why I was so wrapped up in what Lee thought of my books, but didn't you want someone you loved to respect what you wrote? Lee was supposed to be the closest person I had. He was supposed to tell me it was good, that it was worthy—and that *I* was worthy of that praise.

But instead it came from a stranger I barely knew.

Ben reminded me of Ann in that way. She'd sat down at my table, and with a certainty as if she already knew that my words were worthy, she asked me to write her romances. She gave me a gift I never thought I'd get. And through her I wrote the stories I wanted to read, and it was so powerful—

I took a deep breath, and put my book back on the shelf. "I don't know how to finish Ann's manuscript."

He cocked his head. "What do you mean?"

"I mean I don't know how. I . . . I don't think I can. But . . ." I swallowed the knot in my throat, and said with certainty, "I'll try."

He was quiet for one heartbeat, then two, then three. And then I saw his shined loafers stop in front of me, and when I looked up he had bent down a little, his hands in his pockets, and he was smiling, "Thank you. Annie would like that. And I'll help you however I can."

"Oh? Gonna write the happily ever after for me?"

"I can give you some ideas."

And I recognized that kind of smile, finally. The kind you didn't really show to strangers. The kind you kept to yourself because the world had been shit, and your heart had been broken so many times by different people and places and stories. He had stories, too. The wedding ring on a chain around his neck. The way he fit his hands into his pockets to look as small as possible. The reason he loved romance.

And for the first time since I cried about Lee in Rose's matchbox-sized apartment with a bottle of wine and a half-eaten pizza, my hair still wet with rain, I wanted to learn a new story. I wanted to read the first chapter in the life of Ben Andor and figure out the words that built his heart and soul. And okay, yeah, maybe also his six-foot-three frame, but honestly even if I *wanted* to climb him, I couldn't because he was very much a ghost and I would go right through him.

I wasn't very good at climbing, anyway.

We left the bookstore after I'd bought the new Sarah MacLean historical romance, and Ben walked me home the last two blocks. By then the storm was at the edge of town.

"So, in the spirit of being a mediator," I began, pausing at the gate to the inn, "I'm obligated to ask if you would like me to pass on a message to anyone."

He cocked his head. "As in anyone I've left behind?"

"Yes. Parents or, um, your grandmother, right? A significant other?" I said that part a bit quieter, thinking about the wedding ring around his neck. It wasn't like . . . I mean, we weren't . . . this wasn't—I wasn't *fishing*.

"Um." He rubbed the back of his neck. "I . . . well." Then he took a deep breath and said, "No."

I gave a start. "No one?"

"Don't look at me like that."

"I'm not—"

"You are."

I forced myself to look away. Down the street. Seaburn was walking the mayor, and I waved to them as they passed. *No one.*

There was a weight to those words. I'd always operated alone, but I knew I had family—Alice and my dad and Rose and Carver. But to be really alone. I'd spent my life with safety nets. I couldn't imagine what it was like to walk a tightrope without them, and then when you finally fell . . .

No one.

I tried to not flinch away from the thought, but it stayed with me. Because loneliness was the kind of ghost that haunted you long after you were dead. It stood over your plot in the cemetery where a lone name sat carved in marble. It sat with your urn. It was the wind that carried your ashes when no one claimed your body.

"I'm sorry," I whispered, once Seaburn and the mayor were out of earshot. "I didn't know."

"I didn't expect you to, but don't worry about it. It doesn't matter."

"It does—"

"No, it doesn't," he interrupted, and placed his hands on the wrought iron fence, and leaned against it. "It doesn't matter, Florence, it really doesn't. Everything is in my will—I wasn't a fool. I'm a thirty-six-year-old bachelor whose close relatives are *all* dead, and I share my apartment with a cat named Dolly Purrton."

"You do *not*."

"I do. She's perfect. And my will was pretty straightforward in regard to her," he added. "I had planned my entire life. How I was going to live it. What I was going to do, and when. Everything had its place. It was neat and orderly."

"Like your desk."

He gave a shrug. "I'm not great with surprises. I don't—*didn't*—take chances. I didn't take risks. On anything—or anyone." He hesitated, and then corrected himself, "*Almost* anyone. And I was fine with that life. I'd even planned on what would happen should

I die before forty, I just . . . didn't think it'd happen. I would've expedited a lot of my long-term plans," he added, trying to joke.

I didn't find it funny, for once. "You can't plan for everything."

"Trust me, I know that now," he said, and there was this hardness in his voice that made me think that it was something he regretted a lot recently. "I thought, before I died, I would at least find . . ." He shook his head. "But of course not."

"Find what?"

He slid his cool brown gaze toward me. "The one thing you don't believe in, Florence." Then he shook his head and said, "I guess if everyone found their big love, then the world wouldn't be such a terrible place most of the time, eh?"

"Ben . . ."

"I don't need your pity."

"Pity?" I mock gasped, undoing the latch to the gate. "Whatever gave you that idea, Benji Andor? I was just going to welcome you to the Singles Club, it's not so bad here. Some people even like it! I envy them."

He snorted and walked through the gate. "I do, too."

At the counter inside, Dana was reading a novel by Courtney Milan at the desk, and I waved at them as I passed up toward my room.

"Good night!" I called.

Ben said, "Sweet dreams."

Dana said, "Night!"

I left up the stairs and went to my room and fell onto my bed.

That night, as the storm blew over Mairmont, I tried to listen to the dead sing through the trees, but as the wind bent the limbs and scraped across the rooftop, all I could hear was the rain. And all I could think about was Ben Andor in the bookstore, bending ever so slightly to me with a lopsided smile, thanking me for trying.

No one had ever thanked me for that before. For trying. Even though I was failing. Even though Ann's expectations loomed over me like this huge, dark thundercloud. I didn't want to disappoint her, and I was beginning to realize how much I didn't want to disappoint *Ben*, either. But more than that, though, I wanted to finish that manuscript so he'd know that he wasn't some empty Sharpie unable to leave a mark. He left them wherever he went, even if he couldn't see them.

Even if no one told him, "Thank you for trying."

18

The Undertaker's Daughters

MONDAY MORNING WAS another breakfast with the family.

I missed it, weirdly enough, when I was in New York. And now that I was back, for however short a time, I'd sunk back into the well-oiled machine of my family like I'd never left. Alice and I didn't even snap at each other when we sat down for breakfast, even though I was still salty from that last chapter. I'd tried to write again when I woke up but—it was the same problem. Jackson didn't get struck by lightning this time, but I still didn't know how to make Amelia stay.

Alice, on the other hand, seemed to be having some trouble of her own.

". . . Never mind the wrong shade of concealer came in," she was saying, spearing another egg. "Honestly—do you think *one* thing can go right for Dad's funeral?"

That caught my attention, and I looked up from my first cup of coffee. The caffeine was beginning to fire off those synapses in my brain. "You ordered the wrong concealer?"

Alice glared at me. "No! The company sent me the wrong refill. And it's stage makeup, so it isn't like I can go to CVS and get a new jar. Ugh, this is a nightmare," she added, putting her face in her hands. "First I ran out of embalming fluid last night, and now this."

Mom patted her on the shoulder. "Murphy's Law, hon."

"Murphy can fuck off for this *one funeral*."

Just as I always wanted to be a writer, my little sister always wanted to be a mortician. Ever since I could remember, she'd followed Dad like a shadow. She went to Duke for forensic chemistry, and on weeknights, just for fun, she got her mortuary sciences and funeral services degree online. A part of me always thought that it was Alice who should've inherited Dad's gift. She would've been so much better at it, and I doubt she would've been run out of town because of it. She was the kind of person to tackle things head-on. Nothing frightened her. Especially after I solved that cold case, and everything got worse. She fought people on my behalf. Another reason why I wanted to leave as quickly as possible when I graduated high school—so she didn't feel obligated to anymore.

"Anything I can help with?" I asked, poking at my waffle.

Alice said quickly, "No."

"Are you sure? You don't have to do everything alone—"

She looked up from her plate, and I instantly realized I'd said the wrong thing. "*Oh?* Are we going to talk about this now?"

"Alice," Mom warned.

My entire body went rigid. "No—what does she mean? What do you mean, talk about this now? What's your problem, Al?"

"*My* problem? It's not my problem I have a problem with," she snapped. "The second things get difficult, you leave. No matter what. We can always rely on you for that."

"That's not fair. You *know* that's not fair."

"Then why didn't you ever come home?"

"Everyone visited me in New York!" I batted back. "Every year. You came up for the lights and the Christmas tree and—"

"Because *Dad* wanted to see you. And he knew you wouldn't come home no matter how much he asked. You can ask Mom. We would've loved to stay home for Christmas just *once*."

That wasn't true. I *knew* it wasn't true. They loved coming to visit me during the holidays—they'd said as much! And Dad never once asked me to come home, not once—

"Mom?" I asked, turning my attention to her. "Is that true?"

She turned her eyes to the ceiling tiles, then closed them and took a deep breath. "Your father never wanted you to come back when you weren't ready."

A sinking feeling burrowed into the pit of my stomach.

"No, we always catered to you," Alice added and shoved herself to her feet. "We all've got ghosts, Florence. You just happen to be the only one who can't handle yours." Then she shoved her arms into her black jacket, and stalked out of the diner.

I didn't feel hungry anymore.

Mom said patiently, "Florence, you know she didn't mean that—"

"I've got to go write something," I said, lying, *obviously* lying, as I excused myself from the table. Carver gave me a pained look, as if to say, *Sorry*, but he had nothing to be sorry for. Mom asked if I wanted to take a to-go coffee mug with me, but there was coffee at the bed-and-breakfast, and god knows I'd forget the to-go container in some unspecified location and never find it again.

The thing was, Alice wasn't wrong.

It was another argument we had been avoiding—for years. And now all of them were bubbling up to the surface.

Not only that, but I had my dead editor to contend with, Dad's funeral preparations, and Ann's manuscript. Everything all at once.

I hated complicated.

When I got back to the bed-and-breakfast, John waved at me without looking up from his *Spider-Man* comic. I climbed the stairs back to my room, and decided that a long and relaxing shower was *exactly* what I needed. Head empty, water hot, nothing but the white noise of the shower echoing in my brain. I didn't want to think right now. Not about anything.

So I pulled out my NYU sweatshirt again and picked up my jeans from the floor, and laid them out on the bed before I went for the claw-foot tub with a shower. As it turned out, thankfully, the inn didn't skimp on water temperature. I let it get as hot as I could—hot enough to boil me alive, exactly how I liked it—and stood under the spray for a long time. Until the steam was thick and the constant shower of water over my head quieted all the buzzing thoughts in my head and my skin was flushed and my fingers began to shrivel.

Too long, probably.

The soap smelled like butterscotch, and I tried not to think. It reminded me of the way Ben smelled in his office, and I tried to stop thinking. How his eyes looked when he had bent toward me and thanked me, warm and soft and ocher. His shirtsleeves rolled up to expose muscular forearms. How he was so big, and his hands were big, and how they would feel against my body, cupping my breasts, his lips pressed against mine, tasting like spearmint and—

No.

I flung my eyes open. Shampoo suds leaked into my eyes, and I cursed and put my face into the hot water to rinse them out.

No, no, no, Florence. He was *dead.*

He was very, very dead.

"Stupid, stupid, stupid," I muttered to myself. What was *wrong* with me? I was home for the first time in ten years for my father's funeral and I was fantasizing about a *dead guy*. I hadn't even thought about anyone else since Lee Marlow ripped my heart out and fed it to the pizza rats.

So why *now* of all times?

Why him?

Because he was someone very safely dead. Someone so very out of reach. And I was that fucked up.

When the water started to finally get cold, I finished washing the suds out of my hair and got out of the shower. The entire bathroom was still so foggy, I had to use my towel to wipe off the mirror.

Something materialized out of the corner of my eye. In front of the bathtub.

I looked—and let out a scream.

Ben spun around to face me—and yelped, covering his eyes. I clambered to cover my . . . *bits*, but I must've grabbed the world's *smallest* towel because I kept having to shift between covering my nips and my bush, and after a few rotations I realized there wasn't a good answer here. So I grabbed the shower curtain and wrapped that around me instead.

"Oh god, my eyes!" Ben cried.

"The *hell*, Ben?" I snapped.

"I didn't mean to—I'm sorry! I just kind of . . . I didn't see a thing—I promise." Then, after a beat, he added, "Though I hear there is a shortage of perfect breasts in the world and yours—"

"Get out!"

"I'm going! I'm going!" he cried as I grabbed the complimentary toothpaste and conditioner, and lobbed them at him. They sailed right through him, clattering against the closed door as he dipped through it—and was gone.

I gave another frustrated cry, wanting to drown myself in the tub instead. "I just wanted two seconds of quiet," I moaned forlornly to myself, and finally unraveled from the shower curtain. The tiny towel had failed me.

It had failed me so deeply.

I wrapped my arms around my breasts, feeling my ears turn red with embarrassment. I can't believe he *saw* me *naked.* After I'd—

Oh god.

No one had ever called my breasts perfect before. *A handful*, sure, but perfect?

I reckoned they weren't terrible.

Complimenting my boobs didn't excuse him from looking, though. The perv. He didn't just look, he *stared*, like he'd been thirsty for years and hadn't seen a watering hole. Well, my—*I* was not a watering hole. He was very dead; he did not get thirsty.

I wasn't even *entertaining* this.

When I finally changed into my waist-high mom jeans and oversized NYU sweatshirt, looking like the pinnacle of unfuckability, there was a text waiting from my sister.

It said three simple words, but I felt like I was being asked to move a mountain:

Write Dad's obituary.

19

A Dying Practice

> Xavier Vernon Day was a loving husband, father, and friend. He grew up in Mairmont, where he inherited the Days Gone Funeral Home and became a paragon and beloved beacon in the community. He is survived by his wife, Isabella, and his three children, Florence, Carver, and Alice Day. He was . . .

My fingers fell silent against the keyboard. He was, what? Dead? Very. And this didn't sound like the kind of obit he would want to have shared in the *Daily Ram*, Mairmont's local paper.

I pushed my laptop back with a frustrated sigh, and reached for my coffee—when Ben materialized *right* into the seat. I jumped in surprise, spilling my drink. The waitress at the diner gave me a strange look before she rushed to grab a towel to help me clean it up.

"The *hell*?" I hissed at him, and then smiled to the waitress as she came back with a towel. "Sorry, I'm such a klutz!"

"You are a terrible liar," Ben remarked, leaning his head on his hand, elbow propped on the table.

After the waitress was gone, I glared at him. "Well if you'd stop just *popping* up in places, I wouldn't be so startled, now would I?"

"I can't help it," he replied, a bit uncomfortably. "It just happens. One minute I'm . . ." He trailed off, and made a motion with his hand, although he looked a bit troubled. "And then I'm here. Where you are. I take it that doesn't happen with other ghosts?"

"Not that I can remember. They just hang around until I help them with whatever they're sticking around for. They don't just pop in when I'm naked in the shower."

He coughed to hide a chuckle, and glanced away, his cheeks burning red. "It was just as awkward for me."

"Was it? Really?" I asked sarcastically, and sighed. "Never mind, we're going to ignore it." I finished cleaning up my mess, and realized I had, in fact, spilled *all* of the coffee. Perfect. I signaled for the waitress to refill my mug, and took out my phone, so that the old guy reading the personals in the *Daily Ram* in the booth next to me didn't think I was talking to myself. "You don't remember where you go when you disappear?"

"No."

The waitress came by to refill my coffee mug.

Ben frowned and waved his hand through the steam rising from my mug. It passed right through his fingers. "It feels weird when I disappear. Like I know something happens but I can't remember exactly what."

I took a sip of coffee. Oh god, too strong. I dumped half the world's sugar supply into it, and tasted it again. Better. "Maybe you go nowhere."

"That's fucking *terrifying*."

"You're welcome."

He leaned forward a little bit, as if to try to look at my computer screen.

I angled it downward. "Rude."

"Working on the manuscript?"

"No. Dad's obituary," I admitted. A part of me wondered if, instead of a letter Dad wrote for us to read at his funeral, he could've taken that time to write his obit instead. Whenever a bereaved person was having trouble with their obituaries, he would help them write the best goodbyes. He was remarkably good at them.

I was definitely not.

"Ah." He sank back in his booth. Tapped his fingers on the table. "I take it by the look on your face it's not going well?"

"My face can tell you that much?"

"Your eyebrows pinch. Right there." He pointed between them, so close I felt the chill of his finger against my forehead.

I sat back and rubbed at the line between my brows. The last thing I needed was *more* wrinkles. "The obit is going about as good as everything else in my life right now, Ben. Fucking *terribly*." It wasn't his fault that I was failing so hard at my dad's obituary, and the second I raised my voice at him I felt bad. I sighed. "I'm sorry. I'm just . . ."

I missed my dad.

And then it hit me again—this grief that stretched like an endless field of all the things I used to feel for Dad. I was so used to compartmentalizing my life, but now the two bled together, and it made my chest hurt. I was having coffee, writing my dad's obit, and *Dad was dead.*

I blinked back my tears and gave him a fake smile. He could see right through it because his dark eyes flickered.

"I'm fine," I lied. "Great. I just—I have to go."

I took out a few bucks for the coffee, closed my laptop, and left.

20

Novel Idea

DANA FIXED ME another rum and Coke when I set up shop at the bar that afternoon. I'd texted Alice after I realized that Dad's obituary was coming along about as well as literally everything else in my life, and she was very short in replying that it needed to be done by Wednesday.

Amazing. Another deadline I would probably sail right past.

I stared at the computer screen, and knowing I wouldn't get anything done today—my head felt like cotton balls—I scrolled over to Google.

Benji Andor I typed into the search bar.

I was surprised to find that there weren't any articles dedicated to his funeral, or at least his passing, but then again, hadn't he said that he didn't have any living close relatives? Then who was taking care of his goodbyes? I didn't know much about Ben at all.

Who was in charge of his funeral?

While I didn't see anything about his death, he *did* have a social media account. I clicked on it, and went to his page. It was an older photo of him, not quite smiling but not dour, either, leaning against the railing of a cruise ship. And there was a very pretty redhead standing beside him, smiling, with one of those fruity umbrella drinks in her hand. His page was private, so I couldn't know who she was, or anything else he might've divulged, but the photo was enough to make me feel a little uneasy.

"I haven't updated that page in ages," Ben said, and I gave a start. He was sitting beside me at the bar, his head resting on his hand, watching me snoop through his life.

I quickly exited out of the internet, my cheeks burning with embarrassment. "Sorry, I wasn't prying. I wanted to see if—there was any news yet. About your funeral."

"Is there?"

I shook my head.

He didn't seem surprised. "I'm sure Laura's taken the mantle on that. She always liked to be in control of things—not in a bad way. Just in a . . . way."

"Laura?" I asked. The redhead in the photo?

"She's my ex-fiancée," he replied, absently rubbing the wedding ring between his fingers, as if it were a comfort. His ring, I guessed, remembering when he said he had no one to contact about unfinished business. He didn't include Laura in that. Then again, she was his *ex*. Lee would be the last person I'd want to see after I died, too.

"Can I ask what happened?"

He tilted his head, thoughtful for a moment, trying to find the right words. "I'd gone on a business trip to the Winter Institute," he finally began, "but I caught a cold and came home early. Didn't tell her because I thought I'd surprise her with a weekend all to ourselves. She was always pointing out how I never had time for her. I was always working. I would edit manuscripts at work, and then I would bring them home, and I would edit them there until I fell asleep." His eyebrows furrowed. "She was in the shower with a coworker of hers. They'd been seeing each other for a few months at that point."

I sucked in a breath. "Oh, Ben . . ."

"It wasn't all her fault. She was right—all I did was work. I did little else. We were engaged but I didn't—I was—" He pursed his lips and trained his eyes on a dark knot in the wooden bar. He scratched at it absently. "What kind of person makes his fiancée resort to someone else for love and affection?"

"*Makes?*" I echoed. "Ben—it wasn't your fault. You can't control what other people do. Her cheating was *her* choice—"

"And if I'd been present with her? If I'd been there and loving and—what I should have been?"

"She could've communicated with you."

"She shouldn't have to—"

"*Yes*, she *should*," I bit back. "Relationships aren't perfect all the time. You have to talk to each other. I'm sorry, but your fiancée was a dumbass, and she made a mistake, but that was *her choice*."

He swallowed thickly and looked away. "She said as much," he replied. "She asked if we could try again."

"But you didn't?"

He shook his head.

I didn't understand. He was clearly still very much in love with her—or at least unable to forget about her. "Why?"

"Because it was my fault in the first place, Florence, and I loved her too much to cause that pain again. She deserves someone better than me."

I clenched my hands tightly into fists. If Lee had contacted me once after we'd broken up, if he'd asked to try again, to meet in the middle, I would've— "You're an idiot."

"Tell me something I don't know."

"So—what—you believe in love but just not for *you*? You believe in romance and grand romantic gestures and happily ever afters but you think there is something so fundamentally wrong with *you* that you don't deserve it?"

"It's better than not believing in it at all, isn't it?" he snapped back.

I rolled my eyes and slammed my laptop closed. "I've got to go—do something. But for what it's worth? You're wrong." Then I hopped off my stool and stalked out of the bar and up the stairs to my room, and he didn't follow. Carver texted me a little while later, while I was pacing back and forth in my hotel room, trying to calm down.

Wanna wash some graves? he asked.

Not really, I replied.

Too bad, sis.

Ugh, fine. After I'd changed clothes into something I wouldn't mind sweating in, I came back down and peeked into the bar, but Ben was gone.

Good. I was too angry to deal with him right now, anyway.

Carver and Nicki were waiting outside on the porch when I came out. Nicki was a short and stocky man with an angular face and thick black glasses to match his thick black hair and warm brown skin. His family owned a hotel in Cancún, so he understood the trials and tribulations of a *family business.* I was at least thankful for that—he understood the little nuances in our family, the weight Dad's death left on us. I was glad Carver had him, especially now.

Carver had always been the one with his heart on his sleeve.

On the front veranda, Carver held up a portable pressure sprayer and a blue bucket filled with sponges and scrapers. "Ready to have some fun?"

"If that's what you want to call it, sure," I replied coldly.

He gave a low whistle. "What's got you all twisted?"

Ben. The fact that he thought it was his fault that—"Nothing. Just work stuff," I added, not quite lying.

"Well, perk up! Because this is work, too," he insisted, and then narrowed his eyes. "*Grave* work."

"That was bad."

"Dead on arrival?" he asked, scrunching his nose.

I snorted. "Let's get going, yeah? The sun's going to set in an hour and I can't be there after dark."

"Hell yeah!" Carver pumped his fist into the air, and then turned, grabbing his partner by the wrist, and led him down the path to the sidewalk. "Nicki loves doing this."

Nicki nodded. "It's very soothing, and gives your arms a fantastic workout."

"All the better to squeeze me tighter."

"You're my tightest squeeze."

They kissed, and I made a face. "Ugh, gross. True love."

"Tastes like a Taylor Swift song," Carver added, and began to hum "The Story of Us," which made me just want to throw myself off the nearest bridge. Resisting, I followed them to the cemetery, trying to shove my annoyance with Ben as far down into my gut as possible.

"Should we invite Alice?" Nicki asked.

Carver shook his head. "Nah. I bet she's about to have a mental breakdown anyway, what with the makeup news from this morning."

"Poor Alice . . ."

Alice was the only one who didn't really care to scrub gravestones. When we were little, Dad would sometimes pick us up from school with a bucket in one hand, and a portable pressure sprayer in the other, and tell us that we were going to visit some friends. The friends always turned out to be gravestones in the Mairmont cemetery—the older ones that'd survived through hurricanes and tornadoes and half a century of grime and moss. Their letters half-hidden in time, their dates worn by wind and rain. Dad said they needed love, too, even after everyone who remembered them was dead.

So we spent some afternoons scrubbing gravestones clean. It wasn't something any of us ever really got out of doing—or wanted to. The cemetery in the afternoon light looked soft and peaceful. In the top left corner, under one of the large oaks, there was a plot taped off. No one had started digging yet, but my throat tightened anyway.

That was where Dad would be.

It looked different in the daylight.

Carver pointed toward the bottom right corner. "Those look pretty grimy. What do you think?"

"I'll take the one that looks like Madame Leota," I replied, pointing to one of the older ones that had at least a century of dirt caked on it. Those were more delicate work. I liked that kind of work. The meticulousness of it.

Carver, Nicki, and I grabbed the scrapers out of the bucket, sudsed our sponges, and went to work. I took the scraper and scraped off all of the grime and moss, and soaked it down with the pressure sprayer. After a while, when I'd finally gotten back into the groove, I'd cleaned it well enough to make out the delicate insets of the face's eyes.

"Remember when you and Alice were playing tag and accidentally broke a headstone and Dad had to glue it back together with Gorilla Glue?" Carver asked, wiping his forehead with the back of his arm.

I laughed at the memory. "Dad was *beside* himself."

"You could barely tell it was broken. I was more worried about your head. You cracked it good against the headstone."

"Alice was so worried," I mused, scrubbing at the name and dates. *Elizabeth Fowl.* "She stayed up all night in my room to make sure I didn't die or something. She was always like that. Looking after me."

"She picked fights for you in high school," Carver added. "Remember when that girl, Heather, tried to cyberbully you, and Al confronted her in the courtyard?"

"Well, I do now," I replied wryly. I hadn't thought about Heather in a long, long time.

"She punched Heather so hard that she ended up getting a nose job."

"I thought Alice was for *sure* going to get suspended for that," I laughed.

Alice had always been like that. Quick to come to my rescue, quicker to throw a punch. I never liked confrontation, but Alice loved me, and she hated seeing me bullied. We'd been inseparable for years, but then I left the first chance I got. I didn't stay.

And that was something I just didn't know how to talk about with her.

"I kind of feel sorry for this Heather girl," Nicki mused.

"Don't be, babe, she's doing quite well," Carver said dismissively. "Still in town, too."

"Hope I don't run into her," I said, and sat back on the grass as Carver stood, taking the pressure sprayer, and washed down both his stones and mine. They looked a good century younger. "I would have to eventually if I moved back here."

Carver gave me a sidelong look. "You're thinking about it?"

"I mean—I do miss everyone," I admitted.

New York was a great place to live if you had roots there. If you were part of it. But some people weren't born for steel jungles and the fast-paced lifestyle and—let's face it—the cost of living. I used to love that I blended in with the crowd, that I was another face among faces, another writer chasing their dreams in the neighborhood coffee shop. But the longer I lived there, the more gum littered the sidewalk and rust crept in.

I didn't imagine being there forever, but I didn't know where I wanted to go, or what felt like home. Nowhere really did, if I was honest with myself. Dad always said it was never about the place, but the people you shared it with. In New York, I had Rose—and for a while I had Lee, and for a while it felt like I finally *had* found home.

Somewhere permanent. Somewhere safe.

Then, in the blink of an eye, I was on the sidewalk with my suitcase in the rain, and Lee was closing the door.

And despite what I told him, if Lee had come to me, asking for a second chance, begging to try again—

I would've said yes.

But I wasn't sure why anymore.

A quiet wind whispered through the dogwood trees. I'd gotten so used to cars and construction and the sounds of people living so close together, I forgot what true silence sounded like. It wasn't silence at all, but a soft sigh between the gravestones. The steady creak of an old and endless house.

Carver cocked his head. "It would be nice to have you home.

But don't come home because you think you should. Come home because you want to."

I didn't know exactly what I wanted.

But it wasn't what I had.

"Let's do a few more stones before the sun goes down," I said, pushing down the restlessness in my head. Neither Carver nor Nicki pushed back, thankfully, and we managed to do three more tombstones before Officer Saget pulled up at the gates.

He eyed me. "Miss Day. Nice to see you."

I strained to smile. "Lovely evening, Officer."

As we left the cemetery, Carver tsked. "You're not even back a week and you're already getting Saget antsy. Scandalous! What'll the neighbors think?"

"I've done nothing wrong," I said dismissively. "I can't help it that he's suspicious."

"You *did* release a rabid possum in the police station."

"Why does everyone keep bringing that up? Possums usually don't get rabies. It was a fluke! I don't see why he can't just move on." Never mind the trespassing violations and probably the slew of other things I did as a teenager to help a ghost move on. "I just went for a moonwalk the other night. That's it!"

My brother laughed. "You should've asked me to come with you. I love moonwalks! Nicki, one time when Florence and I were—what? Twelve? Ten?"

"Something like that," I agreed, already knowing the story he was about to tell.

"Anyway, it was right after a storm and we were all up and pretty wired. The lights had gone out. So Mom and Dad took us for a moonwalk . . ."

I listened as we walked back along the side street to the main part of town. Most of the shops were emptying out for the evening. Nothing stayed open late here in Mairmont, aside from the Waffle House and Bar None. It was so unlike New York, where everything was busy and frantic all the time. Here it felt like the world was in slow motion. Everything took its time.

I felt like I'd already been here for a year, and it'd only been a few days.

"How's the obit going?" Carver asked as they dropped me back off at the bed-and-breakfast.

"Great," I lied. "I should be done soon."

More lies.

"Can't wait to read it. Dad'd be glad you wrote it," he added. "He was proud of everything you wrote."

"Oh, yeah, the one thing." *That he knew about*, I added to myself.

Carver opened his mouth to respond, but I turned away before he could—I didn't *need* consoling—and I walked into the bed-and-breakfast.

Ben wasn't around, so I took my laptop out of my room and went down to the bar again, and ordered myself another rum and Coke. I slid onto my barstool and opened my laptop.

Deleted the paragraph I'd written. Cracked my knuckles.

And stared at the blank Word document.

I didn't know how to form the words for what I wanted to write. I didn't know how to take all the jumbled feelings in my head and put them onto paper. There weren't words big enough or strong enough or warm enough to encompass Dad. He was untranslatable.

I was sure someone like Ben, who had words for everything—and always seemed to have the *right* ones—wouldn't have had this sort of problem. I bet his brain was as neat and orderly as his desk had been, and his thoughts as ironed as his shirts.

Writing Dad's obit was a different kind of failure than writing Ann's books.

One had too many words I wanted to say, and one didn't have any at all.

I moved my mouse over to File > Open Recent, and scrolled down to the first one. Ann_Nichols_4. I never titled the books until I was almost done, and most of the time the titles came directly from the text itself.

The document opened to where I left off.

A year ago.

I remembered, so viscerally, the beginning of the end. When I had looked on his laptop, convincing myself that I *did* trust him, but I wanted to know what his book was about. I remembered that he'd gone out for laundry and left his laptop open to the Word document. I remembered setting down my laptop—opened to this very scene—and crawling across the couch to where he had just sat a few minutes before. The space heater hummed softly.

And as I read, my world began to break apart, piece by piece, like a puzzle coming unglued. When he came back to the apartment, his laundry in tow, he froze in the foyer. I didn't look up from his computer.

"*When the Dead Sing*," I read, and finally turned my gaze up to him, refusing to believe what I read. "Babe—is this . . . is it about me?"

"No, of course not," he said dismissively, dumping the laundry on the ground. He came over, took his laptop from my lap, and closed it. "Your stories gave me inspiration. You're my muse," he added, and kissed me swiftly on the lips.

As if it would shut me up.

As if it would make everything good again.

Spoiler alert: It didn't.

How could I write about two characters, Amelia and Jackson, reconciling, trusting each other again when—when I myself *couldn't*? One moment I had every grand romantic gesture right at my fingertips, I had faith these two characters would come back together, and I could sow them a happily ever after. But then it felt like the story had been ripped apart at the seams. I didn't feel them anymore. I didn't know who they were, this woman who always knew what she wanted, and this world-weary musician with a heart of gold. I didn't know the kind of love they had, or if they even believed in it.

I knew I didn't.

Hesitantly, testily, I placed my fingers on the keyboard, feeling the rigid bumps on the F and J keys. It was like stepping back into old, worn shoes that had gone stiff without a partner to dance with.

I took a deep breath.

The only way out was through—

Wait.

I took a big gulp of my drink, and then settled my fingers back into position.

Now I was ready.

"You can do this, Florence," I muttered, and sank into the scene.

> Amelia didn't want to hear his confessions. About the lies he wove about a life he didn't live. She knew why he left. Why he abandoned her. The facts stuck to her skin like her wet clothes in the rain. He had lied to her—omitted the story that was most stitched into his

life as though, if she learned about it, she'd look at him differently.

Well, he was right in that regard. She did learn about his ex-wife, and she *did* see him differently. "Were you ever going to tell me?" she asked. "About her?"

He hesitated, rubbing nervously at the scar on his hand that she thought was from one of his wild party nights, but had been from the accident. "I didn't think you'd understand."

"Did you give me the choice?"

"I—"

"No, you just made it for me."

"Amelia, I—" Suddenly, Jackson went pale and dropped dead from all his lies—

"Nope." I deleted the last sentence.

~~Suddenly, Jackson went pale and dropped dead from all of his lies.~~

Amelia didn't want to hear his explanations. "You lied. You *wanted* to. Why should I trust you now? Why do I still love you?"

"Because the heart wants what it wants."

"Then my heart's a motherfucking joke if it wants you."

"That doesn't help, Florence." I sighed, and deleted it again.

I stared at the cursor, but all I could hear was my fight with Lee, our voices growing louder and louder until we were screaming at each other—and I wondered if it was me.

If I had just overreacted. And why couldn't I get *over* him? Why did it still hurt?

Why was I so weak?

> "Because the heart wants what it wants."
>
> ~~"Then my heart's a motherfucking joke if it wants you."~~
>
> She gave him a sad, defeated look. "But why you?"

"That's going well." This time it was not me who said it, but a voice to my side that made me jump. Ben sat on the stool next to me, leaning over just enough to read my screen.

I slammed my laptop shut, cheeks burning. "*Rude!*"

Dana leaned forward over the check-in counter to give me a puzzled look.

I smiled politely at them and said quieter to Ben, angling my face away from them, "It's rude to look at someone else's work."

Especially when it's as bad as mine.

He sat back with his arms crossed over his chest. "I have a feeling you are writing from a very raw place right now."

"No shit," I deadpanned. "Whatever gave you that idea?"

He visibly winced at that one, and looked a little ashamed of himself. "I thought you were working on your father's obituary. I didn't mean to spy on your writing."

I narrowed my eyes.

He held up his hands in defeat. "I promise, darling, nothing more."

Darling. A knot caught in my throat and I quickly looked away. I thought I hated all kinds of pet names. *Dear*, *sweetie*, *honey*, but I guessed I hated it when Lee called me *bunny*, because he said I looked like a startled rabbit when something caught me unawares. He said it was endearing.

It wasn't.

But then why did the word *darling* get my heart racing?

"And," he added, "I wanted to apologize for earlier. I snapped at you, and I had no right to."

"I'm sorry, too," I replied. "I had no right to judge you or your life when mine's a mess. Clearly," I added, motioning toward my laptop. "I'm so fucked up I can't even write a kissing scene."

He tilted his head, debating quietly. He was choosing his words. I liked that about him, that when words mattered, he thought about them before he said them. "It was . . . nice, actually, to have someone tell me it wasn't my fault. Even if I don't agree."

"I hope you change your mind someday."

He smiled a little sadly. "I don't think it matters anymore." Because he was dead. I opened my mouth to say something, to console him, to tell him it still *did* matter, when he said, "So, what has you stuck? Remember: I said I'd help if I could. I'd like to."

He didn't want to talk about it anymore.

I drained my rum and Coke. "Okay, so: Here's my problem. I haven't been able to write for about a year now. I don't see the point anymore. I used to believe in love, but I really don't now. Every time I try to imagine it, I can only think about how mine ended."

"One relationship doesn't—"

"One?" I shook my head with a soft laugh. "If it was *one*, Ben, I'd be lucky. Dad said I had a string of bad luck, but I don't really think that anymore. Guys just . . . don't want someone like me. Or maybe they do, but they just don't want *me*." My eyebrows furrowed as I stared at the condensation on my glass, but all I could see were the times I'd been dumped, broken up with, left outside in the cold April rain—*literally*. "Maybe I'm the problem."

He pursed his lips together, not knowing what to say.

But the worst part?

Dana slid me a shot of something clear with a sad sort of nod and said, "I feel you, sister."

And I realized that they thought I was talking to myself. Commiserating with myself. Throwing my own solo pity party. And what was a party without a shot or two?

"Thanks." I threw back the shot of—oh god, *vodka*. I hated vodka. I set the glass down with a cringe and swooped my laptop into my satchel.

I needed to go for a walk. Get out of here. Do something—anything—else, because clearly writing wasn't happening today. No kind of writing. *At all*. I used to write my way out of utter despair, but now I couldn't even write myself out of a sex scene.

It was embarrassing.

But as I turned to leave, Ben was there.

I jumped.

"I didn't even startle you!"

"It's been a long day," I said, fumbling for my phone. I gave Dana another pleasant nod on my way back up to my room, and Ben followed me like a vulture waiting to pick my carcass clean.

"I have an idea, if you're willing," he proposed when we were out of Dana's earshot.

"Oh, this should be good."

"It will be."

I looked him up and down. He was such a conundrum. Too tall and too broad and too neatly organized, he didn't fit into any of the boxes in my head reserved for *leading man* material. He was doggedly smart, and insistent, and somehow he always ended up being so very polite to me even when he was angry (and I began to tell when he *was* because a muscle in his jaw would twitch).

I unlocked the door to my room and motioned for him to go inside, and I closed the door after him, and pulled off my NYU pullover. While the night had gotten chilly, the heater in my room definitely worked well.

"Okay, shoot," I said, turning to him. "Let's throw all the spaghetti at the wall and see what sticks."

He smiled, and there was a glint in his brown eyes that turned them almost ocher. "Meet me in the town square. Tomorrow at noon. Don't be late." Then he turned on his heels, and departed right through the closed door, and I was left in the quiet room, baffled and a little bit—okay, a *lot*—intrigued.

What the hell could Benji Andor be up to?

21

The Crime Scene

I YAWNED AND poured myself coffee into a paper to-go cup and dumped half the jar of sugar into it. Without Starbucks right around the corner to give me my triple shot soy chai lattes in the mornings, I had to make do with what I had. Which meant terrible-tasting coffee so sweet the grains of sugar crunched between my molars every time I took a sip.

Last night I couldn't get to sleep, trying to balance myself somewhere between the sadness that still felt like a rock in my gut, and wondering what the hell Ben had planned. My mind liked to wander at night and shut up in the mornings, at the exact opposite times I needed.

Rose always told me that I was a goblin. I did my best work between ten at night and five in the morning, when most normal people were either asleep or getting down to business (to defeat the Huns). (Sex, I mean sex.) Meanwhile, I was writing about couples banging it out to Fall Out Boy. I missed those days. When I could write. When I didn't just sleep all day, and stare at my ceiling all night, and scroll through Twitter to see who else in the writing community got book deals and went on tour and hit bestseller lists. It was a certain kind of soul-sucking year I'd had, and I didn't realize how empty I was until I needed to write.

And by then, I couldn't.

Last night felt a little different, though, as I stared up at the smooth ceiling of the bed-and-breakfast. What if Ben *could* help me? What if it was as simple as turning on a switch, and I'd just lost it?

And a deeper part of me asked, *How can you think about Ben and writing and books when your dad is dead?*

I thought about them because if I thought too much about Dad, that stone in my stomach would weigh me down to the center of the earth, and I'd never crawl out again.

So I sipped on my battery fuel and trained my mind on the thing in front of me—namely, Ben.

The main thoroughfare of the town was already filled with people walking to work, and moms pushing their strollers, and high schoolers playing hooky from school. There was a couple sitting in the gazebo, setting up two cellos, and a man in a business suit reading a newspaper on one of the benches in the green. On the other bench sat a man no one else could see. He was leaning back, his arms folded tightly over his chest, his face turned up toward the sun. Every time I saw him, he looked a little less put together. A button was undone on his shirt, or his shirtsleeves were rolled up, or his hair had fallen out of its gel. This morning it was a little of all three.

I tried not to linger too much on his forearms. He had a tattoo on the underside of his right arm, halfway up toward the elbow, though his arms were folded so I couldn't see the whole thing. Though I really wouldn't mind. Some people were shoulder people, some people were back people, some people were butt people—

I, for all intents and purposes, was a forearm kind of girl.

As I watched him, he cracked open an eye to look at me. "You're late."

I checked my phone. "By ten minutes!"

"Ten minutes is still late," he replied, and sat up straight. I joined him on the bench and took another sip of coffee. The grains of sugar crunched between my teeth. He eyed the cup. "I miss coffee."

"Connoisseur or lifeblood?"

"I liked the notes in some very limited roasts that I procured from—"

"Connoisseur, right. You'd hate this stuff, then. Definitely motor oil and sugar."

He wrinkled his noise. "That sounds disgusting."

"I drink the battery acid juice so I can go zoom-zoom," I replied. "Okay so—why are we here? How is this going to help me? I'm wasting time. If I'm not writing, I should be helping my family with the funeral arrangements—"

"This isn't a waste of time. Put your zoom-zoom juice down, take a deep breath, and trust me, yeah?"

I eyed him. "I'm keeping my zoom-zoom juice."

He let out a laugh, said, "Fine, fine," and motioned out toward the center of town. The man sitting on the opposite bench reading the paper. The mothers rolling their strollers to brunch. The kids playing hooky from school. The mayor taking a leak on a fire hydrant. (Hell yeah, stick it to the man, Mayor Fetch!) "This is a trick I learned—just sit and watch people. Set their scene. Imagine who'd they'd be."

"Really?" I deadpanned. "This is stupid." I began to get up, when he cleared his throat. I sat back down with a huff. "Do I have to?"

He raised a single thick eyebrow. I hated it. It was so—so *perfect.*

"Fine!" I threw my free hand into the air. "Show me the way, O great Jedi master."

"Learn you shall, young Padawan." Ben leaned toward me and nudged his chin toward a couple walking their Pomeranian. "They met on Tinder last week. One-night stand. But then they matched again the next night—and the *next* night—"

"Tinder does suck around here," I agreed. "Not a lot of choices."

"And on the fourth night, he called her up. Asked her on a date. They've been inseparable since."

"And the dog?"

"A stray—kept following them around everywhere. So, they decided to adopt it. Together."

I looked at him, baffled. "Wow, you're so *wholesome.*"

"I know, isn't it charming?"

"It's annoying," I replied. "It's like you walked out of a Hallmark movie."

He pursed his lips into a thin line. "Fine," he replied, and motioned between the two of us, "then set this scene."

"You mean between you and me."

"Perfect dynamic. A refined editor and his chaotic gremlin of an author."

"Oh, thanks."

"Call this practice—a warm-up. What kind of scene would we be?"

"The kind that doesn't happen."

"And yet here we are." He cocked his head. "You write for Ann Nichols, for god's sake. Your imagination has been praised as 'illuminating' and 'masterful'—and I'm confident that it still is. So please"—he shifted on the bench to angle toward me—"give me a scene."

"Well . . . we're two people. On a bench."

"A refined editor and a chaotic author," he reminded me.

"But the editor isn't nearly as *refined* as he thinks he is."

"Ouch."

"And the author is tired. And maybe she was never good at writing to begin with. Maybe she never really understood romance. Maybe she's not cut out for love stories—"

He leaned in close to me—so close that if he were alive, I would be able to smell the cologne he wore, the toothpaste he brushed with, the shampoo he used—and he said in a low voice, "Or maybe she just needs someone to show her that she is."

The tips of my ears began to heat up. They were turning red. *I* was turning red.

Stupid Florence. He's a ghost. He knew he was. And he was professional, goddamn it, and orderly, and very straitlaced. The thought of throwing me onto the bed and ripping off my clothes probably hadn't even crossed his mind—not once.

Not that it'd crossed *mine*, either, but . . .

Damn it, I was in trouble.

Then he lifted his eyes a bit beyond me. His eyebrows furrowed. "Is—is that your *sister*?"

"My what?"

The sound of an engine revved behind me, and I glanced over my shoulder in time to watch Alice peel out of a side alley on Dad's motorcycle, and disappear down the street. Well, I guessed it was fixed now.

And the noise brought me back to my senses.

This was bad—this scene, this moment, this tightness in my chest—

"I—I need to go run some errands," I said, standing, and quickly left the town square. When I was well and truly out of earshot, I glanced back and he was still there, lounging back on the bench. Then a car passed between us—

And he was gone.

22

Grave Matters

STOP THINKING! I chastised myself, slapping my cheeks to wake myself up. *Snap out of it.* He was dead, I was alive. There were *tragedies* written with this premise. There were no happily ever afters between an undertaker's daughter and her ghost.

He knew that. I knew that. I wasn't going to misread his intentions. He wanted to help me so that he could move on. Ghosts never stayed. It was one goodbye I was accustomed to. Why would he *want* to stay? Where only I could see him? He wouldn't. He was being nice.

That was all.

With the flowers still impossible to obtain and Elvis booked for the funeral, it was high time to get the receipt from Dad's will and visit Unlimited Party. Karen was the head counsel at the local law firm in town, next to the bookstore. I purposefully averted my eyes as I passed the store's window display and dipped into the brick building at the street corner. Luckily, I caught Karen between clients, so I quickly borrowed the receipt from the files and slipped back out again.

Unlimited Party was a good fifteen minutes away, in a larger strip mall, but at least the Uber driver was quiet. He was listening to a murder mystery podcast—it made me think of Rose. It was one she was obsessed with. She'd seen the ladies live at Comic-Con more than once. I missed her.

What're you up to? New York still there without me? I texted.

Work must've been slow because Rose responded immediately.

Somehow. The apartment is SO creepy there alone tho. I miss you.

I'll be home by the end of the week, I replied quickly.

Take your time! How's everything back home?

Oh, I guess I hadn't updated her. So I did. About how finding one thousand wildflowers was somehow a lot harder than it appeared. About how I somehow booked Elvis to sing at my father's funeral and needed to write Dad's obituary. About the mysterious letter Dad left for his funeral. And now how I was heading toward Unlimited Party because—well—Dad had beat us to the kazoos and streamers, apparently.

I read down the receipt with a growing despondency. Half of the things were smudged out because sometime between 2001 and today, it had gotten wet. Did he think we were going to throw a frat party instead of a funeral?

Probably, in all honesty.

Your Dad always sounded rad, Rose texted. Then there were dots; she was writing. Then nothing. Then dots again. Finally—

Are you doing okay? You know with . . . everything.

Everything. I wished I could tell her about Ben. I wanted to. About the strange, muddled feelings in my chest. I was mourning, but I was blushing. I was so *fucking* sad, and yet there were moments when the tide would go back out and I wasn't drowning anymore in it—and they were all moments, I realized, with Ben.

Because of Ben.

He took my mind away from my sadness, when all I wanted to do was burrow myself in that sadness, make a nest of it, live there clinging to what was left of my dad.

Even though Dad would've rather me fall in love than fall into a depression.

I'm fine, I texted back, and thanked my driver for the ride as I got out of his Honda.

The cashier at Unlimited Party looked bored as he played a game of solitaire on his phone. I came up to him and handed him the receipt, and gave him a tight smile. "Um, I'd like to pick this up, please."

My phone vibrated. Rose again? I ignored it.

He asked, dumbfounded, looking at what he had pulled up on his screen. "Uh, are you—are you sure?"

"Yeah, why?"

"Well, because it says here—"

My phone vibrated again. That usually wasn't Rose's MO. "Excuse me for a moment?" I asked, and turned around to read the text.

It was from my sister.

COME TO THE FREEZERBOX NOW!!!!

Then, a minute later: **PLEASE!!!**

When Alice used *please*, it was an emergency.

"Okay, new plan. Yes to whatever you were going to ask"—I mean, Dad had already bought the stuff, so whatever he had bought I couldn't exactly say no to—"and deliver it to the Days Gone Funeral Home?"

"Uh . . . we can deliver the items on Thursday?" the poor cashier suggested.

"Perfect! Thank you!" I waved as I left the store and hailed another Uber. The same guy in the same Honda pulled up to the curb, and I got in. "Oh, this is a great episode," I said, and he nodded in agreement. The drive back to town was another fifteen minutes, and by then it had started to rain.

The front path was slippery, and I almost bit it hard as I hurried up to the front porch. Carver cracked the front door open as I righted myself again. "That step's slippery," he warned.

I stuck out my tongue. "A bit late, bro."

"You're in a better mood."

Was I?

Carver opened the door wider to let me in. "Alice is in the freezer freaking out."

"About what?" I asked, taking off my shoes in the foyer so I didn't track mud through the halls. He gave me a long-suffering look. Freezer, Alice being down there—"Ah. Dad."

"Yeah."

"And you couldn't do anything?"

"You know I hate the basement."

"You weren't locked in there overnight," I muttered, but I supposed that was the responsibility of being a big sister.

I shrugged out of my coat as I came in, and realized that Seaburn's and Karen's coats were hanging on the rack too—and Mom's white faux mink jacket. I frowned. "Is there a meeting or something?"

Carver hesitated. "Just some stuff—about the estate and the will."

"And everyone was here for it but me?" I inferred.

"It's nothing, Florence."

"Nothing—like when everyone met at the Waffle House early before I was told to be there?"

He closed the door, and breathed out through his nose. "Florence, it's nothing personal. You haven't really been a part of the family business in a few years. And you haven't come home in a decade. We . . . didn't think you wanted to be a part of it."

"Of course I do, Carver."

"Well, we thought you didn't want to. I mean, you knew about it, right? You didn't ask."

"That's kind of a shitty way of turning the blame back on me, bro."

He rolled his eyes. "Sorry."

"Whatever," I sighed. The funeral home was quiet as I shuffled down the hallway to the very last door that led to the mortuary. It smelled like it always did, of flowers and disinfectant. Mom was in the kitchen making tea, it sounded like. There were already a few bouquets delivered for tomorrow's wake. Then Thursday we'd say goodbye.

Time was both passing too fast and not fast enough.

The basement door had a latch on the outside, but it was unlocked. When I'd been trapped down there for a night, I hadn't been afraid of the corpses in the freezers. They were like shells, and when the person was done with them, the shell cracked and broke.

I didn't start hating corpses until much later. I didn't like their stillness, or how blue always—*always*—crept through the heavy foundation, or how they smelled after being, you know, embalmed.

Alice was downstairs, a black-and-white-striped cloth headband in her short hair. She looked like a black smudge in an otherwise soft gray room. Even her latex gloves were black. On the steel table in front of her was—

I fortified myself. It was fine. This was fine.

Alice glanced over her shoulder, and threw up her hands. "*Finally!* What took you so long?"

"I was at Unlimited Party," I replied as I reached the bottom of the stairs, and one foot at a time, one step closer and closer, I came toward the corpse on the table.

No, that was unfair. I couldn't say it was a corpse because it wasn't just *any* shell.

It was Dad.

And Alice had done such a wonderful job, he looked like he was simply sleeping. She already had him dressed in his favorite tux—the tacky red one with the long tails and the golden lapels. He had on his favorite cuff links, gold skulls he bought from some boutique in London several decades ago, and they matched his earrings, and his favorite skull and crossbones and sword rings.

He used to spin those rings when he was anxious—especially the one on his thumb. My eyesight began to blur.

Alice shifted, tapping her foot on the ground. "*Well?*"

"Well what?"

"Does he look okay?" she burst out. It was only then I noticed the makeup kit on a rolling tray on the other side of her, concealer and eyeshadow and lipstick scattered across it. "Does he look like himself? I got his color right? It's not too much?"

"He looks—" My voice caught in my throat, cracked at the edges. "Fine."

Dad looked like I remembered, a too-still snapshot from my memories, and I curled my fingers into tight fists to keep myself from grabbing his shoulders, shaking him—asking him to wake up. It was the kind of prank he'd pull. Pretend to be dead. Then he'd sit up in the casket at his funeral with a "Surprise! I'm retiring!" but . . . that was the kind of happily ever after in my head. The kind that didn't exist.

Because the longer I looked, the stiller he seemed. Frozen. Unmoving.

Dead.

Alice went on. "He had a lot of bruises from the hospital, but at least the tux jacket covers most of that, and his cheeks are a little sunken but—the wake's tomorrow and I think he doesn't look like himself at all so I keep checking the pictures. Is my memory of him already going or—"

"Alice," I repeated. "He looks like Dad."

She hesitated.

"Why would I lie to you? If he didn't look like him, I'd tell you."

"He doesn't look too . . . Tony Soprano?"

"He loved *Six Feet Under*—"

"Florence!" Then, after a beat, "Those aren't even the same shows!"

I rolled my eyes. "Dad looks great. Trust me, you're good at what you do. Better than Dad, even."

That, at least, made her a little calmer. "I can never be better than Dad," she said and crossed her arms tightly over her chest again. She shifted her weight between one foot and the other, staring down at our father. I never could have done what she did. I couldn't even look at Dad for very long before I burst into tears, so I decided to leave *that* spectacle for tomorrow.

I'd already cried more times than I could count this week—if I kept this up, I'd die of dehydration myself.

Instead, I bumped my shoulder with Alice's. "C'mon," I prodded gently, "you're done. Dad looks great. Pop him back in the fridge and go watch some anime or something."

She bit the inside of her cheek to keep from smiling. "Dad used to say that. 'Oh, just let me pop 'em back in the fridge! I'll meet you up top'—god, Florence, I miss him."

"I do, too."

I waited for her to return Dad to one of the freezers before we climbed the steps together. Alice locked the basement behind us, and somehow I managed to convince Carver to take her to dinner. They invited me, but I wasn't really hungry.

I made an excuse. "I've got work, sorry." And it was only a half lie. "The obit won't write itself."

"It's not supposed to be a book, Florence," Alice said.

I gave her a polite smile. "It's hard to find words sometimes."

"If you need help . . ."

"No, I'm fine."

And suddenly, the comradery we had in the basement melted and she rolled her eyes. "Whatever, just don't be late on it," she said, and went to go fetch Karen, Seaburn, and Mom from the kitchen. They decided—loudly—to go to Olive Garden. My family was a lot of weird things, but sometimes they were just predictable. And that was nice.

Carver put on his coat and began to button it up slowly. "You two okay? You and Al?"

"She didn't snap my head off this time," I replied. "Well, at least not until the end there."

"Maybe after all of this, you two should have a talk."

"Carver . . ."

He gave me a look. "Listen to your middlest brother for once."

And the voice of reason. Somehow. The longer I stayed in Mairmont, the deeper the town burrowed into my skin. It was too small and too comfortable and too steeped in everything I loved about Dad. And my family. And why I left. It hurt just being here.

I said, "I will."

He held up his hand, pinkie out. "Promise?"

"Promise," I replied, hooking his pinkie, and he left with Alice and Karen and Seaburn out the door.

Mom lingered for a moment, slipping into her ancient faux mink coat. With it on she reminded me of Morticia Addams and Cruella de Vil and soft winter evenings in the funeral home, closing the curtains and turning out the lights. "Are you sure you don't want to come eat, Florence?"

"The endless salad and breadsticks *are* tempting," I replied. "How did the last two funerals go?"

"Without a hitch. Now all we have is the big one, and I think we'll close for the rest of the week after that. Give us some time."

The Days Gone Funeral Home never closed before. Not for snowstorms, or hurricanes, or floods.

It was fitting it took Dad's death to shutter the doors for a few days.

"I think that's a good idea," I replied. "And thanks, but I sort of want to stay here for a while. I just want to . . . sit. In the quiet."

Mom nodded and pulled me into a tight hug, and kissed my cheek. "I can't see things like you can," she said, "but I know he's here."

I didn't have the heart to tell her that he wasn't. That his ghost didn't roam the creaky halls and sit in his favorite parlor chair and that the whiff of cigar smoke, strong and sweet, was just her memories playing tricks.

"I'll order you some chicken Alfredo to go and keep it at the house if you want it later," she went on, and with one last lingering look at the foyer and the oaken staircase and the parlors, she left and closed the door quietly in her wake.

And I was alone.

The funeral home felt so empty, and big, and old. I sat down in the red parlor—Dad's favorite—in his favorite high-back velvet chair, and sank into the silence. The evening was so quiet, I could hear the wind creak through the old house.

The dead singing.

I wondered if the wind was Dad. I wondered if he was in this gust, or the next one. I wondered if I would ever recognize the sounds through the floorboards, the wind swirling between old oak wood, making sounds that, perhaps, could have been voices.

It all finally became real. This week. This funeral. This world—spinning, spinning, spinning without my father in it.

And the wind rattled on.

23

The Casket of True Love

"FLORENCE?"

I glanced up at the voice, quickly wiping the stray tears out of my eyes.

Ben stood in the entryway to the parlor, his hands in his pockets, but all I could see was his faint outline, his face shadowed in the yellow streetlight pouring in through the open windows. Of course he would appear now. When I least wanted him to.

"Great timing," I muttered, sniffing. God, I probably looked hideous. Half of my eyeliner had already wiped away onto my palm.

He came into the parlor, his footsteps silent against the hardwood floor. "Is . . . everything okay?"

I took a deep breath. If it wasn't already obvious . . . "No," I admitted, "but it's not really something you can help with. Thank you, though. For asking." Then, a bit quieter, my voice cracking at the edges: "I miss him. I miss him so much, Ben."

He came over quietly and sat down on the floor in front of me, and for the first time—ever—he had to look up to meet my gaze, and he gave me something that I hadn't really thought I wanted: his undivided attention.

"What was your dad like?" he asked, because he was decent. Because he was good.

What was the song Dad liked? "Only the Good Die Young"?

I was quiet as I tried to think of the right words, afraid to open up. To tell him my story. Ben and I were strangers, and he never knew Dad. Never would. And even though Ben was being decent, and kind, and made me feel like my hurt was worthy of this wasted time—

I was still afraid.

Had I always been this guarded? I couldn't remember. I'd been closed off for so long, locked tightly, that it just felt safe and natural. I tricked myself into thinking that I could live like that forever, and until Ben showed up, I thought perhaps I could.

But now . . .

"My dad was kind, and he was patient—except when his soccer matches were on, then he would get *so* mad at the TV. He smoked too much, and he drank too much at his Thursday night poker games, and he always smelled like funeral flowers and formaldehyde." Talking about him out loud felt like a relief, in a way, as though I were slowly dismantling the dam I had built, brick by brick, memory by memory, until I could feel again. I wish I could say I wasn't crying, but I was because I tasted my tears as they slipped into my mouth. "When I was little, we lived here—in this old funeral home, and sometimes I caught him and Mom down here in the parlors, windows thrown open, dancing to a song they heard in their heads. He was the one who said I should be a writer. He said that my words were so loud and so vivid and alive they could wake the dead." I laughed and said a little quieter, because it was a secret—one I'd never told anyone before, "Somewhere, under one of these floorboards, I've got smut hidden."

"Oh? Scandalous."

"You'll *never* find it," I added. "Carver looked for years. Finally gave up."

He laughed, and I really loved the way he laughed. Soft and deep and sincere, and it made my uptight muscles and my rigid bones relax. It was endearing. I mean, for a dead guy. He leaned against my chair, his head resting on the armrest, eyes closed. I clenched my hands because I wanted to run my fingers through his thick black hair. And I couldn't.

"So, did the great Benji Andor always want to be an editor?" I asked.

He tilted his head to the side, thoughtful. "I never wanted to create words, I always wanted to bury myself in someone else's. But to be honest, I became an editor because I'm chasing this feeling I felt when I read my—" He quickly stopped himself and cleared his throat. "When I read my first romance."

"Which one?"

Ben shifted. He didn't say anything for a long moment, as if he was debating whether to tell me the truth or tell me at all. I doubted he would lie to me at this point—I didn't think he could lie his way out of a paper bag if he had to. "*The Forest of Dreams*."

That . . . was *not* what I was expecting. "Seriously? An *Ann Nichols* novel?"

He shrugged. "I was eleven maybe?"

"You must've been a popular kid."

"I mean, I read Tolkien and played Dungeons & Dragons, if that's any indication."

"Wow, yeah, *really* popular."

"I feel like you're roasting me," he commented dryly, turning his face toward me, and there was a smile tucked into the corner of his mouth.

I gave a half laugh that might've also been the remnant of a sniffle. "Admiring you, really. Do you know how healthy it is for a kid to read something other than 'boy books' aimed at boys?"

"So I've heard. I just like love stories, I guess. I like the way they paint the world in this Technicolor dreamland, where the only rule you have to follow is a happily ever after. And I've spent most of my adult life chasing after that high."

"And then I came into your life and declared that romance was dead. No wonder you hated me."

"I didn't hate you," he clarified. "I was caught off guard. Here was a beautiful young woman declaring that romance was dead."

I shook my head. "I'm not that pretty, Ben."

He gave me a strange look. His eyelashes were long, and the ocher flecks in his brown eyes glimmered in the dim evening light. "But you *are*."

My breath caught in my throat. Because here, sitting in the dark with both my mascara and my nose running, he thought I was beautiful? At my worst, selfish and needy and cold?

I quickly looked away.

Suddenly, a gust of wind whistled through the house. The beams creaked; the windows rattled. Ben gave a start.

"It's just the dead singing," I replied. Maybe it was Dad, somewhere caught on the wind.

"The dead singing?" He had a peculiar look in his eyes. "Like Lee's book title?"

I didn't answer. He didn't really need it.

"Florence . . ."

"Surprise." I picked at my cuticles, something that Rose had tried to get me to stop doing for years, but she wasn't here and I was nervous. "I thought Lee was it, you know? I thought he was the one. My whole family is made of these impossible love stories—and I thought this was mine. I mean he was *Lee Marlow*. Executive editor at Faux. And he liked *me*. For the first time, a guy I dated looked at me like I mattered, and wanted to know every weird little thing about me." I shrugged, chewing on the side of my lip. I didn't like admitting how stupid I was. Even a year later, it was all still so raw. "He was the closest person I ever told about my . . . *gift*. About the ghosts I helped. I chickened out, though. I told him they were stories I wanted to write one day. I put up a barrier because I couldn't face how he'd look at me if I told him it was real. I should've known better. I just became a story to him, too."

And when the story was written, I wasn't any use to him anymore.

A crow cawed somewhere outside. They were perched in the dead oak, unsurprisingly. There was a certain kind of silence that permeated places of death. The sound was closed and private, as if the spaces where the dead were honored were separate from the rest of the world. When I was younger and my brain was full of anxious spirals, I would lie down on the floor between funerals, and press my cheek against the cool hardwood, and listen to the house's silence. It always gave me space to think.

Now, I feared the sadness in my soul was sopping up the silence like a sponge. I felt heavier with each breath. It was no longer a soft silence, but a still one.

He lifted his head from the armrest. A muscle feathered in his jaw. "That *bastard*."

I gave him a surprised look. "Come again?"

"That *bastard*," he repeated a little louder. "Of all the fucking shitty things to do to you, he ruined your memories. Things you told him in private—in *trust*. That fucking dead-eyed narcissistic *asshole*."

Behind him, a vase full of orchids began to rattle. I didn't think Ben knew he was doing it. "The next time I see him I'm going to—"

"Whoa, tiger, you're dead."

The vase stopped rattling almost instantly.

He folded his arms across his chest tightly, and harrumphed. "Minor inconvenience."

His anger took me so off guard, so far out of my range of emotions about what happened to me, I dunno—I just lost it. I began to laugh. And cry. But mostly laugh as I slid off the chair and onto the ground beside him. It was one of those spiraling sorts of laughs, because I didn't realize how I was supposed to feel about this story until just now—

"Am I that funny to you?" he lamented tragically.

"No—yes," I added, but my voice was tinged with nothing but adoration. For a guy I barely knew. "Do you know how long I've wanted someone to get angry for me? I thought I was going crazy, that maybe I wasn't *allowed* to get angry because I told Lee they were just stories. I thought maybe . . ." And I hesitated, because had I said too much? I usually didn't talk about these things—with anyone, not even Rose. They were my problems, and not anyone else's. But he leaned in a little closer, as if gently asking me to go on, and I felt safe admitting, "I thought it was what I deserved. I thought that's what I got for . . ."

"For having the audacity to trust someone you loved unconditionally?" he asked, and the anger was gone from his voice. It was softer now, warm like amber.

I quickly turned my head away from him. Looked toward the foyer, and the colorful moonlight that slipped through the stained glass window.

"It isn't your fault he's a dick, Florence," he said. "You deserve so much better than that fuckhead."

"Strong language, sir."

"Do you disagree?"

I turned my head back toward him, the specter sitting so still in the parlor room where I had buried my hopes and dreams beneath the floorboards. "No," I replied simply, and then I smiled. "You know, you being angry on my behalf is kinda sweet. I wish I'd met you sooner when you were alive."

He returned the sad smile. "Me, too."

24

Such a Scream

KEYS JINGLED IN the front door as Mom unlocked it and stepped in. I only took my eyes off Ben for a second as I scrambled to my feet, but when I turned back, he was gone. Disappeared again, though I didn't know where he went. Mom jumped when she saw me standing in the parlor, and put a hand over her heart.

"Don't scare me like that. I thought you were your father," she said.

"Expecting him?"

"Would I be crazy if I said yes?" she ventured with a secretive smile.

I shook my head. "Not at all."

"Good! I'd hate for my own daughter to think I was crazy," she said with a laugh, and held out a takeout box from Olive Garden. "Well, since you're still here, take your Alfredo."

She handed me my food after I pulled on my coat. "Thanks. I haven't been here for that long, have I? You guys just left."

She shrugged. "It was weird without Xavier. We couldn't stay."

"Everything is weird without him."

"Yes, though not sad. Your father wouldn't want us to be sad." Then she fixed my scarf and wrapped it once more around my neck. "If you're on your way out, would you do me a favor and escort your old mother home?" she asked nobly, crooking her arm so that I could take it, and I did.

She was taller than I was, and thin like Alice. They both had dark hair, and when Alice was going through her rebel phase, she would steal dark lacy dresses from Mom's closet and wear them to school like a real-life Lydia Deetz, though by then I was already in college and well away from Mairmont.

Mom locked the funeral home doors on the way out, and we stepped down into the brisk April night. There was still a chill tucked into the wind, but I could remember the way April warmed so suddenly to summer it was almost a shock. One week there were coats, the next shorts and flip-flops. Maybe tonight was the last cold one, maybe tomorrow, but either way time *was* passing, slowly ever on, leaving people behind like a flower losing its petals one by one.

"I'm glad you're home," Mom began, looking ahead of us. "The occasion I could do without—but I'm glad, nonetheless. Xavier said he'd get you back here one way or the other."

"I doubt he'd have planned this."

"Certainly not! But it does suit his style," she said with a soft laugh. "Oh, he was gone too soon, Florence. Gone much, much too soon."

"I wish he was still here."

"I do, too, and I will for the rest of my life." She squeezed my arm tightly. "But we're still here, and he'll be with us long after the wind is gone."

I swallowed the knot in my throat. "Yeah."

We passed the ice cream parlor where she and Dad went every weekend when I was little and she was pregnant with Alice. She always craved pistachio ice cream. If I closed my eyes, I could see Dad in the booth by the window with his sundae, feeding Carver with a small plastic spoon. "Here comes the Douglas DC-3 aircraft in for landing! *Zzzzzzoom!*"

But the parlor was different now, with a new coat of paint, a new owner, new ice cream flavors. However much Mairmont stayed the same, it kept shifting ever so slightly. Just enough for me to feel lost, for my past to feel like another lifetime ago.

"I should've come home, Mom. Years ago. I should've visited. I should've . . ." My voice cracked. I swallowed the knot in my throat. "I can't remember how many times you tried to convince me. But then you stopped."

"Trying to change your mind was like trying to lasso the sun," Mom replied. "You're stubborn—like your father—and you take everything on your shoulders like he did. Everyone else's problems. Never his own."

"But I'm the opposite. I'm selfish. I—I never came home. I should've. I never told Dad . . ." That I was a ghostwriter. That I *did* keep writing novels after I failed, like he wanted me to. That, although in the strangest sense of the word, I'd done exactly what he believed I could do. And he never knew it.

"I hated this town after they chased you out," she said scornfully.

"They didn't chase me, I left."

"Because other people couldn't stand that a thirteen-year-old did something they could never do."

"Talk to ghosts?"

"Help people. Listen. Do something so incredibly selfless, you had to leave for it—oh, don't give me that look." She added, "You didn't have to go to the police, but you *did*. You helped them solve a murder they wouldn't have otherwise, and then when you told them the truth—it wasn't your fault they didn't believe you. For all I care, this entire town can fuck off."

"Mom!"

"I said what I said. That boy's body would still be buried on the Ridge if you hadn't said something."

And his ghost would probably still be badgering me about trying out for the debate team. He was adamant that I could argue my way out of trouble if I had to. And I proved him right my junior year of high school when Officer Saget caught me one too many times doing something slightly illegal for very good reasons.

Halfway back to the house, Mom said with a sigh of remorse, "Oh, what are we going to *do* when Carver and Nicki get married? It isn't quite like I can dance with your father's corpse."

I nodded seriously. "You don't have the upper arm strength."

"I couldn't carry that sort of deadweight!"

Gallows humor.

I missed it. I missed talking about death like another step in the journey. Lee Marlow *hated* my humor. He thought talking about death was gross and immature. And the guy before Lee—Sean—thought I was weird when I joked about death. William didn't much care. And Quinn absolutely would not hear of it.

I missed my family.

I missed *this*. Mairmont's quiet evenings, and the black dots that were palmetto bugs skittering across the sidewalk, and the moths fluttering around the streetlights, and the sound of the evenings buzzing with insects and the wind through the trees. I missed the certainty of Mom, and the defiance of Alice, and the middleness of Carver, and the steadfastness of Seaburn, and the slow bloom of Mairmont.

It seemed like New York was changing every time I blinked.

One way one moment, and then completely different the next—a chameleon of a city that never fit into one box, that never clung to one descriptor. It was always something new, something exciting, something never before seen.

I loved that for a long time, the steady march to something impossible, the ability to reinvent itself again and again despite hurricanes and pandemics and elections. And I loved everyone who I met on those streets, the Williams and Seans and Lee Marlows . . .

But the sky was always dark, and only the brightest stars shone through the light pollution of the city that never slept.

Dad said that I'd miss the stars too much, and their permanence. In New York, it was hard to pick any out, but here in Mairmont, I could see them from horizon to horizon, and the spring thunderstorms that bubbled up on the southern edge of town.

The kind of thunderstorms Dad loved.

The ones that never made it into Lee Marlow's book, and with a sudden realization I understood why I had felt so uncomfortable here. Coming home was one thing but—ever since I'd been home, I'd kept Mom and Carver and Alice at arm's length. It wasn't because I didn't love them, or didn't miss them.

I was ashamed, but talking with Ben helped me realize that I had no control over what Lee Marlow wrote. That it wasn't my fault.

I couldn't shoulder every burden, and especially not his.

"Mom?" She stopped on the porch, and turned back to me with a raised black eyebrow. I took a deep breath. "I have something I have to tell you. Before—before you find out from someone else."

"You're pregnant."

"No!" I quickly replied, repelled. "No—no absolutely *not*."

She breathed out a sigh. "Thank *god*. I don't think I could bury my husband and welcome a grandchild all at once. My range of emotions is not that flexible."

"Mine neither," I said with a laugh. I motioned to one of the rocking chairs on the front porch, and she sat in one, and I in the other. "I . . . remember that man I dated? Lee Marlow?"

"The asshole who kicked you out onto the street?"

I hesitated. "There's more to it than that."

And then I took a deep breath—and I told her. About Lee Marlow, and the stories I told him about our family. I told her about his book deal, and how I found out, and the last conversation we had before I found myself outside in the rain. It had been my choice to walk out. My choice to leave.

But really, what was the other option? *Staying?*

"I think what's worse," I said finally, "is that Marlow wrote Dad wrong. He wasn't weird or cryptic or terrifying. I think that's the worst part about this entire nightmare—Dad's immortalized by that asshole, and he did it *wrong*."

Mom crossed one leg over the other, and took out a pack of cigarettes from her back pocket. "Fuck him," she quipped.

"Mom!"

"No, truly," Mom repeated, lighting her cigarette. "Fuck that son of a bitch for twisting every good memory you told him into some deranged *Twilight Zone*. We aren't a gothic horror novel. We're a love story."

I . . . never thought of myself, my story, my life, as anything more than a boring book shelved in a boring library in a boring town. But the more I thought about my family, about the summers I and my siblings ran around in the sprinklers, and played hide-and-seek in the cemetery, and the Halloweens Mom dressed as Elvira and Dad hid in a coffin and popped out to scare every poor kid who came trick-or-treating, and the years Alice and I played dress-up with the vintage clothes we found in the attic, and the summers collecting animal bones, and lighting candles for midnight waltzes through the parlors, and sitting so quietly in the kitchen with Dad to listen to the wind sing—

There was nothing but love in those memories.

We might've been a family in black, but our lives were filled with light and hope and joy. And that was something that Lee Marlow never understood, never wrote in his cold, technical prose.

It was a kind of magic, a kind of love story, I didn't think he'd ever understand.

From the oak tree in our yard, a crow cawed in the branches, and a few of his friends echoed. My chest tightened.

Ben.

"And someday," Mom added surely, as certain as sunrises and spring thunderstorms and wind through creaky old funeral homes, "I know you'll write our story the way it was meant to be told."

"I—I don't think I could—"

"Of course you can," she replied. "It might not be in one book. It might be in five or ten. It might be little bits of all of us scattered throughout your stories. But I know you'll write us, however messy we are, and it'll be good."

"You have a lot more faith in me than I have in myself."

Mom tapped me gently on the nose and smiled. "That's how I know I'm a good mother. Now, these old bones need some rest," she sighed, and stood. She kissed me on the forehead. In the porch light, she looked older than she ever had. Weighed down by sadness—but held together, still, by hope. "I'll see you at the Waffle House in the morning. Sweet dreams, dearest."

Then she went into the house, and closed the door behind her.

I sat there for a while longer as the wind began to howl through the trees as the storm grew closer. A flash of lightning streaked across the sky.

In my memories, I could see Dad sitting on the steps of the

house, smoking a stinking cigar as he watched the storm roll in, a beer in one hand and a smile on his face, Mom leaning her head against his shoulder, a glass of merlot in her hand, her eyes closed as she listened to the rumble of thunder.

"There's nothing like the sound of the sky rattling your bones, you know?" he once told me when I asked why he loved thunderstorms so much. "Makes you feel alive. Reminds you that there's more to you than just skin and blood, but bones underneath. Stronger stuff. Just listen to that sky sing, buttercup."

Another streak of lightning crawled across the sky, and I finally stepped out into the night.

The air was heavy and human. Alice said she couldn't smell the rain, but I never understood how she *couldn't.* It was so distinct, so full, so *alive*, like I wasn't only breathing air, but the movement of electrons sparking together, igniting the sky.

As I started back toward the inn, thunder rolled across the town in a booming, house-shaking rattle that left my ears ringing. I hoped that when they eased Dad into the ground, the dirt would part for the thunder. I hoped the sound would rattle his bones still, make them dance, like they did mine. I hoped that, when the wind was high, blown from some far-off shore, I could hear him singing in the storm, as loud and high and alive as all the dead I'd ever heard singing.

"Florence?" I heard Ben, and suddenly he was walking beside me.

"It's going to rain soon."

"Shouldn't you be heading home?"

"I already am."

I passed the inn and kept walking toward the town square. It was empty with the night and the coming storm. And then the rain came with a soft, low hum. First a droplet, then another, and then the air broke and the humidity rushed away to cool, sharp pinpricks of water. I tilted my head back, face toward the thunderous sky.

In Lee's book, when it rained, Mairmont smelled like mud and pines, but standing in the middle of town, my flats flooding with water, the world smelled sharp from the oaks that lined the greens and the sweetness of the grass. He said that when it rained the town was quiet.

But my ears were full of noise.

I was soaked in a matter of moments. The rain passed right through Ben. He looked as dry as he had been before because he wasn't real anymore. He was a ghost.

But he was *here*. Now. In the moment. Nevertheless.

"You'll catch a cold if you stay out here much longer," said Ben.

"I know," I replied.

"And you're getting wet."

"I already am."

"And—"

"I don't have an umbrella, or a coat, and it's cold and it's storming and what if I get struck by lightning?" I finished for him, and tilted my head back, and let the rain wash my face. "Don't you ever do things you aren't supposed to?"

He didn't respond, so I guessed he never did.

My entire life was built on those kinds of things that I wasn't supposed to do. I wasn't supposed to move away, and I wasn't supposed to ghostwrite for a romance author, and I wasn't supposed to fail in turning the last book in, and I wasn't supposed to fall in love with Lee Marlow, and I wasn't supposed to come back here.

Not like this. Not for Dad's funeral.

"It probably worked out better for you," I said to him. "Thinking everything through, following the rules, being who you're supposed to."

To that Ben replied, "Well, I'm dead and I have nothing to show for it. Nothing to exist after me. I was just here and now I'm . . . I'm gone." He sounded frustrated and sad. "I had so many *plans*—so many. And now I will never be able to do any of them, and I just—I want—"

"You want to scream," I filled in.

He looked at me in surprise. "Yeah. I do."

"Then do it."

He paused. "Do it?" he repeated. And suddenly—Ben screamed. Just a loud, vicious yell that echoed off the storefront windows and the town hall.

I stared at him, startled.

He said, "Like that?"

A smile curved my mouth. I didn't think he'd actually *do* it, but . . . "Do you feel any better?"

"Not yet," he replied.

And he screamed again. In his voice there was aggravation, and heartache, and sadness, because he was a ghost, and he had left his life behind, and he had died in the prime of it—and I hadn't even thought about what he must've been feeling. To be dead. To be ignored. Invisible.

I was the only one who could hear him screaming.

But he didn't do it for other people. He didn't do it to be heard.

So I took a deep breath, and I screamed with him. I screamed into the howling storm, and my voice was carried off in the wind, it was struck down by thunder, it was dampened by the rain. I screamed again. And again.

And it did make both of us feel a little better.

25

Deadweight

BY THE TIME I made it back to the bed-and-breakfast, I looked like a drowned rat and my teeth were chattering, but I didn't really care. I felt okay again—better than I had since I landed at the airport. Like a weight had been . . . not lifted, no, it was still there, but it had gotten a little lighter. Dad was gone, and I was grieving, and it was going to be okay.

It wasn't yet—but it would be. I didn't know you could feel like that. I didn't know *I* could feel like that again—okay.

Not good, but better.

"Thank you," I told Ben once I latched closed the wrought iron gate to the inn, and started up the stone path to the front porch. There was a light burning in the foyer; Dana sitting at the desk reading. I paused inside the porch, so I was no longer getting rained on, and turned on my heels back to the ghost of my dead editor. I was almost eye level with him standing on the third step, though he was still a little taller.

"I should probably be saying that," he replied, his hands in his pockets, sleeves rolled up to his elbows to expose the tattoo on his forearm again. It was numbers. A date, I realized. From about five years ago. And half of a signature that looked familiar, but it was half-hidden by his sleeve. He looked less put together than he had a few hours before. The top three buttons on his shirt were undone, his tie lost somewhere in the netherworld between here and there.

He asked, "You always take ghosts to scream in the rain?"

I tore my eyes away from his forearm. "No, I only take people I like."

"Then you like me?"

"I haven't exorcised you yet."

He barked a laugh. "Another talent of yours?"

"You should've seen the last ghost. Had to shoo him away with holy water."

He laughed again, and shifted on his feet. We stood awkwardly. My heart hammered in my throat, and I curled my fingers tightly into my palms because all I wanted to do was reach out, brush his floppy hair out of his face. He needed a haircut. Then again, I liked his hair when it wasn't gelled to perfection. It curled at his ears and at the nape of his neck, the kind of curls I'd wrap around my fingers and toy with.

This felt like one of those moments when I should've said something. Anything. How much I appreciated his help, and how much I liked him near, and how sorry I was that he was dead—

We were on a boat passing under a bridge, for a second in the shadow, a moment—*the* moment—like the moment I felt with Lee in that private library, when I accepted his hand and let him pull me toward places unknown, like the moment with Stacey in the college bar in SoHo, when he asked my favorite ice cream flavor, and Quinn when he offered me a stick of gum in civics, and John in high school, inviting me out to pizza with his friends after prom.

Small moments you catch, and keep in glass jars like fireflies, or you let go.

I couldn't catch this moment; I couldn't keep it—I couldn't keep *him*. Better than anyone else, I knew what happened when I got too close to someone already dead, when I opened my heart and let someone in. It had happened before, and I found his murdered corpse on the Ridge three days later. A stupid, small part of me had thought he was still alive. But he wasn't. He was a ghost.

Ben, too, was a ghost. Not alive.

Not *real*.

If I wasn't careful, I'd make that mistake again.

And he knew it was a mistake, too, because we both let the moment pass, and found ourselves on the other side. He was meticulous. He thought things through. Of course he wouldn't do anything, he wouldn't say anything, he'd keep me at arm's length for both of our sakes.

But then why was I so frustrated that he did?

He cleared his throat and nodded toward the door. "You should probably go inside before you catch your own death."

"Yeah, you're right," I replied, and quickly turned away from him and went inside.

Dana was sitting at the front desk, reading another book. An N. K. Jemisin fantasy this time. They looked up when they heard the bell above the door chime, and jumped off their stool. "You're soaking wet!" they cried, grabbing a towel from underneath the desk, and coming around the side to hand it to me.

"Thank you so much." I took the towel from them, and dried my hair before it dripped all across the hardwood floor. Then I wrapped it around myself and gave a shiver. "Damn weather tonight."

"You're telling me," they replied, returning to their post. "The weather apps didn't even give us a warning—"

"Oh, look, there's our *famous* author," came a voice from the living area. A chill curled down my spine. And there, sitting so properly in one of the IKEA chairs in the living area, was Heather Griffin.

Everyone had that *one person* who made their high school career unbearable, and Heather was mine. We had been friends for a brief moment, until she came to the conclusion that I was crazy after the murder case. She never believed that I talked with ghosts—she thought I was looking for attention. She was also one of the main reasons why the rest of Mairmont thought so, too.

"Who were you talking to outside, Florence?" Heather went on with an innocent look. She was accompanied by a group of women who looked like a book club, laughing behind their copies of Ann Nichols's *Midnight Matinee*.

"I was just—you know—talking. To myself," I mumbled. Idiot. I was an idiot to get so comfortable in Mairmont. I should've known better.

Out of the corner of my eye, Ben moved slowly into the lobby, his hands no longer in his pockets but on his hips. He stared in at the book club with pursed lips.

Dana, bless them, leaned forward on their stool and said loudly, "How's your stay, Florence? Do you need anything? Towels, shampoo? Peace and quiet?" they added pointedly, darting their eyes at Heather.

She smoothed on a smile and poured herself a glass of lemon-infused water from the dispenser on the far side of the desk. "Well, I know when I've overstayed my welcome. It was nice to see you, Florence. Maybe we should catch up sometime," she added, scrunching her nose with a grin, and clipped her way back into the living area, where book club resumed.

I sighed and leaned against the desk. "Damn. For two seconds I'd forgotten about her."

"Lucky." Dana laughed. "I could send you up with a bottle of wine? We've got a new red in from the Biltmore that is *gloriously* bitter."

"Don't tempt me! I still have Dad's obituary to write. And I somehow have to find *wildflowers*."

"There's some growing in the back garden if you need them."

"A thousand of them?"

They winced. "Yikes, sadly not."

"See, that's my problem. And wildflowers are so *vague*—never mind I don't have a thousand dollars to spend on a florist to find me some."

In the lounge, the book club tittered some more. I would be lying if I said I didn't want to hear what they were saying about *Midnight Matinee*. Ben was leaning against the doorway, hands crossed over his chest, listening in on them. His face didn't tell me anything, except that he was either bored with their analysis of my writing or he wasn't paying attention to them at *all*.

"Hmm." Dana drummed their fingers on the oak desk, thinking. "You could try the Ridge, maybe? It's become part of the state park now. You might find some there, if the season's not too early."

I winced. "Yeah, I've thought about the Ridge." Hadn't been back there since that day. Of course wildflowers would be there, the one place I didn't want to look. But it turned out, I might not have had the choice. "Thanks. I'll hike up there tomorrow and see it."

"Great, and lemme know how it goes?"

"Sure thing. You're a lifesaver."

"Shucks!"

I grabbed one of the mints from the bowl and began to head up the stairs when my name caught my ears—a bare whisper, but there. From the living room. The women in the book club were talking about me now, and if who they had been in high school was any indication, it wasn't anything good. My shoulders tensed.

Dana mouthed that I didn't have to go, but I did. I'd spent ten years running from these assholes, and I was sick and damn tired of it.

Ben warned as I passed, "Don't pick a fight."

Oh, I wasn't.

Heather quickly righted herself in the chair with an air of innocence. She'd been bent in toward some of the other women, whispering over their bookmarked novels. I wondered if they'd even read it, or if buying romance novels to never read and gossip over them was the newest trend. Heather looked like I remembered her, pretty brown hair and pretty brown eyes and a pretty smile over soft pink lips. She wore a sleek black skirt and a paisley-printed blouse. I remembered Dad once telling me that Karen had hired her as a clerk at her legal firm in town.

She smiled with strikingly white teeth. "Would you care to join us? We're big fans of Ann Nichols."

I bet she was.

I swallowed the rebuke bubbling up in my throat and sat down on the fainting couch beside her. "I love *Midnight Matinee*."

"Nichols hasn't written a bad book yet," said one of the other book club attendees happily. "I devour all of them the *second* they come out."

"I hear there's a new one this fall," said another woman. She was older, with curly gray hair and in a leopard-print sweater. "Haven't heard anything about it yet, though."

I could *feel* Ben staring at the back of my head at that comment.

Heather asked me with a fixed smile, "What was that one book you wrote, Florence? We'd love to read it for our book club next month."

I returned the smile, and it was a real one. "Seaburn said you already read it when it came out."

"Oh? Must've forgotten . . ."

I was sure she hadn't. I took a deep breath. Wrestled my emotions under control. I was an adult, and I wasn't running anymore. "I know you don't like me, Heather, and I know it was you who spread those rumors about me in high school—that I was crazy or a devil worshipper or whatever."

She went rigid and darted her gaze around the rest of the book club. A few of them went to high school with us. They knew. The others had a passing, vague recollection of what happened. It *was* a small town, after all. "It was hardly just me. It was Bradley and TJ and—"

"I forgive you."

She blinked. "Excuse me?"

"And I forgive me, too," I went on. "I was so wrapped up in what everyone else thought of me I didn't recognize that I actually did something good."

"You found a body, Florence," she said dismissively, rolling her eyes. "It wasn't like you *solved the case* of what's his name—"

"Harry. His name was Harry O'Neal." My mouth flattened into a thin line. "He was in our grade. He sat right behind you in math."

She narrowed her eyes. Did she remember? Probably not. She probably hadn't thought about the boy murdered on the Ridge in fifteen years.

"The thing is, Heather," I went on, "I believe people. Even if it's weird, even if it doesn't make sense, I want to believe them. I want to see the good in them. I give my heart to everyone I meet and I put it in everything I do. And sometimes it hurts—often it hurts, actually . . ." And I glanced back to Ben, wishing I had taken that moment on the porch and trapped it in a jar. "I can't ever control how someone else treats me, but I can control how I choose to live and how I choose to treat others. And I'd worried about what other people thought and what other people wanted from me for *years* because I actually thought it mattered." My eyebrows furrowed as I realized that I wasn't just talking about Heather now, but Lee, too. People who had taken what they wanted from me, twisted my good intentions, and turned them into something sour.

"Florence, I don't know where this is coming from," Heather said, feigning shock, but the rest of the book club was quiet. Some had opened their books; others were scrolling through their phones. I didn't know what they thought of me, but I realized I didn't give a single fuck.

"So I forgive you," I said to her, "because you don't understand, and I'm not going to explain it to you. He liked you, though. Harry. Right up until the end." Then I stood and took one of the cookies from the coffee table, and bit into it. "Have fun, y'all," I added, and left the lounge area.

Dana gave me a weathered salute as I climbed the stairs and mouthed, "Holy shit."

Holy shit indeed. I didn't let myself pause until I was almost at the top of the stairs. My hands were shaking.

I let out a solid breath and dug around in my satchel for my key card.

Ben came up the stairs behind me. "Harry? He's the boy you helped?"

"Yeah. When I was thirteen, Harry—his ghost—came to me one evening like you did, but I didn't think he was dead because, you know, I'd *just* seen him that day at school. But he was. We didn't know why he was still around. He couldn't remember how he died, either. So I . . . helped him find out." I tried not to think about that year, the police investigation, the national news coverage, the rumors at school where people called me crazy at best, an accomplice at worst. "You know the rest."

He said, a bit sadly, "You liked him."

"I always have had to learn things the hard way." I tried at a joke, but it fell a little flat.

He reached out, but then stopped himself and crossed his arms over his chest. His biceps strained his tailored shirt, not that I was looking. Because I wasn't. Because he was so very off-limits.

The lock clicked and I shouldered the door open. "And anyway, thank you for tonight."

"Sweet dreams," he replied and pushed off the wall to leave.

A thought occurred to me as he made his way back down the hall. "Where do you go?" The question surprised him because he turned back around on his heels toward me. "I mean—ghosts don't sleep, so . . ."

He shrugged. "I wander. Until I disappear, then I usually just come back somewhere near you."

"And you still don't know where you go?"

He shook his head.

"Well, you're welcome to . . ."

Sit in my room, but that sounded weird. It *was* weird. For all I knew I was inviting him to stare at me while I slept á la Edward Cullen. He said he was a romantic, so it was really a coin toss on whether he'd be flattered to role-play *Twilight* or aghast that I'd remotely consider it. I shook my head and said, "Never mind. Have a good night, Ben."

"You, too, Florence."

I closed the door and pressed my back against it, because I felt my heart beating—so fast it felt like it wanted to jump right out of my chest. He had been so close to me, so close I noticed the thin scar under his right eyebrow, and the beauty mark above his lip, and the fine black hairs on his arms and—

"I am in *so* much trouble," I said under my breath as I opened my laptop.

And not just because I was falling for—

I *wasn't* falling.

I couldn't.

I tried not to entertain the idea as I pulled up Dad's obituary again, and stared at the blank document.

Then I took a deep breath, and remembering what my Mom told me earlier, I started with a simple story.

I started with goodbye.

26

Ridges of the Past

I WASN'T THE outdoorsy sort of person. In fact, I really hated nature that wasn't grown in a cemetery. I hated the bugs, the hiking, the snakes you had to watch out for, the palmetto bugs, the ants, the ticks, the weird hairy caterpillars, the *raccoons*. One time in high school, on my way to my car in the morning, I was chased by an opossum with a bent tail. *Chased.* Straight to my car!

I gathered very early on in my life that nature didn't like me, either. Even when I moved to New York, pigeons dive-bombed me and sewer rats always seemed to zero in on skittering over *my* feet. I didn't want to talk about the Godzilla-sized cockroaches that lived in my first apartment. I will never be able to sit down on the toilet and pee in peace for the rest of my life because of that damn infestation.

So it was safe to say, hiking up to the Ridge the next morning, I was *not* having a fun time. Never mind the history with the Ridge. It wasn't so much that I avoided it but . . . coupled with hating nature, I never really had a reason to come back.

What was worse, I hadn't seen Ben all morning. I wondered where he was. Usually he waited for me in the living area downstairs, but this morning when I went to fix my daily cup of battery acid to head to family breakfast, he wasn't around.

I couldn't wait for him, either, so after my waffle and eggs I headed for the Ridge. There was a forest path on the far side of Mairmont that trailed up to the fields. Now that I thought about it, Dad *did* used to pick wildflowers when he went for walks around the Ridge. He'd gather a bunch of different colors and bring them back down the trail with us, and present them to Mom at home.

The trail had changed in the decade I'd been gone. There were now benches along the path to commemorate Harry, and the dirt trail was more defined, but the trees were mostly the same—large old oaks and pines unfurling their leaves for spring. New York seasons were wonderful, since you actually got to *experience* all of them. In Mairmont, it was either winter or summer, with a week of spring and fall in between. This week must've been spring, and I'd come down at just the right time. The morning air was brisk, and the sun was bright, and the woods were quiet.

It was just me and my gasping breath as I trekked up the path.

When I was almost at the top, I leaned against a pine, bent over, to catch my breath. Sweat was dripping down my back and that was *not* a comfortable feeling.

"You know, most people don't hike in flats."

I pulled myself ramrod straight—and almost blacked out. Ben gave a yelp, flinging his hands toward me, as I caught myself on a tree. I blinked the spots out of my eyes. "What were you gonna do, *catch* me?" I asked, annoyed.

"It would've been rude not to try," he replied.

"Oh, well then, thank you for the attempt."

He mocked a bow. "Trying to find those wildflowers?" he asked as I pushed myself off the tree and climbed the final few steps to the top of the trail.

The tree line abruptly ended, and in its place stretched a wide meadow nearly a football field long before it dropped off a bit—the "ridge"—and more trees began. There was a bench over to the left of me, and a trash can that smelled like it hadn't been emptied in at least a week. On the far side of the Ridge was a small plaque, donated by the town and placed by the town council, where I'd found the body. Harry's dad didn't think anyone would find him out here for at least a few years, so it surprised him when police came knocking on his door a week later.

Last I heard, he was rotting in the state prison.

What surprised me most about the Ridge, though, was that the field was covered in small white puffs. Dandelions. Stretching on and on like a fresh powdering of new snow. It was beautiful, struck against the contrast of the clear blue sky. I could lie down in it and be buried beneath the blooms, totally submerged, and sleep there.

They were weeds—technically wildflowers, I guessed, but not the kind I was looking for.

I let out a long breath. "Well, *shit*."

Ben stood beside me, looking out onto the field. "Lots of wishes there."

"What?"

"You know, *wishes*," he replied, motioning to the field. "Didn't you ever blow on dandelion tufts?"

"Of course I did," I replied defensively. "It's just dandelions are useless to me right now. They're not what I need."

"No, but . . . do you think we could stay a little longer?" he asked, and motioned for me to follow him into the field. In the sunlight, he looked a little more washed out than he did in the shade, a little more ghostly, sparkling like he was made of the twinkle lights I strung up in my dorm in college. The dandelions bent softly in the breeze through his ankles, and I wanted to walk with him.

"Just a little," I agreed.

He waited for me to catch up, his hands in his pockets, patient and tall as always. "Imagine how many wishes you could get out of these. At least one is bound to come true."

Ben never stopped fascinating me. "You believe in dandelion wishes?"

"Statistically, one is bound to come true with all of these dandelions, so yes."

"And if you only made one wish? On all of them?"

He tilted his head, actually debating the question. Finally he decided, "It depends on the wish."

What kind of wish would that be?

I plucked a dandelion and twirled it around between my fingers. "Then set the scene," I began. "What would a refined dead editor wish for? He's walking with his chaotic author. It's midmorning—well, probably afternoon now—and there are hundreds of thousands of dandelions to wish on. What would he wish for?"

The edge of his lips twitched. Then he bent down close to me, and my skin prickled at his nearness, and he said in a soft rumble, "If he tells her, then it won't come true."

My breath caught in my throat. "She won't finish her manuscript on time."

"He wouldn't wish for that. He knows she's perfectly capable of it on her own. She just needs a little more faith in herself." His ears started turning pink. "Because even though she can't see how talented she is, he knows she'll figure it out someday."

"And if she doesn't?"

"Maybe that's what he wishes for. That she does."

I quickly looked away, my cheeks burning in a blush. "That's a terrible wish," I forced out. "Wasted potential—my editor would circle that and tell me to recast."

He quirked an eyebrow. "Fine, then what would the author wish for?"

"World peace," I replied smartly because I couldn't bear to tell him the truth.

That I'd wish that this moment in the field would last forever. That we never had to leave, that we could freeze time and live in this moment where the sun was high and warm and the sky was a crystalline blue and my heart beat bright in my chest and he was here.

I wanted a moment that never ended.

This moment.

Standing there in the middle of the dandelion field, looking up into Ben's soft ocher eyes, I began to realize that love wasn't dead, but it wasn't forever, either. It was something in between, a moment in time where two people existed at the exact same moment in the exact same place in the universe. I still believed in that—I saw it in my parents, in my siblings, in Rose's unabashed one-night stands looking for some peace. It was why I kept searching for it, heartbreak after heartbreak. It wasn't because I needed to find out that love existed—of course it did—but it was the hope that I'd find it. That I was an exception to a rule I'd made up in my head.

Love wasn't a whisper in the quiet night.

It was a yelp into the void, screaming that you were *here*.

Ben took a breath. "In truth, I'd wish for—"

A roar of wind swept across the trees, and when it hit the field, it plucked up the white fluff of dandelions like a roiling wave on the ocean. It swept across the field and rushed toward me in a whirl of seeds that looked like snow. I shielded my face as the wave splashed against me, over me, around me, and carried the dandelions across the rest of the field and up into the crystalline sky.

I whirled around and watched them go. “Holy shit, talk about spring winds. Right, Ben?” There was no response. “Ben?”

But he was gone.

27

Ghost of a Chance

WHEN I REACHED the bottom of the Ridge, Carver's blue Ford pickup truck was parked in the lot. He dipped his head out of the open window, a John Deere hat flipped backward on his head, and waved me over. He had a beautifully carved wooden birdcage in the passenger seat that he'd made himself, strapped in for safekeeping.

I let out a low whistle when I saw it. "Is that *mahogany*?"

He scoffed. "Hell no. It's cherrywood. What do you think I am, made of money?"

"You do have a steady high-paying job in tech and can take all of the vacation you want *while* working from home so, like, yeah, I do," I replied.

He playfully slammed me on the arm. "Shush. Just wait until you sell the next Harry Potter. Then you'll be rolling in the dough and everyone'll want you to be their best friend—perhaps with benefits, if they're lucky."

I rolled my eyes. "No one will sell the next Harry Potter. It hit a zeitgeist that'll never be re-created, and because there is so much to *choose* from now, it's near impossible to predict the next publishing trend—"

"Okay, okay," he groaned, "I get it! Uncle, I call uncle!"

I stuck out my tongue, and then nudged my chin toward the birdcage. "What's that for, anyway?"

He grinned then. "I got an idea for a part of Dad's will."

"You were thinking about that?" I asked, surprised.

"Of course I was! What do you take me for, a nonmeddling middle brother?"

"Touché."

"Okay, I say we feed the little fuckers who keep stealing the squirrel food, trap twelve of them, and let them go during the funeral."

"Those are going to be some mad crows . . ."

"So? What're they going to do? Shit on my windshield?"

"Steal your Rolex."

He looked annoyed. "Do you have a better idea?"

"No, but I do like the birdcage—can you give me a ride back to the bed-and-breakfast?"

"Sure, hop in. Just be careful with the cage," he added as I walked around to the other side. I slid in, and noticed a copy of the *Daily Ram* on the seat. I picked it up, and flipped through to the back. "The obit was lovely," he added as I found it.

Good, they used one of my favorite photos of Dad. It'd been taken a few years ago, when everyone had come to New York to celebrate the New Year and we'd all grabbed our champagne and climbed the fire escape to the roof. He had a cigar in one hand, laughing into the night, his face lit by New Year's fireworks. I smiled at the memory.

Carver pulled out onto the road again and made a U-turn back into town. "You know—you don't have to do all of this alone. I love scavenger hunts."

I folded the newspaper back up and stuck it between the seats. "I know, but you're all so busy. I'm the bum of the family."

"I wouldn't say that," he replied. "You ghostwrite for Stephenie Meyer."

"Not even the same genre, bub."

He shrugged. "Worth a shot." He picked up a Slim Jim from the console and tore open the wrapper with one hand. "Want some?"

"I can never stop chewing it."

"Half the point." He bit into the end and tore it with his teeth. "I heard you had a run-in with Heather . . ."

I winced. "Word gets around that fast?"

"Dana couldn't stop gushing over how cool you were when I ran into them at the coffee shop this morning," he replied. We rolled to a stop at the only stoplight in town. The mayor was making his rounds with a high school dog walker, and he was the happiest boy as he crossed the street in front of us. We waved, and the high schooler waved back. "I also heard you talked to Mom about feeling excluded."

Seriously, was *nothing* sacred in this town?

I rolled my eyes. "It's fine, she explained it—"

"I'm so sorry," he interrupted.

That surprised me.

"I wasn't thinking. Neither was Alice. We just . . . you never wanted to . . . we thought it would be too much," he confessed, "especially after we noticed that you started talking to your—" He changed course quickly. "Someone we can't see again. Like Dad did."

I clenched my hands into fists. "Did you think he was crazy, too?"

"I don't think you're crazy, Florence."

"Then tell me, what *do* you think?" I snapped. Even though it'd been ten years, that same anger was quick to simmer beneath my skin. "That I'm talking to some imaginary friend? That I'm losing it?"

"You know I'd *never* think that—"

"*Faking* it—?"

"Is it Dad?" he interrupted. *Oh.* "Would you even tell us? Or keep it to yourself? Like you keep everything else to yourself? Florence, the lonely island!"

That was it. I was out.

First it was Ben, who did a miraculous Houdini act at *just* the right time, and now Carver was laying into me about things I obviously did *not* need to work on.

My patience was already thin, but now it was absolutely demolished.

I reached for the handle and forced the truck door open, forgetting I was still buckled in. So I unbuckled my seat belt, after almost strangling myself, and shoved my way out of the car. "I'll see you at the wake, Carver."

He cursed. "No, wait, Florence—!"

I slammed the car door before he could finish whatever he was about to say. I didn't want to hear it, anyway. Florence, the *lonely island*, was tired and sweaty, and she didn't want to talk about her faults before a nice hot shower.

And what was more worrying was that *someone* caught me talking to Ben, and the rumors were at it again. I pulled my jacket tightly across my chest, folding my arms together, as I hurried back to the bed-and-breakfast. People weren't looking at me as I passed—but what if they were? What if they were leaning in toward each other, whispering, "There goes the ghost whisperer," and laughing under their breath?

Stop it. They weren't.

It was my stupid brain turtling. This wasn't high school anymore. I was a decade out of it. I was older. I was wiser. And despite Carver, my head was still filled with the memory of dandelions in the wind—and I realized that the rest of this didn't matter.

And I was okay.

Somehow.

28

Dancing with the Dead

I HAD BEEN to plenty of wakes before, but never one like this.

As I slipped on my kitten heels on the front porch and made my way down Main Street toward the Days Gone Funeral Home, the townsfolk, wearing blacks and reds, began to close up their stores, carrying platters of cheese and crackers and lasagna and fried chicken and collard greens and various oven bakes.

For an hour, Mairmont had paused, all save for the lone Victorian house with black shutters and wrought iron fencing on the parapets. The closer I got, the more people there were. A sea of people, spilling out of the front door and down the sidewalk.

Seaburn was standing at the front gate in a brown suit, an orchid in his pocket. He saw me as I crossed the road, and pulled me into a tight hug. "Why're they all outside?" I asked.

"Well"—Seaburn extended a hand toward the front door—"see for yourself."

I walked up the pathway to the front steps, and hesitantly opened the front door—and stopped dead in my tracks. Because two of the three parlor rooms were full of flowers. Not just any flowers—*wildflowers*. All separated by color in clear glass vases. There must have been . . . there must have been a *thousand* of them.

I was baffled. "How . . . how did . . ."

Mom came out of the red parlor room, where Dad's casket sat. "Oh, Florence! Aren't all these flowers *lovely*?"

"Who . . . how did . . . when—"

Then Heather stepped out of one of the parlor rooms, wiping her hands off on a handkerchief. What was *she* doing here? I began to ask that exact thing when she outstretched her hand to me and said, "Your dad was a good man. We will always want to help when we can. And you were right. But people change. Even me."

I looked down at her hand, then at her again. "You . . . did this?"

"Dana helped me," Heather replied, not retracting her hand, waiting. "We organized donations last night and this morning to buy and deliver the flowers needed. I'm sorry," she added.

I didn't know if she was telling the truth, or if she had some ulterior motives—to look better if word got out about our confrontation? To paint me as the spoiled woman who never grew up? See? Heather *did* change, it was Florence who couldn't let the past die!

Or . . . maybe that was my brain being cold and bitter. Thinking everyone had an ulterior motive when maybe, this was just what it looked like.

I took her hand. "Thank you," I said.

We shook.

Then she took the vase of blue wildflowers and disappeared into the blue parlor room. Mom motioned for me to come into the viewing room when I was ready.

Seaburn elbowed me in the side. "Go see your old man so we can open up the house."

"Yeah, I should."

I breathed out a long breath, steeling my shoulders. One step at a time. Carver and Alice were waiting inside the red parlor room—Dad's favorite room—and outstretched their hands to me. I took them, and squeezed them tightly, and together we walked up to the dark mahogany casket decorated in wildflowers of blues and reds and yellows and pinks, to begin to figure out how to say goodbye.

The afternoon was a blur of people drifting in and out of the funeral home, shaking my hand and giving me their condolences. Casseroles began to pile up in the refrigerator in the kitchen, and more than one bottle of champagne was spilled on the hardwood floors. The entire town was here, crowded into the old Victorian house and across the lawn, in their best black clothes. They paid their respects to Dad one at a time, and the three Day siblings stood off to the side, our hands clasping one another's, keeping ourselves upright. Mom was stalwart, sipping on a glass of champagne, so gracious to everyone who came to say their goodbyes.

"Of course he'd be buried in that god-awful red suit," Karen said, dabbing her eyes so her makeup wouldn't run. "Of course he would."

"Alice did a great job," John said, in his best black boater shorts, black shirt, and pizza hat. "Looks like he's still kickin'."

Someone else said, "He was so proud of you."

And everyone else just went by in a blur. I barely registered their faces.

"You three are the best kids an undertaker could have."

"So proud."

"Great guy."

"He was so proud."

"Such a good man."

My bottom lip wobbled, but I bit it to keep myself firm. Whenever I felt myself giving way, Carver would squeeze my hand tightly, as if to ask, *Do you need a moment?* And I would squeeze back that I was okay, and tighten my grip on Alice's hand, too. The world spun on, and we were still here.

When the last of the visitors finally left, including Mrs. Elizabeth in a pretty pink suit because, she said, "Black isn't my color," with her ghostly husband in tow, I closed the front door and locked it. The smell of the wildflowers was so overpowering, we elected to keep some of the windows cracked to air the place out. But even with them open, the funeral home felt so quiet, I almost couldn't stand it. Mom busied herself in the red parlor room, picking up the dried flowers off the ground and situating the wildflower vases. The arrangements wouldn't be moved until tomorrow, when we had the graveside service, and I had to wonder how we'd get all of these damn flowers hauled over to the cemetery.

I leaned back against the front door and breathed out a long breath.

"Everything okay?"

I glanced up toward the voice. Ben was standing awkwardly in the middle of the foyer, his hands again in his pockets. I hadn't seen him since he disappeared on the Ridge, and I felt instantly better just *seeing* him. His presence was a balm.

"You missed all the fun," I said in greeting, wiping the edges of my eyes. Thankfully I'd worn waterproof eyeliner today.

He glanced around. "The wake . . . is over already? How long was I gone?"

"A few hours," I replied. The Ridge felt like an elephant in the room. What had he been about to say? What would he have wished for?

"Are you okay?" he asked, worried. "I mean—that's the wrong question. Is . . . is there anything I can do?"

Even though he couldn't interact with the world, even though no one else could see him, even though I was the one who was supposed to be helping him . . . "You're very thoughtful."

"You're hurting. It's hard to see."

"Am I *that* ugly a crier?"

"No—I mean yes, but no—I mean . . ." He pursed his lips. "I wish I could do something. Anything. Take you in my arms and hug you and tell you that things are going to hurt for a while, but it gets better."

A knot formed in my throat. The grooves on the front door pressed into my back, I leaned so hard against it. Isn't that what I had wanted to tell him, what felt like eons ago? "Does it? Get better?"

He nodded. "Bit by bit. I lost my parents at thirteen in a car accident, and my grandmother adopted me. This is my dad's ring," he said as he took off his necklace, felt the ring between his fingers. "I keep it with me so I don't feel so alone. She told me that you don't ever lose the sadness, but you learn to love it because it becomes a part of you, and bit by bit, it fades. And, eventually, you'll pick yourself back up and you'll find that you're okay. That you're *going* to be okay. And eventually, it'll be true."

"Your grandma sounds like my dad," I said, and sniffed, wiping my eyes with the backs of my hands.

He curled his fingers around his ring and put it in his pocket. "I'm sorry, Florence. I know you've heard those words a lot today, but . . ."

"Thank you," I replied. "You've been really great." And then I couldn't help it—I laughed. "Oh, god—I just realized. Ben and been, get it? Your name? It's a play on—I'm sorry, you're trying to have a serious moment and I'm . . . a mess." I scrubbed my face with my hands, mortified.

"You've Ben waiting to make that joke, haven't you?" he commented wryly.

"I've Ben resisting, honestly."

He sighed, and then gave the smallest chuckle. It cracked the sides of his face, and there was a smile. I almost couldn't believe my eyes. I bent toward him to get a better look. "What?" he asked.

"I wanted to see if you were actually smiling, or if I was hallucinating."

"You're so strange."

"Absolutely. Don't you wish you'd never let me walk out of your office?" I joked.

"Yes." He said it so resolutely, it made me blush.

Was that your wish? The one from the Ridge? I wanted to ask, but it wouldn't do any good. I was here to help him move on, and he was here to leave.

Ghost stories never had happy endings.

"Well, you got off lucky, then," I replied, grabbing the tiny trash can from beside the door, and I started picking up trash the guests left behind. Plastic champagne glasses and napkins from the finger foods outside. It was like people forgot trash cans existed.

For the next twenty minutes, I walked around the funeral home in the silence, righting everything, cleaning the tables, closing the guest book.

When I rounded to the red room where Carver stood, looking down at Dad in the coffin, I paused. He was muttering quietly under his breath, and slowly reached out a hand to Dad's, folded so neatly over his chest, and rested it there for a moment.

Quietly, I backed out of the room.

Ben leaned against the doorway, looking into the room with my dad's coffin. He said, "I like your Dad's style. Great tux."

"It was his favorite," I replied.

Carver gently closed the lid of the coffin. For the last time. Then he moved out of the red parlor room where Dad was and gathered up the cups from the end table. I lugged the trash can with me, and held it out for Carver to dump the cups into.

A stereo sat atop the table, usually reserved for some sort of somber organ music during wakes and visitations. I couldn't remember if we had it playing today.

My brother gave a sad sort of smile as his fingers skimmed across the stereo buttons. "Remember when Dad played music while we cleaned up?"

I groaned. "He had Bruce Springsteen on *repeat*."

He chuckled. "Remember that time he pulled his back out wailing on an air guitar to 'Born to Run'?" His eyes squeezed at the edges, prickling in the only way he knew how to cry. His voice was thick as he said, "God, Florence, I wish he was here."

"Me, too. And—I do need help. With the will thing. Mostly the crows. And your . . . cherrywood birdcage."

He gave a mock gasp. "Oh. My. God. Is Florence Day actually asking for *help*?"

"Please don't make this a big deal—"

"Al!" he called to our youngest sister, in the blue room. "Florence actually asked for our *help*!"

Alice poked her head out of the doorway. "Fuck that," she replied.

"So that's a yes?" I rebutted, and my sister stuck out her tongue and withdrew into the blue room again.

Carver bumped his shoulder against mine. "*Always* a yes." Then Mom called him from the third parlor to help her move some vases, and he scrubbed me on the head as he went. I smoothed down my hair again, muttering to myself.

"Question," Ben said, coming back to me as I finished cleaning the table with the stereo. "Did Lee get anything right?"

"Hmm?"

"In his book."

I tilted my head. "He wrote that we listened to Beethoven's *Für Elise*—Carver went through a classical music kick—and that Dad danced with skeletons. Which he did," I added, "but only on Halloween."

He snorted a laugh. "I bet it was terrifying."

"Oh, absolutely *not*. He'd do this thing where he'd throw his voice and move Skelly's jaw—it was funny! He was funny. And maybe a little funny looking," I conceded, and absently ran my fingers across the stereo's buttons. "I think the worst part is that Lee thought my childhood was something sad and lonely. And maybe sometimes it was. And it wasn't always great—but god, Ben, it was good. It was broken a little, and banged up, but it was good." I pulled open the drawer beneath the stereo to show Ben the CDs we had, the ones Dad played. "It was so good."

Because Dad collected songs and danced Mom around the parlor—and together they taught us how to say goodbye. They taught us a lot of things that most kids rarely even thought of. They taught us how to grieve with widows, and how to console young kids who didn't quite know death yet. They taught us how to put makeup on corpses and drain out the blood to replace it with formaldehyde, how to arrange clothes so the hospital bruises from the IVs and shock paddles and stickers weren't quite as prominent. How to frame flowers on a casket to disguise how few some people received. Mom and Dad taught us so many things, and all of it led to this.

They gave us the tools to figure out what to do when they were gone.

And now Dad was.

I took out the topmost CD. A burned silver disc with Dad's scratching scrawl on it.

Good Goodbyes.

I couldn't remember how many times, after long viewings and sad wakes, Dad would call us to the funeral home to help clean up—just like this. Just like now. The Days Gone Funeral Home was small, and Dad didn't like overworking his employees if he didn't have to, so he worked *us* instead. I always made like I hated it, the too-clean smell of disinfectant and floral bouquets, the bright rooms, the dead people in the basement, but I had a secret:

I never hated it as much as I said I did.

By the time Mom had dragged me and Carver and Alice to the funeral home, usually on school nights, Dad had already shrugged out of his coat, his sleeves rolled up to his elbows, exposing the tattoos he'd acquired in his youth (that most of Mairmont would gasp at if they knew). He'd put on this CD, and beckon us into the house of death with a smile and a good song.

"Want a listen?" I asked Ben, showing him the disc like it was a secret.

"What is it?"

I put the CD into the stereo, and pressed play.

The hiss of the speakers sighed through the parlor, and I closed my eyes, and the music started. The antiquated bop hopped from room to room, the shake of the tambourine, happy and joyful and light, and finally—*finally*—I felt like I was home. The song settled into my bones as if it wanted me to move, like it wanted me to throw my arms up, to twirl, to jump.

I didn't need to see where I was going. Every corner of this funeral home was my childhood, every inch seared into my soul like a long-lost treasure map.

I remembered Dad standing by the stereo. I remembered the snap of his feet. Pointing to Mom, beckoning her close with an orchid in his mouth and the shake of his hips.

"I didn't expect this," Ben remarked, surprised.

"We are full of wonders, Benji Andor." I mimed the tambourine as I bopped down the hallway.

Carver, putting the guest book away in the office, looked at me like I'd lost my mind as Mom poked her head out of the smallest parlor room. A smile tugged at the edges of her rose-red lips.

"What's that music, babe?" asked Nicki, fixing his rolled-up sleeves. He must've been the one helping Mom situate the flowers for tomorrow.

"Dad," Carver replied, and he was fighting a smile as I wiggled the invisible tambourine.

I undid my hair from its tight bun and shook it out, because the wake was over, and began to sing along to the Foundations' "Build Me Up Buttercup." Dad used to turn up the stereo as loud as it would go, so loud I was sure the corpses rattled in the basement, and take Mom by the hand, mouthing the words, and she'd laugh as they danced through parlors so accustomed to death, and they looked like home.

They were home.

This was home.

Because Dad left us things—little things—so that we wouldn't be alone. So *Mom* wouldn't be alone. So he could still be with us, even if just in the melody of a song. Any song. Every song. Not just the Foundations, or Bruce Springsteen or Bon Jovi or Fleetwood Mac or Earth, Wind & Fire or Taylor Swift.

Whatever song, whatever made us feel *alive.*

Carver grabbed his partner by the hand, and pulled him into the hall to dance.

The good goodbyes.

I always thought the CD was meant for the people laid up in coffins, with floral arrangements and bouquets and guest books—and maybe it was.

But maybe it was for the living, too.

To keep us moving forward.

Ben watched with a baffled look, so misplaced in a funeral home filled with light and sound, and before I could stop myself I reached out to try to take his hand, to get him to dance with us—when my hand fell through his.

He gave a sad sort of smile, and outstretched his hand. "We can pretend."

"I like pretend," I replied, and reached out my hand again, hovering it over his. Then I mimed taking his other hand and he played along—

And suddenly we were all moving and singing. He twirled me out, and back in, and I laughed in a way I hadn't in years. And Ben was smiling. Really, truly smiling. It sent a shock straight through my core because he'd never smiled like that before. At least not for me.

He was beautiful.

It made my heart skip at the thought, and then the music, rattling in my bones so brightly, and I recognized—quite suddenly—this feeling. It was the kind I wrote about years ago, the kind he talked about, the kind that itched just beneath my fingers, lost on the doorstep of some Brooklyn brownstone—or so I thought.

It was the answer to a question, soft and subtle, but it was there—the kind of feeling, this hope, that had just been hiding, waiting for some specter to take my hand and dance me across the floorboards.

It felt, for a moment in time, like happiness.

29

When the Dead Sing

"PIZZA'S HERE!" ALICE called as she brought a box of Domino's into the kitchen. We were all sitting around the kitchen table at the house playing spades—Mom, Alice, Carver, Nicki, and me (well, and Ben, but he was sitting on the counter beside the sink, well out of the way of anyone after Nicki accidentally passed through him earlier, shivered, and said, "I think someone rolled over my grave"). Alice took down the plates from the cabinet and set them down beside the pizza box, before grabbing a helping for herself and Mom. "No one looked at my cards, right?" she asked as she sat back down at the table.

"Not a soul," Carver lied. Nicki pushed his chair back to get plates for them both.

Alice eyed our brother. "Liar."

"Sister! You hurt me!"

"You've never *not* cheated at spades," I pointed out, leaning back in my chair to grab a slice. My hand was absolutely terrible and I was losing, but I was too stubborn to give up. The loser had to clean up the kitchen—and it was not gonna be me. I had skirted that responsibility for ten years.

I'd be damned if I was gonna start now.

Carver thanked Nicki for the plate and casually kissed him on the cheek. We were all still technically in our wake clothes, but we'd lost our jackets and shoes and most of our jewelry by then. A half-empty bottle of Maker's sat on the table, along with everyone's glasses.

"I am, by no means, a cheater. Nicki, tell them I'm a good and honest man," Carver went on.

Nicki patted Carver on the shoulder. "You are honestly something."

"*Babe!*" he cried.

Ben chuckled against his shoulder. I didn't think he noticed me watching him, not at first, not as he took in my family. Alice and her chipped black nails and Carver and his boyfriend sneaking soft touches to each other and Mom humming "Build Me Up Buttercup" quietly to herself as she rearranged her card hand again and again. It was endearing, the way he pushed his fingers through his hair, and leaned forward to sneak a look at Carver's hand, and how he laughed whenever Alice mumbled something smart to herself.

And I thought—with a pang of sadness—how much Dad would've liked him.

He finally caught me staring, and quirked a thick black eyebrow. I was in the middle of shoving pizza into my mouth, and quickly looked away. "So, where were we?" I asked between a mouthful of cheese, setting the pizza down on the table like the heathen I was. He didn't catch me looking, I lied to myself.

He didn't see *anything*.

"Nicki and I were about to kick y'all's asses," Carver replied.

Mom sat quietly at the head of the table. She took another sip of her drink. "Now, now, sweetie, Xavier and I never raised you to lie."

"*Mother!* Now I'm getting sniped from *both* sides?"

"Obviously I'm winning," she added, and with that drew a card from her hand and set it down on the table. A jack of hearts. Which meant, in spades, that if you had a heart, you had to play it, and we had played hearts only once before during this game. If you didn't have a heart, you could trump with a spade.

I, sadly, had a heart left. Two, actually.

Alice flipped a card out of her hand. She tossed it into the middle. A four of hearts. Excellent. Carver played an eight of clubs. Which meant he either didn't have hearts *or* spades . . . or he decided to throw a card. Because he knew Nicki would win the hand.

Carver made a ticking sound with his tongue. "Your turn, sis."

I chewed on my thumbnail.

"Or do you got nothing? If you lose this hand . . . it's dishes for you," he added.

"Thank *god* I don't have to do them for once," Alice sighed.

Ben eased himself off the counter and came around the kitchen. He leaned over me, his hand anchored on the table, a *hmmmmm* soft in his throat. Where he was near me, my skin tingled with cold. It felt like when your hand goes numb, quite the opposite of if he were alive and leaning so close. I wondered what he had smelled like when he was alive. What cologne he used, what shampoo, what he looked like naked—

"Tough choices," he mused. "You're in a real pickle."

"Shush, I'm trying to figure out what to do," I said, telling myself that my cheeks were burning because of the whiskey, and drained the rest of the glass. The ice clinked at the bottom.

"You should play that one," he suggested. "Nicki has a heart left and—"

"I'm not going to *cheat*—"

"What are you whispering?" Carver asked through a mouthful of pizza.

Alice added, tongue in cheek, "Your *ghost* friend helping you out?"

"*No*," I rebuked.

Carver agreed. "If she had a ghost friend helping, she wouldn't be losing so badly."

Nicki slapped him on the arm. "Be nice!"

"I am!"

Ben bent down against my ear and said, the words a low rumble in his throat, "Annihilate them."

I was thinking the same damn thing. It wasn't cheating if no one knew. I pulled the queen of hearts from my hand and slammed it down in the middle of the table. And, like Ben said, Nicki had to play his hearts. I won the round.

And the next one. My family would play their hands and then Ben would advise me on what to play next, his voice tickling my ear.

When I took the fifth round in a row, Carver crossed his arms over his chest. "Well, this isn't very fair."

"Whatever do you mean?" I ask.

Mom recorded the score. "Florence, you're only twenty behind."

He threw his hands up. "That! You're not this good."

"What if I am?"

Mom set down her pen and gave me a level look. "Florence, is your ghost friend here?"

Alice rolled her eyes. "Mom, you know she won't talk about it—"

"He is," I interrupted my sister. Maybe it was the glass and a half of Maker's in me, or maybe it was just being in proximity to Ben, feeling like I was safe. In a way I hadn't felt in a very long time.

"*He?*" Carver enunciated.

Alice narrowed her eyes at me. "You're cheating. Tell your *ghostie* friend to stop looking at my hand!"

"It's Ben, preferably," the ghost said.

"He'd rather be called Ben," I told Alice.

"Sure, sure, *Ben*," she said, and—as if sensing Ben moving over behind her—snapped closed her hand and put the cards facedown on the table. "Tell him if he's going to be sitting here looking at our cards, he can at least play with us and let me kick your ass."

"Strong words coming from someone whose highest card is a ten of puppy-toes."

I blinked at him. "You mean clubs?"

"Puppy-toes," he repeated with a shrug.

Alice eyed me suspiciously. "What about clovers?"

"Clovers? It's clubs."

"As I said: clovers."

I ignored her. "He said you've got strong words for someone whose highest card is a ten of *clubs*," I told her, and her eyes widened. She jabbed a finger at me. "Oh that's not fair! Automatic dish duty! *Cheater!*"

Carver pressed his cards against his chest. "Has he seen *my* hand, too?"

"Seriously?" I added, baffled. "Not 'Oh my god, ghosts are real!' Or 'Oh my god, this house is *haunted*!'"

My family shook their heads—even Nicki.

"Xavier did the same thing, sweetie," Mom clarified.

Carver agreed. "How else do you think he always won at those poker games?"

"Can your ghost—Ben, sorry—play spades?" Mom asked.

"I haven't in a while," Ben mused delightfully.

I nodded. "Yeah, he can."

"Good! Because you're terrible, sorry, sweetheart. He can help you—but no more cheating, are we clear?"

"Crystal, Mrs. Day," Ben replied.

"He said"—and I adopted my best Ben impression—"'Crystal, Mrs. Day.'"

"I do *not* sound like that."

"You definitely do," I replied.

Mom laughed. "Tell him to call me Bella. I hate *Mrs. Day*. Nicki, dear, it's your turn."

And that was that. Ben came back around to stand behind me and point at cards, muttering about the probability of my family members having certain hands, and which were safest to play. I always threw down cards as a chaos agent, but he was meticulous and strategic, much like how he kept his office. Sometimes when he leaned over me to point at a card, muttering low and quickly, a shiver would crawl down my spine because I loved the way he talked softly, pinpoints on the edges of his words—

Loved.

Oh.

A few rounds later, we all decided to call it a game. Carver had won, which was no surprise to any of us, and Nicki politely thanked "the ghost" for playing. They left the kitchen, laughing about how I was still saddled with the dishes despite having ghostly help. I could hear them in the living room, talking loudly about the visitors from the wake.

As I pulled in all the cards and shoved them back into their box with the jokers, Mom said to me as she cleaned off the table, "He was always torn, you know, about the gift you shared. He wished you could've chosen instead of being burdened with something you didn't want."

That surprised me. "I never thought about it that way. I always thought . . . it would've been put to better use with someone like Alice or Carver. They're so much better than I am."

"I think you all would have had hills to climb. Alice is hotheaded and Carver is fickle. You give too much of your heart. Like your father." She put the dishes in the sink and turned on the water, waiting for it to warm.

One of my biggest flaws. "What do you think's in the letter that I have to read?"

Mom gave a think. "I'm not sure, actually."

"You've gotta have *some* idea."

"I do," she agreed, "but I'm not sure. Though whatever it is, he wanted you to read it."

"But why? Alice and Carver are *much* better at speaking in front of people!"

"Because he probably felt like you needed to the most," Mom replied, and squeezed Dawn soap over the plates in the sink. "Honestly, you think I understood everything that went on in that man's head? Of course not. He always surprised me. I think he will again. Are you helping this ghost friend of yours?" she added, changing the subject.

"She's doing a wonderful job," Ben commented.

"I'm trying to," I replied, deciding not to dog her about the letter anymore. "He's leaning beside you. Against the counter. To your right—I mean left."

Mom turned to her left and said, "You're welcome here anytime, Ben."

"It would be a treat," Ben remarked, and I bit in a smile because I wondered what Mom would really think of him, so tall his head almost brushed against the top of the doorframe, his dark hair floppy and his eyes bright.

"He says thank you," I translated.

"Good. Now—"

"Dishes!" Carver pointed at me, sticking his head back into the kitchen. "You lost!"

"I did not!" I argued.

"You cheated and you *still* lost! Mom, stop doing the dishes—"

"I got them," Alice interjected, shouldering past Carver.

"But, Alice—"

"Chill. I don't mind. You look tired," my sister added to me, taking the sponge from Mom. "You should probably get some sleep. We'll see you tomorrow."

I hesitated. "But I can do them . . ."

She rolled her eyes. "Fine, we can do it together. Mom, I think Carver wants to go set that wooden cage out to see if he can trap those damn birds, and Nicki's scared shitless of them—"

From the other room, Nicki cried, "I am *not*!" Then, after a moment, he added, "But they *are* terrifying!"

Alice gave Mom a look. "Can you help him so he doesn't hurt himself?"

Mom sighed. "If I must . . ."

"I don't need help!" Carver argued, but Mom took him by the shoulder and guided him out the back door.

Alice and I did the dishes in silence. Ben had left the kitchen, but I didn't know where he'd gone instead. Hopefully to oversee my ridiculous brother, because I had very little faith that Mom would do anything other than nod sagely without really knowing what to do.

I kept *wanting* to say something to Alice—this was the first time we'd really been alone together, not counting Dad's corpse in the mortuary—but nothing sounded right in my head. I used to be so *good* at talking to Alice. We were best friends, with all the inside jokes of sisters who actually got along.

And then we weren't. I didn't really think about how leaving Mairmont would hurt everyone I loved, but especially Alice, and I couldn't get our last fight out of my head. Well, the last *few* fights.

"I'm sorry," I began, "that I never came back."

She almost dropped one of Grammy Day's favorite dishes. "Oh my *god*, warn me before you do that."

"I just apologized!"

"Yeah—I know. *Gross.*"

"Fine," I said, a little hurt because honestly, I *meant* it, and took the plate from her and dried it furiously. "I won't do it again."

"Please don't," she agreed, scrubbing another plate angrily. Then she sighed, and her shoulders unwound. "You're apologizing for the wrong thing, anyway. I don't really blame you for *leaving*."

I blinked. "You don't?"

"I'm not a monster. Leaving was the only thing you really *could* do. And I don't really blame you for not coming to visit, even though I said I did. Dad never asked you to come home. He never asked if we were okay with going to visit you. We just *did*." She sighed and shook her head. "I just . . . for a long time I was just so mad you didn't take me with you. Do you know how many fights I got into over you?"

I actually had to think about that one. "Thirteen?"

"Fourteen! I got into one after you left. You know Mark Erie?"

"The football guy Heather married?"

"Bingo. Cracked his jaw. Had to sip out of a straw for a month," she replied triumphantly. And then she sighed and took a sip of her drink. "And, I guess, after a while I started just being mad *at* you. Because even though you were gone, you were just as tight with Dad as you always were. I was jealous of that. Of you and Dad and y'all's ghosts."

I didn't know what to say—I'd never thought about it that way.

That the one thing that I had run away from was also the one thing I remembered most fondly about Dad—and the one thing that neither Alice nor Carver nor Mom could ever have with him.

"Dad was a good man," she went on, "but he wasn't perfect. He saved that part of him for you. I saw him every day. I got into fights with him. I watched him neglect his health because he thought giving other people their goodbyes was more important than sticking around for *us*. I thought he'd forgotten about us."

"Alice . . ."

"He just forgot about himself. And I couldn't *do* anything." She sniffed, and I stared at her with my mouth open because her eyes were wet, and Alice *never* cried. She didn't cry when she skinned the side of her leg in third grade while trying to skateboard. She didn't cry when she broke her first finger when Carver accidentally slammed the car door on it. She hadn't cried at weddings or funerals or graduations—so I didn't know what to do.

I dropped the towel, torn between hugging her and calling for help. My voice wobbled. "Alice . . ."

Because she was about to make *me* cry, too.

She wiped her eyes with the back of her hand. "Maybe if you were here instead—"

"Don't," I cut her off. "Don't finish that."

"But it's—"

"*Not true*," I stressed, mortified that she'd ever think that. "Dad not going to the doctor was Dad's fault, not yours. It never will be yours."

She looked at me, and her eyes were rimmed red, and her bottom lip trembled. "I couldn't protect him," she sobbed.

"I c-couldn't either, Al."

We pulled each other into a tight hug, and cried it out on each other's shoulders. It was cathartic in a way that nothing else had been this entire week. I kept holding all of the pain in, and I couldn't imagine how Alice felt this whole time. I should have asked her. I should have wondered if she was okay because none of us were.

But we would be.

After a moment, she squirmed out of my hug and pushed the remaining tears out of her eyes. "I can finish the dishes alone."

"You won't hold the dishes against me?" I asked suspiciously, wiping my own eyes.

"Obviously I will," she replied with a laugh, telling me that she was going to be okay and needed some space, and shooed me away.

I grabbed my coat from the rack and slipped it on as I caught a glimmer of Ben sitting on the floral couch in the living room. He was relaxed out on it, his eyes closed, one leg crossed over the other, his arms softly folded over his chest, almost as if he was asleep. Over the past few days, he had slowly unwound in front of me, first his hair becoming disheveled, his shirtsleeves rolled up, his trousers cuffed, his tie lost somewhere in the netherworld between Friday night and here, and now—ever so slightly—there was the shadow of a beard crossing the strong angles of his chin. I'd never seen a ghost change before. They were immovable. Stagnant. Then again, I had never paid close attention, either.

He cracked open an eye. "Ready to go?"

My heart twisted. It felt so familiar in the weirdest way. As if in some other universe he was here, real, *alive*, sitting on the couch, waiting for my sister and me to finish the dishes so we could go home.

Perhaps in another life.

I nodded. "Yeah."

He stood and came over to the foyer as I put on my shoes, and we left together down the front steps to the sidewalk. "Walk you home?" he offered.

"Oh, how gentlemanly of you."

"I am occasionally."

It was nice, walking beside him back up the street to the inn. He asked about my sister, and if we were okay, without ever prodding, and I told him about our conversation. I didn't know Alice had been hurting so terribly, and her hurting made me want to punch whoever made her hurt. But in this case, it was Dad. And me, to some extent. I knew that Alice didn't *like* me leaving, but I didn't think . . .

I just didn't think.

"It's okay, at least you talked," he said gently.

"Yeah."

Lee never escorted me home until we lived together, and even then sometimes I would duck out of his publishing functions early and take the train home alone. I always said to myself it was because I never wanted to *bother* him while he made connections, but the truth was I usually felt like an unwanted purse, standing quietly beside him as he talked to executive editors and poets laureate and god knows who else, feeling like an outsider even in an industry I was very much a part of.

Even if only secretly.

I wrapped my coat around myself tightly. Ben glanced over at me, frowning. "Are you okay?"

"Fine," I muttered. "Just . . . exhausted."

"This is exhausting," he agreed softly. "All of it. Pretending to be okay while the world changes around you and leaves you behind to sit with whatever loss you found."

It did feel exactly like that. "But you got through it, so I think I can, too."

"I know you can. You're braver than I could ever be. I couldn't do what you do. Helping ghosts like me move on. You have to say goodbye so often."

"It's different with them—erm, you—because I *get* to say goodbye. The last thing I said to Dad was . . ." I hesitated, trying to remember my conversation with him. Friday felt like so long ago, and the conversation was already a blur. Had I told him I loved him? I knew I did, but I kept second-guessing it. What if I hadn't that once?

I couldn't remember.

I blinked the tears out of my eyes and cleared my throat. "*Anyway*, I appreciate your help during the card game."

He snorted a laugh. "Well, you do suck at spades."

"I do *not*!"

"Oh you absolutely do." He cocked his head, and a curl of black hair fell across his forehead. "But you know, that's kind of what I like about you."

"*That's* what you like about me? I thought it was my perfect breasts?"

The tips of his ears went pink, and he quickly looked away. "Yes, well, they're not why I like *you*. They're a bonus. Like a book sale. Buy two, get one free."

I chewed on the side of my cheek, trying to hide a smile. "And that's what I like about you."

"My broad and very perfect chest?"

"It is very broad," I agreed, and he laughed. It was soft and throaty, and I really liked it.

The last crisps of winter clung to the chilly evening air as a spring wind blew its way through the budding oaks and dogwood trees, and I felt the itch in my fingers to write this all down. To paint the sky in dark blues and purples and silvers and paint the sidewalk in shards of glittery glass, and wax about how it felt to walk quietly beside someone who enjoyed your company just as much as you did theirs.

I couldn't believe that I was swooning over the bare minimum—*decency*.

Dana was at the counter when we came into the inn, and they smiled at me over another romance novel. This time Christina Lauren. "Evening, Florence."

"Good night, Dana!" I greeted.

Ben walked me up the stairs to my room at the end of the hallway, where he stood and waited as I fished my room key out of my purse. "Your family is really cool."

"Oh, you saw them on a good night."

"I've seen them every day this week while dealing with the worst," he reminded.

I winced. "True. Imagine us during *weddings*. We're a riot."

"I'd love to see that," he replied with a soft sadness. Because the chances were, he wouldn't. I'd finish Ann's book and release him from this weird half-life before any of that happened.

Trying not to think too much about it, I found my key card at the bottom of my purse and waved it over the lock. "Honestly, it's not *that* special—Ben?"

He'd gone pale, suddenly, and caught himself against the side of the wall to keep from falling. I dropped my key and reached for him, but my hands passed through his arm.

"Ben—Ben are you okay?"

"Do you hear that?" he asked. His eyes had gone glassy.

"I—I don't hear anything."

"It sounds like—like—" But then he winced. The lamp on the table began to rattle.

Dana called from downstairs, "Florence? Is everything okay?"

"Fine," I called back, hoping they didn't come up the stairs to see the portraits slowly sliding wonky on the walls. I shoved open my door. "Inside, please," I whispered, and he nodded and slipped through the wall into my bedroom.

Well, that was one way to do it.

I got inside and closed the door. The lamp outside stopped rattling. "Please, sit. I'm worried."

He was holding his chest, shaking his head. "I'm fine."

"You are *not*."

He pursed his lips, about to rebuke me, but he must have thought better of it and eased himself down on the bed. He swayed gently. Did he look fainter than usual? Paler? I couldn't decide—though I did know that I was frightened enough that it killed my buzz.

"You're not fine," I decided. "What's wrong?"

"Nothing," he replied, rubbing his face with his hands. "It's nothing."

"It's not *nothing*—"

"I'm dead so why does it matter?" he said, and his voice was gruff and thick. "I'm dead and every time I disappear I come back a little less. I'm dead and I can still hear my heart beating in my ears, fainter and fainter. I'm dead and gone and I'm here and it's not the book—it can't be the book, Florence."

"Of course it is."

"I don't want it to be. Because when you finish it . . ."

My heart jumped into my throat. "You're just tired. You can stay here and rest all you want. I'm going to wash my face, okay? I'll be back." And as I left for the bathroom, I thought I felt a chill of cold brush through my wrist, but I ignored it because if I didn't, I was afraid we would start dancing on a tightrope, and the ground was too far down.

I took a long time in the bathroom. Too long. I didn't know if I wanted him gone by the time I got out, or if I wanted him to still be there sitting on the side of my bed. No, I did know what I wanted, but I was afraid.

I wanted him to stay.

"Ben—" My voice caught in my throat as I left the bathroom, and found him lying on the bed, turned onto his side. He was so long that his feet almost reached the end. He was still—of course he was, he was dead—but it unnerved me until I crawled gently under the covers on the other side.

His eyes fluttered open. "Mmh, I'll get up—"

"Stay," I said.

"You're very bossy. It's cute."

"And you're stubborn." Then, quieter: "Please."

He put his head back on the pillow. "On one condition."

"What?"

"Tell me to stay again."

I scooted closer to him, so close that if we were alive, our breaths would mingle and our knees would knock together and I could pull my fingers through his hair. I said softly, a secret and a prayer, "Stay."

30

....

Strange Bedfellows

MORNING LIGHT POURED in between the violet curtains as I woke up, and I rolled over to check my phone. Eight thirty. Thursday, April 13. Today was my dad's funeral. I hugged a pillow tightly to my chest, and buried my face into it—when I remembered Ben.

He was lying beside me, eyes closed, still as stone. Ghosts didn't breathe, and they didn't sleep, either, but there were the beginnings of dark circles under his eyes. There was a bit of stubble on his cheeks, too, and I thoughtlessly reached to touch it when he opened his eyes.

I retracted my hand quickly. A blush crept up my face. "You're awake—sorry. Of course you are, you don't sleep. Good morning."

"Good morning," he replied softly. "Sleep well?"

I nodded, and hugged the pillow to my chest tighter. "I don't want to go today."

"I know. I'll be there."

"Promise?"

He nodded. "Though I don't know how much it'll help."

"More than you think," I replied, pressing my mouth into the pillow, my words muffled. He looked doubtful, so I pushed the pillow down and added, "I don't feel so sharp or raw with you around. I feel . . . okay. I haven't felt that in so long—like I don't need to put on any masks for you. I don't have to pretend to be cool or cute or—or *normal*."

His eyes softened. "I like being around you, too."

"Because I'm the only one who can see you."

"Yes," he replied, and my heart began to sink into my chest, until he added, "but not because I'm a ghost, Florence." Then he reached to brush a strand of hair out of my face. When his fingertips passed through my cheek, it felt like a bloom of cold. I shivered—I couldn't help myself. He retracted his hand, his lips pursed together. "I'm sorry."

I shook my head. "I'm the one who should be sorry. I haven't finished that manuscript. I don't know when I will. I—I feel like I just keep failing you."

"There's more to life than work, and you are grieving for your dad right now. Asking you to do that . . . no. I don't expect you to kill yourself trying to finish it."

"Says the workaholic."

"I wish I wasn't. I wish I'd taken a vacation—done *something*." He rolled onto his back, and stared at the popcorn ceiling. He swallowed hard, and his Adam's apple bobbed in trepidation. "I wish . . . I had closed my office door after you walked in and kissed you until you saw stars."

I let out a squeak. "You do *not*!"

"Oh yes I do," he replied. "I would've asked first."

I could imagine that, in some alternate timeline. Where he stood, and shut the door behind me, and knelt down beside where

I sat, clutching a cactus, and asked me in this exact soft, growling voice—"May I kiss you, Florence Day?"

And I would've said yes.

I shook my head fervently. "No—no *way*. I—I had unwashed hair! And I wore my Goodwill tweed coat! And my scarf had *coffee stains* on it!"

"And you were sexy as hell. But you couldn't meet my gaze," he said with a laugh. "I thought you hated me."

"Hated you? Ben." I pushed myself up onto my elbow to look him in the eyes, and said very seriously, "I wanted to climb you."

He barked a laugh, loud and bright. "Climb me!"

"Like a goddamn tree," I moaned regretfully. *Let me die of mortification here*, I thought. At least then I wouldn't have to attend the graveside service today. "I couldn't look at you because I was having a minor crisis in my head *over* you. I mean—here you were, this gorgeous new editor, and I had to do the one thing that no author in the *history* of books wants to do: admit that I hadn't finished the novel."

"To be fair, I *did* know that the ghostwriter would be coming to meet me," he pointed out as I rolled over to the edge of the bed and pushed myself to sit up. He followed me with his eyes as I went over to my suitcase and began digging through it for today's clothes. "A woman named Florence Day."

"And there I was showing up with a cactus."

"Which you promptly told me to stick up my ass, basically, when you left."

"I know, I feel bad about that. It was a good cactus." I cocked my head. "I don't remember you at many publishing functions, though. Didn't you go to any?"

"Not many, but I *did* go to the publisher of Faux's party for the release of *Dante's Motorbike*."

I picked my dress out of the suitcase and froze. "Wait—a few years ago?"

"Yeah. You had on those heels with the red bottoms? You couldn't walk in them to save your life."

"Louboutins," I corrected absently, hanging the outfit over me as I judged whether I needed tights or knee-highs, but my mind was years away—back in that cramped private library, feet throbbing from those shoes. "You were there? That was the party where I met . . ."

Lee.

He nodded at the unspoken name, his hand absently going to the ring around his neck. He rubbed at it thoughtfully. "You were in the library and I can't remember how many times I told myself to just go over there. To talk to you. This stranger whose name I didn't even know."

"A novel idea."

"For *me*, it was. But I'd just met Laura, too, and I'm nothing if not torturously monogamous. And then . . . the moment was gone. Lee walked up to you, and that was it."

To think, he had been there since the beginning. We had passed each other like ships at sea and I never knew. All of my heartache could have been circumvented—all of his pain could have been mended. What kind of people would we have been if he had found me in that library? Or if I had mingled with Rose and found him instead?

"I wish we had met instead," I whispered.

"I would've been terrible for you," he replied, shaking his head. His voice was softer, closer. He'd gotten out of bed and came around toward me. I watched him in the mirror, and his eyes were trained on the carpet. He couldn't meet mine. "I would've been terrible for everyone. I was terrible for myself."

"Laura cheating on you wasn't your fault."

He didn't respond.

"It wasn't. It was hers. You told me that after that you felt like she deserved better. Someone who would keep her from cheating but—you're wrong." I took a deep breath because this was something I had to come to understand, too. That worth wasn't dependent on someone else's love for you, or your usefulness, or what you could do for them. "It's not her who deserves better. It's *you*, Ben."

He swallowed thickly. "How come when I told myself the same thing a thousand times I didn't believe me, but when you say it, it feels true?"

"Because I'm rarely wrong."

"You did say romance was dead."

I tilted my head, looking at his reflection in the mirror. "Aren't you?"

He chuckled, and finally looked up again, and his eyes were a warm, melted ocher. Like in the dandelion field. "I don't think this is what you meant," he replied, his voice soft and gravelly, and I realized how badly I was burning up on the inside. I wanted him to touch me, to run his fingers across my skin. I wanted his face in the crook of my neck, his lips pressed against the freckled skin there. I wanted to fold myself into his sharp angles and stay there. Exist there. Because there—*there* I was sure I wouldn't fall apart, I wouldn't disassemble, I wouldn't feel broken.

Not because I couldn't exist on my own, but sometimes I just didn't want to.

Sometimes I just wanted to let my guard down, let the pieces of me fall to the ground, and know that I had someone there who could put me back together without minding the sharp bits.

"Though dead is what you make of it," he mumbled, his dark gaze almost feverish, if he weren't so polite. "There are so many things we can do. We can talk books, we can wax about the romantics—Lord Byron and Keats and Shelley—"

"Mary or Percy?"

"Mary, obviously."

"The only choice," I agreed.

He laughed. "And I want to complain about all the youths and their TikToks and sit on park benches together making up stories and go for walks in graveyards at midnight."

"I feel like we've done a few of these . . ."

"But I could never touch you."

"I'd be okay with that."

"No one else will ever see me."

"That means you'd be all mine."

He sighed and sat back on the edge of the bed. Morning sunlight slanted in such a way, it carved a stark golden shine across him. "That sounds awfully similar to the plot of *The Forever House.*"

"One of Ann's best."

"And it's the only one without a happily ever after."

I gave him a strange look. "What do you mean?" I asked as I gathered up my clothes and went into the bathroom to change. I left the door cracked. "They got together in the end!"

"You think so?"

"Of course. She moves into the house and then the doorbell rings. Of course it's *him.*"

"Come back from the dead?"

"Stranger things happened in that novel," I pointed out, and through the crack in the door I watched him think back on the time travel and the maybe–maybe *not* werewolf neighbor.

Finally, he said, "Fair. How'd you come to start ghostwriting for Annie?"

"Why do you keep calling her Annie?" I shimmied into my

hose—the knee-highs weren't going to cut it—and tucked my white blouse into the skirt.

"A habit, I guess," he replied in that aloof way that very much sounded like bullshit, but I didn't press it. Maybe it was a weird editor thing. "Did she contact you?"

"No, actually. Well, sort of. I met her in a coffee shop about five years ago. You know, the one on Eighty-Fifth and Park?"

"Oh, they've got great scones."

"Right? Totally the best. Anyway, it was empty, and I'd just broken up with my agent after my publisher dumped me, so I was writing some saucy smut—"

"Noted, you write sex scenes when you're depressed."

"Just some good foreplay. Very titillating stuff. *Anyway*, she sat down at my table and critiqued what I was writing. She'd been reading over my shoulder, apparently, and I asked her what the hell and that was that. She critiqued my work and then asked if I wanted a job."

"Five years ago?" he asked, perplexed.

"Yeah." I tugged on my skirt, and zipped it up in the back. "Why?"

"Because I was—what the hell could you have been writing to attract her?" he asked, though I got the feeling that he wanted to ask something else.

I poked my head out of the bathroom. "Guess."

"Had to be something off the cuff. Alien barbarian erotica?"

"No, but I'd read that."

"Omegaverse?"

"*Anyway*," I said loudly, pulling my hair back into a bun, and left the bathroom. "She gave me pointers on a confession scene. She said that people usually weren't overly eloquent, and grand romantic gestures are obtuse and obsolete because they're too corny. I argued the opposite—that people like grand romantic gestures because they *are* corny. Because people need more corny in their lives. Like this"—I outstretched my arms to encompass the room, this moment—"is corny. All of it. Right down to how much I want to touch you, and how I can't."

"And do tell, how much do you want to touch me?"

"You're terrible."

"You brought it up! And I would point out that this scene is not so much corny as rife with romantic tension. If it's corny, then perhaps you're writing it wrong."

"Oh, then tell me, how would you write this scene, maestro?"

"Well, first off," he began, and turned his dark eyes to me, "I would ask you what you wanted."

"Ooh, consent. That's sexy."

"Very," he murmured in agreement, his voice low and gravelly. He stood and stepped close to me. The hairs on the back of my neck stood on end. "Skip the banter, shelve the soul-searching. It's morning, and the sunlight is glorious on your hair, and you are exquisitely stubborn. You'd never tell me what you'd want."

"Ha! Go on." I tried to keep my voice level. "Then what do I want?"

He came up behind me, outstretching his arms, hovering over my skin as he traced the contour of my hips to my middle. "I have an inkling that you would like me to reach my hand beneath your pretty lace underwear," he whispered, his lips pressed close to my ear, "and stroke you slow. And while I did, I would kiss your neck and nibble at your ear."

I felt myself flush, my heart beating in my throat as quick as a rabbit. I held my breath as he bent closer still, closer than he'd ever been, never touching, his fingers painting over me like a sculptor's, relishing in my design.

"And then?" My voice was tight. Controlled.

I'd written more intense scenes than this. This was nothing.

Then why was *this* getting me all hot and bothered?

It was the look in his eyes, that dark glimmer. The promise that he would do exactly what he was telling me. For a man who liked his lists, and liked his order—that was powerful.

His mouth hovered beside my ear. "Romance isn't a sprint, Florence. It's a marathon. You start slow. With your blouse, one button at a time. You said I was meticulous, but I would show you just how meticulous I could be." His fingers mimed undoing the buttons of my blouse. "For each button, I'd plant another kiss on your neck, your collarbone, and finally your perfect breasts . . ."

"You really are a boob guy, aren't you?"

"They're nice," was his response.

"Yes, but I see one problem here," I said, perhaps a little too loudly because this was getting—I was getting—right, yep, a problem. "There is very little pleasing *you* in this scenario."

The edge of his lips twitched. "Oh, who's to say it isn't for me, too? I am quite the selfish man when it comes down to it—"

"So, getting me off gets *you* off?"

"Why's it about me at all? Why not just you? You are worthy of that."

I swallowed the rock lodged in my throat. I was? Worthy of that kind of undivided attention? Because I never felt that way with Lee, not even as he kissed me and told me what to do, where to plant my lips.

"God," I half laughed, "you really do read too many romance novels."

He chuckled. "I wouldn't call that a fault. Would you?"

"Depends. Where would this scene go?"

"I would ask you—"

I took a deep breath. "Then ask me."

In the mirror, his eyes found mine. They were sharp, considering, thinking. He said this was for my pleasure, but I was terrible at being selfish. I could see it in the glint of his eyes, the swallow of his throat. He wanted nothing more—for how long? Since he first saw me? Before I ever knew his name?

I heard him take in a shaky breath. Then, "Unbutton your shirt. Slowly."

My fingers slid down my wrinkled business shirt, undoing the buttons one by one, until they were all undone and the shirt hung loose over my bra. I relaxed my shoulders, and the shirt dropped down, puddling around my elbows, exposing what he very much considered to be very good breasts in my very best lace bra. "Like this?"

He made an agreeable noise. "You are perfect."

"Am I?"

"Do I need to repeat myself?"

"As often as I deem necessary."

His fingers twitched, and he curled them tightly into fists. "You are perfect," he said again. "I like admiring the view." Then, "Close your eyes."

I did.

"Imagine the scene. I would pull my fingers through your hair; I would rake my teeth across your skin—I would undo that pretty lace bra of yours and caress your nipples with my tongue. I would slip a finger inside of you—two, and you would be so wet and I would pleasure you so slowly, as slow as you wanted—"

"I would drive you crazy," I commented.

"*Florence*, you already do."

I laughed, and opened my eyes, only to find his hands over mine. I turned around, and finally looked at him—truly—for the first time, and pulled my shirt back up onto my shoulders. "It'd be a good scene," I said, and my voice broke a little, my fingers buttoning my shirt back up. "Corny, but in a good way."

"I like corny," he agreed, his gaze lingering on my lips.

My alarm went off, making both of us jump. I quickly stepped away from him and hurried across the room to turn off my phone. And reality crashed back in, because today was my father's funeral, and I still had two things to check off his will. "I—I'm sorry. I have to finish getting dressed. So much to do. So little time."

"Can I help?"

I tilted my head, and smiled. "No, you just being here is enough."

"Can I, then?" he asked, sitting up a little straighter, his hands curling into nervous fists. "Can I stay? Like this—with you?"

My heart leapt into my throat. *But what about Ann's last book?* I thought, but I didn't want to voice it. I didn't want him to change his mind because—"I'd like that."

Because people always left. If they had a choice—they left.

And Ben wanted to stay.

I cleared my throat, tucking my shirt back into my skirt. "I better hurry up. Dad won't bury himself," I added, and went back into the bathroom to brush my teeth, but my blood rushed with the thought of all the corny moments I could have with Benji Andor. Even though he was dead.

It didn't mean he was gone.

31

Bring Out Your Dead

ACCORDING TO MOM'S text, we were all going to meet at the funeral home before walking over to the cemetery. And I, in true Florence Day fashion, was miserably late. My siblings were already outside, about to leave for the cemetery.

"Sorry, sorry!" I cried, hurrying up the stone path to the porch. "I lost track of time."

"We figured," Carver replied. "The flowers are already at the gravesite. A few guys came by to take them there this morning."

"And Elvis has the program list," Alice added. "We gave him the list of songs you left last night. Almost couldn't read them because of your chicken-scratch handwriting, but Dad's handwriting was just as bad."

List of songs . . . ? I put the question away for later. "Thank you, guys. And the crows?" I asked Carver hopefully.

He sighed and hefted up the empty cherrywood birdcage. "Yeah, didn't catch a single fucker."

"I told you to use your Rolex."

He gasped, stricken. "Never!"

Though I figured the murder didn't leave the rooftop of the inn last night, since Ben hadn't left, either. That was . . . just slightly my fault. Not that I'd admit it. Alice cocked her head and looked up into the old willow tree. Beneath it, Ben was standing with his hands in his pockets. He looked up, too. She nudged her head toward the murder of crows perched in the tree. "Do you mean those bastards?"

"Imagine that," Mom said. "You know, your father used to say they only showed up when—"

"Ben's under the tree," I supplied.

"Well that's our lucky break," Carver said. "Do you think we have to catch them?"

"Nah, they'll follow," I replied, and gave Ben a wink. He rolled his eyes. I told my family to go ahead without me, that I'd catch up in a moment. I still had to put on my makeup, and I wanted to do one last round through the house. I waited until they were down the street before I climbed the steps to the funeral home, and peeked inside.

I took a deep breath. "Dad?"

My voice echoed through the building. I waited patiently, but there wasn't a reply.

"I know you're here. I didn't leave Alice any song list." I paused. "But you did."

The house creaked in reply.

"Everything dies, buttercup," he once said as we sat on the front porch, watching a storm roll in. Carver was toddling in his play pool, and Alice was gurgling on his knee. "That's a fact. But you wanna know a secret?"

And I had leaned in, so sure it was a cure for death, a way to bat it away—

"Everything that dies never really goes. In little ways, it all stays."

Not in the horrific way Lee wrote it. Not with moaning ghosts and terrifying poltergeists and living dead, but in the way the sun came back around again, the way flowers browned and became dirt and new seeds bloomed the next spring. Everything died, but pieces of it remained. Dad was in the wind because he breathed the same air that I breathed. Dad was a mark in history because he existed. He was part of my future because I still carried on.

I carried him with me. This house carried him.

This town.

"Florence?" Ben asked timidly. "Are you okay?"

I squeezed my eyes shut, willing the tears to stay back. I was going to cry enough today. I didn't want to start early. "Yeah. We should probably bring the crows over."

"At least I'm useful for something."

"That's why I keep you around," I teased—and he suddenly pitched forward. "Ben!" I cried.

He caught himself on the doorframe. Shook his head. "Sorry—I—dizzy," he muttered. His hands were shaking, and his skin had dropped to that pale, sickly tone from last night.

A knot formed in my throat. "You're not okay."

"No," he replied truthfully, "I don't think I am."

The doorbell rang.

Ben and I exchanged a look.

It rang again.

My heart fluttered. The last time I answered the doorbell, it was Ben. Perhaps this time . . . maybe this time . . . I hurried to the front door, almost crashed against it, and flung it open—

"Rose?"

My best friend stood on the doormat to the Days Gone Funeral

Home, a duffel bag in tow. She flipped down her Ray-Bans in awe. "Holy *shit*, bitch! You didn't tell me you lived in the Addams Family house!"

"*Rose!*" I threw my arms around her and hugged her tightly. "I didn't know you were coming!"

"Of *course* I was. I know you can handle it alone, but—you don't have to." She took me by the face and pressed our foreheads together. "You're my little spoon."

"You never cease to make it weird."

"*Never.* Now where's your bathroom? I have to piss like a racehorse and have to change into my Louboutins."

"It's an outside funeral, Rose."

She gave me a blank look.

"Never mind, c'mon." I let her into the house. She dumped her duffel bag into my arms and sprinted to the half bath under the stairs. I put her luggage in the office, where it'd be safe while we were at the funeral, and went to check on Ben in the hall. He was sitting on the bottom steps, his head in his hands.

"Hey," I said quietly, giving a knock on the doorframe. "Is everything okay?"

"Mmn, no. A little? I'm . . . not sure. I keep hearing things," he said. "It was quiet at first—but now it's so loud."

"What kinds of things?"

"Talking. Voices. Sounds—"

The toilet flushed and Rose stepped out of the bathroom in her red-soled high heels, the same ones that I wore years ago to that horrible *Dante's Motorbike* book launch, and grabbed me under the arm. "Are you ready to say goodbye to the old man?"

I hesitated with a look at Ben, but he smiled at me to give me some comfort and promised, "I'll see you there."

She jostled my arm. "Florence?"

I squeezed her hand tightly. "Yes. Let's."

Rose was my copilot. My rock. My impulsive, wonderful best friend.

And I was so, so glad that she was here.

32

It's a Death!

THE CEMETERY WAS peaceful, and the grass looked like a watercolor painting against the pale shale of the tombstones. They stuck out like jagged bottom teeth, some crooked, most cleaned. As we passed some of the darker, mold-grown stones, I made a mental note to come back and scrub them pretty again—and then stopped myself.

I wasn't here to work. I was here to mourn.

Though I was sure Dad would have done the same.

Almost the entire town came out, with lawn chairs and picnic snacks. The wildflowers they had donated—all one thousand of them, arranged by color—sat stacked around Dad's casket like a mountain of petals, as Elvistoo crooned "Suspicious Minds" from his portable karaoke machine.

And—perhaps best of all were—

"Oh my god, those *balloons*," Rose gasped. "Does it—does that actually say . . ."

I couldn't help but smile. "Yeah, they do."

Unlimited Party had delivered—and decorated—the funeral home lawn, tying balloons to the backs of chairs and hanging streamers from the oak trees that read IT'S A DEATH! and HAPPY DEATH DAY! They had also passed out party hats and kazoos, and some of the town kids were playing "The Imperial March" near a statue of a crying angel.

Rose and I joined my family in the front row of chairs that had been set out, and it looked like Alice was nursing a migraine.

Carver said regretfully, "The balloons got her. She almost had a stroke, she was so livid," while Alice, poor Alice, was muttering, "I'm going to kill him. I'm going to *kill* him—"

"Al, he's already dead."

I introduced Rose to my family. Whenever they'd come for Christmas, Rose had gone home to Indiana, always missing each other by mere hours at the airport. But finally, now, they got to meet. Mom leaned over Alice to shake Rose's hand. "Pleasure, though I'm sorry it's under these circumstances."

"I'm sorry for your loss," Rose replied.

"Did he have to order the *balloons*?" Alice wailed, and Nicki patted her on the shoulder comfortingly and asked Rose how her flight was.

I scanned the crowd for Ben, but I didn't see him. Had he disappeared again? I hoped he was okay. One by one, the crows landed in the nearby oak tree and quietly ruffled their feathers against the wind. So he had to be here somewhere. That gave me some relief.

After a few minutes, Elvistoo's rousing rendition of "Return to Sender" interrupted my thoughts, and I glanced down at the set list.

"You're up," Carver whispered.

Right.

Dad, in his will, said he didn't want a preacher or a bishop or any sort of holy person. We weren't really the organized-religion kind of family, even though we dealt in death. All he said by way of a speaker was the letter he wrote.

I took it from Karen, Dad's lawyer. The paper was soft and crinkly. "It's showtime."

Alice looked worried. "Florence . . ."

"I can do it. Really."

"You don't have to do all of this alone—"

"I'm not," I interrupted gently. "Because I want everyone up there with me. If that's okay."

The tension that had coiled Alice's shoulders a moment before unwound, and she agreed. Carver bumped against me gently, giving me a little nod. I took Mom's hand, and she took Alice's, and Alice took Carver's, and we made our way to the space in front of Dad's casket. Elvistoo handed me the microphone.

I always went about everything on my own. I thought I could solve everything myself—though I guess I never really had to. I had family, and I had friends, and I had parents who loved me and would always love me until the end of time and—

And there were people out there, too, that I didn't know and wanted to, like Ben, who saw me for all my chaotic flaws and my stubbornness and still wanted to stay.

He wanted to stay.

I wanted him to stay, too.

I cleared my throat, and looked out over the cemetery, and all of the people who had come with their lawn chairs, wearing party hats and telling the kids to shush on their kazoos. "Hi, everyone. Thank you for coming. This is going to be a different kind of funeral than you're used to—though I think if you know my dad, you're already expecting that." I opened the envelope, and took out the letter. "Dad gave me a letter to read to you. I don't know what the contents are, so let's find out together."

My hands were shaking as I unfolded the piece of yellow stationery. Dad's handwriting unfurled like a story. He must've written in the quill I gave him for his birthday a few years ago, because of the ink stains and the way the letters bled together.

"'My dearest darlings,'" I began, my voice already shaking.

What the letter said didn't really matter. It was an explanation of why he asked us to go through so much for his funeral. It was an apology for not being able to stay longer. It was a goodbye filled with horrible puns and the worst dad jokes imaginable.

It was a letter addressed to me. To Alice. To Carver. To Mom.

It was a soft goodbye.

Wildflowers for Isabella. A thousand flowers with ten-thousand petals for every day he would love her to eternity. Songs we danced to in the parlors, soft and good and bright goodbyes. Banners and kazoos and party hats for all of the birthdays that he would never get to attend. A murder of crows, to remind us to look for him still. Because he would be here.

Always.

And for me to read this letter—because he knew I would try to do these impossible tasks alone.

Carver covered up a laugh, and Alice elbowed him in the side.

He hoped I asked for help because asking was not a weakness—but a strength. He hoped that I would ask more often, because I would be surprised by who would come into my life if I let them.

Not all of my companions would be ghosts.

I wish I could say that at that moment wind rustled through the trees. I wish I could say that I heard my dad in the wind, telling me those words himself, but the afternoon was quiet, and the black birds in the oak tree cawed to one another as if I had made a particularly funny joke.

And Ben stood at the back of the crowd, his hands in his pockets, and I felt a safe sort of certainty that everything was going to be okay.

Maybe not right now. Not for a while.

But it would be—eventually.

Not all of my companions would be ghosts, but it was okay if some of them were.

Because Dad was right, in the end, about love. It was loyal, and stubborn, and hopeful. It was a brother calling before a funeral to ask how the latest book was going. It was a sister scolding her older sister for always running away. It was a little girl on a stormy night tucked into the lap of an undertaker, listening to the sound of the wind through the creaky Victorian house. It was a ballroom dancer spinning around in an empty parlor with the ghost of her husband and a song in her throat. It was petting good dogs, and quiet mornings waking up beside a man with impossibly dark eyes and a voice with the syrupy sweetness of third-shelf vodka. It was a best friend flying in from New York on a moment's notice.

It was life, wild and finite.

It was a few simple words, written in a loopy longhand.

"'Love is a celebration,'" I read, my voice wobbling, "'of life and death. It stays with you. It lingers, my darlings, long after I'm gone. Listen for me when the wind rushes through the trees. I love you.'"

I folded the letter back up and whispered softly, privately, one final time, "Goodbye, Dad."

33

The Last Goodbye

"AND NOW, ELVISTOO take it away," I said, voice cracking, and handed the microphone back to the man dressed in white.

As soon as Bruno introduced himself again and starting to sing "Love Me Tender," Alice and Carver and Mom embraced me, threading our arms together in a hug. I loved them so much, I started crying—or maybe I was already crying? I couldn't remember when I started, and I couldn't remember when they started crying, either, but we hugged each other as tightly as we could. Because there was a secret about all the Days—we cried whenever we saw someone else crying. So if one Day cried? All the others followed, and at that moment I wasn't sure if I'd started it, or Carver, or Mom (definitely not Alice, never Alice), but it didn't matter.

"You're t-terrible at speeches," Alice said after a while, wiping the tears out of her eyes. Her eyeliner smeared, and I cleaned it up with my thumb.

"I know," I replied.

Carver took a breath. "I think I'm going to propose. To Nicki."

Mom gasped, "Oh, darling! I'm so happy!"

"Here?" Alice asked, flabbergasted.

"No—course not! But soon."

"Good, because I could imagine Alice doing it here, but not you," I remarked, earning a pinch from Alice. "Ow! Hey! That was a *compliment*!"

Alice stuck out her tongue. "I don't even *have* a partner."

"Doesn't mean you won't forever," Mom said sagely, dabbing her running mascara. "Love comes when you least expect it. Why, when your father and I first met . . ."

I glanced over to Ben, on the far side of the funeral, with the good mayor happily keeping him company, as Mom recounted when she first met Dad at a conference that was one-third furry con, one-third ballroom-dancing championships, and one-third mortuary seminar. It was a good story, but we'd heard it a thousand times.

We could hear it a thousand times more.

I couldn't tell those kinds of stories about Ben. Half of the people wouldn't believe me, and the other half would think it was a tragedy. Maybe it was. Dad said I wouldn't keep ghosts as companions my whole life—but what if there was one I wanted to keep?

What if one was different?

Ben must have felt me staring, because he turned his dark eyes to me, and mouthed, "You did great."

And I couldn't help but smile.

"Oh, she sees her ghost boyfriend again," Alice mock whispered to Carver.

My shoulders squared. "He's *not* my boyfriend!"

"Mm-hmm," Carver replied skeptically. "Oh, come on, you were basically over the moon for whoever helped you cheat last night."

"I wish I could see him," Mom mused.

"I still wish it'd been Dad—no offense to your ghost guy," Alice added with a half-hearted shrug. "But I realized you probably wouldn't have kept that a secret."

"Yeah, no. I haven't seen him," I confirmed a little sadly. My siblings exchanged the same look—before I took them by their hands and squeezed them tightly. "He knew we'd have each other. He didn't need to stick around."

Alice tugged her hand out of mine. "Ugh, this is getting too mushy for me. Go get your ghost boyfriend or whatever."

"He's not my . . ." But just as I began to argue, my siblings split for opposite ends of the funeral to talk with other people, and Mom wiggled her eyebrows before she joined the small group of people moving back and forth to Elvistoo's rousing rendition of "Build Me Up Buttercup."

Ben stood and tilted his head toward the far side of the cemetery, where we sat a few nights ago, and as I thanked the people for coming and accepted their condolences, he patiently waited under the oak tree.

"The flowers are beautiful," I told Heather, who agreed in that *I told you so* way of hers, and I found that I really didn't care. She came through for me when I needed it most, and that counted for something. Not everything—I could forgive her, but I wasn't going to forget how she made me feel in high school.

But she wasn't worth any more of my time, either.

I didn't manage to make my way over to the bench until Elvistoo was on his second glass of champagne and had devolved into singing anything the crowd shouted, so he was currently howling through "Welcome to the Black Parade."

"I can honestly say I've never been to a funeral this fun," Ben said when I finally sat down beside him. "People are *literally* dancing on graves."

"Well, *around* graves. It'd be disrespectful to dance *on* them," I corrected, and noticed that his hands were white-knuckled fists on his knees. "Are you still hearing them? The voices?"

He nodded. "They're louder. And it's—getting harder. To stay here."

A chill crept over my skin. "But I haven't worked at all on the book! You shouldn't be *going* anywhere," I replied in alarm.

To which he swallowed thickly. Pursed his lips. And admitted, "I don't think it's about the manuscript, darling."

"It *has* to be. That's the only reason you would be here, haunting me, and—"

"It's not," he interrupted resolutely, and winced in pain.

I narrowed my eyes at him. "Why? What haven't you told me?"

He shook his head. He hadn't been able to meet my gaze since I came over to the bench. Why was I just noticing this? He couldn't meet my gaze because he knew I'd see the truth if he did. "I . . ."

"Ben."

He clenched his jaw.

"Benji."

"It's a long story," he began, staring down at a patch of dying grass by his left loafer, "but I think I need to tell you. I think I *should* have told you from the beginning."

I clenched my fists. I wasn't sure I wanted to know. If he wasn't here because of the manuscript, then . . . what else could there be? "Okay. What is it?"

"Ann Nichols was my grandmother."

I forced a laugh. *Really?* "*Ben!* C'mon, I know you love her. She was like the matron saint of romance to all of us—"

"I don't mean like that." Slowly, he drew his eyes to mine. They were glassy and wet. The world slowed. Oh no. "She was *my grandmother.*"

There was a lot of information in that sentence that could have surprised me. The fact that he hadn't told me the myriad of times we talked about his grandmother. The slant of his nose that perhaps looked a bit like hers. The sharpness of his jawline. How much he *knew* about Ann Nichols. How he always called her Annie.

No, it wasn't any of that. What surprised me was one simple word: "*Was?*"

He took a deep breath and closed his eyes. "She passed away five and a half years ago."

Five . . . and a half *years*? Just about the time when I met her, when she sat down across from me and offered me a job. I was shaking my head vehemently. "That—that can't be right. No, we met at that coffeehouse . . ."

"She couldn't have," Ben replied gently. "She had been bedridden for at least a year prior while she was writing her last book—*The Forever House.* We had a quiet funeral. She wanted it that way, because she had an idea. There were four books left in her contract, and she wanted them written, but she didn't want the cloud of her passing to define them. So she laid out a plan to find a ghostwriter and finish those books. She also told me not to notify her publisher."

"And her *agent*?" I could just imagine the flames spitting from Molly's mouth when she found out—

"Molly knew."

I wasn't sure if that made things better or worse, actually. I tried to keep myself calm, but I was anything but. My head was spinning. "And—you—the estate—just *let* me? Without knowing she was *dead*?"

"No." He finally opened his eyes, and faced me. "I had been on the hunt for a ghostwriter for a few months at that point, but none of the writers fit. Then you asked, and I thought perhaps Annie had reached out to you before she died and just never told me." He shrugged a little half-heartedly.

"But she didn't. She asked me herself. *After* she died," I realized, and sighed. "I took a job from a ghost. Never had *that* on my bingo card . . ."

Ben let out a soft laugh, leaning close to me. His hand was so near mine, I could almost reach out and take it if he were alive. "Annie did used to say the universe sends you the things you need exactly when you need them, and I want to think it sent you. I don't know about afterlifes or what happens after—after *this* but . . . finding your book was divine. Giving you Annie's legacy and watching it flourish under your pen was a blessing. And this?" He looked into my eyes, and suddenly this no longer felt like a conversation. It felt like a goodbye. "These last few days have been . . . beautiful. It's a good ending, darling. As your editor, I have no notes."

My throat constricted. "Ben . . ."

"I'm sorry, but I—I think I know why I'm here. With you. It isn't because of Annie's book. It's because of *yours*. To thank you." And he smiled. It reached his eyes, but in the way smiles did when you were trying to swallow down a sob. "The last year of Annie's life was hard—I was her only family left, and she was mine. I can't begin to express how much your book helped me. That entire year was bleak, but I could open it and get lost in your words, and in those moments it felt like everything would be okay. I don't know why it was that book, exactly, but it was. So, thank you for giving me words when I didn't think there were any left. I hope you never stop giving the world your words."

I couldn't count how often I wanted to hear those exact words from someone—anyone—and here was this man telling me he *loved* them. Cherished them.

My mouth grew dry, and I didn't know what to say. If I said, *You're welcome*, would he disappear in a sparkle of dust? Would the wind carry him away into the afternoon?

"I'm sorry I have to go," he said softly, guiltily, "but I promise that not all of your companions will be ghosts, darling."

I'd heard that before. "Not even the ones I want to stay," I replied. My heart was breaking.

"I'm sorry," he repeated, and gave me a sad sort of pleading look. It twisted my gut. "I want to be with you—but not like *this*. I want to grow old with you. I want to wake up every morning and see you on the pillow beside me. I want to cherish every moment of our lives and—"

"We can't," I interrupted. "I know."

Something inside of me gave then. Not hope, exactly, but the small thread of happiness I had this past week, because it couldn't support me. I was balancing precariously on a string that snapped, thinking it was made of sturdier stuff.

"Florence—" he began, and winced again. He clutched his chest. "I—I want to stay but I . . ."

He couldn't. He was begging me to let him go.

I took a deep breath. The good goodbyes were what you made of them. Elvistoo crooning The Supremes' "You Can't Hurry Love" in the background, Mom laughing through her tears as Seaburn spun her through the grass.

I turned back to Ben, and I smiled the only kind of smile I could muster. It was sad and broken, but it was mine. "Thank you, Benji Andor, for letting me live in your grandmother's world for a few years. And thank you for wanting to live in mine."

All I wanted to do was take his face in my hands and kiss him, but as I reached out to try, his eyes widened. He sucked in a short breath.

As if he saw something past me. Something I couldn't see. Something I never would.

And then he was gone.

Forever this time.

34

Ghosts in the Floorboards

IN THE CORNER of the Days Gone Funeral Home, beneath a loose floorboard, there was a metal box full of my deepest dreams and my smutty fanfic. When you grew up in a family where everyone knew everyone else's business, you had to find ways to keep your secrets. Carver hid his in the backyard. Alice wrote poetry and stashed it in a tree somewhere on the Ridge. And I hid mine beneath the floorboards.

"I'm gonna fix myself a drink. Do you want anything?" Alice asked, hanging up her coat and heading down the hall to the kitchen. I had excused myself from the gravesite soon after Ben disappeared, and Alice asked if I needed company. I think she sensed something was wrong.

Something beyond burying Dad, anyway.

"Whatever you're having," I replied, and headed into the red parlor room. I knew exactly where the loose board was, hidden under an end table, and wedged a fire poker between the planks of wood, and pried it up.

I took out the box and dusted it off.

Then I opened it.

There was a letter on top, written in that familiar loopy hand. Dad's handwriting. He must've found it while cleaning the parlor—stepped on a loose floorboard, and pried it up to see what was underneath.

Or maybe I was never that sneaky.

Maybe he always knew I hid my secrets here.

I'm so proud of you, buttercup.

And stapled to the bottom were receipts. A sob caught in my throat. They were sales from the bookstore in town. *A Rake's Guide to Getting the Girl*, *The Kiss at the Midnight Matinee*, and *The Probability of Love*. He had bought them. And he knew they were mine.

He knew.

I hugged the note to my chest.

And if he knew, then that meant—when the bar owner interrupted Bruno. The half-finished sentences about my writing. Ann Nichols's new books in the window . . .

Alice found me in the red parlor room like that. She froze in the entryway, eyes wide, holding two glasses of whiskey on the rocks. "The hell? This is some Goonies shit here."

"It's my stash," I replied with a hiccup. She came over and slid down to the floor beside me, and set down our drinks. She picked up *Midnight Matinee* and flipped it over to the back. "He knew, didn't he?"

"Knew what?" Alice asked, feigning innocence. I could tell she was lying—what kind of older sister would I be if I *couldn't* tell? I glared at her and she shrugged, putting the book back into the lockbox. "I have no idea what you're talking about. He definitely didn't tell the whole town."

"Alice!"

"Oh I'm going to *kill* whoever told you."

"No one did. Well . . . Dad did." I showed her the letter.

"Good," Alice declared. "Turns out no one wants to piss off the guy who'll put them in a casket. Don't wanna be looking like a clown."

"Oh my god, he didn't threaten anyone, did he?"

She gave a one-shouldered shrug. "I am sworn to secrecy." We put the note and the rest of the books back into the box, and I slowly began to shuffle through the rest of it. Journals, concert stubs, little notes filled with smaller stories. She watched, stirring the ice in her glass. "Dad found mine, you know."

"Your stash?" I asked. "Yeah, it's in the knot in the tree out near the Ridge."

She gave me an astonished look. "You *knew*?"

"Carver found it *ages* ago."

"His is—"

"Under the woodpile in the backyard," we said together, and laughed.

I took a sip of my drink. It was a lot stronger than the drinks Dana made. It personified Alice—she was there, in your face, unable to be forgotten. I admired that about her. She wouldn't have let her ex-boyfriend steal her stories and publish them. She would've chased him down, and shit in his shoes, and penned an article for the *New Yorker* painstakingly detailing how much of a liar Lee Marlow was. Not just to me—but to his colleagues, to his friends, to journalists, and to colleges and deans asking him to be their guest professor.

She would have annihilated him.

As the sun began to sink across the evening sky, the shadows in the parlor grew longer and darker, but we didn't get up to cut the lights on. There was a certain kind of softness to the way the golden light filtered in through the windows and kissed the dark corners. We knew this funeral home with our eyes closed, anyway, and the floor wasn't that uncomfortable yet.

"So, I've something I've been meaning to tell you." Alice shifted to sit cross-legged and downed half of her drink.

"This should be good," I teased.

Alice squirmed. She did that when she was trying to keep a secret that was physically trying to escape her body. "Karen read most of the will before you arrived, so you missed this part of it." She pursed her lips tightly together and was quiet for a long moment. "You had your ghosts with Dad, and I thought I had nothing. But . . ." She looked around the parlor, as fondly as Dad always did. "I had this place. Well, I *have* this place."

I realized with a gasp. "Dad gave you the business?"

She gave the smallest nod. "After Mom dies, of course, but—he put it in his will. He said it went to me. And Mom said she'd happily turn it over before she kicks it but I really don't want it *that* badly and—"

"Oh, Alice, I'm so *happy* for you!"

"Really?"

"Yes, *really*, you idiot! I'm so freaking happy! You're the only one who understands this place—*really* understands it. I can't imagine it in better hands."

Her bottom lip wobbled, and then she threw her arms around me. "Thank you," she said into my shoulder.

I hugged her tightly. "I know you'll do a great job, Al."

She finally let go and sat back on her feet, and wiped her eyes. "I think I met my crying quota for the year."

"It's okay to cry sometimes."

"Not with thirty-dollar mascara on!"

"Well, whose fault is that?"

"Impossible beauty standards and my lack of thick eyelashes?" She sniffed indignantly, and took a drink of her whiskey. "So, what're you doing with your secret stash? Afraid someone found it?"

"Oh, no. I guess I was just looking . . . for something," I replied. She cocked her head in question. "An answer, I think. Someone who just left told me that my book was his favorite. He thanked me for it. That—that was why he was here."

Alice's eyes widened. "Oh, sis. Ben?"

For some reason, someone else saying his name made me sad all over again. Tears burned at the edges of my eyes, but I dutifully brushed them away. I'd helped dozens of ghosts in the past. Most of the time I just had to listen to them—to a story—before they left.

"I don't understand why I'm so messed up right now," I admitted. "I've said goodbye to so many people—shouldn't it be easy now?"

Alice gave me a strange look. "Who told you that lie? It's never easy. It's also never really goodbye—and trust me, we're in the business of goodbyes. The people who pass through here live on in you and me and everyone they touched. There is no happy *ending*, there's just . . . happily living. As best you can. Or whatever. Metaphor-metaphor-simile shit."

I bit my cheek to keep from laughing.

"And that goes for the ghosts you help, too. I think you'll see him again."

I wiped my nose with the back of my hand. "He's gone."

"Tell that to the wind."

Maybe there was some truth in Alice's words, though I didn't really believe them yet. As I took out my fan fiction and leafed through my journals, there was a certainty in that teenage girl's words, in what she wanted, in who she was, the parts that I clung to, the parts of my first book Ben loved. She believed in happily ever afters and grand romantic gestures and one true loves that stretched on beyond their canon endings. I wasn't that girl anymore—or so I always told myself. But maybe I was.

And maybe that wasn't a bad thing.

Lee Marlow had said that romance was only good because you read it with one hand.

He was wrong. He had stolen my stories and rewrote them into some literary circle jerk with *award potential*, but I had the memories of my parents waltzing in the parlors, of Carver and Nicki kissing in the cemetery, of Alice pinning a wildflower in her hair when she thought no one was looking. He might have had the plot, but he didn't have the heart.

Ben was gone, but Alice was right. He was still here, and I still had a book to write. And now I finally knew how to write it. I still didn't know how to write Amelia and Jackson's ending, but I knew that I could. I knew that I was capable.

I think knowing that would've made Ben proud.

"How did I get such a smart sister?" I asked her at last.

Alice grinned and punched me in the shoulder. "About damn time you realized how smart I am! You can call me Saint Alice if you please."

"That's going a little far."

"*Sage* Alice—"

"Really?"

"And name your next book character after me."

"Absolutely *not*," I laughed, when there was a knock on the front door and Rose's voice echoed into the foyer.

"It's just me! And I *so* need to piss—oh my god, is that a *secret stash*?" Rose asked when she saw us sitting on the parlor floor with my box of secrets, but then she quickly hurried to the bathroom. Alice and I were still drinking on the ground when she came back out. "Wow, look at all this smut. Maybe your editor'll take one of these for your next book," Rose joked, glancing over an *X-Files* fanfic. "Ben doesn't seem the Mulder-Scully type, though."

I gave her a strange look. "Who?"

Rose said, "Your editor—I mean," she said, and glanced at Alice, "*Ann*'s editor."

Alice waved her hand. "I already know."

"Rose, that isn't funny." Ben being gone hit me again, right in the stomach, and it made me want to puke.

My best friend took her phone out of her bra. "Erin texted me when I was coming back from the cemetery. He just woke up."

"He's dead," I said.

"*What?* No—I could've sworn I told you he got hit by a car."

"Yeah and that he died!"

Rose shook her head slowly, about three types of confusion crossing her face. "I . . . did *not* say that."

Didn't she? I mean—it didn't matter, Ben was right *there.* He haunted me. He was dead, he *had* to be. But the more I thought back to our conversation the less I became sure about it because . . . I wasn't sure if she *had* said he died, or if I inferred it. She said that he was hit by oncoming traffic, and I inferred the rest.

I mean, he was a fucking ghost.

And now he was gone. I watched him fade into the wind, but—

What if . . .

What if that wasn't because he moved on?

"And—and he woke up?" I asked, my voice brittle. I got to my feet and faced Rose, my chest tight with anxiety and disbelief and—and hope.

It was *hope.*

Rose showed me the text message from Erin.

HOTTIE MCHOTCAKES HAS RISEN! He's awake!!

"Hottie McHotcakes?" I echoed, reading the text over and over. It was so outlandishly funny. Because I'd just said goodbye to him. I'd watched him pass on and here someone was talking about him as if he was—

As if he *was*—

"He's alive."

The times he disappeared without warning. The voices he heard. The sounds. The pain—I'd ignored most of it because it didn't matter. He was dead because my stubborn ass said he was. But he *wasn't*, and while he existed here, some part of him was still being pulled back to his body, wrenched back, even though he kept trying to stay *here*, thinking that wherever he was going was worse.

If I'd been more perceptive. If I hadn't written off his weird experiences. If I'd just *thought* a little, that things weren't always the same, not always certain.

I pressed my hand over my mouth to muffle a sob.

Rose took me by the shoulders. "Florence? Babe? Are you okay?"

I shook my head. The world blurred with my tears. "H-He's alive," I said between sobs. "B-Ben is alive."

Alice looked up from her spot on the ground. "Your ghost boyfriend, Ben?"

To that, Rose asked, "A *ghost*?"

And that made me cry even harder, and Rose pulled me close to her and wrapped her arms around me, even though she didn't understand. He could feed his cat again, and he could go to bookstores, and read his favorite novels, and he could take all of those vacations he never did before, and meet new people, and find a new family and—

And me. He could find *me.*

I wanted to have memories with Ben. I wanted to see him on the front porch and sit with him and make up silly stories about the people that passed on the sidewalk. I wanted to share a beer with him down at Bar None, and I wanted to dance with him—*really* dance with him, our hands intertwined, my unruly heart beating so loud it gave me away.

I wanted to kiss him, obviously, but it was so much fucking *more* than that.

When I was with Lee, I could see my entire life unfold around him. I knew where I fit in, I knew what part to play and how to play it. I had a place in his life, and I boxed myself into it as best I could, and I tried to be the perfect girlfriend for someone who was looking for a saint.

But when I thought about Ben, about his disheveled hair, his timid smile and soft voice, a heartstring pulled so taut in my chest it almost broke, and it hurt. Because I thought I could—

I thought I could *love* him.

Cautious and organized and stoic as he was. *Just* as he was. He didn't need to fit into a perfect place in my life. He just . . . needed *to be.*

He existed. And the rest of my world made room.

He was right in the end. Romance wasn't dead, after all.

35

Unruly Hearts

USUALLY WHEN YOU flew into LaGuardia, you kissed your ass and hoped for the best. I hated flying into LGA—the turbulent air, how you're going *right over the water*, how *you think you're going to land in that water* when at the last minute the tarmac comes up and your plane juts down and—

I didn't like flying.

At all. But I braved it. In fact, I didn't quite mind it at all. Because I was going to see *Ben*.

After the funeral, I had thought to stay a few days longer, but as soon as my family heard about what had happened—from Alice, because she was about as good at keeping secrets as my dad was—they all told me to go. Catch a flight back with Rose, come home in the morning, go to his hospital—to *find him*.

"Good things don't wait, and neither should you," Mom had said.

Perhaps this wasn't my grand romance, but this was my story, and whether I was the rule or the exception, I didn't care. I just wanted to see him. I wanted to make sure he was okay.

Rose's phone pinged with a few texts. Probably all from Alice. They had gone on a date last night to Bar None, and Rose hadn't been able to shut up about my sister since. I loved it—and hated it. My chaotic best friend and my smart-ass younger sister? It was a recipe for trouble.

What were Ben and I? Were we anything? I wondered. I didn't know. I thought back on my last conversation with him, and I was filled with mortification all over again. His grandmother was Ann—he'd read all of my sex scenes! He'd seen me *naked*!

I wasn't sure which was worse.

They were all pretty bad.

Though, did he remember any of that? Or when he woke up, was it like waking from a dream? Erin had told Rose that his injuries were minimal, and the doctors hadn't known why he wasn't waking up. Because he wasn't there. His soul—spirit—whatever. I wasn't sure what made us tick. The memories in our electrons? The wind in our lungs? The echo of our words? Whatever it was, he was awake now, and even though it felt like an eternity since I sat in his office and gave him a cactus, it had only been a week to everyone else.

"Oh, hey." Rose elbowed me in the side. Passengers were beginning to file out of the plane and onto the jet bridge. "Erin texted me while we were on the flight. He's taking visitors now!"

"Oh."

I wanted to puke.

Leaving the airport was always a lot easier than coming, but LaGuardia made it hard no matter what. It was like whoever designed the place wanted everyone who came through it to suffer as much as they could. All of the open gates were on one side of the airport, but the line for the taxis was across the parking garage, down an incline, through a construction zone, at the far end of what was probably once a bus stop. It took thirty minutes to get there, and calling a car would've taken just as long because the pickup area was right *next* to the taxis.

But we finally managed to nab one, and Rose told our driver to take us to New York Presbyterian in Lower Manhattan—and take the shortest route possible. Because of the layover in Charlotte, we didn't actually manage to get back to the city until rush-hour traffic, so a drive that usually took thirty minutes took an hour and some change. That was one thing I didn't miss about the city. At least in Mairmont, there weren't enough people *for* an hour and a half's worth of traffic.

By the time we pulled up at the hospital—and the right building—I just wanted to go home, but Rose was nothing if not stalwart.

"Don't you *want* to see him?"

Of course I did. That wasn't the question. It wasn't if I wanted to see him but—this last week had been strange, and otherworldly, and who was to say that he wanted to see *me*?

Rose paid for the taxi and dumped her duffel on the sidewalk beside a fire hydrant, out of the way of most of the people. "I'll be out here," she said, waving me inside. "I don't really like hospitals."

"I don't, either—you know, the whole *ghost* thing," I hissed.

"And one's waiting for you upstairs. Five thirty-eight. Don't forget!"

As if I could. I'd been repeating the number over and over in my head for the entire taxi ride, but a small voice, one that I had been trying to ignore, trying to shove away, kept asking, *What if he doesn't remember you?*

What would I do then?

I didn't know, but I didn't think about it, either, as I got into the elevator and hit the fifth floor button. A moment later, an older woman stepped in with me. She had on the loudest sweater I'd ever seen—every color of the rainbow vomited onto it and knit together. I'd seen a sweater like that only once before.

"What floor?" I asked.

"Oh, I think it's finally time to head to the top."

"Sure thing." I pressed the highest number.

The older woman leaned toward me. She smelled like lilac perfume and dumplings. "Thank you, Florence."

"You're welc—" But when I glanced over, she was gone. A chill slithered down my spine. I could've sworn she was here, just a moment ago.

And that sweater—she looked like—

She looked like Ann.

The elevator doors dinged and opened to the fifth floor. I stepped out and glanced back one more time to make sure that the woman wasn't there, but of course she wasn't. She was dead. Five years dead.

I didn't have time to think about Ann, because as the elevator doors closed, I heard a familiar voice say my name. And it wasn't the voice I wanted to hear.

"Florence?"

I turned around, and standing there in the lobby, with blond hair and a trimmed beard, was Lee Marlow. He was holding a bouquet of yellow flowers in his hand with a card stuck in them that read GET WELL SOON!

I felt myself go clammy all over. "Lee—h-hi."

"What a surprise!" He seemed confused. "What're you doing here?"

"Um—I'm here to see Ben."

He frowned, as if trying to puzzle out exactly how I knew him. And I didn't know where to start. Though I should've known better, because it turned out, Lee didn't much care. "'Course he's popular with the ladies."

Ben? Right. I'm sure he told himself that because no one came to see him when he had his appendix out on our two-year anniversary.

"It's nice to see you made some connections at all those publishing parties I took you to," he added.

He really couldn't think about a world beyond himself, could he? Charming and suave, of course he was, and the world he knew danced around him like planets around the sun.

I forced my lips to smile as my hands balled into fists. Just one punch. Just one—

No, Florence.

You're better than that.

"I just asked the nurses," he went on, and pointed down the hall. "He's right down this way. We can walk together."

I didn't want to, but I didn't want to do this alone, either. My chest was beginning to feel tight. This wasn't how I pictured seeing Ben again, with Lee Marlow to witness, but I began to care less and less about *how* we met again and just that we were *going* to. Because Ben was here, and the panic in my veins was slowly, with each step, transforming into excitement.

He was here. In this building. *Alive.*

Ben was alive. Ben was alive.

Ben was alive.

Hospitals didn't look so different from publishing houses—at least not Falcon House. Glass walls separated patients from everyone else, sometimes frosted but never private. The cacophony of beeps coalesced into this jagged sort of rhythm that had no rhyme or reason, and my heart was louder than all of them, beating in my ears like a funeral march.

Lee never knew how to do anything in silence. He didn't like quiet. He had to be either talking, or listening, or *doing* something. So, as we went together down the hall, he talked. "It's good to see you—are you going somewhere?" he added, once he noticed the suitcase I was rolling with me.

"I just came back from visiting home."

"Home? No shit. You always hated home."

"My dad died," I replied, and his eyebrows jerked up.

"Oh. Florence, I'm s—"

"Is that his room?" I interrupted, looking straight ahead. Toward the end of the hall, to room 538. I could see the number on the plaque. And through the frosted glass, there was a shadow—a shape—sitting up in bed.

I knew that shape. I knew *him*.

"Oh, what a surprise. Laura's still here," Lee observed. I didn't notice the woman sitting in the chair beside Ben's bedside until he said something. Soft red hair and a heart-shaped face, snuggled in a blanket. The same red hair from the social media photo. The same soft face.

"Laura?" I echoed.

"She hasn't left his side since the accident," he went on, and I didn't think he told me that in malice because—he couldn't know why I was here. Or what I felt. "I keep telling her to go home but you know how it is."

I came to a stop.

Fifteen feet away, in room 538, Ben laughed at something she said. It was loud and bright and—and *happy*. He was happy. I didn't need to see him to know that.

"I think she still misses him," he said. "Maybe he'll give her a second chance now."

A second chance. What Laura had begged of Ben, after she cheated, and Ben had wanted that. A second chance—but he didn't think he deserved it, because what guy drove his girlfriend to cheat? But it was her fault. She made the choice.

And he made his.

But . . . she had been at his bedside this whole time. Waiting for him to wake up. She loved him. *Really* loved him—and they had the kind of shared history that Ben and I couldn't have in the seven days we knew each other.

I . . . knew very little about Ben. What was his favorite food? His favorite music? What was he afraid of—what did he do on the weekends? Did he own one of those squatty potties? Questions I hadn't thought to ask in the last week.

Then again, I'd been grieving. I was *still* grieving. It was hard to make space with a sorrow that full.

"Why didn't you come after me?" I asked Lee abruptly. "When I left?"

He gave me a strange look, and oh, I wished he could've said that he missed me. And I wished he could've apologized. And I could've told him that my stories were real, and that they were precious, and that I wanted to tell them someday. Because ghost stories were just love stories about here and then and now and when, about pockets of happiness and moments that resonated in places long after their era. They were stories that taught you that love was never a matter of time, but a matter of timing.

And this was not mine.

Lee Marlow said, of all the things he could've, "I don't think we would've worked out, bunny. I don't like dating rivals, though you got a while to go. I didn't want to see you jealous—"

My hand was already in a tight fist.

It would've been a shame to waste it.

So I turned and I slammed it straight into his motherfucking nose.

He gave a howl of pain, backpedaling in surprise. His nose wasn't broken. I didn't know how to throw a punch that hard. But it *did* hurt my knuckles. He whirled back to me with wild, angry eyes. "The *hell,* Florence?!"

"I'm not your rival, Lee Marlow," I told him, shaking my hand because it hurt. "You're not even in my league. But you better watch me," I added, and grabbed my suitcase handle again, "because I'll be the writer you will never be."

Then I left down the hallway, back toward the elevators.

And I didn't look back.

Even as he shouted at me to stop, told me he'd call the cops, file a report—I didn't care.

It felt good, and he deserved it.

And I was never going to think about Lee Marlow again.

Rose was still waiting for me outside, and the look on my face must've said it all. Her eyebrows knit together and she shook her head. "Oh, honey," she whispered, and pulled me into a tight hug.

I told her I couldn't do it. I didn't tell her why, but it didn't really matter anymore anyway. It wasn't my move to make, and this wasn't my part of the story to tell. I had helped him get his life back, and he had helped me through mine—and if that was it . . . then it was. He was happy, and so it was time that I was, too.

I went home with my best friend in the entire world, to our small apartment in New Jersey, and I finished writing a love story.

36

Lovely Meeting

Amelia Brown stood in the rain, and she knew she didn't want to be alone.

"I'm sorry," Jackson said, and he met her gaze and held it. His eyes were the deep blue of a summer sky back home, and however angry or sad she was at him, she still found herself yearning for those skies whenever she looked into his eyes. "I was a shit, and I shouldn't have lied to you about Miranda—it just hurt. And I thought if I just forgot about her, the pain would go away. But I was wrong. And instead, I hurt you in the process. I was afraid."

"Of what?" she asked, making herself stand her ground. In the dim lights from the house behind her, he looked like a specter from her dreams. Come to haunt her. She had wanted him to return, but she didn't think he would. "Did you think I'd use your past for a little money and fame?"

"Didn't you try?"

She winced. "I never sent in that article. I couldn't." Because she had realized over quiet dinners at the kitchenette and saving dogs and running from paparazzi—she realized she didn't want that. She didn't want a loud life.

She just wanted a good one.

He said, "I know. Thank you."

She hugged herself tighter. "We're even, then."

"You rented the house for another week, I hear."

"I love the weather," she replied, shivering in the cold.

"It's quite good. Would you . . . want the company of a messed-up, burned-out musician?"

She cocked her head. "Depends. Is the guitar included?" She motioned to the guitar slung on his back.

"I was going to serenade you if you wouldn't listen," he admitted a little sheepishly, and wiped his eyes. He was crying, though he'd tell her it was the rain.

She took a step toward him, and they were close enough that all she had to do was reach out her hands and take his, and pull him into the warmth of her house on the Isle of Ingary. "What would you play?"

He reached out slowly, softly, and took her hands in his. "Don't worry," he replied, "it would be a song with only the good notes."

I wrote. And I wrote. For three months, as April turned to May, turned to June and into July, I polished and I edited and I cleaned the draft as I sat in front of a fan and drank sweet tea and fell in love over and over with Amelia and Jackson and their magical Isle of Ingary. I checked my texts, though they were mostly from Rose checking in on me, and Carver asking about plans to propose to Nicki, and even Alice a few times! Though whenever she texted it was mostly about Rose.

I could see that trouble coming from a mile away. My best friend and my little sister? God help me.

I ate takeout Thai from the restaurant down the block and went to bed too late and woke up at noon to fix myself a pot of coffee I would take one sip of before abandoning it as I fell into the story again.

I hadn't written like this in years, not since I first began writing for Ann.

It felt like everything over the last year, all of my pent-up frustrations, all of my failures, all of my wants and hopes and dreams, they all came tumbling out of me. On the page I could make sense of all of them, mold them into a beginning, a middle, and an end—because all good love stories ended.

And then, just like that, I was no longer in the dark night. I was stepping out into the daylight, into the happily ever after, and it felt good and whole and bright.

And something to be proud of.

One evening, Carver called to tell me, "He said yes," on a video chat with Nicki, showing both of their golden engagement bands. "And we're gonna have the wedding in a few weeks at the funeral home. I figured since Alice *basically* owns it now, she could bump a wake or two and give us a family discount. Bruno is officiating."

"Elvistoo?" I asked, surprised. "I didn't know he did weddings, too."

Three weeks later, on the hottest day of July on record, I finished the last book I would ever write for Ann Nichols.

And it was good.

I sent the novel attached in an email to Molly, who then forwarded it to Ben's new assistant editor, Tamara, the one who had done a lot of the heavy lifting while he was away on medical leave. Tamara knew I was Ann's ghostwriter, too. I wasn't expecting to hear back. It had been three months, and if Ben remembered me, if he *missed* me, then he would've found me. He knew how.

A few minutes later, Molly called. And offered me representation.

"I know your work is good, and since the contract is over, I thought I'd poach you before anyone else got you," she said frankly. "So, what do you say?"

I told her I'd think about it, just to make her sweat a little for keeping Ann's death (albeit a secret) from me. Molly was one of the best agents in the business, and I liked working with her, so it was a *no-brainer*, but you know, I had time to sit and think on it, since I wasn't sure *what* I wanted to do next.

I'd just finished a book, after all.

Was Ben going to love it? No, I already knew he would. He was going to love it because for a few days during a chilly spring in Mairmont, he loved *me*, and like Jackson singing a song with only good notes for Amelia, the book was filled with only the good parts of us.

That evening, instead of takeout, I decided to make some celebratory mac and cheese while Rose stopped by the discount liquor store to get our favorite pineapple wine on her way home. My phone dinged as I was draining the noodles. An email.

I looked at who it was—

And my heart slammed against the bony cage of my chest. I almost dropped my phone into the hot noodles.

The email was from Ben.

Miss Day,

It was a pleasure working with you. I wish you all the best on your future endeavors.

Best,
Benji Andor

And that was all it said.

For the next four hours, I paced the apartment trying to decode every secret message within those twenty-two words with Rose and a bottle of pineapple Riesling.

"We didn't even work together!" I cried, carving a hole in the hardwood floors the faster I paced. "What does he *mean*?"

Does he remember? No—he couldn't. If he did, then he would have contacted me so much sooner than this. That couldn't be it.

Rose watched me pace from her perch in the middle of the couch, sipping on her wine. "Perhaps it was just a polite email?"

"I didn't even get one of those from *my* old editor."

"You should respond."

I stopped pacing. "*What?*"

She took another large gulp. "Tell him you'd like to meet, and then finish up your unfinished business."

"I don't *have* any—"

"Florence."

"Rose."

"I love you, but you do."

"I love you, too, but you just expect me to waltz into his office and—and tell him what? That I'm a chaotic mess? Seven drunk ferrets in a trench coat?"

In reply, Rose forcibly set down her wineglass onto the coffee table and reached behind her on the couch to our bookcases. She grabbed one and presented it to me. "Sign, seal, deliver."

I stared down at my own book, *Ardently Yours*. The book that Ben said was his favorite in the whole world. And I let out a very long sigh. "Remember your last idea involving Ben?"

She shrugged. "You got to punch Lee, didn't you?"

She had a point.

So, the next morning, while I nursed a hangover and ate congealed oatmeal, I wrote a reply email.

Mr. Andor,

It was a pleasure. Though I do have something for you. Do you think we could set up a meeting?

Sincerely,
Florence Day

Miss Day,

Would this Friday work, at noon?

Best,
Benji

Mr. Andor,

Noon would be lovely.

With all my best,
Florence

And that was that.

I second-guessed my email the entire week. Was *lovely* too strong a word? Should I have signed it Miss Day? Should I have addressed him as Benji instead of Mr. Andor? Rose told me that Wednesday that if I spiraled any more, I'd drill myself to the center of the earth.

So I tried to spiral more *quietly*.

I think I might've had a full-on panic attack if it weren't for having to finalize plans for Carver and Nicki's wedding that weekend. Right after the meeting with Ben on Friday, I was to take a taxi to Newark and hop on a plane home for their wedding on Saturday. Friday was the rehearsal dinner and bachelor parties, and as the big sister who did absolutely *nothing* to help with the wedding while I was in the deadline trenches, I had to at least show up for those. I reserved my room at the inn (to John and Dana's pure ecstatic joy), and walked Mom through the whiplash of "I'm so happy!" and "My baby's all grown up and leaving the mortuary!" *and* I managed to talk Rose into coming with me purely because I was the best eldest sister in the entire world and I knew for a fact that Alice would *never* ask her. She was bold at doing absolutely everything, except when it came to her own happiness.

I guess it ran in the family.

So I gave myself a little leniency when I realized that I hadn't brought any sort of WELCOME BACK! OR GLAD YOU LIVED! card to go with Ben's gift until I was already in the elevator going up to Falcon House Publishers. I bounced on my heels, quite unable to stop moving.

"Beautiful day," I commented to a man sweating through his Armani suit. He grunted and patted his forehead.

It was summer in the city, and the men in the elevator looked like they were about to sweat to death in their ironed business suits, the women in flouncy skirts and kitten heels.

And I was in what I felt best in, an oversized blouse and straight-leg jeans with a hole in the left knee, and red Converses. I didn't look like I fit in here, but looks were deceiving, and best of all?

I didn't really care anymore. It didn't matter. What mattered was where I was going.

I wasn't scared of the looming floor number that we rose to meet. Executive editor Benji Andor had been back in the office for a little less than a month, though I was beginning to suspect he had done more than a little work from home before that. He apparently still had a lot of catching up to do, from what Erin told Rose. Then again, when did editors *not* have a lot of catch-up work to do? As long as I'd known Lee, he'd been *majestically* behind on every deadline. But I had a feeling that, unlike Lee, Ben actually wanted to catch up—but then why would he agree to entertain a meeting with me?

I was nervous. What if he thought I was some sort of weirdo who wanted to give him his favorite book? Couldn't be any worse than a weirdo giving him a cactus, I guessed.

Because it *had* been three months, and I wasn't going to lie, quite a few of those nights I spent drowning in a bottle of wine, wondering what happened with Laura. Wondering if she stayed. If he wanted her to. If they decided to try anew.

I was alone by the time the elevator stopped at the floor for Falcon House Publishers, and I stepped out into the clean white lobby. The glass-cased bookshelves looked exactly the same. Ann Nichols's bestsellers sat on a shelf all to themselves, and the glass reflected me, freckled cheeks and dry lips and messy blond hair pinned up into twin buns.

Erin was reading a book as I came up to the front desk, but she quickly put a sticky note on the page and closed it. *When the Dead Sing* by Lee Marlow.

It came out this week.

"Florence! Good morning!" Erin greeted. "How's Rose? Is she alive?"

"You two *really* need to stop going to that wine bar," I replied, remembering Rose stumbling into the apartment last night and immediately passing out on the soft shag rug in the living room.

Erin gave a pout. "But they have *such* a good cheese plate."

Rose wasn't going to work today; she'd already caught her flight to Charlotte, where Alice would pick her up to drive to Mairmont. After this meeting, I'd be on my way, too. I asked if I could stash my suitcase behind Erin's desk, and she happily agreed. "I'll ring Benji and tell him you're here."

"That'd be great, thanks."

As Erin called Ben's office phone, I leaned against the front desk to get a better look at Lee Marlow's novel. The cover was decent, I guessed. A bit too much like *The Woman in the Window* for my liking. It wasn't as if I could *forget* that Lee's book came out this week. It had been everywhere in the city—on subway ads, in magazines, an entire article in the Sunday edition of the *New York Times*, and even in my favorite indie bookstore. It wasn't something I could quite escape, but I no longer felt under the shadow of it, either.

Lee ended up *not* filing a police report after I'd punched him at the hospital. Probably for the best, because I had secrets that could make his life very uncomfortable for a while, and he didn't need that sort of bad press before the release of his instant bestseller.

After a moment, Erin hung up the phone and said, "That's odd, he didn't answer, but he should be in his office. You can head back there, if you want. His door should be open."

So took a deep breath, and I went.

37

The Dead Romantics

I REMEMBERED THIS walk three months ago. I remembered how terrified I was, how I hoped whoever this new editor was would give me a little slack. I did end up getting the extra time I needed, but it didn't quite go the way I had planned. I passed meeting rooms separated by foggy glass, and assistant editors and marketers and publicists working diligently to make the machine that was publishing run.

It really was a miracle that anything came out on time. Well, a miracle and way too much caffeine.

At the end of the hallway, Ben's office door was open like Erin said it would be, and there he sat as if he'd always been there. As if he hadn't been a spectator during the worst week of my life. His hair was a little longer and wavy, not gelled back like the last time I'd met him, and curling gently against his ears. His sleeves were rolled up, and the slightest hint of his father's golden wedding ring peeked out from beneath his collar. There was a shallow scar running slantwise across his left cheek, still a little red and tender, but healing. He wore large thick-framed glasses, though they didn't seem to help him see any better because he was still squinting at something on his computer screen, a pen hanging out of his mouth.

It was a snapshot of his life. I wanted to take a photo of it, memorize how the door framed him in a perfect setting, the window behind him with midday light flooding gold into his office.

I steeled myself—and my heart.

Even if he didn't remember me, it was okay. It was going to be okay—*I* was going to be okay.

I rapped my knuckles against the doorway.

He gave a start at the noise. The pen dropped from his mouth, but he caught it and shoved it in an accessory drawer in his desk. "Miss Day!" he greeted in surprise, and quickly stood to welcome me in, knocking his long legs on the underside of his desk. He winced at the pain. "It's a pleasure to see you again."

He held out a hand over his desk, and I took it. His was warm and calloused and I thought I had prepped myself for this sort of meeting, but at that moment I realized how woefully underprepared I actually was. Because he was *alive*. When so long he had been a specter that faded in and out of my life, first a ghost and then a memory and now—

Now he was standing in front of me and no matter whether he remembered me or not, he was here. The feeling of his hand in mine made me happy in a strange and comforting way.

And that sort of happiness, even bittersweet, made my heart so full it might just burst.

I squeezed his hand tightly. "Thank you for fitting me into your schedule," I replied, smiling. "I've got to get to Newark, so I won't be staying long."

"Going somewhere?"

"Home!" I replied happily. "My brother's getting married this weekend."

"Congratulations! Well, then by all means, let's get to it. Please, sit," he said, and motioned toward the IKEA chair facing his desk, and I sank down into it. The last time I was here, I had all but begged him for another deadline extension. I had even argued that *love was dead* in order to write a different genre. Nothing worked.

The Swell of Endless Music would have been a damn good revenge fantasy.

But it was a better romance.

To my surprise, he had kept my apology cactus. It was sitting on his desk beside his monitor, and it was still alive. He'd made room for it, on his tidy desk where everything had its place.

I had changed so much in these last few months, and I wondered how much he'd unknowingly changed. If somewhere deep down beneath his flesh and bones there was an echo of moonlit walks in graveyards and screaming in the rain and dandelion fields and funerals.

Or were they my secrets now? I held them close either way, though not as close as I held my purse right about then.

"So, Miss Day—"

"Florence, please," I corrected, tearing my eyes away from the cactus.

"Florence, then. Sorry," he added. "I was just rereading Ann's manuscript when you walked in and compiling some final notes for her. We'll probably do a small round of edits and send it off to copyedits—it's really quite solid already."

"See what Ann could do with a few more months?" I joked, tongue in cheek.

He smiled softly. "You were right. And the title? *The Swell of Endless Music* is so lyrical and soft. It's great. I think we might use it—where's my manners? Would you like something to drink? I'm sure the break room has tea or burnt coffee, if you'd prefer that?"

"Battery acid at noon? Oof, I'll have to pass."

He grinned. "Might be for the best. Your zoom-zoom juice might backfire on the flight."

I gave a start. "My what?"

"Oh—um, your coffee," he corrected himself, his ears turning red with embarrassment.

We sat for an awkwardly quiet moment.

Then he cleared his throat. The redness of his ears was inching down toward his cheeks now, and he checked his watch. "Anyway, there's a reason you wanted to meet with me?"

Yes, but I didn't want to leave after this, and go on about my life. I wanted to stay in this uncomfortable chair as long as humanly possible, because I knew when I left, I would never be coming back again.

Dad once told me that all good things came to an end, eventually.

Even this.

I opened my purse and took out a book-shaped present wrapped in brown paper. "I wanted you to have this. As a thanks. Or—I don't know—a get-well present? I was thinking about getting you a card, but it just felt weird to write, 'Glad You're Not Dead!' on it, you know?"

He laughed—*actually* laughed. It was deep and rumbly. "Apparently, I was pretty close to dead for a few days. I dreamed that I was."

My throat began to constrict. "Well, good thing it was just a dream."

"It felt real enough," he replied, accepting the gift. He opened it very meticulously, one edge at a time, barely tearing the paper. His eyebrows furrowed when he finally unwrapped it and read the title. Books didn't always find success, but they found where they needed to go, like Dad had said. Ben flipped open the book to the title page and ran his fingers along the black Sharpie I used to sign it. I'd only signed a handful of books before, so I didn't really have a signature or a certain way to sign. It was just my name, plain and simple, next to his.

He was quiet for a long moment, too long.

Oh god, had I become the weirdo who gave him a cactus *and* a book now? This was a terrible idea. I knew it was from the beginning. I was going to put googly eyes on *all* of Rose's vibrators for *ever* suggesting this.

"Oh, look at the time!" I gathered my things and quickly popped to my feet. "I really have to go. Hope you enjoy the book, you know, assuming you haven't read it, because why would I assume you've read it, right? No one's read that book and, um, it's definitely a different Florence Day and—"

"Florence," he whispered, his voice cracking, but I was already at the door. "Wait—*Florence*—please. Wait."

I stopped in the doorway, and steeled myself with a breath, and turned to face him. He was staring at me strangely. Then he was on his feet, brown eyes wide, and the way he looked at me, I could have been the ghost.

Maybe I was.

"What would this scene be like?" I began, hope making my chest hurt, knotted tight. I might've just been that weird girl who gave him a cactus and a book, but maybe—just maybe—I was *more.* "A refined editor from a prestigious romance imprint and—"

"A chaotic ghostwriter who takes graveyard walks at midnight and shouts in the rain and unironically orders rum and Cokes and bites her thumbnail when she thinks no one's looking."

"I do not," I lied, my voice cracking, as he stepped closer still, and suddenly he was in front of me, and cupped my face in his hands, the recognition in his eyes blooming like dandelions, and the ache in my chest turned into something warm and bright and golden.

"I knew you once," he said so ardently, it made my heart flutter.

"I think you still do," I whispered, and he bent and pressed his lips to mine. They were warm and soft, and tasted vaguely of Chap-Stick, and I wanted to savor it. Because he remembered me. He *remembered* me. And I just wanted to kiss him forever, because he smelled like fresh laundry and spearmint gum and his hands were so warm cupping my face and he was *kissing me*. Benji Andor was kissing me. I was so happy I could die.

Metaphorically.

"It wasn't a dream," he whispered against my lips.

I shook my head, and my heart was beating so bright I could barely stand it. "I'm one hundred percent real. I think. But . . . maybe kiss me again to see if I'm actually here?"

He laughed, deep and humming, and kissed me again in the quiet corner office of Falcon House Publishers. "I'm sorry I made you wait. I'm sorry I didn't realize."

"Wait, wait." I eased away from him a little, thinking. "Does this mean I'm *literally* the girl of your dreams?"

He scrunched his nose. "Wouldn't that be a bit cliché?"

"You're right, you'd probably flag it for being too unrealistic."

"Especially considering one of us thinks love is dead," he agreed.

"Okay, to be fair, you *were* mostly dead." I ran my fingers across his face, his stubbly jaw and red scar, and twined into his raven-soft hair. "But you aren't anymore, and I was wrong."

"I'm glad you were," he agreed, and bent his head down to kiss me again. His stubble brushed across my cheek, rough and real, and I wanted to drink all six-foot-whatever of him in like one of those stupidly large cowboy-boot beer glasses at roadside bars. Then he anchored my head and kissed me deeper, and for a moment I knew

I was still in Falcon House Publishers, but I felt like I was shooting through the stars, infinite, with my heart beating brightly.

Until my starry-eyed ass came back to earth like Armageddon. "Oh—oh god," I gasped, pulling away. "What about Laura?"

He snapped his eyes open and gave me a strange look. "*Laura?* She just wanted my Nora Roberts books if I kicked it, I assure you."

I unwound with relief. "That must be one hell of a collection."

He chuckled. "I'm proud of it. Do you want to get dinner tonight?"

"I would love t—" I froze, remembering myself. "Oh—oh *shit*, what time is it?"

Ben glanced at the analogue clock on his desk. "Almost twelve thirty—wait, didn't you say you had a flight?"

"Definitely. At three, and if I miss that flight, Alice is going to *kill* me, so I can't do dinner tonight because I'll be in Mairmont but I—"

I didn't want to say no. I didn't want to leave. And then I found myself thinking about what came next. Dates, and movies, and holidays, years passing in a single blink. He'd keep his hair floppy, and I'd cut mine short, and we'd be somewhere else in the story, or maybe secondary characters in someone else's. And I thought about years after that, when he'd gotten used to my chaos and I his caution and the world was a little blurry. I didn't know where we would be, or if he would get tired of me, or if I would break his heart—

But I thought—I thought I wanted to find out.

I said, "Come home with me."

He didn't even think. He didn't weigh any odds. He didn't pause to find his words. They were there, as sure and certain as his smile. "Can we swing by my apartment first on the way to the airport?" he asked.

"Only if I can meet Dolly Purrton."

"She'd love that," he assured, and kissed me again.

38

Body of Work

"FLORENCE! NICE TO see you again," Dana greeted with a smile, and put down their current read.

The North Carolinian afternoon was sweltering hot, so all the windows were opened to let the golden sunshine spill in. Mairmont's only bed-and-breakfast looked so much different in the summertime, with the wind catching on the sheer curtains, and the sound of insects humming through the old house. All of the flowers and bushes outside in the garden had flowered into blooms of reds and purples and blues, and ivy and jasmine crawled up the terraces on either side of the house. It was oddly picturesque.

I hugged Dana as they came around the desk. "It's nice to see you! How's John?"

"Insufferable as always," they replied endearingly. "He's trying to convince me that we need a goat—a *goat!*—for the backyard. I want chickens instead."

"Tiny dinosaurs or a lawn mower, that's a tough choice," Ben commented, his hand finding mine again, so naturally that it made my heart flutter. I never thought I was the heart-fluttering kind of person, but it wasn't so bad.

At the airport, he used the miles he had accrued from years of traveling to writing conferences and book expos to buy a ticket, and he'd traded seats with a nice older lady who had never flown first class before, and she was delighted. Ben squeezed himself into the aisle seat beside me, and curled his fingers through mine, and it was as simple as that, as if he had always been a part of my life, and I had been a part of his.

He did this thing where he rubbed small circles around my thumb joint with his own thumb, and it made the skin there tingle. We talked about our favorite places we'd been, and he was a lot more traveled than I was thanks to Ann's book tours, and he hated flying almost as much as I did, but we both wanted to take a cross-country drive. He hated skiing, but we both liked snow tubing and burnt marshmallows. His comfort food was ranch dressing on Hot Pockets, while mine was box mac and cheese, and neither of us cared about that new hipster deconstructed meatball joint in SoHo. We were indifferent about the beach, but we *loved* beach reads, and the two-hour flight felt like two minutes.

Then we'd rented a car from Charlotte, and he'd rolled up his sleeves and said that he could most definitely drive an SUV, but after accidentally knocking the car in neutral and almost running into the airport bus, we swapped places and I drove the distance to Mairmont. He was much better at picking the driving music, anyway.

I squeezed his hand tightly, too. It was a reassurance to myself, standing in this small bed-and-breakfast, that he was actually here. Real. The girl who saw ghosts standing beside a man who had once been a little bit ghostly. Mairmont's gossip ring could eat their hearts out.

Dana's eyes flicked to Ben. "And who's this?"

"Ben," he greeted, and outstretched his other hand. "Nice to see you again, Dana."

They accepted it. "We've met before?"

"Um—no," Ben quickly corrected. "You just—I was—"

"I'd talked about you a lot is what he's trying to say," I covered for him quickly. "You make a mean rum and Coke, so I had to brag."

They grinned. "I do, don't I?" They checked us in and took a key off the hook behind them and dangled it from their finger. "Enjoy."

I took the key. "Thanks," I replied, and grabbed his hand again, and we disappeared up the stairs with our suitcases in tow. I liked how he felt beside me. I liked the company we kept. And whenever he brushed his thumb against my knuckles, there was a shiver that went from my toes all the way to my scalp, and I couldn't stand it. Not in a bad way.

But in a way that drove me crazy.

At the end of the hall was the hotel room with the wolfsbane on the door. I'd booked it again for old times' sake, before I'd ever asked Ben to come with me. I thought I would be spending it alone. Funny how a few hours could change everything.

I unlocked the door, and he rolled our suitcases inside. Sunlight spilled through the sheer curtains, catching the dust motes that floated in the air. I remembered a lot about this room—from the fake wolfsbane in the vase on the dresser to the knot in the hardwood I kept toeing the night I wrote my dad's obituary because I couldn't stop pacing to the side of the bed where Ben slept the night things started to spiral, the night before Dad's funeral.

The hotel room hadn't changed at all. Still could use more purple, but I was far from caring what color the room was. All I could see was Ben drawing a shadow against the window, sunlight shining golden on his dark hair, and I'd read about aching before. *I* had ached before.

But this was—I was—

I remembered the morning we woke up together, and the things he said he'd do to me, for me, and it all came back in such vivid detail I had to tell my brain to slow down. Breathe. I wasn't some weirdly horny teenager anymore—I was absolutely a refined woman with exquisite taste in rum and Cokes, *thank you very much*, and—

Oh, who was I kidding.

"Well, it's nice to be alone finally," he said, turning back to me, pocketing and unpocketing his hands, as if he wasn't sure what to do with them.

"I feel like we need a chaperone," I tried to joke, coming up next to him. My skin felt like it was on fire.

Don't climb the man mountain, I told myself. *Don't climb the man mountain. Don't climb—*

"Florence, I think—"

"Don't."

Then I took hold of the front of his jacket and pulled him close, and to my surprise he met me halfway. Our lips crushed together, and then he pulled away, whispering, "Sorry, sorry, you're just so beautiful and I finally get to touch you and—"

"I feel the same way," I replied, our lips lingering together for a moment longer, before he decided to follow with another kiss, rougher this time, biting. He was so hot—like, furnace hot—and when his thumb brushed against my cheek, it was warm. *He* was warm, and a knot formed in my throat because how much had I wanted this months ago, when we were in this very room together? How much did I want him to kiss me—on my neck, behind my ear, trace my collarbone with the edge of his teeth, murmuring devotions into my hair?

A lot, it turned out.

In a scattered mess we tipped back toward the bed, stepping out of our shoes, dropping my purse to the carpet, his tie abandoned somewhere on the bench at the foot of the bed. He lifted me up and sat me on the bed, and kissed me like he wanted to devour me, teeth scraping against my skin, nibbling my lip, and I couldn't get enough of him, either.

I wanted to explore the curve of his neck as my fingers slid down it, and I wanted to ask about the scar just above his collarbone, where his father's wedding ring always seemed to catch. He kissed the birthmark under my left ear that I always kept hidden because it was shaped a little like a ghost and that was *too* on the nose for me. It was electric, our contact skin to skin, as if little sparks ignited between our cells every time we touched. If our pasts sang in the wind, our present was in the touch of his hands on my waist, the way his fingers trailed across my body, the breathless kisses he planted against my mouth, as if he wanted to write me into his memory—burn it there.

My fingers tentatively found their way underneath his charcoal-gray jacket as I began to slip it off his broad shoulders, and he shrugged it off the rest of the way. It puddled on the floor. He leaned into me, deepening his kisses, and I just wanted to sink into him, and bury myself into the crook of his body, and stay there forever.

I pressed my hands against his hard chest—and paused. Came back to myself for a very, *very* brief moment. "*Wait.* Wait-wait-*wait*," I muttered to myself, and started to unbutton his pristine white work shirt. He didn't have an undershirt on, and I most definitely had felt— "Oh sweet chiseled Jesus." I traced my fingers across his hard chest to his abs and very *distinctive* V cut into his trousers. "What are you—an *underwear model*? Are these suckers airbrushed?"

His ears went red with embarrassment. "I'm an anxious person. I swim when I'm anxious. Which means I swim a lot."

"Lucky for me."

"You're ridiculous," he said, not unhappily, and planted a kiss at my jaw. "But I like that about you."

"Oh, I am going to be even *more* ridiculous when I demand to put googly eyes on all *six* of those abs—"

He pressed his mouth against mine, still ravenous, and made me shut up. And you know? It was sexy and I was super okay with it because whatever I'd been about to say succumbed to the part of my brain that seemed to always go offline whenever he kissed me that hard. And quite frankly, my brain had been on for way, way too long. It needed a hard reboot.

"Do you . . . ?" he asked, breathless. "Want to?"

"*Please*," I whispered, and we melted into each other, exploring each other's soft hidden corners.

At some point he undid my bra, and at some point, I slid off his belt, and at some point he was kissing me—everywhere. He pressed a kiss between my breasts, then just below them, then against my soft stomach. He went lower and lower, muttering in a love language of tongues.

As an English major, I had studied rising actions, I had charted climaxes. Making love and making stories were close to the same thing. You were intimate and vulnerable and wandering, traveling across the landscape of each other, learning. You told a story with each gesture, each sound—every kiss a period, every gasp a comma.

And the way Ben touched me, the way he played his tongue across my skin and burrowed his fingers into me, made a story with my body—the way I bit my lip to hush a moan, and curled my fingers around the duvet—I wanted him to read every word aloud until the very last page, when our lips were swollen and our bodies intertwined into each other's spaces, and he threaded his fingers between mine and raised them to kiss my knuckles.

After a moment, he asked, "I have a question," in a soft and thoughtful voice.

I shifted a little to look at him better, flattening out the fluffy feather pillow. "I might just have an answer."

"What are we?"

My eyebrows shot up. "You ask that *now*?"

"Well—yes," he replied, a bit embarrassed, and his ears began to turn red again and travel down the length of his cheekbones. "I mean—how are you going to introduce me to your family? I want to start with a good impression. They mean a lot to you, and that means a lot to me. So . . . what do you want me to be for you?"

I thought about it for a moment. "Well, this—us—we're a bit strange. Technically we've only known each other for a week and some change but . . ."

"It feels longer than that," he admitted, rubbing circles on my thumb knuckle again. "Ever since the accident, I've thought about you even though I was sure it was a dream. I scoured forums, talked with other coma patients, but nothing helped. I couldn't get you out of my head. I thought I was going crazy."

"No crazier than a girl who can see ghosts."

"I don't think you're crazy, Florence." And he said it so seriously, I pursed my lips together to keep them from wobbling, and rested my cheek into his shoulder.

"Well, then what do you want to be?" I asked.

He closed his eyes, and there was a moment of pause when he was searching for the right words. "I like you a lot, bordering on the bigger word, but . . ."

I tilted my head. "But?"

He admitted, "It's a bit cliché this soon, and if we're going to tell our children this story in ten years . . ."

I laughed, because of *course* he would flag that in this story. "Then I'll say it first," I said as I sat up and leaned close to him, my hair falling in a curtain around us as I pressed my forehead to his. "I love you, Benji Andor."

He smiled so wide it reached his brown eyes, and turned them ocher, as if that were the happiest thing he'd ever heard. "I love you, too, Florence Day."

"Then I think we should most definitely be platonic friends who swap video streaming service passwords and only see each other once a year at holiday parties."

He gave a long sigh and sank farther into his pillow. "Okay, we can do that—"

"I was kidding!" I exclaimed, sitting back again. "I didn't mean it!"

"Too late, I've already lost my will to live."

I playfully shoved him in the shoulder. "*Fine.* Let's be bunk-mates, then."

"Only?"

"Gym buddies?"

The light began to leave his eyes.

"Pocket pals!"

"You're ridiculous."

"And maybe partners. In the romantic sense," I added, our hands still intertwined, and I squeezed his tightly. "A suitor. A paramour. My courter. My second-best friend."

He quirked an eyebrow. "*Second?*"

"Rose will always be number one."

"*Fuck yeah I am!*" came a voice from the doorway as I realized a split second before my sister and Rose burst into the room that I had forgotten to lock it. Alice screamed and covered her eyes while Rose took a long drink from a champagne bottle. Clearly, they'd started the party early.

"Wow," Rose noted, giving a thumbs-up. "We sure have good timing. Great sesh, bestie."

"*We're leaving!*" Alice added, grabbing Rose by the arm, and pulling her back out the door. "*Put a sock on the door next time!*"

I thought Ben was going to die—again. When the door was closed, he pulled the covers over his head and disappeared beneath them. "Please kill me," his muffled voice moaned. "End my misery."

Grinning, I pulled the covers off him again, and he looked dejected and mortified in the deathbed of pillows. "Absolutely not, sir. If *I* have to live with them, so do you."

"It'll be a quick death. Just suffocate me in your perfect breasts."

"They aren't that big."

"But they *are* perfect."

"So you keep saying." I combed my fingers through his hair a few more times because, poor guy, he really didn't know how to handle mortification, and then I kissed him on the lips. "Let's get dressed and go help Mom keep those heathens in line."

I began to crawl out of bed, when he grabbed me by the arm and swallowed me up underneath the covers with him. "Just a few more minutes," he said, his breath hot against my neck as he held me tightly.

"Only a few," I agreed, though in my heart I knew I would've been happier with forever, but just this moment would do for now.

39

....

Ghost Stories

WE DID NOT end up catching *either* of the bachelor parties that night, but I was very certain neither Carver nor Nicki remembered the night very well anyway. From what I heard, there'd been an impromptu concert where Bruno almost threw out his back howling the laments of Dolly Parton, Carver accidentally lit the bar counter on fire, and Alice mooned Officer Saget right in the middle of Main Street. Sad that I missed *that* part, but I was glad we didn't end up going. *Someone* had to be coherent on the wedding day.

I busied myself with final wedding preparations, rearranging the flowers in the parlor rooms while sneaking tastes of desserts in the kitchen. I wasn't sure how Carver talked Alice into letting them have it in the funeral home for *free*, so I made a mental note to ask him what sort of blackmail he had on Alice for her to be so agreeable about it all.

The Days Gone Funeral Home looked like it was decorated in a flower crown, with large sunflowers on the porch and white ribbons draped across the old wooden roofbeams, and the once-suffocating floral-and-formaldehyde smell was replaced with the scent of bright and beautiful sunshine. The windows were open, as were the doors, and every so often a clever, happy wind raced through the old Victorian house, and the foundation creaked and groaned in hello.

Ben looked so at home in the red parlor, helping me arrange the sunflowers in vases kept from Dad's funeral, as if he'd been here all this time.

Alice elbowed me in the side and said, with all honesty, "Good catch, sis. Not my type, but good catch."

"Yeah, I think so, too."

"That does it for the flowers," Ben said, finishing up the vase he was working on. He wiped his hands on his trousers and said to Alice, "Nice to formally meet you."

Alice gave him a once-over. "You take care of my sister, you hear?"

"Yes, of course."

"And no more cheating at cards."

He raised his hands in surrender. "I wouldn't *dare*."

"Mm-hmm." Her phone vibrated and she took it out of her back pocket and quietly cursed. "The caterers are here—ugh. Can you two finish setting out the decorations?"

I gave her a salute. "Aye, aye, boss."

"Weirdo," she muttered and left out the front door, shouting at the caterers to move the van around back—"No, not through the *grass*, you *heathens.*"

When she was gone, Ben took a sunflower out of one of the vases and tapped me on the nose with it. "Your sister's doing a great job with the business."

"She is, isn't she?" I looked around at the parlors, strewn with colorful flowers and pearly white ribbons, and I wished Dad could have seen it. A wedding in a house of death. I kissed Ben on the cheek. "Thank you for being here."

"Thank you for inviting me. There's nowhere else I'd rather be than beside you."

I rolled my eyes and playfully shoved him away. "Stop being so sappy," I complained, hoping he didn't notice my reddening ears. If he talked like that much more, I was going to be in a permanent state of blush.

He liked me; it was still so hard to believe.

Benji Andor *adored* me.

And for the first time since Dad passed, everything felt almost perfect. The sky was this almost-perfect crimson—the color of Dad's suit when we buried him—and the sweltering July heat had abated to a soft humidity that still felt sticky, but it was as close to perfect as you could get in the summer, and the entire town had come to watch my brother and his husband say their actually perfect vows.

They slipped on each other's rings and professed their love under the ancient rafters that had echoed more sobs than cheers, and the purpling light of evening eased softly in through the windows, painting everything in shadowy hues of rose, and it was a fitting wedding for a funeral home.

Dad would have loved it.

After the wedding we popped champagne and played Dad's favorite burned CD and danced through the parlors to all the good goodbyes, because endings were just new beginnings. And right now, we were happy, and Carver and Nicki were dancing with each other, and Rose and Alice were flirting in the kind of way that would lead to something else.

(What kind of romance writer would I be if I didn't see how they fell?)

Because the same look was on my face, too, every time I looked at Ben. When he left to get us a refresher of champagne, Mom slid up beside me and gave a hard sigh. "Would it be frowned upon if, during the couples' dance, I danced, too?"

I offered out my arm to my mom. "I'm not Dad, but I can dance with you."

"I'd love that, sweetheart, but I was referring to your man."

And just as she said that, Ben swooped in and offered his hand to—my *mom.* I gasped, scandalized. Ben said, "Patience makes the heart grow fonder."

"What charm!" Mom cackled and wiggled her eyebrows at me as she let Ben lead her into the throng.

He winked.

(Ugh, this was for saying I'd put googly eyes on his washboard abs, wasn't it?)

I moped about on the edge of the parlor like a lonely island, swilling the red punch that was *most definitely* spiked. Everyone had someone to dance with—even the *mayor.* And here I was, left to lean against one of the tall tables with the owner of Bar None and Bruno. They were smoking cigars that reminded me of the ones Dad liked—strong and sweet.

Bruno nudged his chin toward Ben and Mom dancing. "I haven't seen your mom so happy in ages."

"He's a catch," the owner agreed.

I bit the side of my cheek to hide a grin, watching Ben trip over his own feet. He and Mom laughed, and it pulled at something deep in my chest. It ached, but not in the way I'd felt when Dad died. It was a good sort of pain. The kind that reminded me that I was still alive, and there was still life to live and memories to make and people to meet.

"How'd you meet him?" Bruno asked.

I tilted my head. The song ended, and I wondered how to explain it. He was a ghost who haunted me after I failed at turning in his grandmother's last manuscript—"I met him at work," I finally supplied. "I thought he was an absolute stuck-up asshole at first."

"And she was a chaos gremlin," Ben replied, surprising me. He put his hand on the small of my back. "I didn't think I stood a ghost of a chance."

"You were *so* deadly serious."

"And *you* were too much of a free spirit. But I think I love that the most."

I turned around to him. "Is *that* what you love the most?"

His lips twisted. "That I can say in current company." Then he offered his hand to me, and I took it. He spun me around, away from the table and onto the dance floor.

"I didn't know you danced," I said, tongue in cheek, because we'd danced before.

A lifetime ago.

He laughed and brought me closer to him. "What love interest doesn't?" We danced across the ancient oak floorboards, around Mom and Alice, and Seaburn and his wife, and Karen and Mr. Taylor, though I only knew that later, because all I remembered was Ben. The music was a little dampened, and the evening light slid through the open window in lazy hues of oranges and pinks, and he looked so perfect painted in it.

We danced slowly, his hands soft on my hips, swaying to a slow song that I didn't know, but I liked it. It was sweet, with violins, with lyrics about want and yearning and everything that you really needed for a good love song.

A glimmer in the corner caught my eye. I glanced over.

An old woman with beautiful wide brown eyes stood in the doorway to the parlor, her hand outstretched to an elderly man in an orange sweater and brown pants, who took it tightly and kissed her knuckles. They shimmered in that star-glitter way spirits did. Ben glanced in the direction I was looking.

"Can you . . . see her, too?" I whispered in wonder, looking from him to the elderly woman and back again. She had gardening dirt under her nails, and a content smile.

"Now he can give her lilies himself."

"You *can*." I curled my hands tightly around his jacket. Because he could see them. He was one, and now he could see them, and that meant—

It meant I wasn't alone.

When I looked back toward the couple, they had already melted into a brilliant flash of sunlight, and Heather walked through the doorway, arguing with her husband about their babysitter, as if nothing had been there at all.

"Would you like to go on a walk? In the graveyard?" he asked, drawing me from my thoughts.

I gave him a surprised look. "You're *asking*?"

"It's not night yet so it's technically not illegal," he replied dutifully. "And it's a bit stuffy in here, and besides, I'd like to see your dad."

"I'd like that, too." I laced my fingers through his, and we slipped out of the reception and down the front steps of the old and sure house of death. And life.

Life happened in old funeral homes, too.

The cemetery was warm and quiet in the summer evening. The iron gate was already closed, but we knew the perfect little broken bit of wall to climb over, and we held each other's champagne as we did. My family had been busy, it seemed, since Dad's funeral. Almost all of the tombstones were washed, gleaming like bone shards sticking up from the hills of bright green grass.

Dad was waiting for us on his favorite hill in the cemetery, in a nondescript shaded plot close to his favorite old oak tree, easily lost in the sea of stones. His marker was pristine and the weeds plucked out. Mom had put fresh orchids in the vase, and I picked out the spoiled leaves with care. His plaque only had a single word—*beloved.* Mom said it was because there were so many things Dad had been to so many people—"Beloved son, beloved parent, beloved husband, beloved pain in the ass . . ."—but secretly I knew Mom had requested only that word because it was her word to him. Her soft *I love you.*

Her beloved.

I brushed a ladybug off the plaque.

It still felt like he was here some days, like the world still turned with him in it. And parts of him still were.

Ben crouched down beside the tombstone, and I let him have some privacy as I followed the path up to the bench under the oak tree and sat down. The night had cooled off, and the wind whispered through the trees, and a murder of crows cawed in the distance. I closed my eyes, and I could imagine Dad sitting beside me like he used to, chatting about rates of flower arrangements and the cost of coffins and Carver's newest chair he built and Alice's latest chaos. I breathed in the sweet scent of freshly cut grass.

And things were okay.

Ben came over to sit down beside me after a while.

"So, what did y'all talk about?" I asked.

"This and that," he replied, rubbing his father's wedding ring on the chain around his neck. "Told him to give Annie a hello. And a thank-you. If she hadn't asked you to ghostwrite for her . . ."

"A ghost asking an author to ghostwrite, that *has* to be a first." I sighed, and leaned my head against his shoulder.

"What're you going to do next?" he asked, folding his fingers through mine. He began to rub circles on my thumb knuckle thoughtfully. "You turned in Annie's last book. Her contract's up."

"Well . . ." I debated my answer. I still had to get through line edits of Annie's book, and copyedits, and pass pages, but those were all things Ben already knew. I also still had to accept Molly's offer of representation, but I'd do that on Monday. "I think . . . I'm going to write another book."

"What'll it be about?"

"Oh, the usual—meet-cutes and high jinks and grave misunderstandings and conciliatory kisses."

"Will there be a happily ever after?"

"Maybe," I teased, "if you play your cards right."

"I'll be sure not to cheat."

"Unless it's to help me win, of course."

"Always. I'm yours, Florence Day," he said, and kissed my knuckles.

Those words made my heart soar. "Ardently?"

"Fervently. Zealously. Keenly. Passionately yours."

"And I'm yours," I whispered, and kissed him in a cemetery of immaculate tombstones and old oak trees, and it was a good beginning. We were an author of love stories and an editor of romances, weaving a story about a boy who was once a little ghostly and a girl who lived with ghosts.

And maybe, if we were lucky, we'd find a happily ever after, too.

Eccentric Circles

IN THE DAYS Gone Funeral Home, in the back corner of the largest parlor, there was a loose floorboard where I once kept my dreams. I kept them locked tight in a box, storing them like treasure, until the day I could take them out and brush them off, like old friends coming to greet each other.

I didn't store my dreams in a small box underneath the floorboards anymore. I didn't need to.

But there was a girl who was a little bit tall and lanky for her age, dark hair and wide eyes, who wrote her dreams on spare pieces of paper and put them in a jar like fireflies, and when she found her mother's old metal box and its smutty, smutty *X-Files* fanfic, she decided to store her dreams there, too.

And the wind that whistled through the old funeral parlor sang sweet and soft and sure.

Like love ought to be.

Acknowledgments

Just as it takes a village to raise a child, it took a village to raise Benji Andor from the dead. *The Dead Romantics* couldn't be possible without a lot of people, most of whom I will probably forget in these acknowledgments, but you know who you are. Thank you for giving Florence and Ben a ghost of a chance.

This book wouldn't be possible without the tender love and necromancy of my agent, Holly Root; my phenomenal editor, Amanda Bergeron, and assistant editor, Sareer Khader; my copyeditor, Angelina Krahn; my wonderful publicist, and the whole team from managing to production to marketing, Christine Legon and Alaina Christensen and Jessica Mangicaro and everyone else. And to my critique partners—Nicole Brinkley, Rachel Strolle, Ashley Schumacher, Katherine Locke, and Kaitlyn Sage Patterson—for being the Rose to my Florence and encouraging me when I was at my lowest.

Speaking of lowest, I would also like to give a very enthusiastic *fuck you* to my anxiety. Thanks for, as always, being the worst.

And finally, to anyone who has proclaimed drunkenly at a bar that love is dead—I've been there and trust me, love is *not* dead. It's simply sleeping off a raging hangover. Give it two Tylenol and tell it to call you in the morning.

Thank you for reading this book. I hope you find a little bit of happiness wherever you go.

The Dead Romantics

• • • • •

BEHIND THE BOOK

I SEE DEAD people.

Kidding. I really don't, and if I did I would probably:

One, talk to my therapist and—

Two, schedule an exorcism.

Joking aside, I *do* kind of see dead people. We all do. We see them in family photos, when we remember the way your grandma used to talk to her flowers; and the way your granddad happily sat in his favorite rocking chair on the porch, watching lightning arc across summer storms; and the way your aunt used to have a laugh so infectious she would light up a whole room. We read about them, all the time. English class is full of dead people. Jane Austen? Dead. Shakespeare? Doth be dead and buried. Charles Dickens? A tale of two deads. We listen to them on the radio, we watch them in films, without really thinking that they—you know—caught the midnight train already.

But, honestly?

Death scares me.

That's the crux of it. Death itself, in all its ferocious unknown, scares the living crap out of me. So why—*why god, why*—do I gravitate toward ghost stories? And if there's a ghost *romance*? You bet your ass I'm going to be up all night reading it. Death and ghost stories go hand in hand, like peanut butter and getting it stuck to the roof of your mouth.

I don't understand my fascination whatsoever, and you know? I'm not the kind of person to think too much on it, because if I do my anxiety is going to start to spiral and then all I will think about is my unknown, eternal end.

Which is probably why I write.

There's this illusionary permanence to writing. My books will be here long after I'm gone. I mean, *hopefully*.

Forever. (Usually.)

People write for different reasons—to feel less alone, to understand their own feelings, to tell stories that make them happy—and people read books for different reasons, too.

For me?

I read because I want to be held. Not like, literally, by a book. (That'd be weird.) But metaphorically. I want to sink into a novel. I want to be romanced by the possibility of sunsets too pretty to describe and kisses that you feel all the way in your toes and love stories too wide and wild for you to ever feel alone.

If anything staves off the creeping unknown of death, I propose that it's a good book.

Maybe not *my* book—I mean, I hope it's my book. Or at least my book is a stepping-stone for what *will* be your favorite book. I hope I can write one for you. I hope I can write one for me, too.

I didn't start writing *The Dead Romantics* to explore my feelings on an author's legacy and what the dead end up leaving behind. I just wanted to write a fun ghost story! A chaotic gremlin of a woman meets the stern ghost of a man (who, secretly, has a cinnamon roll–flavored heart of gold)! They have sexy high jinks! Everything turns out fine in the end!

Well, I was the fool, apparently, because little did I know, I had the talent to do *both*.

Somehow.

It might be a one-time deal, so I am *relishing* in this moment. I managed to do something I didn't realize I could. (Well, *two* things. I didn't think I'd be able to write anything in 2020 but I showed myself that anything is possible with a few healthy coping mechanisms and nowhere to go during a pandemic.) Most of the time, I talk around my own insecurities and make fun of them until the person I'm talking to gets fed up with my turtling and tells me to just write a happy novel.

Well, I did! So joke's on them! It's also sad! And a little sappy!

But you know? I like a little corny in my life and I hope that you do, too.

I think, as readers, we all have a comfort read, the one book that protects us in the exact ways it needs to—whether it is a romance or erotica or a thriller or a crime story or a fantasy. A book that we find ourselves in, like looking in a mirror. *Oh, you, too?* It will ask, as it fills that soft, hollow place in your heart that nothing else dared to touch. I think we all deserve a book like that, whatever yours is.

It's not about how many books are sold or whether they are turned into films or re-released with different editions that makes a book's legacy. I think it is the readers, whether there are only seven of them, or seventy thousand. You're the legacy, you're the life beyond the story I give you.

Florence's dad said that the people we love are in the wind, and I believe it. I think that the people we love can be in the pages of books, too.

I hope you find yourself in a book someday.

And I hope that book lives forever.

DISCUSSION QUESTIONS

1. Florence is a ghostwriter for Ann Nichols. Do you think books written by ghostwriters are just as important to an author's legacy as those written by the author themselves?

2. Usually, keeping secrets can shake a person's trust in someone else. But Florence's dad kept the secret that he knew who Florence ghostwrote for and had read all of those books. Do you think some secrets can actually *build* trust once revealed?

3. Throughout the novel, Florence struggles with trying to write the perfect ending. If you could write any sort of happily ever after, how would it go?

4. Both Ben and Florence find comfort in romance novels. What are some of your favorite comfort reads?

5. There are many depictions of afterlives in the media—ghosts, reapers, spirits—from all different cultures. Why do you think the theme of death is so universally explored in stories and the concept of life (or some semblance of it) after death?

6. What is a book you loved that you believe more people should read? What did you love most about it?

7. Death, and how a person handles it, is a big part of the novel. If you could leave a list behind for your loved ones, like Xavier does in the story, what would be on it?

8. If Ben and Florence were put in a punderdome, who do you think would win? Kidding—but in truth, do you think humor and tragedy go hand in hand? Why or why not?

9. Do you feel Lee Marlow was justified in writing *When the Dead Sing*? Do you think original ideas exist? Or do we all pull inspiration—knowingly or not—from the experiences we've had and the people we've met throughout our lives?

10. If Ben and Florence had a sequel, what do you think it would be about? How do you think Ben will handle his newfound power of seeing dead people?

11. What do you think Florence will write next?

ASH'S COMFORT READS

- *Howl's Moving Castle*, Diana Wynne Jones.
- *Beach Read*, Emily Henry.
- *Dragon's Bait*, Vivian Vande Velde.
- *The Proposal*, Jasmine Guillory.
- *Dating You / Hating You*, Christina Lauren.
- *Well Met*, Jen DeLuca.
- *A Winter's Promise*, Christelle Dabos.
- *Boyfriend Material*, Alexis Hall.
- *The Princess Bride*, William Goldman.
- [*That one fanfic that will never be named*], Unknown.

Photo by Ashley Poston

ASHLEY POSTON writes stories about love and friendship and ever afters. A native to South Carolina, she now lives in a small grey house with her sassy cat and too many books. You can find her on the internet, somewhere, watching cat videos and reading fan fiction.

CONNECT ONLINE

AshPoston.com

HeyAshPoston

AshPoston

HeyAshPoston